KINGDOM

OF

CARDS

Emmaline Leigh

This is a work of fiction. All of the characters, organizations, and events portrayed in this novel are either products of the authors imagination or are used fictitiously.

Copyright © 2023 by Emma McGeown

All rights reserved.

Cover designed by Kelly Ritchie

ISBN: 9781738150724

For Heather and Liv,

I hope you love this book as much as the first time.

To my parents,

Thank you for everything. I love you.

And to you, my dear reader:

Keep your cards close–it's all just a game, after all.

One should not surrender completely to Twisted Magic.

For if they do, they will never recover.

— The Order of Crowns. 1886 Edition.

PART ONE
THE DEALER IS DEATH

Emmaline Leigh

ONE

AURA

London 1889

Aura didn't remember wielding the knife. She'd been blind, consumed by a hatred she hadn't known she possessed; an anger that was not her own. She was cursed, or perhaps that was too simple of a term. Blood flashed before her memory, not a new sight for her, yet tonight? Tonight, it had been different. She hadn't been in control of her mind, and for all she knew, maybe she wasn't. She took a steady breath, attempting to get her mind in order, then she looked at the facts.

Aura Wrentroth hid behind a facade; a fact.

Aura Wrentroth was going mad; possible, but false.

Aura Wrentroth had been destroyed the night her brother, Alon, had died; the night she learned that good people could lie. Now, she was bound to her own set of lies, if only to keep her neck out of the noose.

A fact. One that inevitably had caused blood to stain her hands.

Aura smoothed her clean hands down the front of her intricate laced bodice, attempting to settle her nerves. Nearly less than two hours ago, she'd been drenched in a man's blood, magic, the Twisted sort, coursing through her veins like her life depended on it.

It didn't.

But in that moment, nothing mattered but the blade in her hand and her mission. Her mission, from her employer. Aura's hands tightened as they clasped in front of her. Come morning, whispers of the Queen of Spades' newest kill, *her* newest kill, would take the upper classes by storm. Her name was a whisper, among the highest circles, a carefully calculated act to rid the population of its cruelest.

Or so she was forced to believe anyway—by the magic, by her shadow of an employer.

Her end was always only two steps behind her, waiting to strike. After all, what would society do if they found out that the once-daughter of a well-bread mother and father, was never the same after they died? What would they do if they found out that the niece of her well-respected uncle, not only had her own dangerous endeavours, but aided him in the mortuaries of the Order of Crowns and Scotland Yard, alike? What would they do if they found out just how scarred her heart was?

She didn't know.

Blood stained her hands, and a life she hardly recognized anymore haunted the very depths of her soul. Perhaps, it had been a mistake picking up that knife, listening to the voice she'd heard in her head, nearly three years ago. At present, had her brother been alive to say it, she was almost certain he'd tell her she was a disgrace. *Hurt if you must, never kill,* those would be his words, though, currently, they were of little use to her.

Aura Wrentroth leaned against a brick building, trying and failing to appear inconspicuous in her rich blue dress. The wind nipped at her bare arms, and she cursed herself for not wearing gloves. In truth, she'd forgotten them in her uncle's laboratory in her rush to get here. *Five more minutes.* She would give herself five more minutes. What she should do, was head inside of the Order of Crowns now, but she was waiting for someone.

A very late someone.

At that moment, a body rounded the corner, but it was only her uncle who'd gotten into a fuss with the carriage driver over payment.

He nodded at her. "Ready to go?"

Aura opened her mouth to say she wasn't, but quickly shut it. Any waiting she had to do could be done inside, out of the damp London air. She and her uncle approached the Order of Crowns, joining the procession of guests walking up the stone stairs leading to the manor. The building itself was two stories of red brick, thick spires lining the roof. Light from the windows cast the shadows dancing along the front of the manor in welcome. Aura had only been here a handful of times, yet each time it didn't seem to get any easier to ease her shoulders.

She was a liar. She did not belong among the nobles she stood with, arguably she hadn't since her title had lost its meaning.

A fact that no one need know.

She was as much of an imposter here as she was in her own skin. The door to the Order of Crowns snapped shut behind her as she and her uncle stepped into the crowd of partygoers mingling in the entrance way. It looked like every other entrance hall in upper-class England, all white-walled, gold-gilded, and marble-floored, finished off with a massive chandelier that dangled over the guests like a million raindrops suspended in air. That, and it practically screamed wealth, which the Order of Crowns—a secret society that, honestly, Aura had very little knowledge about other than the fact that her uncle did occasional work for the Duke—seemed to love showing off. Aura stepped away from her uncle, retreating off to the side, desperate for a glimpse of her usual acquaintances, not that she came to these sorts of things often. Usually, she was off prowling the London streets, dagger in hand. Or in the morgue.

People swarmed the foyer, dressed in the finest silks to the softest velvets, the dresses creating a colourful sea amongst the duller colours worn by the men. *How many are pretending to love this life of theirs?* Aura, for one, saw no appeal in it at all. There was too much waiting, and patience had never been a particularly favourable virtue of hers.

A few people glanced at her before turning and whispering to their friends. *These whispers,* Aura knew what they were about. She was used to them by now and had been ever since her parents had passed. Aura was practically one of the most powerful Optical Magicians in London, well next to Duke Brittenworth's—the leader of The Order's—youngest son, Xavier. The magic was a curse as far as Aura was concerned, allowing one to see as far into the past as needed, and arguably one of the worst magics to be manipulated by Twisted Magicians. Part of her hated it, part of her believed her magic was useful. Either way, she hardly remembered her own past. People wished to know how a girl like herself, whose memories of her parents were so hazy they might not even be real, was blessed with such power. In truth, she didn't know.

She wasn't sure she wanted to.

"How's it been at the morgue?"

Aura clenched her hands into fists at the sound of his voice, fearing she might be tempted to slap the man. Carefully, she turned to face Sir Avery Waltzeen. He had bright red hair, the colour of fire, and a thousand or so freckles that made his face appear younger; even though he was a few years older than she was. He wore a velvet waistcoat (copper, she catalogued—like his hair) over a white shirt and black trousers. He smiled, and she resisted the urge to walk away altogether. She'd known him for quite some time, yet she wasn't entirely sure where he was from.

Her magic, previously, had revealed to her he'd been a military trainer for a couple of years. He'd travelled until he landed a job as the second in command to Duke Brittenworth. He had the hint of a Scottish accent, though it sounded as if it had been flattened by time long spent in the Americas, causing a slight lilt when he spoke.

He was also the sole communicator between her and her employer.

"Delightful," Aura replied. "Bloody cadavers and exposed brains are quite a joy in my early hours."

Aura was pleased to see Avery's smile fall. "Yes, I suppose removing Twisted toxins from the dead would make for a great morning activity."

She ignored him. "You were late."

"And you were impatient."

Aura rolled her eyes. "What do you want, Avery?"

"I?" Avery shook his head. "I don't want anything. *He* does."

Aura stiffened. By *he* Avery meant her employer had another job for her.

Looking away, she surveyed the room around them. The foyer had emptied out quite a bit since she'd entered, most guests retreating to the ballroom, probably eager to see the heir's coronation as the next leader of The Order. That, or his decision on marital prospects.

Avery leaned forward, lowering his head. "But first, you should have something for him."

Aura slipped a ring off of her middle finger. She'd got it from the man she'd killed earlier, and though wearing it felt wrong, she hadn't had much of a choice. Her employer had asked for it. She wasn't sure exactly what it did, all she knew is it must do something if her employer wanted it. *Something* related to Twisted Magic. That had been the deal Avery had explained to her three years ago, get the ancient artifacts by killing the wealthy who didn't deserve them— who were supposedly crooked. Even if she wanted to argue, once the magic took control, she lost her own.

Avery took the ring from her, its red gem glistening in the light, before stuffing it into his waistcoat pocket, though not before Aura noticed a look pass over his face. He seemed to be moving slower, as if to play with her.

"What does he want, Avery?" Aura asked, sharply.

"The coronet."

Aura frowned. "You *work* here. You get it."

Avery only shook his head. The coronet was said to be an ancient artifact spanning all the way back to the beginning of the Order, sometime in the early fourteenth century and, according to records, around the exile of Twisted Magicians. This coronet was said to hold special magical properties that could heal an individual from Twisted attacks. Having worked closely with Twisted Magic and the poison they leave behind, she knew that the magic, if left untreated, resulted in death. Why Aura's employer would need it, she had no idea. But she supposed she had no idea what he did with half of the things Aura stole for him. He could have someone break into the palace, but it's rumoured that Queen Victoria keeps *her* crown with the same magical properties close to her at all times.

"You see," Avery continued. "If you don't, someone close to you will have to die."

She turned to face him. "Avery—"

"You'll do it. This time there are stakes, Aura. That is the condition I'm supposed to relay."

She needed a way out of this conversation.

Avery frowned just as Aura felt a hand at her back.

"Dearest Aura," she half-turned her head to see Locklyn Henry Mortsakov, son of Marquess Alexander Mortsakov and Marchioness Amelia Mortsakov—and arguably, her best friend in all of London, remove his hand from her back to hold out his arm to her. "I've been looking for you everywhere. Come now, we're late to the party."

Aura took his arm as Avery inclined his head in a bow. Aura knew he was mocking Lock, but he had no choice but to withstand certain *societal* expectations. "Lord Mortsakov."

"Ah, Waltzeen. I do believe I overheard Duke Brittenworth speaking about a rather alarming issue. I'm sure, as his second, he'll be wondering where you've run off to, no?"

"Yes, of course." Avery grimaced, met Aura's gaze and waited for her to nod before striding off all together.

Aura breathed a sigh of relief, letting go of Lock's arm to face him fully. He was dressed in a crimson waistcoat worn overtop of a white stiff collared shirt, and black trousers. A small gold anatomical heart had been pinned to his tie; a black frock coat layered over everything.

"Thank you, Lock. You just saved me."

He regarded her levelly. "Did I? From what?"

He was playing the fool. Though he didn't know Avery's role in her life, he knew that any conversation with Avery for more than thirty seconds was what one might call *insufferable*. As for lack of acknowledgement on the subject, she didn't care. When Alon had died, Lock had sat with Aura for hours until the tears subsided, huddled together in the corner of Rien's laboratory. He'd been there when her world had been ripped apart at the seams. He didn't know that her brother's death was what made her into the person she hid behind, a place for her to put her rage, but that was for his benefit. She knew very well where he lay with the idea of the Queen of Spades. With *her*. Not that he knew that.

Still, it didn't matter.

She had been there when he'd been at his worst—out of his mind—and she'd stayed. For the most part, Aura tried to forget their early years of friendship, filled with all the horror that it was. She was trying to heal—*a half-truth*. *S*he wasn't sure she could heal until she found a way to wash the blood off her own hands. Aura shook her head, pulling herself from her thoughts.

"Avery Waltzeen," she whispered, and he laughed softly. The laugh sounded more like, *I cannot believe that this is still a problem,* rather than actually finding the situation funny. It was, after all, not a joke. Lock indicated they should walk, and she placed her hand on his arm once more. As they strode away, she cast a quick look over her shoulder to make sure Avery was not watching and was very pleased to see he was deep in conversation with another woman. She was blonde, though didn't quite have the posture of a duchess. Aura paid her no more thought as she turned forward once more.

"Still a shock I have to swoop in, really," Lock was saying, amusement lacing his voice.

Aura turned back to him. "I swear, next time I see him, I might just fake my death so he can leave me alone."

Unprobable. Her employer would kill Avery before *ever* touching her. She was too *invaluable*, as Avery had once told her.

"Oh, come now, I don't think you'll have to go to that extreme."

"Won't I?"

"I'll help you," he said, suddenly serious. "I do happen to have excellent skills with a sword."

"Thank you. I'll be sure to let you know." She laughed, though she knew he was completely serious about his offer. He practiced fencing when he was *bored,* which was quite often, as he told her. He gave her a look, and she bit down hard, trying to swallow her smile at this perfectly inappropriate time and the rather handsome tilt of the dark brows he arched at her.

Lock steered them toward the ballroom, but Aura stopped them before they entered. "Not in there."

"Why?" he asked, looking down at her curiously. He wasn't that much taller than her, but he could be intimidating if he wanted to be. Thankfully this was not one of those times.

"It's a vow I made with myself."

He hummed, sarcasm playing in his voice. "How about you make a vow with me?"

"I did."

His gaze snapped to hers. "*That* vow has kept us out of prison."

"Indeed, it did." She looked away. She hadn't meant to speak about their past indiscretions, of the secrecy that bound them together. Lock seemed to have moved on, however, and was steering her away from the ballroom, the sounds of music and laughter, and instead brought her through a hallway and up a set of stairs. Aura tucked a strand of short brown hair behind her ear as she reached the top of the stairs, regretting not pinning it away. As she did, her dress shifted at her collarbone, stinging a fresh scar. She winced; half-forgetting Lock was behind her.

"Aura?" He was before her in moments.

She blinked at him, realizing she'd just stopped walking. She wasn't *supposed* to remember, she didn't want to—it'd seem her memories of earlier this evening were taunting her. Lock's gaze flicked to her collarbone, where the scar burned beneath fabric, the tiniest nick visible with the neckline of her dress, before flicking back up to her face.

"Are you okay?"

"Yes."

He stared at her for only a moment longer before turning away, and Aura sincerely hoped that his magic wouldn't sense anything. He had Emotive Magic, which made it very difficult to lie to him, though she'd done a decent job over the past three years.

They walked along the corridor in silence for a few moments and Aura was glad to be away from the crowds—she could never quite handle them after Alon—until they stopped before a door, one she knew led to the library. Lock had just braced a hand on the door handle just as Lock's mother called down from the way they'd come. Lock swore, more out of annoyance than frustration at the interruption.

"Locklyn."

Aura saw Lock flinch at the use of his proper name.

"Your father and I would like a word."

Lock shot Aura a rather exaggerated wink before adjusting the sleeves on his coat and clapping his hands; Aura could just see the purple colouring starting to peak above his stiffened collar, his eyes beginning to glow before another voice boomed, startling them both.

"Locklyn Henry Mortsakov, don't you dare use magic on your mother."

"Yes sir," Lock mumbled, though his father was too far to hear. Aura motioned for him to go and that she'd be fine.

"The ballroom. Fifteen minutes," he said, lowering his voice. "Obviously I would ask more politely, but I'm a bit pressed for time, and care little for gentlemanly ideals. And, I am aware of your vow, but surely rules can be bent if someone *invites* you."

He didn't give Aura a chance to reply before spinning slowly on his heels. Aura stood there for a moment, marvelling over his magic like she always did. Emotive Magic allowed anyone that possessed it to sense what someone was feeling or give people dreams, though from what she understood, the latter took a toll. Lock had a way of making it seem easy; effortless, like his magic didn't make him exhausted or dizzy. Purple fluorescence flowed through him like blood, like it was natural, and that was what she admired. Though the colours of his magic were the reason she was always hesitant to use her Optical magic. After all, glowing blue eyes didn't do too well in a dark room surrounded by enemies. Aura rolled her eyes at his retreating figure before slipping into the library beyond.

It was circular like a spyglass. At the top, a circular window sat looking in on the books, and had it been day, the light might have reached the delicate pages. The shelves stood like centuries in the middle of the bottom floor, the second floor looking down onto them. Her veins were buzzing. *No, no—*

"Where is your dagger?" A voice infiltrated her head, making her dizzy, and she stumbled forward gripping the railing.

"I don't need it," she muttered, quietly, should anyone else be in the library.

"You have enemies everywhere."

"Not as Aura Wrentroth. Now, get out of my head."

"Can you hear his heartbeat?"

Aura pressed her forehead to the cool metal. "Whose?"

There was no answer.

Twisted Magic was like a poison, slithering into one's mind whenever it wanted. The Twisted possessed one of the four magical abilities—Optical, Emotive, Auditory, or Perceptive—and used them against their victims, playing tricks on their senses. In Aura's case, her employer used Perceptive to give her thoughts, not read them. Aura's hand slapped against the railing.

Anger would do her no good.

Aura breathed a heavy breath before letting it out slowly. It was not every day her employer spoke to her; indeed, it'd gotten less and less in recent years.

So why now?

Today?

She didn't care to ponder the idea.

Instead, she turned on her heel and marched out of the library, ignoring the lingering dizziness from being affected by Twisted Magic.

"*Kian*," A woman was saying just as Aura pulled the door shut behind her. "The deal is—"

Aura turned.

She was blind.

Where the hallway should have stood was a searing darkness. Aura stumbled backwards, only for her back to collide with the ground as she fell to the floor. Aura scrambled up, no longer hearing anything. Her hands were shaking, she didn't do well feeling trapped, and right now—

She blinked.

Everything was back to normal.

Aura clasped her hands together to keep anyone from noticing the way they shook before she turned and descended the staircase, ignoring what she'd witnessed. Her breaths were coming fast, and she needed to calm down. The foyer was nearly empty now, which was a relief, but still, a sense of dread filled her. She thought she might drown. She'd vowed that she wouldn't step one foot in that ballroom, but if she wanted a chance to speak with Lock while her uncle wasn't around to ask any questions, she was going to have to. Besides, weren't some promises meant to be broken anyway? Still, the thought of braving the den she'd been avoiding all night did nothing to help with the foreboding feeling she felt whenever she so much as spared a glance at the accursed room. *Breathe,* she told herself. It was just a room. *Breathe,* she'd told herself when she found that she wasn't while fighting an opponent. If she was going to do this, she'd better take it as a warrior. Otherwise, she would stand there until the room faded into a collection of cobwebs and dirt. She watched the couples dancing, the women's giant skirts swishing with each chassé as the men guided them gently across the floor. In the far corner, a group of gentlemen were laughing over something another had said moments prior. To them, it was a joy; to her, it was a place to be aware of because she never knew what would come at her. *This is not a battleground,* she thought, though it might as well be. She was doing this for Lock. *If* she gathered herself, *then* she could spend a few more moments with her best friend.

There. It didn't sound so terrible when she put it that way.

The beautiful sound of melodic string instruments cascaded over the crowd, and a feeling of eagerness crept into her bones, though it was quickly put out.

"I heard the next thing the Queen of Spades will go for is the coronet," a woman whispered as she strolled past, a gentleman on her arm.

"Don't be ridiculous. She isn't foolish. Unless she wants to get herself killed." The gentleman led her away before Aura could hear more, and she turned in the opposite direction. If only they knew she had no choice.

She shifted in discomfort as commotion drew her attention behind her, where a Lady spoke in hushed tones to a gentleman. The Lady had a weariness about her, her blonde hair flowing down the back of her red gown, her face tilted into a gentle frown. The gentleman seemed to pay her no mind and only seemed to squeeze her arm tighter. The woman's face fell back to neutrality, smiling when she caught Aura watching. Could this have been the woman speaking with Kian Brittenworth? A flash of something caught Aura's eye, but it was gone before she could even see what it was. She pursed her lips, watching the couple exit before heaving a breath and stepping into the crowd, cursing every minute. A dance, that was it—not that she was one for dancing, but she didn't necessarily want to turn Lock's invitation down either. She weaved her way toward the wall though she may as well have been all the way on the other side of England. A thrum of nerves started inside her veins, and she clenched her hands into two tight fists. She was sure that her nails would leave half-moon shapes pressed along her palms, but she didn't care. Not now, not as she was in the battle zone of prying eyes and whispers, not while the echoes of her earlier crimes were in her ear, and certainly not while she felt this exposed. She longed for her familiar hooded coat and the rush of adrenaline as she slung her knife through another swindler, but that was so very far away. She shouldn't crave it—death—but it called to her, no matter how much she wanted it to stay away. She plastered on a grin, tensing her shoulders, and hoped that nobody noticed her sharp gaze, assessing all exits and the faces of the crowd. She jumped as someone cackled loudly, sending a pulse through her.

She squeezed her eyes shut for a moment, then, wishing for her knife, something to fiddle with.

But tonight, she was not that person.

Indeed, tonight, she had a role to play.

And a job to do.

TWO

LOCK

This was the equivalent of a slow death. Time, it seemed, was intent on torturing him. He'd spent nearly fifteen minutes in the ballroom, only to be paraded with ladies his parents so diligently arranged to grace his presence. In that short amount of time, he'd turned down each and every single one of them. In fact, he told them he was busy, which irritated most of them, indeed they probably thought he was crass. However, he simply was not interested, and couldn't care less about his parents' *wishes*. This would have gone a lot quicker, had he thought to talk about his past unbecoming issues, however it was not *proper* to talk about them. Apparently, it's improper to tell people that he once poisoned his ex-classmate and went to a party the next day as if nothing had ever happened—or that beneath a tree, at the far end of the lot, where their own manor stood, his classmate lay rotting.

No one would believe him anyway.

Apparently, it was improper to tell them that he, a lord, was plagued by nightmares. He almost scoffed. His parents would probably perish if they found he was capable of such horrors, and yet, had they gone to the furthest point, in their own plot of land, and dug, they would have found what had been a person. Even more lovely, they would have found out that their son, Lock Mortsakov, had been a cold-blooded killer.

He was guilty, his hands bloody, and no one knew what he hid beneath his lordly facade. No one knew that perhaps, he'd even enjoyed himself a little. Or that most days the guilt was almost enough to drown him.

No one but Aura, who'd helped him make the poison.

They were bound together by secrets, and perhaps as a consequence, his heart was bound to hers. In debt, so to speak. She'd saved him from Hell, metaphorically, of course, but saved nonetheless.

Well, as much as he could be, anyway.

Rien had called for him and Aura down in the Order's mortuary, located in the basement, and he couldn't have been more grateful as he'd weaved his way through the crowd of twirling couples and cocky gentleman, who spared him little more than a cursory glance. Indeed, until Rien had called upon him, he'd been waiting for the coronation to be over so he could go back home—back to pretending the Order didn't exist. Lock himself wasn't one of them. The feud between the Order and this so-called Society they hunted was too messy; the affairs of secret societies were not one he liked to concern himself with.

The place reeked of pressure, and that, he found, would only lead to disaster, the need to fit elsewhere. He'd been seven when his father told him to mature. He'd been thirteen when he decided he didn't care, fifteen when he'd killed for the first and last time. Three years later, here he was, fighting his way out of the categorical confine he'd placed upon himself.

Killer.

The word haunted him, a reminder of what he'd done and who he'd done it for. Though, the Twisted Poison pumping in his veins was often reminder enough. His blood ran black, not that he let anyone close enough to see that lest he be exiled, as the Twisted were *supposed* to be. He could feel it, too, the poisons swimming beneath the surface, a curse on his heart, a reminder that time was running out. Ignoring the situation, as he often did, didn't change that fact. The night he'd killed, he'd been coaxed by a voice of the Twisted, and as he knew from Aura's studies, their magic left lasting impacts if not dealt with. The only issue: extraction was either illegal if the victim was still alive or a science experiment if they were dead. Neither seemed particularly appealing if he was being honest with himself. He was a monster just waiting for the right time to rip out from beneath his skin. He was, by definition, very angry—that is the fatal flaw to emotive magic—and the Twisted Magic slowly eating away at him didn't help matters.

Regardless, he was still a good man.

And he had done what he did for the right reasons.

Though it wouldn't take much for those lines to grey, and that terrified him.

None of that mattered, however, if he was dead. That's why he was here, tonight of all nights. He hated Order parties, but tonight, the coronet would be on display. Tonight, Kian Brittenworth would take a wife and take up the position as the head of the Order of Crowns. It was a coronation, for all intents and purposes. Though it wouldn't be, not if Lock got to the coronet first. It was, after all, a matter of life or death.

It could suck the Twisted Poison from his system, break the curse, so to speak.

None of that could be done while he was downstairs in the mortuary. Regardless, he was Rien's apprentice, aiding in defining the cause of death, meaning he didn't mind the work as he spent most of his time with Aura anyway.

His head was pounding, a feeling he was used to now, as poison circulated through his system. Lock shut his eyes. The pain of that night was still very much circulating within him. He'd never talked about what he'd seen, what he'd done, except with Aura, who'd been there when he'd done it. But he liked it that way; it was a secret held between them—a simple sign that at least one person might not see him as the monster he saw in the mirror.

The only secret she didn't know was how cursed that night had left him.

"Lock." Aura snapped her fingers above his face as he squinted at the ceiling. He lay on one of the wooden mortuary tables in the Order's basement, the ones *meant* for dead bodies. Beside him, Aura was glaring at him, her apron splattered with blood and Twisted toxins over her blue dress. It was somewhat of an amusing sight if he were being honest with himself. The corner of his mouth lifted in a smile, though he fought to hide it. Rien was upstairs doing business with Duke Brittenworth, so that had left Aura to do most of the work. Well, and him.

"Is something amusing?" Aura asked.

"Not at all." Lock swung himself into a seated position, looking down at her. "I just think that if you're going to wake me up, you should do it as if I'm the prince of your dreams."

Aura rolled her eyes, turning away from him and back to the body on the table next to the one he'd been laying on. "Put an apron on and help me."

"I'm usually a better help if the *entire* autopsy weren't already performed," Lock said, sucking in a breath, the stench of antiseptic stinging his nose, before eyeing the filled vials of Twisted toxins on a side table next to an exposed heart taken from the body.

Aura cast him a look over her shoulder. "You're going to sew him up."

Lock gave her a look, but she ignored it. In truth, he didn't mind getting his hands dirty, but he was very aware of the time ticking away. Surely, he only had a few minutes until the coronation, and the coronet would become a lot more difficult to get his hands on. Pushing off the table, Lock moved to the door where the aprons hung and slipped one over his head, tying it around his waist quickly. It was a practiced movement, one he knew how to do ever since he'd started working with Rien three years ago, after he'd excelled in Rien's class at his past academic institute. Pushing his dark hair back, Lock stepped up beside Aura. To him, the body was nothing compared to the story behind it, the story its insides revealed, whereas Aura's area of expertise lay in the magic side of things, the facts used to connect dots. Aura handed him a needle and thread, which he threaded before bending over the body. Three years ago, he might have gagged at the putrid smell or the blood, but now it hardly bothered him as the thread wound in between flesh.

"This is not how I expected my evening to go," he muttered as he started the branches of stitching that made a Y over the chest.

"Maybe if you'd stayed awake—"

"I was awake. Ever heard of thinking?"

Aura hummed, taking a syringe filled with white liquid—Twisted Auditory toxins—and dispensed it into a vial. "You have blood on your shirt."

Lock looked down to see that he did, indeed, have a spot of blood on his cuff. However, he couldn't just roll up his sleeves, exposing his darkened veins. Lock pretended to not have heard her as he finished off the stitching.

"They thought he'd gone insane," Aura said, carefully flipping the man's wrist to show the blue gem, the imprint given to all Order members.

"He doesn't look like he was," Lock said. Externally, he looked fine. There wasn't even a sign of tiredness beneath the eyes. Reaching over the body, he grabbed the file, proving himself correct. He had no medical history and no history in an asylum.

"No, *Locklyn* Mortsakov, thank you for your *astute* observation." Aura held up the vial filled with Auditory toxins. "He'd reported hearing voices—"

"Manifested by the Twisted," he finished.

Aura nodded, setting the vial back down. She took her apron off as he wheeled the table with the body on it into an adjoining room where it would be disposed of. There were about four cadavers in the room, each a little different than the next, and he wondered, with all those bodies waiting to be buried, how their lives had ended. In tragedy? He shook his head; he supposed dying was a tragedy in itself, regardless.

When he returned, Aura was writing notes in a small notebook to give to Rien so he could write a report, though it was clear that the cause of death was self-infliction. Aura shut the book just as he hung his apron on the door, opening it for her.

Together, they moved along the corridor swiftly, mounting the stairs two at a time, as per routine. They didn't speak. In his case, he was concerned about getting the coronet, and Aura was probably lost in thought. They'd just made it to the top of the stairs as Rien barrelled into them. He stepped backward, apologizing. Rien was a tall man, streaks of grey through his once-brown hair. His face was pale, though even more so now, clearly having been scared from running into them.

"I was just coming down to see you two. Is it done?" Rien asked, straightening his hands down his black jacket.

"Yes," Aura said, handing him the notebook.

"Excellent."

Lock and Aura stood there, almost awkwardly, as Rien read through the notes, humming in approval before he snapped it shut. Without another word, he turned on his heel and left, presumably to inform the duke of their findings.

Lock sighed. "You know, I'm starting to think he's just using us."

"Lock, we are under his *apprenticeship*. What'd you expect?"

"Correction, he's *your* uncle."

"Yet, here I am, doing the work while you doze off," Aura said before moving into the hallway. Lock stood there for a moment, staring at her. His Magic flared, his veins beginning to glow purple. Ahead Aura stopped walking, staring at him.

His heartbeat was suddenly erratic.

He brought up a shaky hand to loosen his tie.

His breath was coming in fast.

Fear.

Not his own, though, and clearly not Aura's. He squeezed his eyes shut, forcing his magic away. His breathing returned to normal, and he straightened his waistcoat, thankful no one else was in the corridor.

Lock frowned. Had that been Twisted Magic or his own? Surely, he'd feel it if it were Twisted.

No. It couldn't be Twisted Magic, this was a noble's party. The duke has guards set up everywhere. It was practically a fortress, seeing as this Society they so eagerly hunt is made of Twisted Magicians. Long ago, the Twisted had been banished from society, their magic too dangerous, too manipulative to stay—what with the false senses they used as their own form of poison on the mind—and Lock hoped that the rumours of them being back were a hoax, though, with every body that turned up at Rien's laboratory or the Order's, he was becoming less and less hopeful.

"Are you alright?" Aura asked, and he blinked, finding her right in front of him.

"Quite."

Aura looked skeptical but did not argue. Instead, Lock held out his arm to her. "Come, Dearest Aura, I told you I wouldn't let you break your vow."

Lock steered them in the direction of the Order's library. He just needed a few moments alone, to regain his thoughts, before he went in search of the coronet.

"Lord Mortsakov?" A voice called from behind them. Both he and Aura spun to see Kian Brittenworth, the heir, striding towards them. Lock frowned, he thought the coronation was bound to happen any minute. Kian bowed his head to Aura. "Miss Wrentroth. Running from the party already?"

Lock nearly choked on a laugh, a lord running away? Certainly, his parents would have a heart attack.

Running made one weak.

Or so he was told anyway.

If only they knew how long he'd truly been running from his own secrets.

Lock was unfazed, however, by the question.

Kian was taller than Lock, with straight golden hair and a pale face, and wore a short blue velvet coat with matching waistcoat over a stiff collared shirt and trousers. His cheekbones were sharp, his chin held high, every bit the heir he was. Kian was made of angles, superiority dripping off of him.

Aura readjusted her arm in his, both seeming to have slipped into a demeanour that was usually reserved for dealing with the duke and merchants. The heir to the Order of Crowns and Lock hadn't exactly talked over the years, but he supposed they got along well enough. Though Kian had a way of always staring like he was always guilty of something. And as if the heir had heard his thoughts, Kian's eyebrow rose, awaiting a response.

"None of your concern, really."

"Isn't it?" Kian said, glancing over their shoulders. "Though maybe you're right, maybe it isn't. Do be sure to be there for my coronation."

The heir strode off, not looking back.

"Strange," Aura muttered, and Lock tended to agree as he led her down the corridor. Kian didn't have a habit to speaking to someone unless he had reason, and so far as Lock and Aura were concerned, he had none. He needed to figure out which of these rooms housed the coronet.

Lock haphazardly dared a glance behind him, feeling a shiver down his neck—almost as if they were being watched. He could have sworn he saw a shadow whip around the corner, but there was nothing when he blinked. In fact, the only sound was Aura and him walking on the wooden floor. The sooner they could get to the library the better.

"*Killer.*" A voice slithered into his head.

Aura placed a hand on his arm. "Are you alright?"

"Fine."

He set his jaw as they continued toward the library, ignoring the magic that pulsed inside him. The magic that made him lie.

And the magic that held the vial for him as he'd poured it into his classmate's glass.

The magic that had made him a killer.

The *magic* that had cursed his heart.

THREE

ISKRA

Iskra Storenné was thinking about fire. More specifically, about setting one. She was not that reckless, nor intrusive, however this party was *incredibly* boring. Hence, she was considering burning something. Since fourteen, she'd endured such gatherings as a member of The Order of Crowns, each year growing more and more annoyed as no progress had been made. In exchange for protection, Iskra had agreed to help Duke Brittenworth and his Order catch a secret society made up of mostly Twisted Magicians, known as The Society. However, it proved they knew how to keep their name out of the news.

And the gutter.

They were a whisper among polite society, and Iskra was beginning to question whether they were even real. No matter, Iskra's reason for attending tonight had nothing to do with the Order's incompetency, and everything to do with the coronation.

"Must you look so miserable?" the youngest son to the Duke, Xavier Brittenworth said. She turned to meet his gaze. They stood in the ballroom, their backs against the wall as if observing the guests. The coronation was set to begin any moment, and anticipation was coursing through her.

"I must."

"Suit yourself," Xavier said, taking a sip of wine that had found its way to his hand as soon as he'd entered the room. Iskra pressed her back to the wall. The ballroom they found themselves in was long, lit by three small chandeliers, their flames casting the room in a brightness that Iskra preferred in social settings. It gave her more room to see potential enemies, more room to locate a way out if needed—the sort of thing her parents had trained her to look for. Whispers of electricity were circulating amongst the upper classes, and she guessed that as soon as he could, the Duke would get his hands on it. After all, the Duke was one for the newest and best inventions, and Iskra couldn't blame him. The idea of electricity was one she hardly could begin to comprehend, but that didn't mean it couldn't excite her.

At the front of the room, on a raised platform the Duke was pacing, and Iskra glanced at a clock that hung just above the entrance way. Kian should be here soon.

So should the coronet.

Iskra's hands itched to feel its silver in her hands before it even *touched* Kian's head. Iskra was no thief, but she would do whatever it took to get her hands on it.

Guests were starting to get restless, the dancing having long since stopped, giving way to bustling conversation. Some about Kian, his coronation, others about this Queen of Spades and a recent kill. Others simply cast looks in her direction, eying her, dressed in a set of black trousers, a white blouse, and a long black coat, silver buttons lining the sides—not a dress, as expected. Iskra didn't care for any of it.

Beside her, Xavier checked his pocket-watch. "If you'll excuse me."

"Where are you going?"

Xavier gave her a sympathetic look. "Somewhere better than here."

She glared at his back as he left. They'd known each other for three years, and here he was, leaving her alone. He'd been gone only a few moments when Duke Brittenworth cleared his throat, pushing his greying hair out of his face. He cast a quick glance to his right, where Kian should have been standing, the only indication that he was annoyed. It was odd, how Kian wasn't here yet. He wasn't the sort of man to miss his own coronation. Silence blanketed the room, and Iskra couldn't help but note the absence of people that ought to be here. Xavier, for one, though she couldn't blame him for wanting to miss it, and Locklyn Mortsakov. Not that she cared, but she would have appreciated his attendance, seeing as he was the only person she'd consider speaking to at events like these, though he was probably off somewhere with Miss Wrentroth, the mortician's niece, whose company Iskra didn't entirely hate either, though *she* was never at these parties.

Duke Brittenworth spoke, this time his voice booming off the walls of the room. "To you all, for another year of trying to break the Society and their crimes. And to celebrate a new era of the Order."

A chorus of voices erupted from around the room, though Iskra stayed silent. The Society, so she'd learned, were killers, employing Twisted Magicians to do their dirty work; a crime that would have Scotland Yard tripping over themselves if the Society was never brought to justice.

A crime that had the Order acting like fools trying to discover their identity.

Kian Brittenworth would only be carrying on a hopeless task. Perhaps it was a good thing he was failing to show up.

Iskra huffed an amused laugh, only to realize too late the room had descended into silence again.

"Miss Storenné, is something amusing?"

She didn't point out that the duke should use a title when addressing her.

"*Je suis désolée,*" Iskra said. "I was just wondering if we've gotten anywhere on identifying the leaders of the Society. It seems we've been doing a lot of dancing without having the correct music. You understand, *oui?*"

The Duke said nothing for a long moment. Finally, it was about to get interesting.

"We're working on it."

Iskra rolled her eyes. They'd been *working on it* for longer than Iskra had ever been around as a member of the Order. She wondered how much of it was just the duke's way of creating alliances in a world destined to hate *him*.

She looked around the room once more, at the Order's faithful members, each pledged with a blue gem on their inner wrist, including her, wondering if any of them actually believed they could stop the Society. It was becoming clear that it was a fool's errand. Iskra had simply been biding her time, until this day when she could get her hands on the very thing that could help solve *her* problems. Iskra huffed a sigh of frustration.

Then she heard it.

The toll of a bell.

The emergency bell.

Duke Brittenworth's guard flooded into the ballroom, shouting orders. Then everything stopped.

Everyone was frozen, a white luminescence creating an aura around the guests, each of their faces stalled in fear. It was as if they were petrified, no longer seeing the ballroom, but their own personal version of Hell. Their eyes appeared to be glazed over, and Iskra knew this was work of the Twisted—like they were being ordered to still, their head filling with the command to freeze. The guards had hands on their weapons. Duke Brittenworth looked mid-shout, and Iskra's hand grasped her pendant that hung at her neck, feeling magic pulse at her fingertips. It was silver, a green gemstone encased in the metal workings, the chain snaking up her neck. It was the only gift she'd ever kept from her parents. It, like the coronet, was an ancient object, passed through generations, meant to aid the monarchs against Twisted Magic. This particular pendant helped Iskra keep her thoughts *her own*. It was a block against anyone—including Twisted Magicians—using Perceptive Magic to stay out of her head.

It was also illegal.

All magical relics were supposed to have been eradicated when the Twisted were sent into exile, save for the coronets. Though, some have since been destroyed, other monarchs accepting or even welcoming death as a result. All other relics that were sent to be destroyed, quickly found themselves in the wrong hands.

Gripping her pendent tighter, she willed herself to move forward. Her magic, Perceptive Magic, allowed for mind reading, yes, but it also meant that Iskra had been trained to keep her walls up from other's trying to read her mind, but that did not extend to Twisted Magic. Her parents had seen that and gifted her the pendent. Perhaps they shouldn't have. Perhaps they thought it'd make her stay in France. Perhaps they thought she was scared, that the pendent would dispel any hesitation. It didn't. Iskra did not fear dying, even then. What she feared was dying, stuck in a gilded cage.

Carefully, Iskra picked her way through the stilled party guests. Her boots echoed loudly in the silent ballroom, and she stopped, fearing that someone might hear her.

But there was no one around to *hear* anything.

Perhaps this was an opportunity. She came for the coronet.

Now she had no witnesses.

A smile flickered on her lips as mounted the stairs and turned down a hallway, leaving the terrified party guests behind her. The halls of the Order of Crowns were silent, Iskra's boots echoing against the mahogany floors, as she passed shut doors. Her blonde hair fell into her eyes, and she pushed it away only to pause as someone exited a room and fell into step beside her.

Iskra let her hand drop away from her necklace, her hands sweaty. She hadn't realized how tight she'd been holding it, her hands marked with the shapes that framed the gemstone. It would seem the Twisted had only targeted the party guests.

"Miss Storenné," the girls voice was formal. Iskra glanced at the guard beside her. Zoialynne Adrennha did not look at her, her gaze straight ahead. In another life, one so far from here, they'd been friends. There was no sign of that now. When Iskra had fled from France, she'd gone to the Americas, where she'd helped Zoialynne flee her past employer. On the journey to England, Iskra had confided in her about the real reason she was running. Since then, Zoialynne had not only become head of Duke Brittenworth's guard but had also become Iskra's personal informant on her parents' whereabouts, should they ever find out where she was.

Now, Zoialynne pretended that Iskra didn't exist until she delivered her monthly reports on the movements of the elegant Viscount Louis Storenné and Viscountess Marie Storenné and their search for their utterly reckless daughter. Iskra rolled her eyes at the thought.

"Zoialynne," Iskra said, matching her stride with the guard. "I need you to do something for me."

Zoialynne glanced at her, a sign for her to continue.

"I need you to go to the docks. I have an informant there who has information from France."

"Iskra, Duke Brittenworth—"

"Cannot do anything if he's frozen. The entire ballroom is."

Zoialynne's eyes flicked in the direction that Iskra had come, before returning to Iskra's. "Fine."

Iskra watched Zoialynne stride off in the opposite direction, presumably to use the furthest doors away from the ballroom. She stood there for a moment before turning down another long corridor. While there *was* an informant waiting at the docks, Iskra had also sent Zoialynne because she'd be out of the way when she found the coronet. The magic didn't hold value to her, more than the actual coronet itself. It was a power symbol, one she could use to show her parents that she wasn't coming back, and that they could not override her say. Iskra was about to move into the room where she knew—and hoped—it would still be, when two sets of footsteps echoed along the empty corridor. She turned just in time to see two familiar figures striding towards her. On the right was Locklyn, and beside him Aura, their heads bent in conversation. As they approached, Iskra cast a glance behind her at the door, eager to step inside. Turning her attention back to Lock and Aura, she forced a smile. Lock looked at her as though she'd interrupted a moment; then again, he always looked like that when minor inconveniences happened.

"Where were you?" Iskra asked Lock.

"Helping our dear scientist here in the mortuary."

Aura scoffed. "I wouldn't call you taking a nap on the mortuary table *helping,* but please, go on."

"I wasn't *sleeping,* dearest." Lock turned his attention back to Iskra. "On a scale from 'stern-talking-to' to murder, how upset were my parents that I failed to show up for Kian's coronation?"

"I don't know, Mortsakov. They weren't causing an outright scene, so I'd say your fine," Iskra said. "Besides, the entire ballroom is currently dealing with Twisted Magic."

Beside Lock, Aura looked curious. "What happened?"

"They aren't moving."

"Twisted Perceptive, then. The good news is, as I'm told, the Duke has a good relationship with the military thanks to Sir Waltzeen so I'm sure it will be no problem to remove toxins from their system later."

"*Oui,*" Iskra said. "Or he might just ask you."

"That would be illegal."

Iskra didn't think Duke Brittenworth cared if it was or wasn't, but she wasn't going to tell Aura that. Besides, going to the military would benefit him as they had extraction tools that were meant to be used on other soldiers who were affected by Twisted Magic; *tools* that worked quickly. Seeing as the Order members were *hypothetically* helping the Crown by fighting the Society, extraction by the military wouldn't be illegal.

Or at least that's how Duke Brittenworth had explained it to her when she's asked about it all those years ago.

Aura shifted. "Do you happen to know if Rien told the Duke about our findings? There is significant damage to the brain, and all signs point to death by Auditory Twisted magic. By the looks of it, the cause of death was done by the dead man." She paused as if realizing she was getting carried away. Iskra shook her head.

She hadn't asked Aura on the particulars of the post-mortem, nor did she know who the Order had asked her to examine, but Iskra wasn't so impolite as to tell Aura to stop talking. Especially when the girl's eyes lit up. Iskra had once been like that, in love with the work she did, but her parents had robbed it from her. Iskra had been a guard for a wealthy estate, just to get away from her own, but when her parents found out, she was forced to resign and take her place as a part of the house. She'd then spent the rest of her time trying to dismantle the empire her parents had created for themselves, only she was getting too close. She'd sent half the place up in flames, and ran. Her parents had called her a criminal, and that was it. Iskra had disobeyed her parents, and it had ruined her life. At least Aura had Rien, who supported her endeavours in the sciences.

Jealousy, Iskra reminded herself, was one of her most annoying sins.

"I didn't see him," Iskra replied, deciding now was not the time to get the coronet. She didn't add that she wasn't exactly looking at anyone either, too focused on the magic pulsing in her palm. Lock and Aura started to move away and Iskra had no choice but to follow them, it would be too noticeable if she didn't. She walked behind them, trying to ignore the sensation of eyes drilling into the back of her skull. The guards were nowhere in sight, probably stuck downstairs, and Iskra had half a mind to do their job for them. *The complete, incompetent fools,* she thought bitterly. Iskra cast another look backwards, but all was silent just as before, but as she squinted, she swore she could have seen a figure slip into a room.

Then, a scream tore through the darkness.

FOUR

SÖREN

Sören Niaheartson cursed Scotland Yard with everything in him. He stumbled on the grass outside of the Order of Crowns, grumbling as he pushed himself up. When Scotland Yard told him to give a letter to his father, the last thing Sören had expected was breaking into the Order of Crowns, and dodging guards and nobles alike. He'd almost been caught in the shadows of a hallway before he'd turned and traced his steps back to the front door, deciding to take a different way in—one that was less risky. He regretted walking into the Yard only three hours ago looking for his father, all but forgetting to avoid Inspector Renyard. If Sören knew anything, it was that if the Inspector could get away with not doing something, he would; hence why Sören had tread all the way over to the Order to give his father a letter. He wasn't even allowed to be here—yet another risky idea. Sören stalked around the side of the estate, his boots falling lightly on the grass. The Duke's manor, and the Order of Crowns headquarters, was two stories of fine red brick and arches that led to intricate gardens. Windows covered the walls, and Sören suspected it might have looked nice had the feeling of anything gold-gilded done anything more than remind him of a world he did not live in. No, he spent his nights in a house, bordering Whitechapel. It had been a nice place once, a home, but the life had long since been snuffed out since his mother died. Sören shook off his musings. He wondered what his father was doing inside; was he cursing the night, or was he providing the Duke with updates on the latest work he did for the Order? Perhaps he was drinking a glass of champagne, celebrating the coronation of the new heir. That was yet another reason why Sören shouldn't be here. The last thing he needed was to be surrounded by aristocrats too drunk to keep their words in their mouth, let alone his father who'd made it clear that Sören shouldn't get involved with any of the Brittenworth's.

    Sören tugged his brown coat tighter around him, nerves settling in his stomach. While Sören's father worked for Scotland Yard, he'd also done work for the Order and Sören was worried the Yard would find out. After all, they didn't look kindly on Secret Societies, especially ones that were out for inevitable war.

    Sören ducked into an archway, manoeuvring his way through what he assumed were servants' halls and found himself in the courtyard. He held his breath in the shadows as the quiet conversation of guards floated past him. He waited for a breath or two, observing his surroundings. Cobble lined the grounds, the moon shining delicately onto the walls of the manor that surrounded the yard. He stood, hidden within the shadows for a few heartbeats, straining to hear for any guards or nobles he wished to avoid. Anxiously, he rubbed a dark hand across the back of his neck, almost meeting his hair which he wore closely cropped to his head before dropping it. Letting out a sigh of relief that he was alone, he began to walk toward the other side of the cobbled grounds where he hoped to find someone who could get his father. There was no way he would be entering the main halls of the building. Not when he was sure to get lost or spotted by an Order member, all dressed up in finery, smelling of alcohol and other things

Sören wished to avoid. High above, the manor seemed daunting, casting long shadows along the ground as he walked cautiously toward the other side.

He tested his auditory magic, but it was blocked, and whether the Duke knew about it, he couldn't say. He placed his hand on the door handle, but it was locked. Sören swore silently—

"What are you doing?" a voice from behind him asked, soft yet demanding. Sören turned to see a boy push away from the shadows of an alcove, discarding a piece of paper on the ground, before striding slowly towards Sören, curiosity in his gate. Sören recognized him immediately as the Duke's youngest son, Xavier Brittenworth. Now, what he was doing here, talking to Sören, he had no idea. A horrid thought came to him. What if Xavier was going to tell his father he was here? Though it wasn't like he knew the real reason Sören wasn't allowed at these parties.

"Breaking into your house," Sören said.

Xavier arched a brow. "Is that so?"

If Sören was looking down on himself right now, he would have slapped himself. He'd just admitted to *almost* breaking into one of the most influential man's estates to *his son*. This was going just splendidly.

"What are you doing?" Xavier asked again.

Sören stared at him. Debating whether or not to tell him the truth, and arguably letting his mind wander. He and Sören had only talked once before, but God, out of all the boys and girls he'd ever been with—which arguably wasn't many—Sören thought he was the most attractive man he'd ever laid his eyes on. Xavier had a pale face, visible freckles dotting his cheeks even in the moonlight, and curly blond hair. He wore a green velvet jacket slung over his shoulder, half covering his pristine white shirt and black trousers. The sight did absolutely nothing to calm Sören's rapidly beating heart. The second-in-line heir was quite a sight if Sören was being completely honest with himself. He had an air about him that screamed of quiet elegance, and Sören admired him for it. He also happened to know that, while Kian and Xavier were brothers, they couldn't have been more different, at least that was what his father always said. Where Kian was sophisticated, Xavier was all laughs and, well, sunshine. But here, standing before him, Xavier seemed to be every bit the heir, except for the fact that he didn't hold the title. Sören felt dull standing next to him, in his brown trousers, and worn coat. The boy lifted a brow as if he expected Sören to answer. Sören scrambled to collect his thoughts, his hands grazing the paper he had so graciously folded into his pocket.

"I have a message for my father from Scotland Yard."

"How lovely. What do the police want?" he said with all the curiosity in the world, his brow furrowing ever so slightly.

"My guess, some investigation," Sören replied, turning to leave.

"You mean you haven't read it?"

Turning back to Xavier, he shook his head once. "No. I'm all for a thrill but meddling in my father's affairs is not one of them."

"Then why, pray tell, do you never attend Order parties?"

Sören was falling. Back into memories of what he'd done. Back to the night, he woke up in an empty room on a mortician's table, no clue of how he'd gotten there. He had woken up, his mind aching and his heart an uncomfortably slow rhythm. It'd been three years since he'd been saved from poison, and yet regret haunted him like a ghost. That was the real reason why his father never let him come to these, and truth be told, Sören had never wanted to come to them either. He was falling and scared to find poison in his hand again, and that one day, the universe would take his life back. But things were different now.

He was different now.

He turned to go. This was a horrible idea. Scotland Yard said it was urgent, but surely Sören could wait for his father back home. He didn't need to be putting himself through this right now. He didn't need memories of his failure following him, and he certainly didn't need his mother's ghost stalking him. *She's gone.* And if he hadn't been damned, maybe he could have saved her. Maybe he could've woken up at university instead of a scientist's morgue table, and she would've scolded him. Because a scolding would've been better than eternal silence.

He had made it to the archway again, where he'd need to find his way out, but Xavier called to him. Despite it all, Sören found himself turning back.

"I didn't know my question would upset you," he said quietly.

"No, I suppose you didn't."

"Let me make it up to you." There was a question in Xavier's words, and everything inside Sören was torn in half. He shouldn't be here, but Xavier was offering a chance for them to speak. Sören stood silently, waiting for Xavier to speak. "Let me help you deliver the letter to your father."

"I—" he paused, a thought striking him. "Why aren't *you* inside?"

"I lost track of time drawing. Besides, I have no obligation to be there if everyone hates me anyways."

Sören eyed the discarded piece of paper only a few feet away, and Xavier snatched it up, putting it in his pocket. He wondered what the heir did to make people hate him, but then again, sometimes being the second-born might've been enough. Sören wondered what Xavier hadn't wanted him to see, but Sören supposed it really wasn't any of his business.

"I see."

"So, will you? Let me help you, that is?"

Sören nodded. Although he should go, part of him had wanted to stay. He guessed want was often greater than need, a force that was hard to ignore because of the craving it left within one's soul. Sighing quietly to himself, Xavier walked ahead of him, pausing once he got to the door, and Soren found him waiting there. As he opened the door for Sören, a haunting chill crept into his heart. The two of them would most certainly not be allowed by the Duke. Sören was no noble, and even though his father was practically indebted to the Duke, it wouldn't matter. He shook his head. He was getting way too ahead of himself.

It was a wonder how Xavier could find his way through the halls without getting lost. Sören thought to make conversation, but by the time he'd worked up the courage to open his mouth, Xavier had turned into a different corridor, ascending a flight of stairs, and Sören could make out the sound of voices in the distance.

"We're almost there," Xavier whispered to him.

"Alright," Sören said. He didn't know what else to say.

"Xavier?" Sören recognized that voice as the Duke's second, Sir

Waltzeen. Ahead, Xavier inhaled and turned around instead of continuing down the hallway, forcing Sören to follow him. Now, where this little detour was going, he had no clue, but he followed him, nonetheless.

I should have gone home. He ran his hand along the wall so as not to trip. They passed a large window that faced out into the courtyard where a woman stood, deep in conversation with the gentleman before her. Sören thought he caught the flash of something, like a blade—no, he couldn't have. This was a party, and frankly, Sören needed to stop looking for the worst in people. He'd been paying too much attention to his father's stories again.

Ahead, Xavier pushed open yet another door, running down a flight of stairs and pushing open a door at the bottom. Sören followed cautiously for fear of tripping over himself. A few moments later, with just the strike of a match, about five candles were dancing on a long worktable. Sören gathered that this must be a small workroom, secluded from the rest of the house. It couldn't have been much further from the servants' quarters. The wooden floor was covered by paint-splattered tarps, and art hung on the wall before the long wooden table that took up almost the whole length of the room. A large window stood looking out into the trees and greenery beyond, stationed on the corner of the manor, and Sören had the distinct feeling that they were now on the complete opposite side of the building. An easel was positioned diagonally as if its painter were to paint the greenery. On the opposite side of the room, a few finished canvases hung from the ceiling, turning the otherwise organized space into what was more of a chaotic one. It was an artist's space, he supposed; *Xavier's space.*

After one final examination of the room, he turned to find that Xavier was no longer there.

Sören had been left alone.

Alone—no. He pushed the memories from his mind, sitting down on one of the hard wooden chairs encircling the worktable. He took several deep breaths. There was nothing wrong with being alone. He was safe here.

He jumped as Xavier put a plate of biscuits before him. Now, where he'd had gotten it, he had no idea, but they looked comforting. He would have thought that Xavier would've ate something fancier, as biscuits were far from it, but Sören didn't care. Truth be told, he was quite hungry. He took a bite of biscuit, watching as Xavier did the same—how easy it was for him to pretend he wasn't related to the Duke as if blood filled with riches didn't flow in his veins.

"Sorry about the letter." Xavier nodded to Sören's pocket, where he'd stuffed the letter as they'd been walking. "I just really, *really,* don't want to see my father at the moment. Avery would've taken me right to him, telling me about how I'm *expected* to show up."

"It's fine." *Was it?* "It's probably best to avoid my father as well. He'd have my head if he knew I was here."

Xavier chewed thoughtfully, looking at Sören. "You know, usually people can't take their eyes off me."

Sören cast him a sideways glance, wondering where he was going with this. "I know."

"But you're different."

"Not really. I'm just trying very hard," he admitted. "You're also rather cocky. Anyone told you that?"

"You, and several others."

Sören took a bite, mulling over the conversation. It was common knowledge that the Duke favoured his eldest, but Sören had never thought that maybe it was because Xavier didn't *want* his father to favour him either. Sören supposed it went both ways: where Xavier was an artist, Kian excelled at business and making everyone else's, his. Sören inhaled. This was the first time in a while he'd felt himself relaxing as he talked with someone. He knew that Xavier wouldn't bring up his past because he didn't *know* about it, and that was something that made him breathe easier. But even if Xavier did know, Sören had the feeling he wouldn't be like the others.

"Sören—can I call you Sören?"

"Depends. Can I call *you* Xavier?"

Xavier scoffed. "It's not like you can call me anything else."

Sören didn't point out that he could address the boy as *Lord* Brittenworth. "Well then, yes Xavier?"

"Can you do something for me?"

Xavier's face had gone serious.

Sören shifted. "Sure."

"My brother is going to be crowned tonight with a coronet. I need it."

"Why?" Sören arched a brow. "Planning on becoming the heir?"

"No. Just—" He fiddled with the cuff of his shirt, the first and only sign that Xavier was not as confident as he had presented himself to be. "I need you to trust me. Can you do that?"

"Yes." Sören had long since been warned about making a deal with someone like Xavier, that it could go bad. But, Sören wanted to help him, and *maybe* the not-so-heir could help him with something in return. "But you're going to need to do something for me too."

Xavier raised a brow. "Like?"

Sören thought for a moment, though his heart knew exactly what he wanted. "I want to work as a Detective. If I help you get the coronet, you need to put in a good word with the Yard."

"Can't your father?"

"My father doesn't want me anywhere other than at home."

Xavier stared at him for a moment, leaning forward. "So, I put in a good word at the Yard with someone who *isn't* your father, and you help me get the coronet?"

"Yes."

Xavier nodded, seemingly pleased with Sören's response. Sören looked down at the table, unsure of what he'd just gotten himself into. But surely, it couldn't be that hard to get the coronet.

"How do I get the coronet?" Sören asked, raising his gaze back to the boy.

Xavier glanced at a clock that hung on the wall. "There's a room where it's housed, second floor, fourth door on the right. It should be there for another twenty minutes."

Sören nodded.

"Sören?" Xavier's voice quieted. "I know this might not matter much, but thanks for treating me like a human"

Before Sören could ask what he'd meant, Xavier reached into one of the worktable's drawers and pulled out a bottle of wine, uncorking it. Sören was eighteen, he could drink, but his heart was suddenly racing again. He turned away, thoughts rushing past him, horrid and regret-filled. He was stronger than this. He watched the red liquid as it was poured into a glass before him—anything could be poison-filled, and poison made people make stupid decisions. He should understand that not every bottle was filled with laudanum. His hands shook, accepting as Xavier passed the glass into his hand.

A flash of memories hit him, causing the glass to drop back to the table with a thump as he stood.

"Sören—" Xavier started, something like worry in his voice, before he started to speak again, though Sören didn't hear it as he muttered a "no problem," to Xavier's previous comment before bolting from the room. He should trust, but he was scared, scared of feeling like he was helpless. Or perhaps that wasn't what he was really scared of.

God, you idiot, you stupid, stupid idiot. You're just scared of falling for him, aren't you? That's exactly what it is? You're scared to open up. Pathetic. He scolded himself but then shoved his feelings away.

What if Xavier was using him as an alibi? No, no, now he was going mad.

His footsteps pounded up the stone stairs that had led them to the room, and finally, he stopped just outside the door, leaning against the wall. He felt dizzy. He shut his eyes, placing his palms against the cool wall. All he could see was Xavier's smile and the way his hair fell into perfect curls atop his head in the candlelight. The door banged open, and his eyes shot open as a hurried-looking Xavier stumbled out.

Sören should've stayed and explained his behaviour. Xavier would try and understand and end up feeling sorry, and Sören couldn't watch that happen.

Not again.

He'd seen it too many other times.

So, despite not knowing where he was going, he did the most foolish thing probably ever done in the history of, well, the universe and ran. Like he always did. He was somewhat disoriented by his surroundings but managed to locate a flight of stairs, taking careful consideration not to trip. It was only when he'd made it to the second floor when he'd finally calmed down. Then, he bumped into someone, swearing loudly.

"Aren't you the detective's son?" a female voice asked, a slight French accent reaching Sören's ears.

"Apologies for bumping into you," he said quickly.

"Sören, why are you here?" A different voice asked, a voice he knew belonged to Aura. Her uncle had worked with his father on a case once. Aura, who had saved him from dying. They weren't truly friends, she was just a person who had done their job, but he still felt indebted to her. He hoped to see that day when she could be recognized for her talents as a poison scientist because God only knows she deserved it. Technically, she shouldn't have saved him; she was no doctor, but she had reversed an antidote, and he'd lived. He'd lived, and he intended to prove to the universe that he was worthy of his second chance. He shook his head, instinctively reaching for the letter in his pocket.

"A letter for my father."

"I hate to break this moment, but are we going to forget about the scream that happened a few moments ago?" a new voice asked. Sören didn't recognize it. Shuffling to move with the others down the hallway towards the noise, he fell into step beside the girl with the French accent. In the dark, he could just make out a pale face and long blonde hair. She was dressed in pants, and Sören admired her, for certainly the Order would've much preferred her to look like a classic lady. She cast him a glance.

"Iskra Storenné." She didn't offer her hand, only cast her gaze forward once more. Ahead, Aura and the boy strode with determination in their step. He knew that Aura would be looking for any signs of poison or foul play for Rien, but he had no idea what made the stranger walk with such purpose. Perhaps it was just the way he walked, being noble, or perhaps it was for reasons only the shadows and the angels above knew about. Sören's father had taught him that many people spoke without words. All one had to do was look for it, but Sören was unsure how one could when even his walk might be hiding something. He shook his head. He'd met a lord, and now he's thinking as if he was a suspect in a police investigation.

"I'm Sören," he said to fill the silence that had surrounded the group, just as they passed the door Xavier had told him housed the coronet. Iskra nodded once.

"As I said, the detective's son."

Ahead, the boy cast a look over his shoulder. "I'm Lock."

"As in Locklyn—"

"I wouldn't finish that if I were you," Iskra warned him. He wanted to press her on what she meant, but kept his mouth shut. Really, it wasn't his place. Besides, he'd be gone as soon as he got this letter to his father, back to his world, where people had to work for earnings in their soot-stained clothes, where some were just getting by. Sören was one of the lucky few, but that didn't mean he was ignorant to the rest of the world. Ahead, Aura had turned the corner. But Sören had paused to look behind him; he could have sworn he'd seen the shadows move. Only for a moment.

"Aura?" Lock asked but paused when he saw what she was looking at. Sören rounded the corner, his gaze locked to where Aura and Lock now stared, frozen in place.

He might be sick.

Lantern light flickered in the darkness that pooled on the floor—blood, he realized. *So much blood.* A knife lay discarded near the puddle, slick with crimson, whispering of a cruel fate.

"I think someone wanted us to see this," Iskra whispered, breaking the tension that had been brought throughout the group. Lock was the first to move into motion as he waved at a passing guard, telling them to fetch Mr. Wrentroth and the Duke. Sören, however, stood frozen and unmoving—unable to take his eyes away from the blood—and who exactly lay there. Sören only registered the blond hair of the victim, his high cheekbones, before his eyes snapped back to the blood, staining his blue waistcoat. It was suddenly too quiet, and only then did he register the lack of people, of guards, overall, the lack of festivities. He would have asked Aura about it, but his eyes were transfixed on the floor in front of him.

Too much blood. He thought, and to his horror, his magic sprung to life following the trail of blood. The sound of a heart thundered in his ears, and it wasn't his own.

    One beat.

    Another.

    Another.

    It faded.

    The heartbeat had sounded strangely like a dying melody, and he knew, for a fact, that he didn't want to hear the rest.

FIVE

AURA

Dead. Kian Brittenworth was dead. A knife through the heart. Once the ballroom had been pushed back into reality, the Twisted having presumably fled after Kian's murder, Duke Brittenworth had dismissed the guests, keeping quiet about his son. He'd then sworn each of them to secrecy. The only people who knew were them, who'd found the body, and Scotland Yard. A thousand thoughts had run through her head last night as she and her uncle returned home. How had the murderer gotten close enough to Kian to stab him? How long had he been lying there? How long would it take for rumours to spread?

For a moment, she feared that she might've killed him, though Lock confirmed that she'd been with him the whole time. He'd seemed worried, when she'd asked, but she had waved him off, not in a place to provide any information. After all, what was she supposed to say? *Dearest Lock, I've become the villain with a head made of fog, so if I have blood on my hands, do forgive me, will you?* She almost scoffed but bit down hard on her tongue.

Kian Brittenworth had been murdered only a corridor down from where they'd been standing. She'd seen him, laying in a puddle of his own blood, a softness to his features that looked as though he had seen true power—godlike amongst a world of people too preoccupied to notice true magic. There had been so much blood, and although Aura was used to seeing it, a cold dread still wound its way around her heart.

Now, standing in her uncle's laboratory only a few blocks from home, a chill ran down her spine as she watched her uncle cut into Kian, the silver of the scalpel cutting flesh. His heart was missing. Her mind switched off like it always did, scientific notes flipping through her mind as she pulled a notepad from a writing desk on one side of the mortuary. She began writing down her observations, but Rien paused her with a hand.

"Come examine the brain."

"Yes, sir." Aura cast her gaze over the usual Y-incision, sown up by a gentle hand, the irritation looking stark against the black thread. Her uncle worked with post-mortems; she was the Twisted poison expert. Usually, Lock would've been here to take on Rien's work, but he wasn't, and she tried not to let her disappointment show. Aura set her notepad on a small desk in the corner and took the syringe he offered her, an odd calm falling over her as it always did. Rien nodded at the body, an indication that she could begin her examination. Rien had already cut across the crown of the head, sawing through the cranium, exposing the brain. Aura looked at it as her uncle *tsked*—a sound that indicated he had been expecting it. The brain, for all its pink colour, was glowing a dark purple, an indication that Twisted Emotive magic had been used on Kian when he died. Usually, the task of examining Twisted victims could be done via syringe, but in the case of murder, all angles had to be examined. Carefully, Aura slowly stuck the needle into the brain and pulled upwards, watching as the syringe filled with the purple toxins. Rien handed her a small vial where she deposited the Twisted toxins before stoppering it. Aura's brows drew together in thought. Had

Kian still been alive, the magic would have had a time limit, leaving lasting effects *in* the body, but the Twisted had acted quickly, making sure that Kian died when he was still in the state of his senses being mystified. Setting the vial onto the desk, she pulled out her notebook, staring at Kian's still body before turning her attention back to her notes. Aura scribbled at the paper, making a small diagram, running through the facts in her head. At present, only one piece of evidence stood out to her, Kian had died because of a Twisted, and that thought alone set Aura's nerves fraying. They were supposed to be in exile, underneath London, not making their presence known. She'd never been so close to the Twisted in relation to their crimes. She only studied their effects on the brain. The fact that one was able to get past the guards, use magic to freeze the ballroom, and most likely got away with murder was a thought that left chills. That is unless the Twisted was also an Order member.

    Her uncle returned from the back room carrying a new spool of thread, and Aura prepared to leave so that he could finish with the autopsy and get it back to the Order. On her way out, she told Rien about the purple liquid and the probable timing of the murder before removing her apron, splattered with the remains of Twisted Toxins and blood, and hanging it on a hook by the door to the laboratory and pulling on her coat.

    She took her time walking back towards the townhouse, letting the beginnings of autumn seep back into her bones. It had rained last night, the streets still damp, and by the looks of the clouds above, there'd be more on the way. Ducking between two parked carriages, Aura crossed the street towards her and her uncle's townhouse. As her boots tapped against the cobblestone, her thoughts began to stray to the previous evening. She wished to forget all the horror of the past day, but as much as she hated to admit it, death fuelled her. Perhaps it was wrong, but when she worked in the morgue, it was another way to prove that she was not just another violent soul with a knife in her hand.

That being poisoned by Twisted Magic time and time again was not her fault.

Her mind strayed to the coronet, to Avery's threat, and how she'd have to plan to go back to get it.

Aura shook her head as if to remove the thoughts from her head. She mounted the stairs to her townhouse but paused.

"Lock," she said, barely masking her surprise in time. "What are you doing here?"

"Apologies." He stood with one hand resting his hat against his back, the other holding an envelope. "I knocked, but there was no answer."

"I was at the laboratory."

A small smile. "I see. I was going to check there next. My apologies for not being able to make it, I was seeing my parents back to their estate."

"I understand," Aura replied.

Lock stuck out his gloved hand, handing her an envelope. It was sealed with blue wax. She peered at him over the letter.

"From Iskra," he explained as Aura broke the seal, reading the letter. Iskra wanted them at the opera, tonight, at nine.

"Does she usually do this?" Aura asked, waving the letter around.

"You mean demand your presence or go to the opera?"

Aura rolled her eyes and he grinned.

"Best get ready," Lock said.

"Best you leave before I consider murdering you."

He placed a hand over his heart. "You wouldn't dare."

Lock was right and he knew it. Aura thanked him for the letter, and he nodded.

"See you tonight, Dearest Aura."

She had already closed the door before she could think of a reply.

Two hours later, Aura was in her carriage on her way to the Royal Opera House. She'd chosen a dress of the richest purple, one eerily similar to the coat she wore when she would run *errands* as the Queen of Spades. Though guilt had clawed its way inside her, she had lifted the floorboards in her bedroom with practiced ease, retrieving the simple dagger from inside. It had a black hilt with a silver spade at the head and a sharp, decently sized silver blade. She had tucked it into a sheath and stored it in one of the hidden pockets near her waist. Now, Aura reached for the dagger as the carriage slowed before the Opera House. *If, then,* she reminded herself, letting go of her hold on the weapon. *If, then.* She sighed; if only it were always that simple. She'd forgotten how beautiful it could be at night. Oftentimes she was stuck in the morgue or conducting her own research or blinded by Twisted Magic coursing through her telling her what to do to truly admire it; all the sparkling lights and the clusters of people living in their own world together. However, the feeling was quickly replaced as she scanned the crowds. People from all walks of life crowded her, from nobles coming to enjoy the show, to pickpockets hoping to pilfer a few extra coins. Aura made a face; she didn't care much for the class system. The way she saw it, there was always another injustice or another person that needed saving, regardless of the blood that ran beneath their skin. Not that she was trying to play hero, she just needed to prove that she could be something more than the pain she'd endured. She was never sure what had coaxed her the first time—to pick up that knife—but every time after, it was because she was someone else, because the magic was too strong to ignore.

She was a shadow that went unnoticed by most.

She was tired of the expectations and the torture that came with being a lady in scientific fields of study—or a lady in this society at all. As the Queen of Spades, she was just human.

And she was feared.

It was that very thought that caused the war in her head; she was a polarity, two magnetic sides joining to forge forgiveness for her grief-stricken soul. She handled both life and death in her hands and sometimes it was too much, guilt ready to drown her. No matter, she slipped her invisible mask into place and adjusted her skirts, feeling her knife once more for reassurance.

The Royal Opera house was an extravagant building with smooth beige bricks, large pillars and windows that cast rectangular shapes of light onto the ground below. Aura alighted from her carriage, her shoes tapping against the ground as she walked to the theatre. Laughter echoed in her ears, but it sounded far away as she scanned the streets, assessing everything.

Calm down, she scolded. The smell of food mixed with expensive perfume lingered in the air. She sighed, stepping into her role. It was the same role she found herself using more often. Not that she was bothered, but it left unwelcome anticipation for when her mysterious employer would want her to strike again. Around her, several other wealthy-looking people made their way into the theatre. Some cast her looks of recognition as her uncle's insane niece; others seemed to be too preoccupied with excitement to notice. She clasped her hands behind her back.

Aura, having noticed Iskra from her carriage, strode up to the girl. Iskra's blonde hair fell down her back, her dress an elegant shade of red with a significant amount of jewelry lining her neck. Several ladies cast Iskra looks, though whether they were out of disgust or admiration, Aura couldn't tell.

"Glad you could make it," Iskra said as Aura took up a place at her side.

"Did I have a choice?"

Iskra huffed a laugh. "You always do, Aura."

"Seems I made the right one, then."

"Indeed." Iskra said. "Have you heard anything from Lock or Sören?"

Aura shook her head. In truth, she didn't know *why* she would know anything. She hadn't had a reason to see Sören or Lock today, though she did know Lock was coming. Sören was not on the verge of collapsing, as far as she knew, so she really had no reason to know what went on in his mind. Though, when she had seen him last night, it was clear he wasn't the boy who had laid on her operating table, whispering words meant for people who have death holding their hearts. He was better, and perhaps it was foolish, but she felt a sense of pride. She gave him a second chance, and that was more power than she should've been able to wield. The poison had been so close to taking him, and she'd played God for only a little bit, just enough to watch his breath fall back into the rhythm of the living. Aura pressed her lips together, ignoring the fear that crawled beneath her skin; she held both life and death at her hands, and it terrified her.

As for Lock, she knew him well enough that he wouldn't miss a night out even if the universe was falling apart.

As if on cue, a black carriage with the symbol of a sword piercing a heart came to a stop next to them. Lock jumped out and muttered something to the driver. He wore an outfit similar to the one he'd worn three days ago; a white stiff-collared shirt, crimson velvet waistcoat, and black tie, but this time he'd added a proper dinner jacket and hat, which he took off as he reached Iskra and Aura.

"I was beginning to think you weren't coming," Iskra said to him.

"Why? It isn't like I have anything better to do." His gaze flicked to Aura, and she smiled at him. She immediately dropped her gaze to her skirts, the weight of the knife stabbing into her guilty mind.

"What about choosing a wife?" Sören said, coming up behind Lock, whose own suit was made of grey cloth, his waistcoat black, decorated with outlines of what appeared to be scales. He looked somewhat uncomfortable in it, but Aura made no sign she'd noticed.

Lock rolled his eyes. "I'm beginning to think all of London knows about my *parent's wishes*."

"That's because they do," Iskra replied before handing each of them a slip of paper with a seat number before they marched inside.

Aura squinted at the brightness of the theatre, playing with the fabric of her dress as she followed Iskra through the crowd—a crowd that reminded her of all too much of *that* night.

She was back, searching for Alon's body amongst a group of people, shouting for the police—and him lying in a pool of blood. She'd been pulled away before she could get a closer look at him. Aura shut her eyes before feeling a presence stop beside her in the crowd. She opened her eyes to see Lock holding his arm to her, almost as if he knew what she was thinking.

"Your sadness is drowning me," he said.

"You could just block it out."

"Perhaps, but your sadness is often best left at home on evenings out, I find."

Aura took his offered arm, "I'm sure you're right."

The tickets Iskra had given them were in a box on the topmost floor, four red velvet chairs placed perfectly, two in front, two in the back, and a curtain behind them to hide the hallway. An enclosed space. She reached for her knife before letting her hand go to the necklace at her throat, a reminder of who she was. She removed her coat and settled it in her lap, taking her time to look around. It was an expansive space, a large crystalline chandelier hanging from a domed roof, casting light onto the audience below. A red curtain covered the stage, though it would be lifted in only a few moments when the show started. A few people were looking around curiously, some lingering on their box—on Lock, more specifically—before moving on. From where he sat behind her, Lock shifted forward so his chest was near her shoulder.

"Dearest Aura, at this very moment, I would be honoured to have you confess your undying love for me," he whispered.

She half-turned towards him. "In that case, *my lord,* I will love you forever if you kindly refrain from speaking."

"Make m—"

"Make me the happiest girl in the world and do as I say."

Lock sat back, amusement flickering in his eyes. "Very well."

Aura rolled her eyes, once again cursing his Emotive Magic. She hadn't meant to feel jealous, but she took comfort in the fact that he didn't like the stares either. Beside her, Iskra shuffled her seat back out of the prying eyes, and Aura wished to do the same. Instead, she got comfortable, squeezing her hands tightly in her lap, partly to help calm her nerves and partly to stop her hands from reaching for her knife.

A bitterness settled over her heart, or rather it had never really left. She shut her eyes just as the lights in the theatre dimmed, and it was like a blanket had been placed over the crowd, silencing them. The only sound came from the odd shuffle of feet or cough from someone down in the main audience. The orchestra started, a symphony that swept over the awe-struck crowd as the first singer came onto the stage. She never understood the opera. Even now, she thought she might doze off if it weren't for the company she kept and the silent promise to leave with more information than she'd come.

"So," Sören said slowly. "Why did you really want us here?"

Iskra turned in her chair to face him. "Find it hard to believe I invited you?"

"Actually, yes." A pause. "You don't seem like the opera-going type."

Iskra gave Sören a look before turning to face the rest of them. "As much as I find you an idiot, Sören, you're right. There is another reason for inviting you."

"Duke Brittenworth's guard isn't available?" Lock mused. Aura frowned. What guard was he talking about? She supposed it really wasn't her business. Lock winked at her, and she rolled her eyes, cursing his Emotive Magic.

"Locklyn, do keep your mouth shut, it really won't help you when I decide to throw you in the Thames."

"Your concern is endearing, but I know how to swim."

"Aura?" Iskra asked. "How mad would you be if I drowned him?"

"Extremely." She paused, ignoring the amused look Lock shot at her. "Now, why are we here?"

Iskra huffed. "I wanted to see how you were after the murder." Sören opened his mouth, but Iskra held up a finger. "And before you say anything about *caring*, I was wondering if you saw anything strange."

"You want to gossip?" Aura clarified.

"If that's what you want to call it."

"I felt this agonizing fear," Lock said, his eyes straying to the singer on stage before returning to them. "Indeed. Dearest Aura and I saw Kian that night, and he seemed fine."

"Not that I've ever been to these parties before, but there was something strange happening, and it was not simply the fact that I was not supposed to be there," Sören remarked.

"How do you figure?" Aura asked, trying to remember any of the events from last night. In truth, they all blurred together. All she saw was Kian and his lifeless body, over and over.

"I heard a dying heartbeat."

Aura clenched her fists tighter. She'd never heard a dying heartbeat, but she'd seen the life drain from the eyes as blood oozed from their lifeless body. That wasn't something any of them needed to know, and frankly, a fact she wished she didn't.

"Aura?" Lock asked, drawing her from her thoughts. "Did you hear what Iskra asked?"

"Apologies, no."

"I asked if the autopsy report shed some light on anything?" Iskra repeated.

Aura turned in her chair, glad to talk about something she knew well. "Kian died with magic in him—Twisted Emotive Magic. There were no traces of any other significant damage, the knife being the cause of death. Rien noted that the knife had entered from the front, piercing the heart directly. It is safe to assume that whoever did it has excellent anatomical knowledge of the body, and that Kian allowed them to get close to him."

The group seemed to sit back. Each, she presumed, was pondering the news, or imagining the scene, judging from the way Sören was digging his fingertips into his knees. She couldn't blame him; it was quite horrific.

Her magic pricked. Before she could shove it down, a blue haze lit her vision, but before she saw anything she felt a cold hand on her wrist anchoring her back to reality.

"Ah yes, use your magic in a dark room for the entire world to see," Iskra muttered, removing her hand.

Aura shot her a look, though she wasn't sure Iskra noticed.

The curtain of the box fluttered as an attendant stepped into the box.

"Miss Wrentroth, there is a Sir Waltzeen here to see you."

Aura rolled her eyes. Of course, he had to be here. She turned to face the attendant, "Please inform Sir Waltzeen," she bit off his name, "that I am, in fact, not here and that he must have mistaken me for someone else."

The attendant looked uncertain but shrunk away after Aura gave him the most withering glare she could muster. She did not want to see Avery, especially after she'd failed to get the coronet. She turned back towards the stage, trying to focus on the vibration that echoed throughout the theatre as the singer hit her final note. Her head felt dizzy, and she braced her head in her hands, a wave of tiredness washing over her. She was sure someone called for her, but perhaps she was imagining it. Her head snapped up.

Her hands itched.

Inhale.

The glint of a dagger.

Exhale.

Avery dead.

A smile.

She left, ignoring the looks her friends gave her and fastened her coat around her. The attendant looked at her when she stepped out from behind the curtain, a frown deepening his features.

"Where did Waltzeen go?"

"Just outside, miss. I believe he decided to leave early."

"I just remembered I must tell him something." The lie formed easily on her lips. More so than she would have liked.

"Would you like an escort?"

She shook her head. She rushed down the hall and ran down the stairs. She passed a gentleman on the stairs, who paid her no mind, letting her easily slip his hat from between his fingers before placing it on her head, tilting it over her brow. It certainly wasn't her usual Queen of Spades uniform and was quite impractical, but it would have to do. She found a side entrance that took her into an alleyway where she found Avery striding back and forth in front of the entrance. She pulled her hat lower over her face, slipping her knife from her pocket. One minute, she was jogging up behind him, being as silent as she could in her shoes. The next, one hand was against his mouth, making sure he made no noise, the other wielding the knife at his throat.

"If I let go, you won't scream," she hissed, the scent of alcohol and dust causing her to wrinkle her nose. Avery clawed at the knife at his throat before grasping it and pulling it away, spinning out of her grasp. Aura's hands shook as he discarded the knife on the cobblestone of the alleyway they stood in, pain slicing through her head—an effect of being controlled by Twisted Magic.

Avery straightened his frock coat, flicking away invisible dust. "So hasty with that knife."

"And who shall I blame for that?" Aura asked, discarding the hat to the shadows of the alleyway.

Avery stared at her for a moment. "Perhaps, you should just listen when you're called."

"I'm not your pet."

"No, I suppose not." Avery inspected his fingernails. "You're a pawn."

Aura ignored him. "What do you want?"

At the entrance of the alleyway, a group of well-dressed gentlemen passed. She didn't catch many words, but she did hear them talking about the Queen of Spades and her most recent errand. Aura brought her gaze back to Avery, glaring at him. He was just a helper, but how easy it would be to blame him. The magic that encircled her system was pounding in her head. Avery sighed, picking up her knife from the ground and handing it to her.

"The coronet is missing," Avery said.

"And *he* still needs it?"

Avery nodded.

Aura turned to go, but Avery caught her wrist.

"I do hope you remember what will happen if you fail?"

"I do." Avery hadn't been specific, but Aura had vowed long ago that no one she cared for would die by her hands. Avery seemed pleased with her answer before going serious.

He inspected his hand. "Maybe your uncle, maybe your lord . . ."

Aura scoffed. "Lock is not *my* lord."

Avery looked up then, a wolfish grin spreading over his face before going serious.

"See me later," he said, though Aura had already slipped back into the shadows, inching her way towards the door, her heart pounding at Avery's suggestion.

A shadow gone unnoticed.

Aura sheathed her blade and stuck it back into her pocket. Removing her coat, she began her slow return to the box. Her brow relaxed, and she braced herself on the staircase's banister for support. Her hands shook, her breath coming in heavy gasps, her mind unravelling from its torture. God, she had been incredibly reckless. What if someone recognized her? Surely not. She was trained enough to know that. A sinking feeling plagued her; she used to be able to control herself.

That hadn't been her.

She had almost *enjoyed* the blood draining from Avery's face as she'd held her knife to his throat, and she wasn't sure if that was the cause of Twisted Magic or not. She wasn't sure she wanted to find out either.

Iskra cast her a strange look as she entered the box.

"Where did you go?" Sören asked after she'd settled herself, hiding her shaky hands in the folds of her skirts.

"Air," she managed, not being able to form a total lie. She glanced at Lock, who knew all the facts about the night she'd found her brother dead; the way she'd felt trapped, how she'd panicked. He nodded in understanding, and she turned back to the performance as if she hadn't just pulled one of her own little acts off herself. She offered no further explanation, and the others didn't ask for one.

The last singer hit her final note before they all made their way out. People dressed in a sea of colours mingled with their friends, laughter plastered onto their too-red faces, and Aura wondered how they could be so happy when all she felt was blood staining her hands.

Outside, the air was refreshing on Aura's face, and it was almost enough to drown out the guilt that held her heart since the incident tonight. She'd come because Iskra had invited her, because the murder of Kian Brittenworth was dragging on her mind, yet she was leaving with no information of the murder, but of herself: she was losing it. Perhaps she *was* Rien's insane apprentice, destined for doom. Iskra had stepped into her carriage as soon as the show had ended, and Sören had set off down the street in search of a Hansom Cab; and Aura had thought Lock had left until he was before her, her guilt-ridden eyes looking into his concerned ones. He fiddled with his hat in his hands.

"Are you—"

"I'm fine," she replied, not wanting to get too deep into the conversation.

"Right," he coughed. "I wanted to say how lovely you look tonight."

Aura smiled a genuine smile. "Thank you. Some might say you don't look too bad either."

Lock scoffed. "Dearest, everyone would say that. This was handmade by the best in London."

"Right, how could I forget?"

"I can think of one reason."

"And what's that?"

"Whatever you're avoiding telling me," Lock replied, donning his hat. Aura stared at him, unable to form words. He only smiled, a playful smile, and Aura knew he hadn't been expecting her to answer. He held out his arm and helped her into his carriage. Aura had been expecting to take a Hansom home, but if Lock was offering, she couldn't refuse it, especially when her bones were beginning to feel like they might collapse in on her at any moment.

Aura awoke when the carriage slowed to a halt. She hadn't remembered sleeping, but at least she hadn't been plagued by nightmares. Lock smiled and nodded goodbye as he helped her out of the carriage. He seemed distant, though she suspected he was just as tired as she was. She strolled to the door, her legs aching. It was somewhere around midnight, and her brain was still foggy from sleep. She barely registered opening the door and hanging up her coat on the stand by the door. She made her way through the dimly lit hallways of her house until she reached her bedroom. Across the way, Rien's light was off, an indication that he was still out, providing Duke Brittenworth with Kian's autopsy report. Aura pushed into her room, leaving thoughts of the dead behind her. Several lanterns had been lit, and she found her eyes closing as she removed the knife from her pocket and stored it beneath the floor. Forcing herself to pay attention, she pulled out a syringe, and got to work removing the Twisted Toxins from her veins. It was illegal, to extract it, as the Crown feared that the venom would be used as poison. But the truth of it was, Aura would rather commit a *crime* than die from the toxins. She stored the Toxins in a small jar, making a mental note to take it when she next visited Avery. Aura placed the wooden panel back into place before standing. She dressed into a soft pink nightgown and, wrapping a housecoat around her, ventured down to the kitchens to grab a glass of water.

When she returned, she placed it on her bedside table and was about to crawl beneath the covers when something caught her eye. There was a letter on the desk that faced the window. She swore it hadn't been there earlier. She walked over and looked out but couldn't see any movement. The hatch on her window was unlocked, the latch flipped over. A chill ran down her spine. How could someone have snuck in here without being seen? Her room did face the street, but surely someone would have been noticed climbing the walls. Whoever had left the letter must have been very skilled at breaking and entering. How could something like this shake her? After all, she'd done plenty of this before. She supposed it was different when it was actually happening to her. She looked at the letter; it was unmarked and had no seal. Cautiously, Aura opened it. In printed type, like the kind they used in the newspapers, it read:

```
Kian's murderer is close to you.
```

SIX

ISKRA

Iskra weaved her way through the busy streets, until she reached the docks. Her heart was hammering in her chest, her breath heavy. It was still early, too early to see how Zoialynne had faired at the docks three nights ago. Clouds rolled over the sky, casting the world in grey. Though, three years of living here, and Iskra wasn't sure that London could be anything other than grey. That is, of course, for when there was sun. Her boots crunched against the gravel, as she slowed her pace. The docks were already busy, shipyard workers bustling their goods into waiting boats, or pushing carts packed with packages to be delivered throughout London. Sailors called orders to one another, half of them getting lost in the clatter of workers. Water lapped against the edge; the sound immediately bringing comfort to her. Long ago, that very sound had reminded her that she was safe, it still did. When Iskra burnt half of her parents' manor down, along with several important documents, and they'd accused her of being a criminal, Iskra had fled and the only thing that eased her worried mind was the sound of open water. It was part of the reason Iskra found herself at the docks. Another nightmare, this one the same as all the others, her running, and ending in death. More and more often, Iskra was finding herself at these docks just to calm her racing heartbeat, reassuring herself that if she were to die, it wouldn't be by her parents' hands.

A ship horn sounded just as Iskra turned down a narrow alleyway, pulling her hat lower to cover her eyes. She did not want to get caught in this part of town, even dressed in her usual trousers and blouse. She was still a woman, and times were difficult, especially after the Ripper Murders. Fear clung to the alleyways like soot, like anyone might be ready to take up a knife. Iskra wasn't scared, per-se, but she was careful in places where she knew she might draw attention. Iskra kept walking until she reached George Yard, walking briskly through the little alleyway. Keeping her head bowed, she shoved her hands into her pockets, as she turned the corner. This street was significantly busier, lined with taverns and shops. A few drunkards sat on the street, presumably from the night prior, though Iskra stalked past them and pushed into a pub known as The White Hart. It looked small from the outside, with its wooden exterior that eventually gave way to brick, glass windows looking in on the dim pub. Lanterns hung just below the sign, still burning from a long night—or, more likely, the barkeep having forgotten to turn them off. Iskra pulled open the door, its hinges creaking slightly as she stepped inside. It was a long space, circular wooden tables scattered throughout the room, with a bar to her left where a barkeep was cleaning glasses. At the end of a bar, a man took a sip from his glass. The barkeep cast her a cursory glance as she passed through the room taking a seat beside the man.

Sir Avery Waltzeen looked at her and scowled. "What are you doing here?"

"Xavier told me where to find you."

It wasn't a lie. She'd been to the Order earlier this morning, demanding to know where Waltzeen was. Fortunately for her, Xavier was not one to withhold information. Even if Xavier hadn't known, Iskra did know that this pub was one that the Duke favoured for business dealings, though Iskra couldn't fathom why. After Kian's murder, The Order had kept quiet about what happened the night of the coronation, and she needed to know why. They weren't saying anything about the Twisted Magic that had been in effect, which brought into question how trustworthy some of the Order members were. When she had pledged allegiance to the Order three years ago, she hadn't signed on to stand next to the killers of an innocent man, regardless of motive. Besides, now she'd need to figure out when she could get the coronet without all hell breaking loose.

Avery turned to look at her, sighing. "Why are you *here*, Iskra?"

"Because Kian wasn't killed over nothing. I wish to know what it is he had, or knew, that left him dead."

Avery, who'd been taking a sip of the liquid in his glass, set it down and stood. "No."

Iskra opened her mouth to respond, but Avery took a step closer, lowering his voice.

"*Miss Storenné,*" he sneered. "As we speak, we are investigating the possibility of espionage within the Order, so I cannot disclose that information to you."

Iskra took a step backward, so her back was against the bar. "Where is the coronet?"

Avery stared at her for a long moment, his gaze intense. He must have decided she wasn't worth his time because he turned on his heel and strode out the door. She could have followed him, instead she turned slamming her palm against the bar, earning an agitated look from the barkeep. Muttering several French expletives, she *hmphed,* turning on her heel and marching out the door. Her efforts hadn't come to nothing, she supposed. If anything, it proved her right. The coronet did have something to do with Kian's murder. It also proved that the Order was investigating the possibility of an imposter, and if someone indeed had committed espionage, whoever it may be, was closing in on the Order and whatever secrets lurked beneath their carefully concealed exterior and had been willing to risk their cover by murdering Kian. Iskra could only wonder what truth they were close to uncovering.

Leaving the docks behind her, Iskra hailed a carriage. There wasn't much to do beside go home and figure out what her next move would be. A carriage slowed, and after telling her driver instructions, she climbed in. Her carriage rumbled along the cobblestone, going slowly as the East end traffic gave into West end. Iskra shut her eyes, sleep somehow finding her even after being so cruel to her earlier this morning. In truth, Iskra knew she wouldn't actually fade away—her mind was reeling and was in no condition for her thoughts to settle themselves in. Beneath her, the carriage rocked along the streets, a calm chaos that Iskra often savoured when she was alone. Bits of conversation reached her ears, and though unintelligible, a small smile found itself placed upon her lips. Her world was spiralling, people were dead, yet somehow Iskra felt none of it for the first time in a long while.

Her carriage lurched to the side, causing Iskra's eyes to fly open. Someone collapsed into the seat opposite her. Iskra wondered how they could have possibly gotten in here without the driver noticing, let alone the carriage stopping. Across from her say a boy with black curly hair, which he wore closely cropped to his head. His dark brown skin was slick with sweat, and a wicked gleam sparkled in his eyes. He raised a hand, wiping at his forehead with a swipe of the white sleeve of his collared shirt. The detective's son—Sören Niaheartson—smiled at her as though he had not just hijacked her carriage, let alone her peace of mind.

"What a thrill!" he exclaimed as if he had just performed a circus act rather than jumping into a moving carriage.

Iskra stared at him. "How do you say it? Oh yes, what the Hell! What, how—"

Sören made a face. "How? The carriage was barely moving, Iskra. I'm not reckless. Why? I have information you want."

"And jumping into *moving* carriages is a regular occurrence for you?"

"Still not over that, are you?"

Iskra offered a slight shake of her head.

Sören only adjusted his sleeves, regarding her as she gained some of her ability to think back. How a detective's son managed to pull that kind of stunt off escaped her. Iskra shook her head; she certainly wouldn't find out about it now, not while there were more pressing matters at hand.

"Tell me something," Sören said. "Do rich people make a habit of sabotaging each other?"

"Considering I set half my parents' estate on fire, I'd say the answer is yes."

Sören looked slightly shocked at her response, though Iskra was too tired to explain herself. Instead, she sighed, leaning forward and placing her elbows on her knees.

"You said you had information."

Sören cracked a smile again. "You'd be surprised what I know."

"*Dépêchez-vous, s'il vous plaît.*" Iskra was growing impatient. At the funny look Sören shot her, she translated. "Hurry up, please."

"You could have just said that." Sören shrugged, then clapped his hands. "I saw you visit Sir Waltzeen."

"How—"

"I live in the area." Sören waved her off. "Anyway, I assume you were asking him about Kian."

"I did. And I presume you infiltrated my peaceful ride home because you thought I needed to know . . . what?"

Sören held her gaze, before he launched into his rather detailed investigation on his father's classified notes and the discoveries the police had made on the night of the murder.

Sören threw his hands up. "Indeed. I might be going to jail soon if anyone finds out. Kindly use your status to help me out."

"I barely know you."

"Even better."

Iskra rolled her eyes as Sören sat back, presumably in his own thoughts.

"It was common knowledge," he said, though Iskra wasn't sure if he was talking to her or himself. "That Kian was supposed to be playing suitor for several guests that night, correct?"

"Yes."

"So, should Kian marry, his father would be allowed to step down, and Kian would lead the Order."

"That's usually how it works. You think someone didn't want him to become the Order's leader?"

"Not exactly." Sören shifted as if he were preparing to tell a long story. "The night Kian was murdered, he had, in fact, chosen a wife and the proposal was to happen that night. My father's notes didn't give her name—presumably for her safety. That was step one to his ascension. Step two would be the coronet."

Sören met Iskra's gaze. "And Iskra? That coronet is missing."

"How did you know I was interested in the coronet?"

"Because Xavier was too." Sören shrugged. "And probably half of the people in attendance at the coronation."

Iskra sat back. "So not only did you look through your father's classified files, you also were willing to steal the coronet for Xavier?"

Sören nodded. "In exchange for something, of course. I also believe that Kian was killed over the coronet. Tell me, why is it so special?"

Iskra did not want to give him a reason to want it, to need it more than she did, so she said, "It's best if you didn't know."

Sören looked like he was about to argue but stopped himself as the carriage slowed. He cast a look out the window before saluting her. "You know where to find me."

She was about to tell him that she didn't, in fact, know where to find him but he was already gone.

Shaking her head, she alighted from her carriage and watched as the carriage drove away. Iskra knew she should go inside and deal with all her contacts in England's correspondents, but she could do that when her mind was less occupied. Instead, she turned on her heel and headed down the opposite way she'd come. Iskra paused, playing Sören's words over in her head.

You know where to find me. Now, she might not, but if she did, the boy could be a huge asset to her—especially when it came to international affairs. Yes, using him as an informant might not be such a horrible idea. Iskra smiled at the thought, then continued her way down the cobbled streets, letting the thoughts consume her.

SEVEN

LOCK

"No one is going to want to marry you dressed like that," Lada said as he walked into the drawing room. It was late and the lamp light cast long shadows on the drawing room walls. Lada, Lock's younger sister, lounged over a chair, her dark hair braided in a crown around her head. For fifteen, she was quite the adult, always telling him information he didn't want to hear. Not that it mattered, since Lock knew he had an impeccable sense of fashion. Lada was a smart girl, but she refused to attend any parties of social standing, which Lock was somewhat grateful for. The parties were what forced him to adapt, and he was worried they'd be for Lada what his education was for him—Hell. Or rather, not the education, but the people that broke him. It had ruined him. He didn't want that for Lada, so as long as she was happy with how she was living, then that is all that mattered. Of course, people gossiped about their family, that he was the perfect child, and she was a shadow, but Lock didn't much care for the lie's others told for pure entertainment. Lada didn't need to know that the world was cruel and bloody, much like he had, or even Aura had.

He could never forget the day Aura told him Alon had died. Aura's brother, three years older, had died from a street fight—being in the wrong place at the wrong time. At least that was what Aura had told him when she had returned to Rien's laboratory with tears in her eyes. At the time, Lock had only known her for around four months, but Lock couldn't forget Aura's face or his own as she was dealt her final blow—the final crack to her worn mind. He suspected he'd looked much the same to Aura the night she'd helped him bury the body of his best friend only a month earlier. That night, Aura had known what he'd done and had helped him anyway. He suspected that the burial was for her as much as it was for him. For him, it had been a way to conceal what he'd done, but he suspected that for her, it was like Alon's very own burial—he never got a funeral. He suspected his torn-up body of peeled flesh and exposed brain had been discarded in other ways, and that Aura would never unsee what she saw that night; the night she'd watched the police drag the body away, the night she had told it all to Lock, that night they'd sat in the corner of Rien's laboratory, hidden away from the rest of the world, just to feel like they were the only people alive. He shook off his thoughts, remembering that Lada was in the room. He swallowed and did his best to keep his features smooth.

"Well, I'm in my own house, and as far as I know or care, I have no interest in marriage right now." He slumped into a chair. With his unbuttoned waistcoat and untidy hair, he might as well have been posing for some portrait. Lada *tsked* and pulled her embroidery from the lamp table beside her.

"Sure, you don't," she said, without looking up as she threaded her needle.

Lock looked at her through lowered lashes. "What do you mean by that?"

His sister shrugged.

"Lada?" he prompted, though he had a sneaking suspicion of what she was going to say.

"Well, it's quite obvious that you fancy someone." She raised her brows, very much reminding him of himself. She wasn't wrong, but he wasn't about to tell her that.

"And it's quite obvious you can't keep your thoughts to yourself."

"Good thing I'll be back with mother and father tomorrow, then," Lada said. Her parents had gone back to their country estate earlier today, but Lada had, to his knowledge, a dress appointment here in London. Lock frowned, fearing Lada had misinterpreted his words. He didn't want her gone, though it was probably best if she was. They came to visit sometimes, and when they did, they stayed in the townhouse they'd gotten when Lock had decided to take up permanent residence in London. It had been two years since then, and he'd made it *his*. The drawing room itself was crowded with books on all sorts of topics, a violin sat propped in the corner next to the faded blue chair, though it had been years since he'd played. The whole townhouse was cluttered, and he couldn't be bothered to keep it in order, but it was enough.

Lock picked up a newspaper from the centre table and flipped around, hoping to find any news of Kian. There was nothing, and he wasn't entirely surprised that the Order wanted to keep it hidden from the prying eyes and ears of the public. He slapped the paper back onto the table just as Lada looked up from her embroidery.

"I heard the Queen of Spades killed again last night; some merchant on the East side."

Lock met Lada's gaze. "Lada. . ."

"Come on, Lock," she pleaded, setting her embroidery aside and standing. "You can't deny it's interesting."

"*Killing* interests you, does it?"

Lada opened her mouth to argue. "I—"

"No, Lada, okay. If you have some fascination with serial murderers, go read last year's newspapers. I'm sure the Ripper would love an admirer, but *please* do not fill your head with this sort of nonsense." Lock stood, holding up a finger. "Lada, it is dangerous out there, do you understand? I care for you and the last thing I need is for you to end up dead."

"It was just a conversation—"

"I don't want to hear it, Lada."

Lada looked at him, her gaze hard, before striding from the room, her gait heavy. He hadn't meant to be so harsh. But mention of the Queen of Spades always left him uneasy, her name whispered in nearly everything didn't make matters any better. Lock sighed, leaving the drawing room and pulling on his coat in the entrance hall. It was late, but he needed air, and time to let his temper cool. Donning his hat, he stepped outside, jogging down the four steps that led from his townhouse. The other townhouses that lined the street were mostly dark, their inhabitants within most likely sleeping. The only light seemed to be coming from his own, where the guest bedroom faced the street. The cool air bit his nose, but it was welcome. Perhaps it would put him out of his fury. Tugging on his hat brim, Lock headed down the street, his footfalls painfully loud in the quiet streets. Turning onto the main thoroughfare, he headed towards the River Thames where he knew of a good pub situated nearby. He made quick work of exiting Marylebone, quickly leaving the district and any anger he'd felt at Lada along with it. Carriages rode few and far between, the horse hoofs distant in only a matter of minutes. As he walked, his mind returned to the Queen of Spades. She deserved every bit of what would inevitably come for her. She deserved whatever punishment the police decided. She deserved to pay. Lock crossed the street and darted into a narrow alleyway, lanterns lighting the way. The pub was in sight at the end of the road, the sound of jaunty laughter floating back to him, along with the sickening smell of ale.

A thud of boots sounded from behind him.

He paused, turning.

The Queen of Spades stood there, a rich purple coat fastened up all the way to her neck, silver buttons trailing down to about her waist before the coat parted to reveal black trousers and booted feet. A hood had been attached, covering her face. Beneath it, she appeared to be wearing a mask, gems seeming to branch over what was visible of her cheeks, like purple tears. Lock stiffened.

She held a bloody knife.

Боже правый, he thought, in Russian, something he only did when he was flustered. He shook his head, correcting himself in English, not wanting to have any ties to his father. *Good God.* As if he hadn't had enough rage for one day. Now, the person he despised stood before him, frozen, watchful. Where had she come from? He glanced up at the ledge of a building. By all Gods, she'd just jumped. He glanced back at her. Her purple hood was pulled low over her face, the long purple coat cascading down the length of her figure, the colour so dark it almost reminded him of the blood she now wiped off the blade, staining the fabric.

The blade with a spade engraved on the handle.

He smiled, though it was filled with nothing but animosity.

"Planning on putting that knife through me?" he asked, watching her.

She sheathed her knife into her coat. *Answer enough.*

He took a step forward. "Have I not done anything worth killing over?"

"You're innocent." Her voice was rough, her back tense. The stance of a killer, he supposed.

He scoffed. "And if I were not?"

"Then I suppose I should kill you right now." She paused. "Though I have no reason to believe you've done anything. Do I?"

He raised an eyebrow. "I'm curious. You kill people, yet they aren't given a chance to give their story. Yet here you stand, prompting a confession?"

She reached for her knife again and began flipping it between her hands like a habit. "They deserve what I give them."

He took a step forward, lowering his voice. "What drives you to kill?"

She caught the knife and pointed it at him. "*That* is none of your business."

Fair enough, he thought. He supposed he couldn't get all the answers. Lock clasped his hands behind his back, taking another step forward. She didn't move. They were close. If he reached out, he could take off her hood. It would be so easy, but truth be told, he was enjoying this little game.

"What drives you to hate me?"

He stilled at her question. *You're a killer. What more reason is there?* But that wasn't true. And for an uncomfortable moment, Lock pondered his state. Why did he care if he told her the truth or not? The thought left him quite disturbed, though he took careful pains not to give his own thoughts away. Recovering, he answered in truth: "You are everything I'm trying to rid myself of."

"A killer?"

He grunted. "And a coward."

He felt the annoyance bounce off her in waves—he didn't need his magic to know it. His fingers reached out. They were so close. Her hand gripped his wrist, the knife at his throat in seconds. He looked down at the top of her hood.

"Don't." Her whisper was venomous.

She pushed away from him, gripping her knife hard, her knuckles white. She seemed to watch him for a moment before she turned, walking in the opposite direction he'd come. Her gait seemed familiar, but he couldn't place from where. She paused, half-turning towards him. "Your heart is cursed."

"At least it is still mine," he muttered, disturbed on how she'd known. *You don't hate her. She's simply a reminder of your sins.* A voice whispered in the back of his mind. A voice he wouldn't listen to. His skin burned, still feeling her hand on his wrist. Her grip was hard and firm, yet beneath it all there was a quiver of fragility. They were antithetical, like birth and death; that was a lie. They were akin in ways that Lock didn't wish to think about.

He blinked, watching her figure retreat. His head was aching, and he doubted he'd be able to see for much longer before the curse took hold. Lock pushed up his sleeves to see his veins. They were getting darker. Swearing, he tugged his sleeve back down as he walked back home. The desire for a drink still lingered, but he needed a clear mind to figure out just how he was going to get the coronet.

Lock took his cup of Earl Grey to the study. He didn't use it much, not even when Rien had asked him to fill out psychosis reports, always preferring to use the kitchen table. The study was a decent-sized room with wooden panelling for walls and a carpeted floor. A desk stood to his right, a fireplace to his left, and bookshelves ahead. No decoration—or *'no room for distraction,'* as his father said. A pile of mail sat on the desk. Most of it was months old, and not of any interest, but the top letter caught his eye. It was new, must've come in when he was out. Setting his tea down, Lock took a seat in the chair, loosening his tie from his throat. Aura's name was written on the envelope in her familiar script, and Lock sliced it open with a letter opener kept in the drawer to his right.

Dear Lock,

Lock blinked, fighting the pounding in his head. It had dulled quite a bit since his encounter with the Queen of Spades, but it would not disappear completely. It never did. Exhaustion pulled at the edges of his mind, which only worsened matters.

I have something of great importance to tell you. I'm afraid it's not pleasant, but I feel compelled to share it. Please come to the townhouse at three to discuss it. I have a feeling Kian's murder is a lot more sinister than we originally thought.

Kindly, Aura.

A small frown etched his lips as he read. Setting the letter down, Lock stood, preparing to retire for the night, his tea left almost untouched. He would need all the rest he could get, especially if he was going to figure out just how to get the coronet.

Lock had just shut his bedroom door when his vision started to blacken. He stumbled to his bed, clutching the sheets in his fist as pain sliced through his head. *Three years.* This had happened every day for nearly three years. His heart was pounding so loud in his chest that he wondered if Lada could hear it from the next room. He clenched his jaw, trying to right himself, just as a wave of dizziness hit. Lock's vision turned black, and he'd only just registered it as he collapsed to the floor.

EIGHT

SÖREN

Sören's nerves reverberated through him. While he'd been expecting to hear news about Kian's murder, he hadn't expected a letter from Aura. Nor had he expected to be roped into a group where no one watched him with pity, not even Aura, who was the one who had seen him hit his lowest point. He supposed he was bound to them whether he wanted to be or not, all held together by a murder. Sören grimaced, yet he'd chosen to come. He had a deal to uphold.

The Hansom Cab rolled to a stop outside Aura's residence, and Sören climbed out, paying the driver. He wasn't sure how long this would take, but he knew he needed to hear what they had to say.

He clambered up the townhouse's front steps, knocking on the door, and was soon let in by Aura's uncle. The entrance hall was all white walls and floral carvings—a pattern that was popular amongst high-class nobles. He was led to the second-floor drawing room, his boots echoing on the floor. Sören felt like an imposter; he didn't belong within these walls, just as he did not belong at the Order. Like downstairs, the drawing room had white walls carved with flowers and a mural on the ceiling. There was a fireplace and four blue velvet chairs seated around a low table. It was the kind of room his mother would've adored. Quickly shoving all thoughts of his mother aside, he set his sights on the chairs.

In three of them sat Lock, Iskra, and Aura. A pot of tea sat steaming on the table, though it looked untouched.

"Hello," Sören said as he sat down, suddenly feeling very uncomfortable. They exchanged greetings before cutting right to business. Lock tapped his foot on the floor while Iskra sat sprawled in her seat next to Aura, watching as Aura unfolded a letter she'd been gripping tightly in her hand. Sören took notice as she glanced around at each of them, her gaze flicking over Lock, a darkness in her eyes.

Aura cleared her throat. "'Kian's murderer is close to you.'" She read from the letter before folding it once more, placing it on her maroon skirts. Sören got a distinct feeling that she was holding something back, but he doubted she'd hide anything as crucial as a matter of the lord's murder.

"Who's it from?" Lock asked.

Aura lifted her shoulders, "I have no idea. It was here when I got back."

She went on to explain her unlocked window and the letter. The story sent a shiver through Sören—someone was watching them, and worse, someone knew what happened the night of Kian's murder.

"And you're sure it wasn't there before?" Lock asked, his face fixed with concern.

"Almost positive. I would've seen it. It's clear someone came in from outside, but how did they scale a wall at two in the morning without being noticed?"

To that, no one had an answer. Sören suppressed yet another shiver; the thought was unnerving. Sure, people were talented in the art of breaking in, but why would they do so to leave a bloody letter?

"Has there been anything else in the news?" Iskra asked, who'd been silent the whole time.

Aura shook her head slightly. "Rien informed me that the Duke wants to keep it quiet, out of the public until the murderer is caught."

The door to the drawing room burst open, and the Rien's head appeared in the doorway as he gripped the handle. "Aura, someone has dropped something off for you."

Sören noticed Lock tense, though he didn't know the other boy well enough to discern what it meant. Aura, however, looked curious as she followed her uncle out of the room. The rest of them sat in silence. *Go on, tell a joke.* He told himself, but there was no joke to break in this silence. Instead, he decided to focus on the letter Aura had received. Who had sent it? Who was smart enough to avoid all notice and get the letter to Aura? If they knew how Kian died, why didn't they just catch the murderer themselves? It made no sense to him, a feeling he hated.

Aura came back into the room, her skirts whispering against the floor as if they could tell him what had made her go so pale. She grasped a piece of paper in her hand, her haunted eyes looking down at it. She looked at them, though the conversational mood she'd been in before had vanished and was replaced with an atmosphere that felt as though it might choke him at any moment.

"What is it?" Iskra asked her carefully. Her French accent dripped between her words. That, he noted, must happen when she was nervous, though he had a hard time believing Iskra could ever feel such a thing.

"This letter—" Sören thought he saw her features clench in anger, but her expression quickly returned to normal, leaving him to wonder if he'd imagined it. It was almost as if she remembered where she was.

Sören's gaze snapped to the letter. "What does it say?"

Aura handed it to him, her hand shaking slightly, as he took it gently from her.

LOOK AT YOU. TRYING AND FAILING. YOU'RE JUST LIKE HIM. THAT'S ALL HE EVER DID, TRIED AND FAILED. THAT'S WHY IT WAS SO EASY TO KILL HIM, WHY IT WAS EASY TO WANT HIM DEAD. I KNOW WHAT YOU WANT, HE WANTED IT TOO. NOW HE'S DEAD.

Sören said nothing as he passed it to Lock, who read it and passed it to Iskra. None of them said a word, and Sören wasn't sure there was much to say. It was obviously sent by the murderer, but why here? Why not the police? *I know what you want, he wanted it too.* Sören assumed it was talking about the coronet, though he didn't know why Aura or Lock would have need of it. He didn't even know why *Xavier* needed it. One thing was clear however, it was worth killing over.

Iskra handed the letter back to Aura who folded it, gripping it tightly in her lap.

"It's very," Lock started, seemingly searching for the right word. "Poetic."

Iskra scoffed. "Or threatening. Surely, we aren't going to listen to it. Are we are simply supposed to believe that the person who killed Kian is *close*? Now, while it does intrigue me, shouldn't we leave the investigating to the police?"

"Not if you wish to get what you want." Sören said, meeting Iskra's gaze, who avoided him. It was clear, she didn't want to reveal her cards, so he added, "Justice for Kian."

As if on cue, Sören felt this sort of understanding. It was an understanding that he had to solve this case. For himself, but also for Xavier, as the coronet would be in the hands of the murderer. Part of him found himself wanting to be greedy. *This is your chance. Take it; take it all.* A voice whispered in his head, though whether it belonged to him or a version of his past self, he wasn't quite sure. It was like a fuse had been lit inside of his head, and everything was clear. They *had* to investigate this. The murder had happened right in front of them, as if they'd been meant to be caught in the chaos. If they investigated, it would ensure that Kian didn't die just to become another dead heir, and it would prove that Sören was a good person—he could prove to his father that he was capable. If *he* solved it, it proved that he could be a good investigator. Whoever the killer was, had the coronet, and solving this investigation would be the only way to get it, the only way to prove that maybe *he* could be a detective. The feeling faded as quickly as it came, but he knew they had to do this. He could see the others felt the same, like an epiphany had found its way in through the closed doors of the mind, an unspoken vow between the four of them.

"For Kian, then." Iskra said, her gaze finally snapping to his. There was a weight in them, though Sören seemed to be the only one that noticed. The others hummed in agreement.

Iskra sighed, muttering something in French. "Where do you start with an investigation? I usually solve all my issues with fire."

Sören raised his brow. "Capable of murder, my dear aristocrat?"

"*Don't* call me that. Anyway, save your charms for the Duke's son you're obviously in love with."

Sören was about to retort, his cheeks heating. He wasn't in love with Xavier Brittenworth. Was he charmed? Perhaps, but how could he not be? Yes, Xavier was a mystery Sören wanted to figure out. His smile was alluring, incapacitating, and contagious, but the now-heir was a complexity. That didn't mean he was in love with him. He was about to tell Iskra just that, however Lock cut in before he could say anything.

"I might have a suspect." He cleared his throat. "Well, it's not concrete, but it seems like a good place to start."

"Who?" Sören asked.

"The Queen of Spades."

"Lock, I love the theory. But she couldn't have been there. I'm almost sure she sticks to thieves and swindlers, not Lords with a habit of being an arse," Sören said.

"Sören, don't speak ill of the dead," Iskra scolded.

Sören put his hands up, feeling light. "If Kian's ghost is in here—" he made a show of addressing the air in front of him. "I'm sorry for telling the truth."

"You're right on one point," Iskra continued. "If the Queen of Spades was in the habit of killing idiot Lords, Locklyn would've been dead a long time ago."

Lock just rolled his eyes. "Fine. I'm willing to admit it was far-fetched."

Lock looked like he had more to say, but nothing came out of his mouth.

Aura paced the room, deep in thought. Her footsteps sounded like a slow heartbeat against the wooden floors. A memory came to Sören, and he found the light feeling disappearing. Flashes of a sweltering room, poison running through his veins, and his heartbeat screaming for one last breath ran through his mind. Sören shut his eyes; when he opened them again, he caught Aura's eye and looked away. *She knows I'm afraid.* But what did it matter? This investigation could prove that he was doing something with his second chance at life, all thanks to Aura.

"We are going to Scotland Yard," Aura said after a moment of silence. "Now."

"We cannot just walk in there, Dearest Aura." Lock said, and Sören felt relief spread through him. The last thing he needed was his father to see him at the Yard.

"We can," she said.

Sören's stomach dropped.

"Because we work for Rien." She strode from the room, and the others were left with no choice but to follow after her. In the entrance hall, Aura was throwing on her coat, disappearing into a room before coming out with a medical satchel. Sören shut his eyes, steeling himself because he was going to have to be brave again, something he had long since stopped doing.

Twenty dreadful minutes later, they all stood in the morgue that Rien used for his Scotland Yard work. A woman's body lay on the table, her bottom half covered by a sheet. Sören had thought seeing his father would be worse than this, but goodness, he'd been wrong. Rien puttered with trays on a different table, and Sören suspected the woman's organs were splayed on each. He didn't dare look. Iskra stood in the corner of the room, and Lock had propped himself up on a table, taking notes, occasionally looking at the body. Aura cut the brain open with a scalpel, the silver harsh against it—Sören shut his eyes, afraid he was going to be ill before they flickered open. According to Rien, the patient was a Lady Cordzig, widow, age thirty. Bruising detailed her neck, indicating strangulation and how Aura could stomach that, Sören didn't know. Dried blood blossomed on her chest, similarly to the way Kian's had. He looked away, still unsure why Aura had brought them here. The crew was silent until Rien left the room, informing them he had a meeting and cautioning them to *not cause too much trouble.*

"What the hell are we doing down here?" Iskra asked, her accent heavy in the darkened mortuary room.

Aura stuck a syringe into the woman's brain, pulling out a blue liquid and putting it into a vial. She took a moment to isolate the brain on the tray for Rien, a sight at which Sören dutifully avoided looking at. "We're here because this woman has been infected by Twisted Optical poison"—she indicated the blue vial

— "been dead for about three days, placing her death one day before Kian. She was an old member of the Order."

"What do you mean?" Iskra asked. "I've never seen her before."

"I said old," Aura said, setting down her scalpel on the table and walking to the woman's wrist where a circular indented scar graced her wrist, where a blue gem had once been embedded. Sören sucked in a breath. "We're here because she, like Kian, is the second person we know of to be affected by the Twisted as a part of the Order. Not only that, but to be stabbed. There was a physical altercation, and at the time Rien believed it to render Miss Cordzig breathless while her attacker stabbed her. I tend to agree. She was found in an alleyway only two blocks away from the Order, being brought here a day after she was dead, or the night Kian was murdered. While the locations are different, the similarities in the two crimes are undeniable."

"Do you think it's the Society?" Sören asked.

"It's too much notice for them." Lock said, looking up from the notebook. "They take pride in their inconspicuous lifestyle."

Aura nodded in agreement. "I wanted you to see—to be here. Should any other evidence present itself."

Sören mumbled in understanding as the group descended into silence. He was aware that should any of them have anything to do with it, this very conversation would be an alibi. Not that he believed any of them were capable of such crimes. *God.* He scolded himself for thinking like his father. They weren't criminals. They were the people that might save him from himself—if he let them. He watched as Aura wheeled the body away into an adjoining room and as the others helped her disinfect the room, the new information running through his head as he stood, helplessly, at the door. Iskra sprinkled sawdust onto the floor, soaking up any discharged liquids, a grimace on her face. The only sounds were the wood chips falling onto the floor, the scratch of Lock's pencil, and the sink where Aura was washing her hands.

Lock sighed, snapping his book shut. "I think we should pay a visit to the Order tomorrow."

"We can try," Iskra said, though didn't elaborate, even as she made her way out of the morgue.

Sören watched her go before he, too, dismissed himself.

His footsteps patted against the stairs as he ascended to the pavement, a small smile touching his face. Regardless of the hour he'd spent wishing he were anywhere else, the investigation excited him—that, and the chance for him to be better than he had been, and perhaps he could even turn it into something.

Sören Niaheartson, criminal investigator, an excellent dancer and a certified coward.

A criminal investigator. The thought made his heart yearn for adventure. As a child, his mother would take him on thousands of trips, exploring the English countryside and its rolling hills, and he loved it with every bone in his body.

"You have a wild heart, Sören. Don't lose it," his mother had said.

I won't—a promise.

He lied.

But, perhaps, this investigation was the key to helping him remember; to remember the fire in his heart that had lit his soul once upon a time. Sighing, he signalled for a Hansom. He had a lot to sift through and somehow he had to work up the courage to speak to his father. What better way to get information than from a detective himself?

"What the devil do you mean you aren't investigating the murder?" Sören exclaimed as his father swallowed another bite of food at their dining table. The lantern light crackled, making his father's glare seem almost haunting.

"I mean I wasn't assigned to the case. For one thing, Duke Brittenworth makes sure Scotland Yard keeps a low profile. Second, I'm under specific instruction not to work on the case from the Duke because apparently, I'm a suspect in an espionage case within the Order."

"And you don't know anything?"

"For God's sake, Sören!"

He flinched, knowing he'd taken his outrage one step too far, but this was frustrating—he was back to square one in his own investigation. Still, he faced his father head-on.

"Or perhaps you're just a coward. You have been since mother died."

Darkness flashed behind his father's eyes, and he stood slowly. It took everything in Sören not to push backwards in his chair. "Or perhaps, I've been assigned to another case. I couldn't investigate this one even if I wanted to." His father stalked from the room, leaving his dinner sitting there. Sören exhaled, trying to release the tension, but that tiny ball of nerves and guilt was still there as he climbed the stairs to his room.

"This can't be real," he muttered to himself. After all, how could Kian just end up dead the exact night Sören had snuck into the Order? How could his father have been assigned another case? And what was this espionage his father had spoken of? He stood, reaching for his door handle as something crashed beyond, causing Sören's heart to stop. He flung open his bedroom door, eyes scanning frantically.

There was no one there. His window had been smashed through, the glass on the wooden floor like tiny crystals from the fairy tales that he used to fill his head with.

Then, a knife grazed his cheek, pinning itself to the wall.

Sören stood frozen, touching his cheek, watching as it came away bloody. His brow furrowed as he turned to the knife sticking out of the wall. There, a letter hung perfectly, as if whoever had thrown the knife had done this before. He took back all his previous thoughts; perhaps this investigation would get him into more trouble than he already was. On shaky legs, Sören reached for the letter, ripping it out from under the knife. It felt cold—like how Sören imagined death was, like how he *knew* it was. He set the dagger down, not turning his back for fear it might stab him in the back. He turned the letter over, though there was no seal. He opened it and swore. Had someone been listening to his stupid mutterings? In black newspaper print, the letter read:

```
It's all real. Every. Single. Thing.
```

Sören crossed the room to his shattered window and looked out. All was still. It was just him, the air beyond, the brick wall in front of him, and *somewhere* out there was the person who had left this letter.

NINE

AURA

Aura fiddled with the folds of her skirt trying, and failing, to remember how she'd wound up at the docks last night. One minute, she was preparing for sleep, exhaustion tugging at her worn mind, and the next she held her dagger, leaning against a wall in some alleyway. She remembered hearing the Thames, the too-loud voices of drunken men, the emptiness of the alleyway.

She *remembered* the blood on her hands.

"Aura?" Lock's voice cut through her thoughts.

They sat in a carriage that rumbled towards the Order of Crowns, where Iskra and Sören would meet them. Aura had intended to take a Hansom Cab, but Lock had shown up early and clearly had a different idea. She didn't mind it, letting the tense feeling in her shoulders ease in his company.

"Yes?"

"Oh, you *are* in there. I was beginning to think I'd accidentally taken a cadaver from Rien's laboratory. Where you obviously spent some time—"

Aura gaped at him. "How did you—"

"You'd be surprised what I know." Lock smiled. "I'm only jesting, Aura. Rien asked if I could aid you, though I had to see Lada off."

Aura nodded before looking away. Perhaps he had been jesting. But the thought of him indeed knowing everything worried her. He didn't, she knew that, but she didn't want him finding out either. She was a skilled liar, but Lock had a way of reading her, and she was afraid that any shift of the eyes might give her secrets away—secrets that must stay hidden for not only her safety, but his.

Traitor. Her mind screamed at her, but she pressed her lips together, a sorry attempt to shut out her mind. Her attention was drawn back to Lock by the tapping of his fingers on his knees.

"Is everything alright?" she asked, not used to seeing him so nervous.

"It's fine."

Aura sighed. A lie, she knew. "Lord Locklyn Henry Mortsakov, you can tell me what is on your mind, or I'll ask Iskra to read it for me."

Lock rolled his eyes. "My lovely Aura, unless you're the queen, there is no need to address me like that. Second, I've been thinking a lot about murder."

"Causing it or investigating it?"

At this, Lock flashed her a grin, all annoyance gone. "It's more fun if you guess."

Aura started to open her mouth, but the carriage slowed to a stop, rocking slightly. A footman opened the door and helped her out, though it felt odd not to clamber out herself. Lock followed behind her, and together they walked up the pathway to the Duke's estate. A grand sort of place, once laced with elegance and purpose, now was wound tightly by dread and the kind of sorrow that only came with death. Loss, after all, was suffocating.

The atmosphere was crisp, leaves already falling from the trees. A change some might say was symbolic, but Aura had never been one for finding meaning where there was none. She feared she had too much of a logical brain, sometimes both a blessing and a curse. She shivered, a bone-chilling wind finding its way inside her despite the coat she wore, earning a flicker of concern from Lock. She pretended not to notice.

Iskra and Sören were waiting for them on the front steps of the manor, each looking like they'd rather be anywhere else.

"Finally," Sören said as he spotted them. "Any longer, and I might've started growing grey hairs."

Aura rolled her eyes at him. "Sure, you would have."

"Let's get on with it. It's cold." Iskra said, already moving to knock on the door and stepping back. It was as if the night at the opera hadn't happened—that they hadn't spoken like they were the kind of people who laughed at unholy hours about the oddities of life, that they hadn't found solace in the company of not being alone. No, Iskra's curiosity had hardened into her usual cold demeanour, and in truth, Aura wasn't sure she'd expected friendship from her. Maybe she just wished for another person who understood her, but then again, that was just another person who would get hurt. *If* she confided her life to someone, *then* there would be consequences.

So, she set her heart out of reach—perhaps then, if she left, no one would grieve her, nor she, them. Aura frowned as they crowded the space in front of the door, all huddled close to stay warm. It was, she noted, quite comforting, though it was quickly replaced by a sense of alarm. They could become friends—they could be more than an alliance—she wanted them to. But she'd never forgive herself if something happened to them *because* of her. And the coronet was the only way to protect them.

"Dearest Aura," Lock muttered, his coat sleeve brushing against hers, purple luminescence just visible at his coat collar. "Your heart doesn't need such guarding. Not here—that's a promise."

"How—" it was like he'd read her mind, not her emotions.

"I wasn't trying to read you, but your emotions are suffocating. You keep your heart in a cage for fear of losing, and I understand why. But, Aura, you don't need to do that here, not amongst them and certainly not with me."

She crossed her arms. "I thought you weren't good at deductions."

"I'm not." — a shrug — "But you're quite easy to read."

"Am I?" *Traitor*. The word echoed in her mind.

"Yes." Lock said, turning forward. "Especially when I can feel your emotions."

"So help me, Locklyn Mortsakov, if you ever use your magic on me while I am wallowing again—"

"Might I remind you that you were the one that got in the way? Oh, and please, let me just stand here and avoid the fact that my best friend is standing beside me, planning how to push herself out into oblivion to avoid sentiment."

Aura sighed. "I'm afraid I must kneel by my sword in defeat."

Lock smirked. "No need. Though you can thank me by allowing me the honour of a waltz in my favour, of course, showering me with compliments about how I'm the best and only friend you've ever had, et cetera, et cetera."

"Mortsakov," Aura said slowly. "Thank you."

He smiled softly, looking down at her. "Always."

It was all he said, and she knew he meant it. Here, looking into the eyes of her best friend, she was safe, unguarded, and so, so guilty.

A quick look around showed that Sören and Iskra had moved away to give them some privacy, much to Aura's appreciation. Only a few breaths had passed, yet there was no sound from the house beyond, not even a creak of the floorboards. Aura watched as Iskra went to knock again, but the door swung open, a breeze of warmth reaching her. She had expected to see the butler, but instead, Duke Brittenworth stood glaring at them with puffy eyes. Aura didn't think that he had an ounce of tears in him, but perhaps she was wrong.

"How can I help you?" he snarled, acidity in his tone. She knew he was usually moody, but never cruel.

"We're investigating your son's murder, and we wish to see the scene," Sören said from where he stood beside Aura, his coat done up to his chin.

Duke Brittenworth scoffed. "Leave it to the police."

"They aren't going to do anything," Sören said, and Aura stared at him. This was new information, and she suspected Sören had learned that bit of information from his father.

"Lies. Besides, even if I wanted to let you in, I can't. Rien, or her—" He jolted his head in Aura's direction, "master is under suspicion for giving classified information to the Society."

Aura stood there, knowing quite well how devoted Rien was towards the Order. Anger seeped into her veins, and she took a step forward. Lock muttered something, but she couldn't hear it over the sound of her next words. "Rien is not my *master*. You should watch your accusations, your Grace, or I might be finding your body in the morgue next?"

The Duke stiffened. "Young lady, you should watch what you say to influential men. I should feel sorry for your husband. My decision is final."

The door slammed shut in their faces.

Aura spun, ignoring the Duke's comment. She was far from a saint, and anyhow, there were far better reasons than her temperament to dissuade courtship. Her mind switched to calculation, looking at this as if it were an equation that needed solving. They needed to find a way in, and if talking wouldn't get them there, breaking in just might. She surveyed the house, the other's quiet talking drowning out as she focused on the plan that was starting to form within her head.

Aura didn't doubt that the others wouldn't mind doing a bit of law-breaking, considering they'd already done it in one way or another; her magic confirmed it.

Her vision sparked blue; Sören and a locked classroom the night she'd saved him; Iskra in what appeared to be a corridor, silent, a lit match between her fingertips; Lock the night they'd worked to cover his tracks. *So,* she thought slowly as the magic faded from her vision. It'd seem none of them were angels, and, she decided, her plan might just work.

Aura and the others rounded the manor, a familiar thrill creeping up inside her. She'd quietly explained the plan as they'd walked, and the others, as expected, had agreed. They located a servant's door, moving aside to let Sören work at the lock, a skill his father had taught him. He was a bit clumsy with it, but she bit her tongue. If she offered her help, questions would be asked, and that was something she was rather hoping to avoid. The door swung open, and after a few moments of waiting they stepped inside.

It was dull compared to the lavish decorations a floor up. The corridor was wide, large enough for two of them to fit side-by-side. Her skirts swished violently as she and the others located a staircase at the end of the hallway and climbed it, slowly, trying not make a sound. At the top, Iskra swung the door open, and they followed her out into the marble-floored hallway.

"Good thinking using the servant's entrance," a voice said from the shadows. Aura spun, nearly bumping into Lock, who steadied her with a hand. Xavier Brittenworth stepped out from an alcove, a book tucked under his arm and a smile on his pale, freckle-scattered face. "Now, don't look so startled. My father and I have a strenuous relationship."

"How did you know we were here?" Iskra asked, her accent slipping out, and Aura suspected that happened when she'd been truly startled.

"I was there. As for how I knew you'd try the servant's entrance? I didn't. But most people wanting to go unnoticed do. Besides, Father has dismissed most of the staff until Kian's funeral."

"Which is when?" Sören asked.

Xavier shrugged, almost sadly. He had the appearance of a tragedy; all sharp angles and hollowed-out eyes. She suspected that she'd looked much the same to Lock the night Alon had died. She shoved down the well of emotion that had sprung to her eyes, closing her hands into fists. Aura felt horrid for her next words.

"Could you show us where Kian was found?"

The heir nodded, or new lord, but Aura doubted his father would simply hand over the Order to Xavier, especially if it was as complicated as Xavier made it sound. Xavier turned on his heel, leaving them to follow.

Aura shut her eyes, magic gripping her soul, as the familiar blue haze cast its view to the past. Kian lay on the marble floor, blood blossoming on his velvet jacket, his blond hair a riled mess. A knife had been stabbed through his chest, piercing the heart. A shadow knelt beside him for a moment before pushing itself up and walking behind the body. They produced a rag from somewhere the vision didn't show her and began to wipe up a trail of blood. The trail led to Kian's bedroom. Not that she should know that, but as kids, Aura's parents had let them play together. But that all ended once the Duke's wife passed.

Aura looked back to Kian, so different from back then, yet somehow the same. His pale face was peaceful, but Aura couldn't help as it screamed at her for help.

This was death: it came so quickly and didn't stay to answer questions.

The dead don't speak. A flash of a memory flickered before her: Lock digging that grave, while she sat by the tree. It was gone as soon as it had come, and Aura was left standing in the hallway filled with thousands of unsaid words and fading magic. The last thing she saw before her magic faded was the shadow disappearing down the corridor, receding into the darkness beyond without so much as a backward glance at the horror they'd committed.

She stood in that very same room—the one Kian had supposedly been murdered in, magic chased away by the end of the vision, like a dancer taking their final bow. The room screamed of secrets, and yet Aura couldn't pay attention to any of them. Supposedly, the murderer had moved Kian to the hallway to make sure he was found, but why? If it were Aura, she would've just kept the body in the room; there was less risk involved that way. She shook her head, focusing on the current room. A bed with a layer of dust sat against one wall, a desk opposite, and a small seating area took up most of the space. The window was latched tightly. There was no way the murderer could've gotten in that way, which meant that they'd been a guest at this party. She tried not to dwell on that but couldn't help the thread of panic that was slowly unravelling within her.

Instinctively, she curled her hands into fists and focused on how the others were fairing in their preliminary searches. Iskra paced the room, allowing for Sören and Lock to finish their magic searches, as hers was the only one that couldn't be used today. Aura descended into silence, not knowing Iskra well enough to start up a conversation on the weather or the politics of England. Instead, she continued to look around, though she knew she would find nothing— it'd been cleaned to avoid scandal. No wonder Scotland Yard wasn't doing anything. She padded her way over to the window when something caught her eye from beneath the bed. She bent, retrieving a piece of paper. There was a tiny blue gemstone, barely the size of a teardrop, folded in between the papers. She turned around to tell the others what she'd found when a voice cut in before her.

"I thought I told you that you weren't allowed in here." Duke Brittenworth boomed, his face red.

They froze, and Aura willed Xavier to come into the room, but somehow, she suspected he was long gone.

"With respect," Lock said, then, before Aura understood what he was doing, he clapped his hands, pushing them towards the Duke. The Duke shouted something, but Aura was too focused on the purple glow of Lock's eyes and veins. The luminescence crept up until it stopped just above his collar. A moment later, Lock rushed to break the Duke's fall into his dreams before ushering them all out of the room with a kind of swift precision she admired in him. Aura tucked the paper and gemstone into her coat pocket and followed the rest of them out. Despite the Duke being asleep on the floor, they rushed down the way they'd come through the servant's entrance. Aura pushed the door open, cold air hitting her as she held the door open for the others. They ran until they were safely off the Duke's property, and they didn't speak until Lock's family carriage picked them up. Aura hugged her arms close, making herself comfortable on the plush seats of the carriage.

Across from her, Iskra huffed. "What a waste of time."

"Not entirely," Aura told her, taking the letter and gem from her pocket. Opening the letter, she scanned the words before reading. "It says 'Don't get caught.'" Beside her, she handed the letter to Lock before looking at the gem.

"Get caught at what?" Sören said, his brow furrowed.

"Infiltrating the Order," Iskra said, raising her coat sleeve to reveal a blue gem stamped into the inner section of her wrist. "It's mandatory for all Order members to take an oath and get a gem sealed into your skin to signify that."

"So, this gem is false, then?" Lock asked, taking the gem from Aura as she held her hand open.

"*Oui*. There's no blood, so it certainly wasn't carved away."

"Kian's mur—"

The carriage swerved to the side, and Aura's heart jolted inside her. Luckily, they hadn't yet made it to Central London's busy streets and wouldn't yet risk colliding with other carriages. The carriage seemed to tip before righting itself again. In the name of the Queen, what was happening? Aura was about to lean forward when a bullet came flying at the glass, shattering the windows of the conveyance. She screamed, sure her heart might beat out of her chest and desperately wished her dagger wasn't hidden beneath the floor back at her townhouse, not that it would be much help in this situation anyway. She racked her mind for anything, any piece of logical information, but she couldn't think over the sound of rushing blood that was filling her senses. The carriage seemed to slow, and Aura looked up to see Iskra picking glass up from her lap. Sören had pressed himself against the seat as if he might disappear into it, his hand on a gun that she hadn't even known he'd carried, and Lock's hand was in her's. If she wasn't so muddled, she might've smiled at the gesture. Instead, her mind felt heavy and fell into darkness.

Aura woke sometime later, her mind in a fog, a blanket pulled high at her chin. Her uncle stood a few feet away, speaking with a doctor. She sat up, not understanding how she was suddenly back in her bedroom, let alone with a doctor.

"My lovely Aura," Lock said from where he sat beside her, with his crooked tie and slightly cut cheek. "I'm quite glad you're awake."

"Why is there a doctor here?"

"Because you passed out. Nothing to fret over, but your uncle seemed concerned. You're alright, it would seem."

Aura crossed her arms, gazing at Rien. He'd never particularly been one to fret over her, but then again, she wasn't usually one to pass out either. Aura fiddled with the cuff of her dress sleeve for a moment. She looked back at Lock. "And why are you here?"

"To make sure you don't die on me," he said, a sarcastic tilt to his mouth. Lock pushed off the chair and knelt at the side of the bed, lowering his voice. "You should know that we all passed out, horrid stuff, Twisted magic."

"Why would the Twisted want us unconscious?" She frowned.

Lock glanced at Rien a few feet away and nodded. "They took the letter and our false gem."

"Why?" Aura's mind was racing.

Lock only shrugged.

"How are Sören and Iskra?"

"Fine. Though, I suspect Sören might be facing his father's wrath. Lucky for me, my parents are more worried about me than the broken carriage."

Aura smiled, despite the dire situation. Their only clue had been taken, but it did reveal something. The murderer could be linked to the Order's so-called espionage investigation. Clearly, the gem had been important—it was more than what they'd thought if the Twisted had been willing to shoot a carriage for it—

especially the Mortsakov family carriage. She glanced back at her uncle. How was she going to explain her situation this time?

TEN

LOCK

Lord Locklyn Henry Mortsakov had told a lie. He'd said to Aura that his parents cared more about him than the carriage, but he'd been wrong. Apparently, Rien had sent a messenger to fetch his parents as soon as Lock had brought Aura to the townhouse, informing Rien of the accident. In the dining room of Lock's townhouse, eerie silence and the scraping of metal against fine china did nothing to dispel the tension. He sat in the middle of it all, pretending he couldn't sense the anger pulsating from his father. He took a long sip of the wine that had been placed before him, only to set the glass down to face his father's fierce glare and his mother's worried one—both were equally unnerving.

"I wish to know what happened," his father demanded as if Lock had a clue himself.

"The carriage was shot at," Lock replied, waving his fork in the air, hoping to cut some of the tension that was eating away at him. "I don't know why or how, but I do know that my friends could've been hurt today."

"So could you," his mother said. "What were you doing with the carriage anyway?"

"We were at the Order." As soon as he had said it, he knew he'd made a mistake. His mother's face seemed to plunge deeper into worry, and his father looked at him with the curiosity of an animal stalking its prey. *Damn me*, he thought before changing the topic quickly. "So, Kian's murder? Horrid business, isn't it?"

"Don't speak of such—"

"Just all the blood—"

"Locklyn. *Stop it.*" His father stood, holding his hand out to his wife. "Come, I think it's time we retire."

Lock sat back; he didn't blame him. His father never liked to talk about anything, least of all how Lock was. Long ago, when Lock had decided to permanently live in London to further his studies with Rien, his father had never said goodbye. His studies had filled that absence for a while, but they'd only ever been a temporary fix.

"Father," Lock said, rising. "*I think it would be best if you left.*"

His father looked like he was going to argue, his face reddening, but Lock's mother simply placed a hand on his arm, nodding at Lock before disappearing from the room. She'd been the balance between them; the one who taught Lock what love was supposed to feel like. He heard the front door shut, and only then did he sit down, burying his head in his hands. His head ached; his veins were getting worse. He only had so much time left. He needed to speak with Aura. He needed to see her, make sure she was alright after the day's earlier events. It was late, but he knew Aura well enough to know she would be far from asleep, and it was dark enough for him not to cause a scandal.

The night was cool against his face, and he inhaled, trying to capture the peace he felt despite the chaos that had cast itself into his life. Murder was always a tricky business, yet if he had gotten away with it, surely, he could figure out how to solve one. He cast a backward glance at the London townhouse behind him, and even as it disappeared, he couldn't keep the thoughts away. His parents were on their way back to their country estate, back to the place where death loomed so close, and yet they had no idea. For a split second, a tree flickered into his memory, where his friend lay, forgotten. Yet there was nothing Lock could do to forget what he had done and the blood that stained his every thought.

As expected, dim candlelight shone through the window of Aura's townhouse. He knew Rien would be at the laboratory carving away at another cadaver, and as Lock pounded up the steps, he wondered what he should tell Rien should he find Lock on the steps. Lock doubted that Aura had told Rien exactly what they were doing, so it was best if he didn't get caught, especially since Rien had already questioned their need to look at the body at the morgue earlier. He knocked, waiting for a heartbeat before the door swung open.

Her apron was covered in whatever she had been working on, her hair done up behind her head, though errant strands fell framing her face. She held a vial in her free hand that she nearly dropped when she brought her gaze upwards from her messy appearance.

"Sorry—Lock!"

He smiled. "Surprised to see me?"

"I am." Aura opened the door for him to come inside. He'd been in this entrance hall a hundred times, memorizing the white walls and direction of the brown mahogany stairs that curved upwards, the way a silver chandelier hung from the ceiling—it'd been his favourite decoration when he'd first stepped foot in this place. He followed her to a room that should be an office but was littered with different chemical compounds, ingredients, and papers scribbled with messy findings; some lists of recipes, others, careful drawings of skulls indicating where Twisted Magic had affected it.

Lock cleared some papers aside and sat on the corner of the desk. "I wanted to see how you were doing."

"Is that so?" She asked, pouring a greenish liquid into a vial.

"It is." God, this was not going how he wanted it to go, not at all. He watched her; only half-faced towards him, he could see her mind was pressed into careful concentration, her very essence radiating with quiet curiosity in the dim lamplight of the workspace. He stood, crossing the room, and plucked the vial from her hands. She levelled him with a glare as she tried to reach for it. Lock raised his brows. "I wanted to see *you*."

She huffed, removing her apron and taking a step away from the worktable. "You should be careful who you mess with when she has poison in her hands."

Lock looked at the vial he still held. "Why would you have poison?"

"To murder you in your sleep."

"Rule one of murder, my lovely Aura, don't tell the person you're going to murder them."

Aura rolled her eyes, and he smiled as they eased into their usual dynamics, which was a whole lot of sarcasm, usually paired with Lock's rising heartbeat. She pulled a chair out from the desk and sat, gesturing for him to do the same.

"You would have known I was quite fine, Lock," Aura said quietly. "So why are you here?"

"Because you owe me a dance."

Aura gave him a look.

"Fine. I need the coronet."

"It's missing."

"All the same." Lock sat forward, pulling up his sleeve to reveal the darkness of his veins. "I *need* it."

Aura grabbed his arm. "Lock, when—"

"Three years ago."

"I could help you."

"And risk getting you in trouble with the law? I'm sorry Aura, but I will not be responsible for that. They already have enough reason to stop you from studying at any institute, and I will not be the one to take you away from your studies."

Aura sat back, letting go of his arm. "Very well."

"Besides, the Magic is too strong, it's been festering for too long. A simple syringe will do nothing."

Aura nodded, a look passing over her face. "So what do you want to do?"

"I wish to see where it was being held, books, anything that might be able to shed some light on my situation. But it's not like the Order will just let us in."

Desperation clung to his soul. Last night's episode was worse than the others, a clear sign that time was running out. He needed to see how the murderer might have gotten to it, and a more selfish part of himself, wished they'd find the coronet, still there.

Aura glanced at him, "Locklyn Mortsakov, you better not be suggesting we break in there. . .again."

"No, of course not."

An hour later, they found themselves in the darkened hallways of the Order of Crowns for the second time that day. The dim lantern they'd brought with them did little to light the pitch-black shadows. They stayed close for fear of being swallowed by the dark, and Lock couldn't shake the feeling of being watched, although it was silent. Locating the staircase, they climbed it slowly, and Lock could just make out Aura gripping the banister as if she was about to fall. As if *he* would let her. He shifted slightly so that she was ahead of him, just enough so that he'd get his head bashed in before her. *How valiant,* he mused, a small smile touching his lips. At the top, Aura waited for a breath or two before pushing the door open.

Eerie. That was the only way he could describe the carpeted corridor, when daylight wasn't streaming through the windows, or an abundance of lords and ladies weren't strolling about in their fineries. It felt hollow, and for all he knew, it was, with one less presence inside of its walls. Lock sensed Aura shift closer to him as they waited for the smallest hint that someone might be awake.

There was nothing.

Lock nodded to Aura for them to continue, though instead of taking the way they'd gone earlier that afternoon, they turned in the opposite direction. Lock wasn't entirely sure what they would find, or if they'd even find anything at all, but he did know that he didn't want them to get caught. The dim lantern cast long shadows against the elegant walls, and Lock couldn't help but think what would happen if the Duke were to find them here, now.

"You know Rien will murder me if he finds out we're infiltrating the Order for the second time today," Aura whispered.

"Will he, then? I thought he was more of the post-murder type?"

"I'm sure he's capable."

"My lovely Aura, the last time I checked, you were also capable of whipping up a quick poison."

Aura rolled her eyes. "I'm not going to poison Rien. Anyway, he doesn't even know about the investigation because if he did, God only knows what he'd do. I lied about how we got into that carriage attack."

Lock didn't say anything because, in truth, he was very aware of the consequences this investigation could hold for them. He paused, sensing a flicker of emotion. *Anger*. He knew it well, or the feeling of it anyway—it was like a pulse, as though the heart was trying to rip itself from one's chest, eager to escape its cage. *Anger*—it wasn't from Aura. A quick glance at her proved as much, so he turned in place, nothing but shadows greeting him. He went to reach for Aura but found she'd already grasped his hand.

"We should keep moving," she said. "Or I'm afraid the shadows will first."

He nodded, and together they made their way up to the second floor, stopping every few paces to make sure they weren't going to run into any monsters—not that Lock believed in such things. He stretched the lantern out in front of them, the light dancing off the reflection of a window. For a moment, the silence was almost serene—his hand entwined with Aura's for fear of getting swallowed. The darkness that loomed in this house was becoming more curious by the minute. Loud voices cut through the silence, and they paused, hearts pounding, and hands entwined.

"What in the Devil do you mean?" a man whispered in a voice he wasn't sure he recognized.

"I need to know." That was the Duke. Then, a shout. And the rattle of a door handle as if someone on the other side braced their hand on the knob. The voices grew hushed, and Lock could no longer hear. Though he was sure that's what his magic had picked up; it was clear the two men were in a heated argument. A shadow peeled away from the wall, and in the faint light, he could just make out the outline of Xavier, his eyes dark. He winked at them just as the door began to open.

Aura inhaled sharply beside him and tugged him into the nearest room possible. He shut the door behind him as softly as possible, pressing his back to the door, sure that whoever was on the other side could hear his heartbeat through the wood. He felt Aura move from his side, venturing further into the room they'd entered. He set the lantern on the floor beside him, and in the dim light, he could just make out a large bed and a bookcase on the opposite wall—rather empty for a bedroom. The footsteps outside echoed, and Lock recognized them as the Duke's, trailing closer to the very room they stood in. The steps paused outside, but this room wasn't elegant enough, nor was it fit for a duke. He searched around for Aura, who was curiously flipping through a book in the bookcase.

"Aren't you worried?" he hissed.

"The door is locked," she said, without looking up from the book. "It's not hard to do. Really you turn the—"

"I know how a lock works."

"Still," Aura continued. "We should get going here because I don't know how long we have."

Lock stared at her, wondering how she had locked the door. While his detailed eye had noticed the lock, he hadn't thought to lock it, but perhaps that was because he was too focused on his rapid heartbeat and Aura's touch to do much else.

"Locklyn Mortsakov, did you not hear what I said about moving quickly, or did you want to end up on the Duke's dinner plate tomorrow night?"

He wrinkled his nose. "My darling scientist, you think such horrid things."

"That I do, my lord. Horrid things that happen to save you," Aura said, pulling another book from the shelf, and it was only in studying her that he noticed the bookshelf in which she stood before—really noticed it. The case was pushed diagonally so that one side was closer to the wall. He walked to where Aura stood before he got on his knees, bending down, inspecting the floor.

"Honestly, Lock? I don't think now is the time for praying."

"I'm not praying," he grunted, standing back up. He hadn't done that since he was fifteen—no amount of wishing, or divine intervention, could wash the sin from his hands as he had slipped the poison into his friend's glass.

The sound of keys clicking into the door sent him into action, glancing at the book titles, though the lantern had blown to smoke. He let his fingers run along the spine, pausing on a book his father had made him memorize—the Order of Crowns handbook of rules. He tilted it, holding his breath as the bookcase swung open, its hinges silent. Aura cursed, and Lock couldn't help but smile. Taking her hand once more, they slipped inside, plunging themselves into darkness as they shut the bookcase behind them, just as Lock could have sworn the door to the bedroom opened. He blinked a few times, letting his eyes adjust. The room was cast in shadow, except for the very centre where light streamed from a single lamp hanging from the ceiling, illuminating a brown pedestal, jewels etched into the corners. Atop, was a plush emerald green cushion, a silver coronet sitting upon it, like a king upon his throne. Red gems seemed to glitter, set into the spires of the small crown, velvet outlining the inside. Relief spread through him, then the confusion hit. The coronet was reported missing. It was not supposed to be here. The entire display seemed to shimmer like it was lit by sunlight rather than a singular lamp, and Lock couldn't help but step forward to get a look at the beauty.

It flickered.

Lock paused, and so did Aura. Unless they were about to faint, that table along with the coronet had vanished before reappearing. Aura's hand squeezed in his, a gesture she'd been doing for as long as they'd been friends.

Darkness.

The Coronet.

Darkness.

The Coronet.

Darkness.

Nothing.

They were plunged into shadow, its inky depths welcoming them with open arms. Lock let go of Aura's hand, instructing her to stay there while he moved forward to where the pedestal had been so only moments before. He braced himself, hoping to hit something, but the room was empty. This was the work of the Twisted, taking advantage of their vision, and he told Aura as much. His head was pounding, the effect of Twisted Magic sinking in. Duke Brittenworth despised the Twisted. All of London did. But it was too coincidental for the Twisted to be here tonight and the night Kian had died. A moment later, the strike of a match whispered through the air, and the light was just dim enough to see the floor and Aura's face, her face which remained calm despite the situation. He looked down at his shoes, only then noticing a small note where the imaginary pedestal had stood only moments before. He picked it up, showing it to Aura.

Power Corrupts us all

Power corrupts us all. The words danced before his mind, yet Lock had no idea what or even if they connected to the murder.

"So, we're back where we started," Aura said.

"It would appear so."

Aura's match blew out.

Lock reached for her hand.

A set of strong hands gripped their arms, pulling them into the shadows, and if Lock didn't believe in monsters, he did now—swearing the shadows were about to swallow him and Aura whole. His mind raced to find an answer, but even as he brought his elbow backward, he got a foot to his knee, causing him to collapse. They spilled out into an antechamber, which was lit by several lanterns, though Lock didn't care to look at much else as he pressed his face to the cool marble flooring, his heart hammering. A door slammed behind them, and Lock turned onto his back, squinting at their attacker.

"You're lucky I know you're friends of Iskra," The girl said as she locked the door before striding further into the chamber. It was a small room, a mural having been painted onto the ceiling, gold leaves detailing the otherwise plain walls. A wooden chair sat against the furthest wall, which Lock assumed was for the girl to sit in, a door leading to the hallway beside it. The girl, however, was staring at them, her arms crossed. She had the skin of deep bronze and rich brown hair that looked almost black. She wore a green uniform used for the Duke's livery, and Lock realized this must be the guard Iskra had been friends with. The girl before them was also the topic of the majority of his conversations with Iskra —by the sounds of it, and as much as Iskra claimed otherwise, this was the girl that meant something to Iskra once upon a time—*truly* meant something.

"Sorry, who are you?" Aura said, sitting up in a pile of her skirts.

Lock pushed himself to stand. "She's Iskra's *friend*. Forgive me, let me correct myself: was."

Aura and the girl gave him a look.

"I'm Iskra's informant," she said to Aura, which didn't really explain anything. The girl seemed to have lost a bit of her fire, and Lock caught a flicker of something steal over her face, but he knew better than to bring it up. "My name is Zoialynne Adrennha, and I am Lord Brittenworth's Head Guard."

"You're also a traitor, in theory," Lock reminded her, feeling the need to point out the irony of their current situation. "By helping us."

"Iskra wouldn't want anything to happen to you."

Lock almost laughed, finding it hard to believe that Iskra would want to save them. They had a professional relationship, and as far as he knew, she and Aura had only ever spoken a handful of times. From what he knew of Iskra, she wasn't necessarily the caring type.

"How did you meet Iskra?" Aura asked, standing and making a slow round, inspecting the room. *Calculating,* he thought, watching as her eyes danced over the painted ceiling, no doubt picking up each and every detail of the room.

"That's none of your concern."

Lock paused, inspecting the now bolted door that they had just come through. "How did you know we were in there?"

"Auditory Magic, my lord. I sit here, listen, and guard the coronet."

Lock made a sound in the back of his throat. "Be a dear and drop the formalities. It's Lock." He paused. "Anyway, were you here when it was stolen?"

"I was out doing business for Iskra the night of the party if you think I did it. She and I have a working deal. I was here for a while, and then I was called away." Lock wanted to ask what she meant, but Zoialynne continued. "Second, the coronet is missing, but for the love of God, if the Duke is not concerned, then neither should you be. My advice? Find the murderer. Do not waste your time on some absurd coronet based on a centuries-old tradition. Look at the facts. Iskra tells me you're both quite good at that."

She didn't know about the Twisted magic; that much was clear, and Lock wasn't about to tell her. It was best to keep it hidden for now. She certainly didn't know that it wasn't the murder that really interested him *but* the coronet. A door behind Zoialynne burst open, and Xavier strode in, taking care to shut it quietly. Zoialynne shot the young lord a look as if to ask what he was doing here, but Xavier ignored it. Instead, he handed Lock a list, and he stared at it.

It was a list of names.

"What is this?" Lock asked, despite knowing exactly what it was.

"The names of everyone who was at the party. I've crossed out the ones I saw at the time Kian was murdered."

Lock watched Xavier; dark circles rimmed his eyes as if he wasn't used to not sleeping. At that moment, Lock saw him as the grieving brother as he ran his eyes down the list. Xavier's own name was at the bottom of the list, and he paused.

"Did you do it?" Lock asked, raising a brow and gesturing to his name. Aura strode over, peering over his shoulder, taking a glance at the list. Zoialynne seemed to have sunken into the shadows of the small room.

Xavier shook his head. "No. But I know a lot. Sometimes, too much for my own good."

Lock nodded slowly. Xavier was telling the truth, his magic confirmed as much, and he watched as he left the room, nodding at Zoialynne. Xavier, to his knowledge, had always been an observer and someone to do the right thing for as long as Lock had known him, and he certainly didn't see any reason why the now-heir would lie about something as serious as his brother's death. Aura called a thank you, although he'd long since left. Zoialynne stepped back towards them and opened another door, telling them to follow the stairs down and leave before they got caught; and they did as they were told, though Lock had a million questions. One thing was clear, however, there were at least two ways to get into that room that housed the coronet.

Aura had gone silent since hearing what Zoialynne had said, and he knew better than to interrupt her when she was like this. She was working through a thousand calculations at once, and while Lock had taken maths and sciences in school, he could never understand how Aura did it sometimes. She looked at life as a puzzle—another problem that needed solving, and she'd do anything to get the answers she needed. It was something he admired about her. While he may be skilled at equations as well, and while he knew Aura well, she would still be an equation he would always find impossible to solve—then again, perhaps he didn't need to. They walked slowly down the lane, to where Lock's carriage was waiting.

Once in the carriage, Lock tapped his fingers against his knees, hoping to ask a million questions, but Aura's eyes were glowing as the carriage rolled to a stop after a ride of silence. Her magic faded, and she smiled.

"Thank you for tonight. I have much to think about." She alighted without another word. He watched her shut the door behind her, sure that her uncle would be long asleep. And for her sake, he hoped she got some sleep. The carriage rattled away in the silence of the night, and Lock let himself relax, emptying his mind of the curiosities—After all, those were problems for tomorrow. He cast one last glance at Aura's street. It was empty save for a gentleman walking slowly, a letter grasped tightly in his hand. Lock rested his head against the cushions, shutting his eyes against the ache in his head.

ELEVEN

ISKRA

Iskra Storenné wrinkled her nose as she stepped into the alleyway where she'd asked Zoialynne to meet her. Iskra had received no news of her parents in weeks, and her nerves were beginning to stretch thin. Zoialynne had disappeared the night Kian was murdered, and Iskra still hadn't heard of any news from Zoialynne from the night she'd left to attend to the call. Perhaps Zoialynne was avoiding her, perhaps not; Iskra wanted to stay alive, and she was going half-mad, staying in the dark. If her parents were closing in, she needed to know—the silence and cool glances Zoialynne had been giving her simply wouldn't do.

Fog hung low in the air this afternoon, and it made seeing Zoialynne difficult until she was right before Iskra. Her hair had been swept back, highlighting her sharp cheekbones, and Iskra scolded herself for staring. She was here on business, and that was it. This was not the boat to England, and this was far from the afternoons they'd shared on it.

That wasn't who they were anymore.

Iskra's boots stamped against the pavement, following Zoialynne wordlessly, although her mind was far away, in a time that had been risk-free of her parents finding her and a time where she was free to do what she liked—a time when her heart had been on fire without a care of getting burned.

Sometimes, she could still picture it: leaving the American docks, where she'd travelled first to get her parents off her trail. After all, her parents, Viscountess Marie Storenné and Viscount Louis Storenné were too proud to even step foot outside of France. Iskra had smiled then, proud of her little accomplishment, as she'd stared out into the vast sea. She couldn't have stayed there, but even now, she wished she could be lost between the waves forever.

"You may as well announce yourself," Iskra remembered saying, sensing eyes pressing into the back of her long blonde hair.

"You really ought to try breathing," a girl replied, stepping out from behind a door. She was the same one Iskra had saved from a vicious employer only two days ago. Her black hair had been bound at the base of her neck, her bronze skin sparkling in the afternoon sun. To this day, Iskra wished she could've captured the way Zoialynne looked that day, but Iskra was no painter, and love was a waste of time—a weakness. Back then, Iskra was running from her parents, Zoialynne was running to something else. Two sides of a story; two hearts met by destiny. But destiny, Iskra had long since decided, is only a useless theory for romantics. Words can't hold such feeble links as friendship, and sometimes, people can become as cold as the icy water they sail on.

"Iskra, are you listening?" Zoialynne snapped in a tone that dragged Iskra from her thoughts, a tone she was used to ever since they'd found themselves in England almost three years ago. It was filled with animosity, only an undertone of what they'd been once shone beneath her eyes. *This is for the better.* Iskra would whisper to herself, but she couldn't ignore the way her heart screamed.

"*Je suis désolée,*" *I'm sorry.* The words that would always mean more to Iskra than they would to Zoialynne. "Could you repeat yourself."

Zoialynne shook her head. "I asked if you were ready for the news."

Iskra nodded, her stomach tightening ever so slightly.

"Your parents have gone off the map." There was no emotion in her voice, and Iskra wanted to scream. *1095 days.* That was the amount of time Iskra's associates had spent keeping track of her parents, making sure that Iskra was safe, and now they were lost. Her parents could very well be on the way to England. This meant that her connections had lost her parents. Iskra scowled.

"Who lost them?"

Zoialynne shrugged. "I don't know."

"Find out."

"There is one more thing." Zoialynne paused. "Lock and Aura are also after the coronet."

"Why?"

"I don't—"

Iskra turned back down the alleyway. The phrase *I don't know* was beginning to get on her nerves. Her world seemed to be falling apart at the seams, guilt running through her for the way she'd spoken to Zoialynne. Her gait was rough, her back tense, trying to focus on her next move. Unfortunately, all she could think of was how angry she was. She whirled to find Zoialynne only a few steps behind her, face flushed.

"Iskra, I do everything for you. Do you understand that? I get that we don't have to be friends, but you could at least have an ounce of respect for me."

Iskra opened her mouth, but Zoialynne pushed past her, and Iskra stayed frozen in place, letting Zoialynne's words sink in. They made her feel worse. *I do everything for you.* The words echoed in her head. *I do everything for you.*

That wasn't fair.

Iskra had never asked Zoialynne to do anything, yet she had done it. She could have left at any point, yet she stayed for reasons that were unclear to Iskra. When she finally regained the ability to move from the alleyway, her mind was a mess of anger. She didn't need friends—she needed connections. She didn't need Zoialynne, no matter how much she wanted her to stay. Iskra focused on the information. Her parents were lost amongst the whispers, and Iskra had no idea what to do. She trusted that Zoialynne would get back to her with the information she needed, but how could they have lost them so quickly? After three years, Zoialynne had only ever reported one other instance where her parents had disappeared, and that was because her messenger had been collateral damage in their crossfire, stupid thing. On top of that, no progress had been made on the investigation into Kian's murder, and it would seem *everyone* was after the coronet—God, everything was hopeless. Iskra tugged her coat tighter around her, hoping it would somehow settle the chill that crept up inside of her bones. Turning down a street, the fog settled before her once more.

"Fire is in your soul, young one. You should consider using it."

The voice was gone, and Iskra was left wondering if it was real or a simple trick on the mind. Iskra reached into her pocket to where she kept a box of matches, shaking her head. She would not become what she had run from, no matter how tempting it felt to watch fire burn the world to the ground.

TWELVE

SÖREN

Sören Niaheartson had promised himself to stay away from Scotland Yard, mainly to avoid suspicion from his father, yet here he was, standing before the blasted building. Its red brick and square window facade seemed to tower before him, and he quickly started ahead before the building toppled onto him altogether. Sören had been to Scotland Yard many times prior, and he didn't waste any time walking to his father's office. Police and inspectors alike passed him, only a few daring to pass glances at him. Sören's father had worked hard to earn his place here, and by extension, so had Sören. It made him feel important, in a strange sort of way. Stuffing his hands into his pockets, he turned into the corridor of his father's office but paused when he saw there was already someone in the glass-encased workspace. Sören kept his back to the wall, observing the exchange silently. He recognized the person who argued with his father immediately.

Xavier Brittenworth.

Now, what Xavier was doing with his father, let alone in a heated discussion, Sören had no clue. It wasn't like the Duke's son was known to come marching down to yell at a bunch of police. Besides, Sören hadn't struck him to be the angry type, but then again, he supposed everyone had their hidden demons. Sören, himself, dealt with cards that he didn't want. Sören's gaze drifted to his father, who, much to his surprise, remained completely calm. Meanwhile, Xavier threw his hands in the air, which could only be used to accuse someone of something.

Sören stiffened.

Had his father done something to upset the Duke? That was another thing; it was likely the Duke didn't even know Xavier was here, considering he'd pretty much told Sören his father was a suspect in Kian's murder. Sören looked around, but it was almost as if everyone had left. If she were here, he knew his mother would scold him for what he was about to do, but the truth of it was she wasn't here. She was six feet below the earth, her heart and kind eyes buried with her. He wasn't sure when he had started seeing his mother as truly gone, but it somehow made it easier to live.

Or maybe he just thought it did.

Sören had spent months scrambling for some semblance of peace, and he'd only found it when he'd let go. After all, hadn't he killed his mother, grief-stricken when he'd turned to everything she'd told him to avoid? He shuddered. Opening old wounds would do nothing to save him. He didn't want to hurt again —he didn't *need* to hurt again. What he needed to do was focus on this investigation. He needed to prove that he was more than his past, that his mind was not shattered. Muttering a quick apology to his mother, he shut his eyes and let his magic work its way between the woodwork of the walls, feeling it run through the corridors. He let it twist its way beneath the doorway until the conversation was as clear as if Sören was standing in the office himself.

"By God, why isn't Scotland Yard doing anything." Xavier scolded. It

reminded Sören of something similar he had asked his father. "Why aren't you doing anything? You're a member of the Order, are you not?"

Sören's father took a deep breath, his dark brow twitching as the only indication that he was frustrated. "Lord Brittenworth, might it surprise you that your father has banned me from doing so?"

Xavier's mouth worked, but no sound came out, so his father continued.

"As for Scotland Yard, they're doing everything they can." He flipped through a stack of papers for what felt like an eternity. "I believe Detective Inspector Thornsbury is assigned to the case, but you'll excuse us if we're still dealing with the public's justified hysteria toward the Ripper Murders last year."

"You have the entirety of the Yard for that."

Sören's father didn't say anything.

"Is there something else going on?" Xavier asked.

His father dragged in a long breath. "I'm sure you've heard of the missing wom—"

Sören didn't get to hear the rest of the answer as his magic rebounded back towards him as someone yelled his name. Someone, being his father, who was glaring daggers at him through the glass. *Shit.* He would rather condemn himself to digging up horse droppings than endure the hell he knew was coming for him. Sören was standing in the middle of the hallway, a place where he hadn't remembered moving to. Xavier had turned as well, his eyes giving nothing away, though Sören thought he caught a flicker of surprise pass over the other boy's features. Questions spiralled in his head, all of which were silenced as he met his father's eyes. Sören tucked his hands behind his back as his father thrust the door to the office open, beckoning him in, then slamming it behind them. Not bothering to ask Xavier to leave, his father said, "What is it you're doing here?"

Sören had no idea what to say without revealing to his father that he was working the case behind his back—an idea that would get him locked up just so his father made sure he didn't do anything stupid. Sören felt like a child again, so small and helpless standing up to the microscopic glare of a teacher after he'd accidentally punched a kid for spreading rumours about one of their classmates. Before Sören could say anything that would ruin him, Xavier stepped an inch closer.

"I asked him here, Detective." Xavier paused. "I thought maybe he could help you see the idiocy of not prioritizing my brother's murder."

Sören's father nodded slowly, and Sören couldn't help but feel like this was the eerie silence before an eruption, the calm before the chaos. "Sören, may you step out with me for a moment?"

Sören nodded and followed his father out, his footsteps pounding in his head. He shut the door behind him, pressing his back against the door as his father turned to face him. Sören had expected a stern face, but instead, he was met with that of worry. It was a face he hadn't seen since he'd woken up on Aura's operating table. He shut his eyes for a brief moment before opening them.

"I want you to stay away from this investigation."

Sören gaped at him. "Why? I was there that night."

"What you're *doing* is getting involved in something much larger than you, do you understand?"

"Yes, but—"

"This isn't up for negotiation."

He hesitated, before saying. "Yes, sir,"

Guilt clutched at his heart—he wouldn't stop. He knew his father knew it too, but his father had already moved on.

"And while you're at it, stay away from Xavier. His father is dangerous, and soon Xavier will be too."

His father gave him a look as if to say *do you understand* before striding down the hall without so much as a glance backwards.

Sören was left staring after his father. What did he mean, *and soon Xavier will too?* Perhaps, Sören didn't want to know. It was too late anyway, they'd already made a deal. He cast a quick glance behind him to see Xavier already watching him, and Sören took in the lord's freckles and kind eyes before turning away and walking down the hallway. Sören hadn't been one to walk away from danger until the danger had landed him with poison in his mouth and a heart beating too slowly. Xavier wasn't dangerous, but there was something about him that Sören couldn't quite place. And perhaps, even if only for a little while, he'd let himself live in oblivion.

Sören found himself knocking on the door of Detective Inspector Thornsbury; after all, just because his father couldn't give him the information he wanted didn't mean Thornsbury couldn't. The Detective Inspector was pale and in his early thirties with rich blond hair and a curling moustache, his suit as clean as the surface of his desk, where papers, too, were stacked into neat piles.

"Mr. Niaheartson," the Detective Inspector said, standing to shake Sören's hand. "To what do I owe the pleasure? Does Nikolas need something?"

"My father is fine," Sören said. "I'm the one that needs help from you."

"Oh?" Thornsbury said, rounding his desk and plopping into his chair, gesturing for Sören to sit opposite him. Sören did as instructed, and only now did he wish he'd brought Iskra or Lock to really influence the Detective, not that he was in the habit of using his friends. That was if they could even call themselves that—it was only that they had a charm that Sören couldn't possess, not in the same way, at least.

Sören clapped his hands together. "What's your acquaintance with my father?"

Detective Inspector Thornsbury frowned. "We've worked on cases before, though I tend to work alone more often now. We don't exactly smile in the hallways, but he's a nice man."

"Then I trust what I have to ask you will be kept between us?"

The gentleman looked skeptical but nodded. For the other's sake, Sören had decided on his way up here that he would leave the others out of it for now until he knew that the detective wouldn't stab them in the back.

"I was there the night Lord Kian Brittenworth was murdered."

Thornsbury sat forward, shifting in his chair.

"I've been investigating it without my father's knowledge because the murder happened around me, blood everywhere, you understand?"

The detective nodded, and somehow Sören understood what he said wouldn't leave this room, not after the weight of the words Sören had just thrown at him.

"I need you to share all the information you find with me, and in turn, I will share what I find."

"Like an apprenticeship?"

Sören nodded. "Sure, let's call it that. Second, this all needs to stay beneath my father's knowledge. Can you do that?"

Thornsbury looked uncertain for a moment but nodded, and Sören reached into his coat pocket and pulled out a sack of coins. "For your secrecy."

The Detective inspector pushed the pouch back at him. "Mr. Niaheartson, I am a fair man. You have a cause, and so do I. One day, I believe that you could make an excellent detective. Your secret will need to be pried from my cold-dead cadaver. Let us shake on it, like men."

Sören shook the Detective Inspectors' hand, relief spreading through him. He pocketed the coins and thanked Detective Inspector Thornsbury for his time, telling him he'd be in contact before he left the office. For the first time since starting the investigation, Sören felt useful in a world of people that acted better than him. He smiled as he began his walk back home. He'd worked his way into an apprenticeship with the detective, and with Xavier's promise to put in a good word if Sören brought him the coronet, there would be no doubt about Sören becoming a detective. It was only a matter of time before the murderer was in their hands. More importantly, it was almost time to prove to his old self that he was better and that his mind would no longer shackle him down to the bonds of a life he didn't want to remember.

THIRTEEN

AURA

Aura watched Rien make an incision on yet another body. She took notes when instructed, but her mind was running over her conversation with him from last night, especially because she stayed awake after Lock had dropped her at home. She also knew that a letter was waiting for her beneath the floorboards of her room, but she very well couldn't have escaped last night, especially since Rien had already known she was out once. If she had, Rien would've been furious; he'd demand an explanation, and when she could give him none, he'd forbid her from working in the morgue until she confessed. Aura tapped her pen against the notebook, taking notes on the heart as Rien instructed. However, all Aura could see was the knife she couldn't remember wielding, a chest cut open, exposed bone, a cut-throat, and a heart left staring up at the night sky. All she could see was the glint of the ring she'd stolen off him before she'd handed it over to Avery the night of the coronation. All she could see was her victims' eyes as the life drained out of them, his lips caught between pain and surprise. She supposed death was often like that: a knife through the heart when one least saw it coming. Aura needed to get back to the house so she could read the letter, and some part inside her hoped there would be no repercussions for doing it a day late. *Or not doing it at all,* she thought, guilt clawing at her chest. Part of her hoped that there would be no letter, that this was all in her head, but she knew it wasn't.

"Has the Duke asked anything of you? Any other bodies found?" Aura asked, trying to focus on anything other than her screaming thoughts. She knew there hadn't been any found, but she needed to broach the subject somehow. Rien peered at her over his thin spectacles before turning back to the body.

"No."

"No questions about the report either?"

Rien all but slammed the scalpel down on the post-mortem table. "For God's sake, no. Aura, you'd be wise to stay away from the investigations and the Order, do you understand? This murder is larger than anything we could even know about, and I don't want you to end up getting hurt, just like you almost were a week ago. You're lucky Locklyn was able to help you."

"Yes, I owe a lot to Lock," she said, and Rien stared at her as if trying to decipher the meaning of her words. In truth, Aura didn't know what she meant by them either; her statement was pure fact. She didn't need an equation to understand that she could never repay Lock for all the things he'd done for her, and for the first time, the weight of her betrayal clawed its way up inside her, and she felt as though she might let it pull her down to its depths.

A flash of blood.

A face she couldn't forget.

A promise shattered in one night.

There was so much to repay Lock for and so many chances to ruin what they had crafted. A bond formed by her witnessing his wrongdoings, secrets binding them as one. Aura shut the notebook, much to Rien's disappointment, and stood.

    She left the laboratory without another word, practically running. Her skirts swished violently at her feet, her heart feeling as though it were going to break through her corset. She'd forgotten to remove her apron, at which people on the street cast her odd looks. She couldn't remember when she had realized that she needed Lock, but by God, she couldn't ruin him. She couldn't be the cause of his pain after he was already hurting himself with his past. He was dying, slowly, and she couldn't be the one responsible for taking away his chance at life. She wouldn't be the reason he wound up dead. That was not what friends did, and if he left, then truly she had no one that understood her. She was a scientist, a mortician's assistant, yet with all the calculations she knew, she couldn't figure out one that would save them. So, she would do the only thing she knew how to; she'd make the Queen of Spades step from her reign and become a whisper made for the past. When he'd faced her in the alleyway, they were two strangers, and Aura couldn't stand to act like that no matter how much burning the sin from her heart would hurt. Around the front of her house, carriages passed without a care for the weight of the decision she was making. But it wasn't just for Lock. It was for her. It was time to let her legend as a killer fade into nothing—that wasn't how she had planned to be remembered, even if all she did was hide behind a mask. She was done with her employer, all the torment he'd caused her. She'd sacrificed herself over and over for *nothing*. She could no longer ruin herself—if her death was the consequence, then perhaps it was worth it. After Alon had died, she'd spent so much time wanting to drown, and the Queen of Spades had only pushed her down further. Now she risked pushing away the only person who'd willingly pulled her away from the freezing waves of grief. She'd wanted to save people, but she was no hero; she didn't want to be. She had wanted to be closer to Alon, but that didn't mean killing herself to do so.

She bounded up the stone steps and thrust the door open, thankful that no one lingered outside the house to witness her like this. Aura's skirts billowed at her ankles, her heart a fast rush. The Queen of Spades had been her life for the better part of three years, and she needed to burn it—she needed to be better because she had people she cared about. Lock, Rien, and even Iskra and Sören. The last thing she needed to do was hurt them as much as she had hurt. She couldn't do that to them. Aura burst into her room, practically falling to the floor. She ripped out the letter, not bothering to read it. Clutching it in her hands, she prepared to rip it into nothing.

A splitting headache.

You need to do this for Alon.

The paper shook in her hands.

The Queen of Spades is helping people.

No, this was Twisted magic, and Aura had to fight. She'd spent years giving into it, and she'd do no such thing today. The Queen of Spades might be helping her employer, but what about helping her? The Queen of Spades was destroying her. Tears leaked from her eyes, and everything in her screamed to just give in. She ripped the letter to shreds, and as if on cue, pain shot through her entire body. Aura doubled over, squeezing her eyes shut. *Foolish girl. You have no idea what's coming for you. The Queen of Spades could've saved you.*

No, the Queen of Spades couldn't have saved her. She wanted to scream.

Aura thought she heard the door open downstairs, and she desperately wanted Rien to bound up the stairs and tell her that it was all going to be okay—that there was an easier way to fight this off. She knew all about Twisted Magic, but the rule book failed to leave out how painful it was. Her body felt like it was burning, her head felt like it had been crashed in, and a loud ringing overtook most of her senses. Opening her eyes, she reached her shaking hands into the floorboards, pulling out her coat and mask and setting it beside her. Reaching in once more, she pulled out the knife.

    The knife that had killed too many.

    The knife that may as well have killed her in the process.

    The knife that she now hurled at the wall.

    Her tears blurred the wall in front of her where the knife now stuck. Aura heaved a sigh, a sob racking her entire body while Twisted Magic pulsed through her. How could she have done this to herself? How could she have let herself continue to do so? She had killed. She'd lied to herself; she was not better. She was worse, and no magic in the world could convince her that she was not simply a horrible person searching for forgiveness in a place that would lend her none. Aura clutched her eyes shut, hoping that this was some odd nightmare.

    But it was not; *A fact.*

    A sound echoed from behind her. It sounded so distant. Still, she fought against the pain and turned to see Lock, his eyes a brilliant purple, his hands together in concentration. He looked elemental, standing there, bathed in a purple glow, and yet she could see the strain fighting this magic was taking on him. The magic, he was fighting for *her*. His dark hair fell onto his forehead, and as Aura drifted off, she thought she noticed a single tear slipping down his cheek. The pain began to subside, but not before the Twisted gave her one final call.

Do you honestly believe love will save you now? Foolish girl, it will kill you.

Then, she let Lock's magic pull her back to safety.

No calculation could save her from the way Lock watched her as he fiddled with the knife he'd pulled from the wall not long after she'd woken. Aura's face was tear-stained and her head rested on a pillow. Lock hadn't said anything since she had awoken. He'd merely leaned back in the chair he was sitting in, and tears threatened to spill once more. His hair was ruffled, his tie askew, and he had the distinct look of someone who'd been crying. Though now, his eyes were unreadable as he watched her. *Your heart does not need such guarding,* he'd told her, so here it was: her heart on display for him to see, oh how horrid it was. And now he was looking at her as though she were not truly real. Lock stood.

"You know when you held this to my throat, I should've known it was you."

Aura looked at him, not knowing what to say. Her heart tightened. She was saving him by doing this.

"Aura, why?" he asked, his voice gentler than before, setting the knife on her desk, the sound echoing through her too-quiet room.

She could've said a thousand things, but it all sounded foolish in her ears. What could she say? That she missed Alon? That anything was better than being buried beneath her own grief? That she'd made a mistake? But, killing wasn't a mistake; it was something far bigger. So, instead, she said, "I don't know."

He looked sorrowfully at her, but his clenched fists gave away his true feelings, and Aura didn't need Emotive Magic to see that. He was the picture of a gentleman, her friend, yet she knew that he was hurting. He turned to leave, but Aura pushed herself off the bed and was going to cross the room but thought better of it. What could she do? Beg him to stay? She couldn't do that. She brushed a hand down her skirts, her legs feeling like they were on the verge of collapsing. She looked at him then, his face distant and cold, his eyes giving nothing away.

"I'm sorry," she said, but it meant little. Her actions were beyond the confines of those simple words. "I shouldn't have listened." *To the magic.*

A frown appeared on Lock's face before he nodded and left, reaching into his coat pocket as if checking to make sure he hadn't lost something.

Aura watched him go because there was no calculation or scientific explanation that would make him stay.

FOURTEEN

LOCK

Betrayal sunk into his gut as Lock walked from Aura's townhouse. Anger ran through his veins like blood, not at her but at himself. How had he been so blind? How could he have walked out on her without hearing what she had to say? How could he have walked out when he'd wanted nothing more than to dry her tears as she looked at him? He should turn right around and tell her all the secrets that hung between them, but he wouldn't—he couldn't. Not while anger still poisoned his mind and not while she was hurting. He didn't hate the Queen of Spades. He hated himself; she had just been the easiest person to blame it on.

Aura was the Queen of Spades.

She was a murderer and a liar.

The Queen of Spades.

The thought echoed back to him, but all he felt was the weight of it all. They both had blood on their hands that they'd never be able to get off, and somehow, he knew that they both needed each other despite their wrongdoings. Aura had stayed when he'd killed the one person he'd promised to save. God, she even helped him bury the body—and he had walked out. *Coward, coward, coward.* Lock shook his head, his anger long replaced by a suffocating feeling. Betrayal would ruin them both in the end, perhaps even destroy them, and Lock could only hope he could say all he needed to before time took advantage of their fragile hearts. At the coronation, rumours had been circulating that the Queen of Spades was after the coronet, that *Aura* was, and if it came down to it, he might just let her have it. He shut his eyes, desperately needing a distraction from himself. As he walked back to his London townhouse, all he could hear was the beating of his heart and the whispers of an apology.

A distraction came in the form of an invitation—an invitation to a place he hadn't been to in a very long time. It was addressed to his parents as well, and he assumed they'd be coming up from the country estate to attend. After all, no one declined an invitation from the Nighvengale's. They were possibly the most influential Marquess and Marchioness in all of England. Their presence felt as though it loomed over the city, knowing everything without ever making an appearance, almost as if they were ghosts. They were, as far as Lock could remember, on good terms with his parents. The Marquess and Marchioness used to attend annual parties, but all that died four years ago. Now, as his carriage rumbled out of Marylebone and towards Notting Hill, he couldn't help but wonder at the sudden invite. Sometimes, when he'd been small, the Nighvengale's had allowed him and Aura to taste the desserts before they were served, but that was when Aura still held value in their eyes: when her parents were still alive. Lock had been too young to remember Aura's parents, his memory proved to be very difficult to reach for from that time, but he did know they'd cared for her very much. Bitterness welled up in his heart; a cruelty meant only for those who decided when people were of value. Then came the sting; he shouldn't be thinking of her, not while betrayal still poisoned his mind. Lock turned his head to the window, watching the fading sun and before long, his carriage rolled to a stop. The white, three-story facade of the Nighvengale's townhouse stared back at him, light from inside dancing along the pavements. He knew that behind the house was an area of large greenery that he noted could be used for a quick escape. He closed his hand into a fist, scolding himself. There would be no need for such escape acts.

He brushed a hand on his waistcoat, waiting at the door. The door knocker, he noted, was shaped like a spade, or perhaps it wasn't. Perhaps his conversation with Aura was just messing with his mind. All he could see was the way she knelt before her coat, knife in hand; he'd recognized it almost as quickly as his heart had shattered. He muttered a curse, grabbing the gold knocker and pounding three times before letting the silence echo through his bones. The butler let him in, music and light conversation greeting him. As he remembered, the inner decor of the townhouse was less like a home and more like a palace. Gold accents decorated the white walls, meeting the high muraled ceilings where chandeliers hung down like teardrops. Lock let his noble mask settle over him like a second skin—a mask of his greatest arrogance and boredom reserved for these kinds of events.

"Locklyn," his mother called, distancing herself from a couple dressed in the deepest purple, a glass of champagne in her hand. "I'm delighted to see you showed."

"I didn't think I had a choice," he replied, emotionless. That was no act. Small talk made him wish he could walk back out and go home. His mother showed no sign of hearing him.

"Your father is speaking with the Nighvengale's. I suggest you go make your presence known. It'll do you good to socialize."

Before Lock could say anything, his mother waltzed away back to the couple. Lock studied them for a moment. The woman had long black hair reaching the length of her back, and the man, his hair cropped short to his head. He recognized them, from the Order perhaps, and yet he couldn't recall their names. The list Xavier had given him popped into his head, but before he could flip through the names from his memory movement caught his eye. In the corner of the room stood Sören next to a gentleman, who looked to be about in his early thirties, a blond moustache curling at his lips. They spoke in hushed tones, and Lock wondered how Sören had been invited. He wasn't someone the Nighvengale's would deem important unless the man he stood with somehow was. He cast a quick glance around the room for Iskra, but he knew her well enough to know that she wouldn't show up. She'd never trusted the Nighvengale's, and for good reason he supposed. They always kept to themselves, yet always seemed to know everything about everyone. Lock noticed his mother watching him, and he cursed himself before walking through an entryway and into a room where his father was speaking with the Nighvengale's.

"Excuse me," Lock said, catching his father nodding in approval out of the corner of his eye. "I'd like to thank you for the invite."

Lord Nighvengale took the hand he offered, shaking it once. The Marquess was a tall man with pale skin, dark brown hair, and silver spectacles. His wife was of similar complexion, though her face had always seemed kinder than her husband's.

"Pleasure to have you," Lord Nighvengale replied. "You're soon to be a valuable asset to us, just as your father is."

Lock managed to smile, though he was confused. He thought his parents hadn't been in contact with the Nighvengale's since their last gathering. Clearly, he'd been wrong. At first, he thought the distance had been because of his parent's association with the Order, but the Nighvengale's made no mention of the secret society. Lock surveyed the rest of the room. He recognized some businesspeople that his father had dealt with in the past, as well as some aristocrats from across the Thames. He paused at the sight of two young women, also a part of the Order and yet he hadn't thought they ran in the Nighvengale's circle. They were lower in the hierarchy, and Lock would have thought the Nighvengale's would've ignored them. One woman had her back to him, but the other he recognized as Lady Elsder, Kian's more obvious choice in marriage. At least, that's what Xavier's list claimed, and what the rumours said. Another thought made him frown. If they were here as lower aristocracy, why couldn't Aura have been here? By all means, she had the title. Or she would've. His fist clenched as the dinner bell rang. There was no way in hell he'd be sitting down at a dinner with so many prying eyes. He let himself get lost in the crowd as he moved towards the dining room. He noted that Rien was here and talking to Lord Nighvengale as if they'd been friends for years, and he took the opportunity to slip out the front door and round the block to the entrance of the back plot of land. In the dark, he could just make out the carriage houses lining the back of the townhouses and the silhouettes of people sitting down for dinner.

"Lockly—" a cough. "Lock," Sören called, striding up behind him in the darkness, no sign of his companion from earlier.

He nodded. "Sören."

"Do be kind and drop the formality," Sören said, doing a rather horrible imitation of what Lock thought was supposed to be him. Lock scowled.

"What are you doing here?"

"Investigating. I'm working with a friend to work on a few leads."

"I see. And your friend is. . .who?"

Sören was silent for a moment. "I don't want to drag you and the others into this just yet. At least until I make sure that he's not—"

"Cheating you out?" Lock suggested, cocking a brow.

"Exactly."

"Very well. What have you and your secret companion found?"

Lock listened with intent as Sören explained about the paper used to write the letters that seemed to help them and how after crossing a few others off the list, it led them to the Nighvengale's.

"Paper is very common," Lock said.

"Aye, but not the ink and paper combination."

"You think like a detective."

"Perhaps. Or maybe I just know where to begin looking."

Lock crossed his arms, but the ghost of a smile crested over his lips. Sören continued to mention the three names at this party that cross-referenced with that of the Duke's: Lord and Lady Liang, Lady Elsder, and Lady Hollisworth.

"My partner is looking into them as we speak," Sören said, glancing backwards at the house.

Lock stored the names in the back of his mind. "While I do think the letters are important, I don't think you're going to find any answers here."

"Why?" Sören asked, frowning.

"Because why would the Nighvengale's send them? They have no interest in Kian."

"Then what are they interested in?"

Lock cast the boy a sidelong glance. "Society. Its secrets. That sort of thing."

"Do you think they know what happened to the coronet? Or if they know what happened to Kian?"

"Difficult to say," Lock mused, though even as he did, his head began to spiral. If the Nighvengale's were connected, then they knew who murdered Kian. And if Lock were hiding something away, he would do it where no one would look. His eyes snagged on the carriage house, and he motioned for Sören to join him. As they approached, music from above filtered through the night air as Lock bent down to try the handle. Sören pulled a set of tools from the inside of his pocket and, kneeling down, began to pick the lock. Lock stared at him but said nothing. It would seem that the son of a detective came with many useful skills. Lock tugged at his gloves while he waited, casting momentary glances over his shoulder every now and then. The door creaked open, and Lock thanked Sören before stepping inside. A carriage and a stable for two horses took up most of the space, but at the far end was a small room. Lock assumed it would be for extra supplies for the horses, but upon entry, he could see that a desk had been set up inside, a small lamp set upon its surface. Behind him, Lock heard Sören rummaging around throughout the various cabinets while Lock searched the desk.

Nothing.

He ran his gaze from floor to ceiling, tapping his shoes against the floorboards. He counted each tap carefully. One . . . two . . . three . . . there. He knelt, taking a glove off before opening the panel. Inside lay a switch and a series of gears. He followed the line to the far wall of the makeshift office before looking back at the switch.

"Lord Mortsakov," The steel in the Marquesses' voice was unmistakable. "What in God's name do you think you're doing?"

Lock sat back on his heels, a mask of calmness slipping over his features. "Dearest Marquess, what does it look like I'm doing? I'm conducting a murder investigation." He cast a glance to where Sören now stood with his partner, who must've come in at the heels of the Marquess, along with a very smug-looking stable hand, who Sören was busy casting glares at. "Now, what's behind the wall?"

"Leave us," Lord Nighvengale boomed, and to Lock's horror, Sören, the blond man, and the stable hand all left. Lock swallowed his fear. It wasn't like today could get any worse. He stood, tugging his glove back on, and brushed invisible dust off his long coat.

"I ask again," Lock said, taking on the same tone as the marquess. "What's behind the wall?"

"Nothing that concerns your investigation."

"Yeah? If I flip the switch, I won't find a knife? A coronet?"

"No! Lord Mortsakov, please leave. I don't want to have to bring this to your father."

"And I don't want to have to bring you to the police," Lock called, dancing around the marquess and into the carriage room beyond. He spun just in time to see the marquess sizzling with anger. "Do you?" Lock asked.

The Marquess swung a gloved hand at Lock's head, and Lock called for his magic, clapping his hands. Energy sparked through his veins, and Lock watched through a purple haze as the man collapsed to the floor. This time, Lock didn't bother trying to catch him. Lock decided he could keep the idea of the wall in the back of his mind, not wanting to stay here a moment longer. The Nighvengale's were definitely hiding something, but it would seem that Lock wouldn't get any information out of them by fighting and certainly not while he was alone. As he stepped out from the carriage house and returned to the party, Lock desperately hoped he hadn't just started a feud with the wrong man.

Lock climbed out of the carriage three blocks from his townhouse. His parents bid him farewell with a promise of returning to London in the next three weeks. Lock's mouth tightened at the idea of having what little he had left of his peace ruined by his parents' insistence on marriage, but that was a matter for a different day. Now, he needed the night air and a place to calm down from the night's events. His veins were lit with the aftermath of a party, sounds of laughter and conversation still floating beneath his skin. It would have felt magical if it weren't for the worry that plagued him. If Sören had found evidence that the Nighvengale's might be somehow entwined in Kian's death, he feared that this investigation would only get more complex. Lock shook his head as he folded his hands into fists. Ahead, in the low streetlight, a figure peeled away from the wall and walked towards him. Lock kept his eyes ahead with his hat pulled low over his face. A moment later, the figure passed him on the street, his own hat pulled low, and handed him a letter. Lock took it before registering what he'd done. He spun, looking for the figure, but it was as if they'd disappeared into the shadows. Lock stuffed the letter into the pocket of his coat, eager to get home before seeing what the devils had to say.

Candlelight flickered at his desk as he ripped the letter open. His room was quiet, save for the distant noise of carriages returning from their respective nights out. *Damn me to Hell.* Lock set the letter on his desk, staring at the letters.

```
Embrace evil and the righteousness of greed,
   but be wary, for you should not let it devour
                    you.
   Protect the one with the heart that bleeds,
      for the devil's kind words only mask what's
                   cruel.
```

FIFTEEN

SÖREN

Sören Niaheartson related to the trees in Hyde Park, what with him all but shivering in the cool winds. He decided his fashion could be sacrificed for his warmth as he buttoned up his coat. Tension gripped the air between Aura, who sat on the bench, and Lock, who paced before it. Iskra sat on the bench as well, muttering rude things about the few people that passed them. She looked bored, not that Sören could blame her. Detective Inspector Thornsbury had informed him just that morning that he'd send Sören to interview the first round of suspects for the murder, and these two seemed the most promising, according to Thornsbury's findings at the Nighvengale's party yesterday evening. Now that he thought about it, he might've just been doing Thornsbury's errands for the better half of the morning. Lord and Lady Liang from up in Chelsea were in London twice a week on business, and spent their lunch hours walking in Hyde Park, hence the reasons for the group's lookout on the bench. Or rather, Aura and Iskra's spot on the bench. He was leaning against a rather uncomfortable lamppost, its edges stabbing him in the back. *Hmph*, he thought, shifting. He spotted the Lord and Lady across the walkway and waited until they got close to interview them. As they approached, Sören took in their dark black hair and silken winter attire.

Iskra coughed. "*Excusez moi*, I'm Iskra Storenné. I'm sure you know me from the Order."

The pair looked as if they might run off.

"I wouldn't," Aura warned, rising as she gestured to Lock. "He has a way of hurting people."

Sören glanced between the two of them. He couldn't help but feel like Aura's words held more weight than they let on, but Lock's face didn't give any such ideas away. The couple allowed Iskra to move them to the bench where she and Aura had been seated only moments prior.

"I'm working with a team to investigate Kian's murder," Iskra explained.

"And you think we had something to do with it?" Lord Liang asked. "Because we didn't."

"It's just a procedure," Sören told them, though he didn't tell them they were major suspects in the investigation. That, he'd learned from his father; never tell the suspects how they are related to the crime committed—but give them enough information to justify their innocence.

Lady Liang put a hand on her husband's arm. "What would you like to know?"

"Where did you spend most of your evening the night Kian was murdered?" Lock asked, his tone more demanding than usual.

"In the ballroom with Mr. Wrentroth. Before then, my wife was with some friends, and I was speaking with the mortician about science—I do have quite the interest in it. Later, we were stuck in there."

Lock nodded at Aura, and Sören assumed it was an indication that Aura would check with her uncle.

"And you knew Kian through the Order?"

"That's correct."

"Do you know anyone that might've had ill intent towards him?"

"No. As I'm sure you know, that dinner was meant to find him a spouse and for him to become the head. No one hated him. They couldn't."

At least not publicly, Sören thought about saying, but kept his mouth shut.

"You were at the Order two days ago. Arguing with the Duke," Aura said. She stated it with no room for answering, and Sören wondered how she knew that piece of information.

"I don't see what that has to do with anything."

"It's best we don't talk about this here. May we stop by your place of residence later this week?" Iskra asked, cutting off Aura, who'd been about to open her mouth. Sören silently prayed that this wouldn't last much longer.

Lord Liang pulled a card from inside his coat with his address on it. "We're back in Chelsea in two days. See us then."

"Yes, sir. Thank you."

Then, Sören was left alone in the park. The suspects were on their way, and Lock and Aura headed in opposite directions. Iskra headed for a café on the corner where he suspected she would buy herself a nice little tea for asking three questions. He shook his head, tugged his coat tighter around himself, and started on his way home.

Sören Niaheartson wasn't one to get many visitors, so when a knock sounded at the door to his house, he was shocked. He'd expected it to be someone from Scotland Yard for his father, but instead, Xavier Brittenworth stood at his door, his coat tugged close to his chin. Soren's father's warning played in his head like a distant memory, but that was the thing about distance—it was easy to pretend he couldn't hear. Sören opened the door wider, leading the heir into an office his father would not use until after dinner. He would have no idea Xavier had been here.

"To what do I owe the pleasure?" Sören asked, shutting the door behind them.

"I'm not sure you'll be getting any pleasure out of this conversation," Xavier said, striding to sit in an armchair in the corner of the room. "I wanted to apologize for the night of the party."

Sören frowned, struggling to recall what Xavier was on about. All he remembered was the blood, that pounding heartbeat, and Kian staring dead at the ceiling.

"You ran from the room. . ." Xavier trailed off as if he was trying to jog Sören's own memory.

"Oh, *that*. It's perfectly fine."

"No, it's not. I feel horrible. I didn't know you. . ."

"Would react the way I did? No, it's my fault, really. I should know that not everything is poison." Sören shut his mouth. That was way more than Xavier needed to know.

Xavier frowned. "I should've been more considerate."

"You didn't know," Sören said, his heartbeat quickening. "Truly, Xavier. It's okay."

The door behind them swung open, his father pausing in the doorway when he saw them. His father dismissed Xavier with a wave. No bow—not at all how he should treat someone of Xavier's standing. If the heir noticed, he made no comment on it before leaving the room. Sören went to his room, not caring for or wanting to hear his father's lecture. He could tell that Xavier had wanted to ask how the investigation was going, and Sören made a mental note to tell him. For now, he collapsed into an armchair in the corner of his room—ignoring the way Xavier had looked at him. He was tired of pity. And no matter how much he tried to keep his thoughts upright, he found himself falling into memories. He remembered the night like it was yesterday, when he'd awoken on Aura's mortuary table, the ceiling blurring together through his tears. His skin had felt heavy. The next sense that had come to him had been his hearing, not his magic, but the normal sounds of voices coming from beside him, or a distance—he couldn't tell.

"He's breathing," Aura had said, though at the time, Sören hadn't yet been acquainted to her.

His father asked what happened.

"Laudanum."

Sören had passed out again shortly after, but since that day all anyone ever saw when they looked at him was someone to pity. He hated it. They always *assumed* it had been self administered—it wasn't. He had just happened to be at the wrong place at the wrong time.

He just happened to say the wrong things.

And he'd ended up with poison in his mouth.

He thought Xavier would have been different, but he supposed he'd been wrong. He would do anything for Xavier to have him look at him without pity, and without regard for his past. Regardless, Xavier had asked him to do a job, and he would keep his word.

Sören sat up in a nearly dark room, dusk spreading throughout his open windows like a hazy cloud. He was awake. *I'm alive.* Another chance at life, and by God, he wouldn't let it go to waste. In fact, having Xavier know about it felt like a weight had been taken off his shoulders. Like maybe it didn't have to be a secret held between him and Aura—a patient and the saviour. He almost smiled because sometimes people didn't get second chances. His mother didn't. And so, he'd do this life for her as well. He'd long ago decided that he would stop letting his past control his life, letting it guide him as if he were to ingest poison forever, with every glass of wine that ever touched his lips. But that was ignorant; God wouldn't grant him another chance at life just to take it so greedily. He sighed. Without another moment to dwell on the memory, he stood. He had a lot of work to do, if he wanted to get the coronet, and it started with going over the facts of the night Kian Brittenworth was murdered.

PART TWO
PEOPLE ARE PUZZLES

Emmaline Leigh

SIXTEEN

ISKRA

The Liang's manor in Chelsea was a dark structure that made Iskra feel like she was stepping into a haunted house rather than a wealthy estate. The thick spires that lined the roof only added to the chill, and she could envision herself being impaled above, even though Lord and Lady Liang didn't seem like the murdering type.

The four of them stood on the steps, waiting for the door to open, the air cold even as Iskra tugged her thick woollen coat tighter around her. It would snow soon, and she wasn't looking forward to it, as snow often brought along a feeling of haziness that she couldn't afford. Not when time felt as though it was always pressing down on her, like she truly was what her parents accused her of: a fugitive on the run. An unwelcome chill ran down her spine. Lord and Lady Liang had been so eager to prove that they weren't killers, yet they took years to answer their door. Iskra huffed, crossing her arms.

"If you scowl any deeper, I'm afraid it might stay like that," Sören said, from where he stood ahead of her, clutching his own arms.

"*Oui.* If you hold yourself any tighter, I'm afraid you might break."

He shrugged. "At least you're afraid for me."

Iskra rolled her eyes, despite the fact that the boy was growing on her. She still needed him for her business assets, but perhaps she'd keep him around after it. Besides, she could use someone to rescue her from her parents, especially since they were in the wind. Not that she would need saving; perhaps she just needed a *friend*. Iskra shuddered, remembering her last conversation with Zoialynne, but it was replaced by a pang of guilt she immediately shoved away. Iskra wouldn't let her feelings get to her, especially not while she was in the middle of an investigation—she knew better than that. The butler opened the door, gesturing for them to enter, seemingly under orders to let them in, which Iskra was surprisingly humbled by. The entrance hall seemed the opposite of the foreboding exterior, with its white walls and intricate silver carvings cascading down the wall until it reached the polished marble flooring. A crystal chandelier hung from the ceiling, an arched staircase leading up to the second floor. The solemn-faced butler led them up the stairs, and instead of showing them into a drawing room, much to Iskra's surprise, he led them into a bedroom. Lord Liang stood immediately when he saw them, bowing to her and Lock and nodding at Aura and Sören. Iskra looked around the room, her gaze settling on Lady Liang, who was dressed in a rich purple, lying still on the bed—her breathing hardly visible. Iskra watched as Aura walked over to the woman, examining her as if she were dead.

"She's still alive, Miss Wrentroth," Lord Liang said, though Iskra thought he said it as much for his own sake rather than Aura's. For all intents and purposes, the lady did have the look of being on the cusp of reality.

Aura cast him a glance. "I can see that, my lord. What I'm looking at is the glow around her brow."

The lord walked over to where Aura stood, and so did Iskra, her curiosity spiked. The fuming lord from yesterday had softened as he gazed upon his wife and brushed her brow. Sure enough, Aura indicated the purple pale glow that emanated at the woman's temple.

"Usually," Aura said, moving to pace the length of the bed, "Twisted magic cannot be seen in an unconscious person unless it's still being used."

"Twisted Magic?" Lord Liang echoed quietly.

"Emotive, Twisted Magic," Aura said, pausing at the windows of the room and looking at the cobbled yard behind the house.

Iskra didn't like the idea that the Twisted were keeping Lady Liang unconscious, but that did lead to one idea—it meant that they were scared she knew something.

Lord Liang turned to Aura, "Can you save her?"

Aura smiled sadly at him, stepping away from the window. "I'm a scientist, my lord, not a doctor."

He turned to look at his wife. "Well, you may as well ask me the questions you've come for. You're allowed to use your magic and search for whatever you wish. If you need me, I shall be here."

"With respect," Lock said, from where he still stood in the doorway with Sören. "We won't be needing any questions other than one. How did this happen to your wife?"

Without turning away from the bed, Lord Liang replied, "It was an assassination attempt once we got home yesterday evening."

"And can you give us the details?" Sören asked.

Iskra thought the lord might not respond, but after a long moment, he turned, fresh tears brimming his eye line. "It was sudden. We got home late last night. And we did as we always do: I retreated to my study, and my wife went upstairs. I usually catch up on Order correspondence the Duke has sent my way, which seems to be more since our fight." He gave Lock a pointed look, that Iskra assumed had to do with what he and Aura overheard when they found the coronet's vault. "When I was done, I found her. No screaming. No pain. She was on the floor, and it was only after that I carried her to bed."

"And you didn't see anyone?"

"No. I wish I would have. Now, if you please, the sooner you can get your investigation over with, the sooner I can focus on what really matters; who did this."

Lock nodded before they all left to let the lord watch over his wife, and as Iskra shut the door, she could tell he was praying; his head bent low before his wife, and Iskra could've sworn she saw his body start to shake with silent sobs.

Iskra knocked on the door to the bedroom, Lock beside her, his mood ever foul since three days ago. She'd meant to ask him about it, but really, she didn't care that much. Most likely, he'd recover. The lord called for them to enter, and Iskra paused in the doorway, unsure if she should continue. While the lord had stopped his crying, he still looked as frail as a flame on a windy day. Lock nodded for her to move into the room as he went to stand by the lord, who was near the large window. Iskra walked to Lady Liang, whose glow had faded, although it was still obvious she was under a spell. Iskra had never tried to break the Twisted barrier before, but she was going to have to if they were going to get the answers they needed. After a quick sweep of the upstairs, she and Lock had split to use their magic while Aura and Sören would continue with the physical investigation. Iskra would much rather have spent her time with Sören or Aura rather than this brooding buffoon, but she couldn't exactly tell him to leave. She needed Lock to tell the emotive state of the sleeping woman, as Iskra's mind sifted through her thoughts. That is, assuming it could be done. Iskra placed her hand on Lady Liang's shoulder, letting her mind latch onto hers. Purple filled her vision, pain shooting through her mind, but Iskra didn't let go; she had felt worse. Iskra pierced the Twisted Magic and sifted through the past events until she reached the party.

"*What do you mean Kian isn't going through with the deal?*" Lady Liang's voice echoed in her mind.

"*I mean he took the money and lost it, Izumi. It's gone—he's lost it or it was stolen. Either way, I've lost my trust in him.*" That was Lord Liang.

"*Kano, this isn't like him. Our business dealings have been all well until now.*"

"*Yes, I think I shall speak with him.*"

Purple shot back at her, and she was flung from Lady Liang—Izumi's—mind. She made eye contact with Lock, who shook his head, an indication that no negative feeling had been addressed. Still, she had to ask.

"What did you tell Kian when you visited him after he lost your money?"

Iskra asked Kano, Lord Liang.

"I asked him where the money might've gone, but that was the last time I saw him. He said it was stolen—that he had no hand in its his disappearance. I believed him. That was a few days before the party."

Lock and Iskra thanked the lord for his time and left him to his solitude. Iskra's was beginning to feel dizzy; that should not have been possible—for her to enter an unconscious mind. Unless part of Lady Liang wasn't fully unresponsive.

Iskra turned to Lock. "Do you believe him?"

"That I do," he said. "I believe he thinks that he forgave Kian, but whether his wife did, it's difficult to say. He is hiding something. I'm just not sure what. I don't suppose you heard anything?"

Iskra shook her head and was about to ask what he meant about Kano hiding something when a servant bounded up the steps, handing a letter to Iskra. She didn't need to read it to know she should go to the Order; the letter was pressed with a blue stamp identical to the gem that graced her inner wrist.

"If you'll excuse me, the Duke is calling," Iskra said, already on her way down the steps.

Lock nodded and turned to where Iskra suspected the others would be conducting their investigations. Iskra called for a carriage, only for worry to wrap itself around her head. What did the Duke want? He hardly ever called on her personally, but perhaps they had finally found something on the Society that would bring them down.

Banned from the Order of Crowns, the Duke's words echoed in her head. They were the first words out of his mouth as she'd stumbled into the vacant room in the Order's lower level. Now, he stood quietly in the corner of the room as Iskra bit down on her tongue, as the gem was removed from her wrist. Her blood thrummed violently, and tears threatened to show her weakness in the task. Blood trickled down her wrist, though she kept her eyes firmly on the Duke. The Order —her once family—was forfeiting her position for working on the investigation. God, she was trying to help them, but apparently, they cared more about finding a mole in their society than Kian's murder. Iskra's knees were in pain, kneeling on the concrete floor of the cellar. Her soul was ripped from her, once again, by people she had thought she could trust. *Trust*; how feeble. Anger coiled in her stomach; how could she have set herself up for such a trap? Her now-bare wrist was attached to a chain, supposedly to keep her still, yet it only made her more agitated. Iskra watched with hard eyes as the doctor plopped the gem into a vial and wrapped a bandage around her wrist. The cellar was dim, but not dim enough for Iskra to miss Zoialynne in her guard livery, jaw hard, as the Duke stepped forward. Iskra tried to meet her gaze, but the guard wouldn't look at her.

"Iskra Storenné," Duke Brittenworth said, "We gave you a home. We protected you. We did everything for you, yet when we warn you to stop your treachery, you don't do the same?"

She glared daggers at him. "I'm helping you."

The Duke inspected his fingernails. "No. You're working with the enemy."

"Who is?" Iskra asked, pulling on a chain with a grunt.

"Does it matter? Not to mention you've been stealing my resources."

Iskra's gaze snapped to Zoialynne's, who looked back at her, levelling her gaze. Iskra shook her head in disbelief, but she couldn't say she was surprised.

It'd seem power truly did corrupt.

With Iskra's free hand, she reached into her pocket, pulling a knife out. She'd started carrying one around ever since Zoialynne had told her about her parents. How foolish of them not to check her. Iskra stuck the tip into the lock of the cuff that held her, and in one smooth movement she was shaking off the chain. She stood, glaring at the Duke, all tears replaced by cold, hard anger. He looked bored. This man had protected her. Iskra had done everything for him, and with one misstep he was removing her. No, there had to be something bigger. There was one possibility, but Iskra pushed it from her mind. Iskra took long strides towards the Duke until the knife was at his neck. Iskra shifted the knife, the metal cool in her hands, pressing hard enough on the man's neck to draw blood. Several guards moved to stop her, but to Iskra's surprise, the Duke held out a hand.

"Go on," he said. "Do it."

Iskra smiled. "You'll wish you hadn't said that."

A dagger at her neck—Zoialynne's.

Iskra turned to stare at her, betrayal seeping into her veins. Iskra removed the blade from the Duke's neck, stabbing it into the fabric of his coat, pinning his shoulder to the wall. In the same moment, she took a step backwards, away from

Zoialynne's blade, ignoring the smug look of the Duke as she strode from the room.

No one made a move to stop her.

A few paces out of the room, a cold hand grabbed her wrist and pulled her into an alcove. She winced at the pain beneath her bandage. She'd expected to see Zoialynne. Instead, Xavier stood there.

He handed her a bottle.

"For the pain," Xavier said.

She remembered a time when she was only fifteen, and he was sixteen running around the Order without a care; that was, until they were caught. Or the time she'd saved him from being hauled away by some of her parents' informants. But those memories belong to the grave, much like her naive self. Still, she took the bottle and drank, wrinkling her nose as it burned her throat. She passed the bottle back to him, which he dutifully accepted, placing it back inside his coat, but not before she caught sight of a bandage beneath his jacket sleeve, matching her own.

"Thank you." She said, blinking tears away from her eyes.

The heir smiled at her. "It's no problem."

Iskra remembered, then, what Sören had told her, about Xavier needing the coronet. She doubted it was for selfish reasons, but standing here, she vowed she wouldn't hurt him when she got her hands on it. She wasn't sure she could handle it; he'd been nothing but kind to her. But this was the price she had to pay. Three years ago, she'd sworn that she would find a way to stop her parents, but there was no other way, other than getting the coronet.

Iskra left the manor with a vow to destroy it, and maybe, just maybe, she'd become what her parents had called her—a criminal. Iskra cast one glance back, imagining flames melting the house down without so much as an apology.

SEVENTEEN

AURA

Aura paced around the small office for what seemed like the thousandth time. She refused to leave it, much to Sören's dismay, but there was something off about the room she couldn't place. Apart from the pale walls and dark oak decor of the room, Aura hadn't the faintest idea of what she was looking for. It'd become obvious upon entry that the room was used often by the lord, the scratches on the doorframe and indents in the floor said as much, and Aura just needed to find *something* that confirmed the lord's personal alibi; to truly check him off the list of suspects. Sören pushed off the desk he'd been perched on, sighing.

"All your optical talent, and it's being put to waste."

She glared at him. "You know that isn't how it works."

He shrugged. "I'm just saying. I think this would be a lot easier if the others were here to help."

"You called?" Lock said, striding into the room. Iskra was nowhere to be found, and Aura shut her eyes, turning back to the room. Lock had done an excellent job of avoiding her all day, and now she needed to do the same. No matter the circumstances of their friendship, she needed to focus.

The rustling of papers cut through her consciousness. "I found this downstairs."

She slid her eyes to Lock, who'd handed Sören what appeared to be drawings.

"Anatomical drawings?" Sören questioned, glancing at the paper then up at her. "Didn't you say that the murderer had a good sense of it?"

"Yes, Sören. I did," Aura said, "but the evidence is all circumstantial. I have excellent knowledge of the body and I didn't murder Kian."

"You murdered someone—" Lock cut off, his tone all jagged edges and scowls. Aura turned away once more, not wishing to point out that he had too, though in a much more noble way. Sören shifted, not saying anything, and she could've thanked him for it. *Silence.* She needed silence. She was vaguely aware of Lock and Sören in the background, though ignored them as best she could as she shut her eyes. The floor echoed and had her mind understanding everything. The floor was hollow where it shouldn't be, and unless the floor was about to cave in, there should be a hidden compartment beneath the floor. She spun to see Lock inspecting the wall and Sören back at the desk, seemingly avoiding all tasks.

"Lock, walk where you just were," she instructed, and to her surprise, he did so. She watched, his coat flicking behind him, his face set into a grim line. *Focus.* She scolded herself. She strode over to him, bending down and inspecting the floor. A few knocks on the wooden paneling proved her hypothesis correct, and she carefully lifted the floorboards from their place.

"Of course, you would know where killers hide things," Lock muttered, and she ignored the jab to her heart. If he wanted to hurt her, that was fair—she'd done worse. But what she didn't appreciate was the distraction from work. She reached into the hole but didn't pull out anything. Instead, she flipped a switch. A series of gears could be heard turning before the painting above the desk popped open, narrowly missing Sören, who shoved himself off the desk as fast as Aura had ever seen him move. She moved to the now-open painting where a section had been hollowed out, lined with velvet. She suspected it must've been a safe, though there was nothing inside. She shifted as Lock came to inspect it, his arm brushing hers. His hand touched hers, though whether it was an old habit or an attempt at forgiveness, Aura didn't know. Tension seemed to reverberate between them, her heart pounding loud inside of her chest. She ignored it.

"Something has been moved recently," he said, and Aura leaned closer, noticing the faint indent of pressure outlining where an object had once been. In the back sat several other items: jewels or money mostly, but Aura was more interested in what had been in the safe. If it was the coronet, as she suspected it might be, the Liang's would have lied and would have a lot of explaining to do to Scotland Yard.

"What do you think you're doing?" Lord Liang's voice came from where he stood at the door. Aura suspected he would have been red-faced had he not been so beaten from the attempt on his wife's life. "I said you could look in our house, not locate my wife and I's most valuable possessions!"

This man was beginning to get on her nerves. "Sir, what was in the box that was recently removed from here?"

"I'd like you to leave."

"If it can help the murder—"

"The coronet. It showed up here after the party. The Duke personally delivered it with a letter."

"Can we see the letter?"

"Afraid not. My wife doesn't like our ties to the Order being public—she burned the letter after reading it."

"But–"

Lord Liang shook his head, somewhat defeated. "If I could help you, I would've done so. Now, leave, or I'll tell the Yard that you broke in."

Aura shut her mouth. She should say more, but she didn't know what, and something in the lord's tone suggested she shouldn't test him.

Lord Liang's eyes strayed to the open floor panel. "You used the fail safe?"

"Why would you need one?" Sören asked.

Lord Liang gave him a look. "*Every* mechanism needs one. Especially if something of value is at risk. Now, if you please, I'll need to now reset it and—"

"One more thing?" Lock asked, folding anatomical drawings in his hands. "If you were to stab someone in the heart, how would you go about it?"

"I wouldn't. It's too risky, with too much room for error. I'd stab the base of the neck, severing the spinal cord. That is, *hypothetically,* if I were to. But I'm not a murderer, Lord Mortsakov. Now, please, leave."

Sören tapped her shoulder and led her from the room. Lock followed after them, and Aura assumed this was Sören's way of making sure they didn't rip out each other's eyes. Aura desperately wished she could speak to Lady Liang, but as long as she was out, they wouldn't be speaking to her anytime soon. Sören asked the butler to inform them when she awoke, but Aura doubted it would be while this investigation was still unsolved, especially if the Twisted were working to keep her unconscious. They left the manor, thick silence stretching between each of them. Lock walked ahead, and she suspected it was to avoid any confrontation with her. She should spin him around and tell him exactly why she had destroyed herself, but it all sounded ridiculous. How could she explain that she needed to avenge a brother that she hardly even remembered?

They strolled quietly down the pathway where they'd hail a carriage back to London. Aura longed for a hot bath, to pretend that none of this existed, and that she had never picked up the knife. Sören made to turn the opposite way to London once they got down the pathway, and Aura stared after him, confused.

"You're going the wrong way," Lock called.

Sören saluted him. "I know."

So much for ripping each other's eyes out. Aura huffed, understanding what Sören was doing, and she appreciated him for it. But an apology wasn't as easy as finding an equilibrium—an answer to the pain she'd caused. No, it was more like proving the answer, step by step, calculating each variable to make sure that all would turn out in the end. And for once, Aura had no idea how to prove her answer—prove to Lock that she was trying to get better. Aura started to turn down towards London. She'd rather walk than face Lock's attitude. Still, he trotted up beside her. It would seem *he* was finally done ignoring her.

"Aura, what happened?"

She didn't look at him. "I did it to save you. For Alon, because of him, and it all went horribly wrong. Did you know it's incredibly difficult to stop, especially when you have someone poisoning you with magic and telling you who and when to strike? What to take?"

"Someone *what*?"

Aura shook her head. "An employer. He doesn't get blamed though, does he? I'm the monster, feral and cold-hearted; forever cruel. I hardly even remember *killing*, Lock." She turned to face him, though he was already watching her, a look she couldn't quite decipher on his face.

He frowned. "You said you were getting rid of the Queen of Spades to save me. Why?"

She quickened her pace, not because she didn't want to have this conversation but because she had no idea what to say. Yes, Aura had wanted to save him—to save herself; She wanted to feel human again, and it would seem that she couldn't achieve all three no matter how hard she tried. If Lock cared or noticed her change in pace, he made no sign.

She paused, spinning around, causing her to nearly bump into him. "Why? Possibly because I didn't want you to get hurt. Possibly because you're *dying*. Maybe because I was tired of being controlled by my employer. Maybe because I wanted to save you because you have saved me more times than I can count. Or maybe it's because I can't imagine what on earth would happen if you left me, but I suppose we're already halfway there."

Aura didn't tell him about the coronet. She couldn't, her veins were buzzing. Aura shut her hands into fists, willing the poison in her system out. She cast a quick look around, but saw no one that could be doing this, then again, the Twisted were experts at hiding.

"And what about saving yourself as well?" Lock asked, his voice quiet.

They were close, his chin tilted down towards her, and Aura could've sworn she saw a flicker of something pass over his face.

Aura scoffed. "I'm sure we're long past that."

"At the coronation," he said, his tone formal. "There were rumours that the Queen of Spades was after the coronet. Were you?"

Aura stared at him. "I was supposed to."

"Would you do it? If I wasn't—"

"I don't get a *choice*." Her words tasted bitter.

"Employer," he said, and at her puzzled look, he added, "You said you had an employer?"

"Yes, but I don't see why I must explain it to you." God, she should apologize, but he was still angry, and no amount of whispered words or dazzling eyes could disguise it. Angry minds didn't wait for tear-filled apologies. No, they lashed and lashed and lashed until the person before them didn't know how to pull them from their own personal purgatory.

"No," he said, and she watched as his invisible mask slipped away. "I suppose you don't."

Aura rolled her eyes, grabbing him by his wrist and forcing her magic into his head. A part of her talent was being able to show what she saw, so she showed him. The letters. The killing. The thievery. The nights when her blood had run red. She showed him everything. The night she'd picked up that knife on her windowsill, everything had spiralled. She left out the parts about visiting Avery and the Twisted, choosing to keep them out—it would only make things worse. The Queen of Spades' story was spread out before their minds like a map on a table; only once that magic faded, Aura wouldn't stick around to see what he thought of her horrid acts. She was sorry and broken and showing that to someone else only made shame crawl its way inside of her heart and bury a hole. *If, then,* she fumbled for an outcome; it was pointless—the damage had been done long before this conversation even happened. The blue light faded from her eyes, and she looked away but not before she saw something unrecognizable on his face. Lock had stumbled backwards, now standing a few steps away from her. His jaw was clenched, his brows furrowed, and he looked as though he was trying to solve an equation, but as far as Aura was concerned, her unspeakable actions had been clear. Her heart thundered in her chest, she had shown him the worst part of herself, and he was unreadable—it terrified her. Aura steadied her dizzy mind, as she always had to when she shared visions, then continued to hail the nearest carriage she saw. She stumbled down the path, her hands shaking from the energy of showing him, and she felt him take a step forward to steady her, but he seemed to remember his place, balling his outstretched hand into a fist. She gripped the carriage door before hauling herself inside.

Lock didn't follow her.

She didn't want him to.

Not after showing him what she'd done. She couldn't face him, especially when the answer to their problem was not yet solved—the only issue was that she had no idea how to solve it.

The streets were busy at this time of night. Aura pulled her hat lower over her eyes, for fear that even in the dim light, someone might see her face. She'd come straight from the Liang's, after checking for Avery at his townhouse, and had only just nicked the hat off a gentleman about to head into a brothel. Her shoes seemed loud against the cobbled streets, though no one she passed spared her a glance. Casting a quick look over her shoulder, she darted into an alleyway until she located the metal door she was looking for. It looked less like a door and more like the bars to a cell, but Aura paid it no more mind as she made quick work of the lock. The metal creaked on its hinges, as the door swung open and closed. Stairs descended downwards and she rushed down, lanterns lit few and far between. It was dim by the time she reached the bottom, the shadows so deep she almost missed the man leaning against the wall, guarding the door, though he looked somewhat disinterested.

"Name?" he asked, pushing to standing, the darkness concealing most of his face. He was dressed like a gentleman, wearing a coat that Aura knew probably housed at least two firearms.

Aura kept her face hidden. "The Queen of Spades."

The man pushed open the door, holding it as she stepped inside. She was nearly through when he caught her arm. Aura stiffened.

"Who you here to see, miss?" His voice was like a snake.

Aura ripped her arm from his grip. "Waltzeen. Now step away or—"

"Or what?"

"Or I'll slit your throat." Avery's voice was calm as he approached them, his shoes crackling against the gravel floor. Aura was pleased to see the gentleman's face sober, though she didn't appreciate Avery stepping in. She strode long strides away from the man and Avery. She'd first checked for him at his townhouse, though he hadn't been there. Now, standing in one of the many underground tunnels that belonged to the Twisted Magicians, she almost wished she'd waited until tomorrow. Bricks formed an arch shape, soot stained, and grit filled. Hooded magicians sat around, some watching her curiously, others playing cards or deep in conversation. Aura had only ever been here one other time, two years ago, when she'd received her disguise from her employer, and even then it felt wrong. She wasn't supposed to know that the Twisted Magicians were exiled beneath the city, no one was. Of course, there were rumours, but no one was ever able to prove it—the Twisted were very careful with keeping this place secure. Pulling her eyes away from the Twisted, she forced her gaze forward, where Avery was now walking, leading her into an office. Unlike the tunnels, the office looked normal, like one might find in any upper-class townhouse in the West End, save for the stone walls. A wooden desk stood at the head of the room, surrounded by bookcases, filled to the brim with books, apothecary medicines, and an assortment of other trinkets. Avery rounded the desk, taking a seat, gesturing for her to do the same.

She stayed standing.

"To what do I owe the pleasure?" Avery asked, once she'd removed her hat.

"I can't do what *he* asked."

Avery sat back. "I see."

Aura stared at him. "That's all?"

"What do you mean, *that's all?*" Avery asked. "I knew this would happen. Just as you know that you can't just walk out of this, Aura. Need I remind you who—"

"No." Aura turned to go. "You don't."

Aura was almost at the door when Avery said, "I am sorry, Aura."

She didn't reply, only tugged her hat on and stalked back past the Twisted Magicians, ascending back up to the world of the living, her heart sinking.

EIGHTEEN

SÖREN

Sören had no qualms about sitting in a carriage with Iskra, except when she spent the entire time glaring daggers at him. Her blond hair hung over her shoulder, back rigid, her arms crossed. Sören sat back as if the seat behind him could swallow him. He almost sighed. For someone younger than him by nearly a year, she shouldn't be so damn scary. Iskra smirked, and he crossed his arms, cursing her magic.

"Are you going to explain why you look like you want to take my eyes out?" he asked as the carriage rumbled onward.

"Non."

He rolled his eyes and picked up his hat from the seat beside him, tossing it at her, which she caught with great precision.

"You, Sören, have an addiction."

He cringed. "What to this time?"

She looked as if she wanted to question him on the meaning of his statement but immediately thought better of it. "You cannot make everyone happy, that is your weakness—an addiction that'll ruin you in the end."

He crossed his arms over his chest. *Addicted.* She was right, of course, except for one thing: it had already ruined him. "Why do you care, Iskra?"

Iskra looked away. "You're the reason Lock and Aura are not here with us now, correct?"

He didn't respond. Had he left Lock and Aura to deal with their problems that he admittedly knew nothing about? Yes. But he couldn't exactly sit idly by and watch as the tension between them spread too thin. Sören wasn't one to meddle in others' business, except when it was affecting the work they did. Lock and Aura investigated well together—he didn't need any Optical magic to see that. God, for all he knew, Lock was halfway in love with her. In Sören's mind, they were magnetic, a polarity—they were two beating hearts that danced around danger, knowing they'd be safe within each other's arms. They were best friends. Sören would kill to have someone like they had each other. Obviously, not actually kill—that would make him a murderer. Sören had done them a favour. At least, he hoped he had. Besides, Sören had seen what pain did to people, and he didn't want that to happen to his friends—that was, if they even were friends. Sören shook his head and said nothing. Iskra wouldn't know anything about apologies. He gazed out the window, watching as the buildings beyond whizzed by until the carriage began to slow. Iskra hopped out without waiting for the assistance of her footman, and Sören followed soon after.

Lady Clara Hollisworth had been absent majority of the night. She was one of Kian's more notable marriage prospects. It was her and a Lady Elsder that were said to have both caught the heir's attention. At least, that was what Iskra had relayed back to him from Xavier's list. Sören had gone yesterday to ask

Thornsbury to check if Liang's words held any truth, but he doubted he'd hear back soon. Besides, the Liang's wouldn't be trying anything, if they were even guilty, especially with all the police around Lady Liang after her attack. Lady Hollisworth, on the other hand, was one of the two candidates in Kian's prospects, and Sören suspected that if Kian had chosen the other one, a nice plot for motive would present itself. He shook his head. Sören needed to focus on the facts—the facts which he didn't have yet. Lady Hollisworth's townhouse stood on the corner of a rather busy thoroughfare, and if Sören didn't get any answers from Lady Hollisworth, he'd march down to Scotland Yard, get Detective Inspector Thornsbury, and question the neighbours about any suspicious activity. He'd wanted to do as such with the Nighvengale's, and although they weren't suspects, there was something off about them. He'd suspected as much when the Marquess had ordered them out. When Sören had told Thornsbury about the exchange between the Marquess and Lock, the inspector had simply shaken his head and told them that they were too powerful. *Marquess Charles Nighvengale could kill the entire population of London and get away with it,* the inspector had said, and Sören believed him. Sören dreaded to think what would happen if they were, in fact, behind the letter writing, or worse. Even if they were, no one could do anything about it. Though, if they were a part of the letter writing, how did they know so much about Kian's murder? He swallowed hard, ignoring all the connections that he and the others would need to go through. Iskra pushed him forward, and he stumbled. He didn't remember when he'd stopped walking. Iskra knocked on the door and paced on the doorstep while waiting. Even Iskra seemed more agitated, and Sören made a mental note to ask her about it later. *That is what friends do, isn't it?* As they waited, Sören turned on the doorstep and watched the houses across the street for any sign of people who could be waiting and watching for the next level of street gossip. Across the way was a house that looked almost as grey as the sky above, its flowers in the window boxes long wilted.

The flutter of a curtain.

A man in a grey coat tucked his collar closer as he walked past the house, casting a glance at Sören before turning down a side street.

He shot a look back at the door, which still hadn't been answered, before bounding down the steps and running across the road. He heard Iskra protest behind him with what were probably several French expletives, but he didn't look back. He followed the way the man had gone—only there was no sight of him. Sören felt anger push from inside him, an anger that he was beginning to recognize as false feelings from the Twisted. He tried to ignore it, clenching his fist behind him. Something brushed behind him, though he spun to find nothing there.

There was nothing at all, just darkness.

He knew that the street was still there, but he could no longer see it. In the center of it was Xavier, a knife stabbed through his heart, his eyes glowing blue as his skin greyed. Sören shut his eyes, the image still there. This wasn't real, an attack of the Twisted, but by God, his heart hurt. Besides, what should he care if Xavier was killed? He shouldn't. He hardly knew the heir. His cheek burned, and all magic disappeared. He blinked, meeting Iskra's furious face.

"Ah yes, perhaps consult me before you walk into a trap," she said, taking her hand off his shoulder. He winced.

"You punch hard."

"You're weak," she countered.

Sören *humphed* but didn't argue.

"Well?"

"Well, what?"

Iskra shook her head before walking down the way the man had gone. "Lady Hollisworth can wait."

Sören followed after her and was about to say that the man was gone, but instead of continuing, Iskra pushed open a gate, turning into the backlot of the house where the curtain had fluttered. It was a thin alleyway, just big enough for he and Iskra to stand next to each other. Doors lined all the way down the row, and he and Iskra walked to the nearest one. Iskra bent down, trying the lock.

"What on earth are you—"

"What does it look like I'm doing?" She took a step backward. "Please break in here."

He raised his brows. "I'm surprised "please" is in your vocabulary." He reached into his coat and pulled out his tools before Iskra could say anything and got to work. As usual, he had the door open within minutes, and they bound up the stairs, making their way to the room. There'd been no signs that the house had been inhabited. Still, Sören was cautious. After all, his little misadventures could ruin his father; but then again, his father might already be ruined. He burst through the door only to find Sir Avery sitting there, a teacup in his hands, legs crossed at the ankles.

Avery inclined his head. "Pleasure to see the traitors are still working together."

Beside Sören, Iskra rolled her eyes. "What do you want?"

"I'm just clarifying that you aren't spreading lies about the Order."

"And why would she do that?" Sören asked as Iskra tugged at her coat sleeve.

Avery shrugged. "I have no idea what goes on in the mind of a mad woman."

A clap sounded behind them, and Avery's head lolled to the side, his tea spilling on his clean trousers. Sören almost laughed at the sight but managed to hold it together as he turned to see Aura in the doorway, Lock beside her, his magic fading. There was something stiff about the way they stood next to each other, but at least they were here.

"Starting the fun without us?" Lock asked, a sardonic tilt to his mouth once his eyes returned to normal.

"It's your fault for being late," Sören replied.

They left the house and found themselves knocking on Lady Hollisworth's door once more. Aura spoke with Iskra quietly, and Sören noticed Aura cast an angered look back at the house. Sören turned back to the door just in time to see a maid open it and lead them into the drawing room. It was flowery, with a pink settee, a dark mahogany table in the centre of the room, and a lit fireplace sending the room into warmth. Not the house of a murderer, he supposed, but appearances could be deceiving. He plopped into an armchair, declining the offer of tea, and crossed his hands in his lap. He felt more uncomfortable in this townhouse than he did at the foreboding residence of the Liang's, and he wanted to leave as soon as possible. They sat in silence, and Sören desperately wanted to make conversation. He was about to open his mouth, when the doors to the drawing room opened, and a lady with curly blond hair and a black dress strode into the room, sitting delicately in a chair as if scared it might burn her.

"Are you in mourning?" Aura asked, a cool undertone that Sören barely recognized.

Lady Hollisworth looked at Aura, anger flaring behind her eyes before seemingly gaining control. "Yes, Miss. I loved Kian, and he is dead. Of course, I'm mourning."

Aura smiled tightly. "Forgive my rudeness. I just hadn't expected it."

"And why's that?"

"No reason," Aura replied. Sören knew there was most certainly a reason, but he'd have to ask Aura about it later.

Lock coughed, breaking the weighty silence that had descended upon the room. "Lady Hollisworth, we are assisting the Order in finding Kian's murderer. If you could be so kind as to answer a few of our questions, it'd be much appreciated. Now, would you care to explain to us where you went when the bell rang?"

Lady Hollisworth swallowed, not meeting Lock's gaze, instead addressing Sören. "I was with Kian, but I passed out in the courtyard."

"Why were you in the courtyard?" Iskra asked.

"Because he was going to propose. Before the coronation, he said he wanted it to be special." Her voice broke, "and then the Twisted came. We were alone one moment, and then black cloaked Twisted were surrounding us. I didn't see what happened to Kian before I passed out."

"Lady Hollisworth," Sören asked, "when did you join the Order, and what was your role?"

"I joined a year ago, just after Duke Brittenworth announced that Kian was a suitor, and that was my role, to charm him."

Across the way, Aura wrinkled her nose. "Your only job was to court him?"

Lady Hollisworth nodded, crossing her hands in her lap. Sören got the distinct sense she was lying but thought it best to leave it for now.

"And can anyone account for the fact that you passed out?" Lock asked.

"Lady Erika Elsder in Brighton, though I'm sure she's also a suspect. The Duke might also relay that I passed out as he was the one that found me. That is, after the Twisted Magic let go of control on the ballroom."

Sören frowned, knowing that they weren't allowed anywhere near the Order. He'd have to ask Detective Inspector Thornsbury to do it, which he didn't have a problem with. He just wished he could see the look on the Duke's face when he found out he was used in a suspect's statement.

"And would you like to account for the Twisted that are currently surrounding your residence?" Aura asked.

Sören sat straighter. He had not seen any Twisted, but that did not mean they weren't there.

"I don—"

"Don't be a fool, Lady Hollisworth." It was Lock that spoke. "My, um, Miss Wrentroth and I saw them."

Lady Hollisworth stood. "If you'll excuse me, I must go to Scotland Yard."

"Care for a ride?" Sören offered.

"No. I think it's best if you leave."

"Are you—" Lock started

"Get out," she said, then seemingly thought better of her words, fiddling with the cuff of her sleeve. "I don't want to put you all in danger should anything happen."

They left the room, but Sören grabbed Aura's arm before she could leave.

"You have a reason for not trusting her, don't you?" he asked.

Aura removed her arm from his hand. "Her voice; at the party, I heard someone talking to Kian about a deal. It was her."

"I see," Sören replied, gesturing for her to leave. Lock and Iskra were waiting for them outside and prepared to depart, but not before agreeing that this wouldn't be the last time that they spoke to Lady Hollisworth, because one thing was clear: she was hiding something, and they intended to find out what.

Sören went straight to Scotland Yard to speak to Detective Inspector Thornsbury about confirming Hollisworth's statement. He tucked his hat lower, should his father see him. Although, if Sören had timed it right, his father should be on his lunch break at a pub three blocks away. Sören bounded up the stairs and caught sight of Lady Hollisworth emerging from an office with several constables. He made a note that she had, in fact, been there, before walking straight to Thornsbury's office. He knocked once, Thornsbury calling for him to come in and smiled when he saw Sören.

"Mr. Niaheartson, I suspect you have a request."

"What makes you say that?"

"If it was just information, you would've waited until your father arrived home to get here."

"Well, well, you are quite the detective."

Thornsbury fiddled with his moustache dramatically, "I have my moments. Now, what is it I must assist you with?"

"I need you to speak to the Duke. He is Lady Hollisworth's alibi."

Detective Inspector Thornsbury nodded slowly. "What exactly did she tell you?"

"That she passed out. And if you wish to speak with her, you should hurry. She's downstairs speaking to some officers regarding the Twisted outside of her house." His mouth curved into a frown.

"You think she hired them?"

"I do. I just can't prove it."

"You're a good lad, Sören. I'll interview the Duke after my lunch break. You and your friends can continue. I'll send correspondence of what I find." He paused. "Speaking of the Duke; he denied going to the Liang's"

Sören's stomach dropped. He hadn't particularly gotten the impression from the Liang's that said: *we just killed someone,* but then again, he supposed murderers didn't necessarily go around preaching their nefarious acts.

"I have a team out there," Thornsbury continued, "and a Twisted specialist with the Duke as we speak."

Sören nodded, though he wasn't exactly sure why he would need one. The Liang's had lied, and how the Twisted were involved, he had no idea. He opened his mouth—

"What's going on here?" a voice yelled, an all too familiar tone.

Sören turned to see his father standing in the doorway, a furious arch to his brow. To Sören's surprise, Thornsbury took a protective step in front of Sören.

"Relax Nikolas. I was just asking your son for his statement about the murder. He'll be on his way."

His father stood there for a moment before nodding and giving Sören a look that suggested Sören should leave immediately. Sören nodded back and watched his father disappear down the hallway. He turned to the Detective Inspector and muttered a thank you before he strode to the door. Pausing, he turned, "Detective Inspector Thornsbury?"

"Yes?"

"I have one more favour to ask."

"Anything, you know that."

"I need you to look into Xavier Brittenworth for me."

The Detective Inspector nodded before plopping himself back into the chair beside his desk. He was surprised at the request, but perhaps it was for the best to prove his father's idea's wrong. Sören left Scotland Yard, an uncomfortable feeling wriggling its way inside him. Sören had no idea what he'd do if Xavier was as dangerous as he'd been warned. He had no idea what to do if the bright-eyed boy found out that Sören's trust in him was slowly deteriorating. Most importantly, Sören had no idea what he'd do if another person he cared for was capable of harm. After all, his father did a great job of hiding his association with London's criminal cases, and Sören didn't need that on his conscience. As Sören stepped into a Hansom, he could tell that trusting blindly would always be his greatest downfall.

NINETEEN

LOCK

Lock couldn't stop seeing what Aura had shown him. He couldn't stop seeing the blue vision of Aura's knife being stabbed through another heart. He couldn't stop pondering over what she'd told him about her employer. She didn't know who they were, and Lock swore that if they ever found out, he would punch them until his knuckles were well bloody. Lock was sick for the way he'd been treating Aura after he found out her secret. After all, Aura hadn't overreacted when she'd watched him commit the worst sin imaginable. Aura had watched him fill his classmate's glass with the poison, and she had still stayed. She'd even helped him bury the body, and she had stayed. She'd stayed, for better or worse, and he had *left*. Lock shook his head as he fell back into his past, remembering the night where everything had changed.

The night breeze had brushed against his face, and he'd pushed his hair back with a dirty hand, pausing with a shovel in his other. The tree above him had whispered faintly about the atrocity he'd committed, but that night, it had been drowned out by the voice of a girl who'd leaned against its trunk, watching as he'd dug the makeshift grave.

"You might want to hurry before Rien realizes we're missing," she'd said, her brown hair blowing in the breeze, skirts wrinkled from sitting. Lock had only been under Rien's apprenticeship for three months, though he'd known her since they were younger, and even then, he could tell Aura was the sort of girl who would do anything to get what she wanted. She'd tried to attend a school before she got caught, though from what Lock understood, she'd been smarter than half the gentlemen there. It was what he admired about her.

"If you'd like to help me dig, I might be faster," he remembered saying.

Aura looked at him. "I'm sure you're capable."

He'd rolled his eyes as he stuck his shovel in the dirt once more. Beyond, his parents lay fast asleep in their manor, unaware that their son was digging a grave behind the tree in their backyard.

"What exactly did he do to you?" Aura had asked quietly, looking at the body that lay a few feet away.

Lock paused, turning to look at Aura, her face so delicate in the slowly declining moonlight, so solemn. "He was going to come to Rien's to kill him, maybe even you, out of some foolish vendetta he has towards me. I couldn't let him do that."

He didn't tell her about the buzz he'd felt beneath his veins, about the dizziness, retribution tasting sweet in his throat as he watched his classmate down the poison.

"So you beat him to it? The killing, I mean?"

"He could have killed *you*."

Aura had been silent then, and Lock turned back, digging another shovel of dirt. He'd paused, and when he turned back to look at her, he found her standing beside him.

"Thank you." It had been barely a whisper. "Death is unacceptable, but I cannot bring myself to be upset. Your hands are bloodstained, and I'd let them waltz me into a dance if you offered. You were doing what you thought was right, and for that I cannot argue."

He'd watched her for a moment. "I'm not proud of what I did. But more people will live because he is gone. He was my friend, and I can't stop but think that was a lie. He was my friend, but for how much longer would that remain true?"

"The dead don't speak, Lock."

He'd smiled, slightly. "And the living never listen."

The body had been buried, and they'd never spoken of that night again. More importantly, they'd never spoken of the words they'd said. Since that night, the magic inside of Lock had only gotten worse, and he feared if he didn't get the coronet, they might *never* talk again. Lock shook his head, pulling himself from his memories as he clambered into his carriage, a sinking feeling in his heart.

As expected, Lady Hollisworth's estate was silent; not even a hint of light flickered in the windows. Lock had alighted from his carriage two blocks back, not wanting to draw attention to himself in the slumbering neighbourhood—let alone notify the Twisted of his arrival should they still be lurking in the shadows. Instead of using the front door as he had earlier that day, he strode around back. There was a black carriage stationed in the small court, taking up majority of the space, but Lock paid it little mind before locating the back where he found the door to the servant entrance already unlocked before slipping inside. He made a mental note to be wary, as it was unusual to find the door unlocked, especially at an hour such as this.

"God," he muttered. He was making a habit of clandestine activities, much to his disdain—he didn't like doing them alone. He'd much prefer it if Aura were here, but he was afraid that wasn't possible at the moment. *I did it to save you.*

But that was just it: he, too, was beyond saving.

The corridor beyond was dimly lit, the few lanterns casting long shadows upon the eerie stone, a silence enveloping him that suggested even the house might be sleeping. There wasn't a creak to be heard.

The main floor was pitch black, and Lock cursed himself for not bringing a lantern. Reaching inside his coat, he reached for his box of matches but paused when a flash of light darted from one hallway into another. Lock stuffed the box into his pocket once more, deciding not to alert the unsuspecting visitor to his existence. He followed just as they disappeared. Lock swore but followed in the same direction. Silence wrapped around him once more in the darkness; alone again, a great place for monsters. Lock watched the darkness move around him as though the shadows were waltzing, without a care that he was in their presence. He inhaled at the sudden change in the air. The rustling of skirts, a familiar set of footsteps; his hand clenched before falling flat at his side.

"Hello, Aura," he said as she stepped from the shadows, producing a lantern from behind her. A rich emerald gown brushed the floor as she took up step beside him.

"Locklyn." She nodded, and he cast her a glance. Guilt piled up inside him, которым he promptly ignored, turning on his mask that was used for investigating.

"May I ask what you were doing in this corridor alone?" he asked.

"I could ask you the same thing," she replied, and Lock didn't fail to notice the quickening in her pace as she climbed a set of stairs to their left.

He followed after her. "You could. Though I assume we're here for the same reasons."

"I'm here to investigate. Not to pester my associate with questions."

Associate? Is that what they were now? Before Lock could answer, Aura pressed a hand to his chest, halting him. They stood there at the top of the stairs, unflinching.

"Don't look so startled, Locklyn. I thought—"

"Forgive me, dearest. Perhaps I thought you'd pull a knife on me."

Aura's gaze snapped to his. He swore he could feel Aura's heartbeat, her eyes flickering in the lantern light. And for a moment, their secrets wound around them, her hand still resting against his heart; the next, they were two strangers who made a bad habit out of secrecy and death. Aura had stepped away, her back towards him, the silence stretching between them.

Somewhere beyond, laughter echoed, though Lock could see no light from beneath any of the doorways. They continued down the hallway—albeit much slower than Lock would've preferred, but there was no indication that anyone was around. They poked their heads into a few darkened rooms before locating the one they were searching for. They slipped into Lady Hollisworth's bed chambers, and though it was too dark to see the decor, Lock didn't need confirmation that this was indeed her room. After all, the small floral sitting space and cabinet of a few dresses beyond gave it away. Time was limited, and so they set to work right away, opening cabinets and examining each surface. Lock pushed a set of newspapers away on her desk, frowning as he read the headlines—a very good reminder of why he hardly read the thing anymore. Another missing woman and the murders of four other women in the past three months—it left a sour taste in his mouth. Shoving them to the side, he did a quick scan of the desk's contents, though there wasn't anything special other than a few writing materials and some dust-covered books. The shimmer of something in the corner of a drawer caught his eye, but a feminine voice echoed from the corridor, and Lock took long strides across the room. He hurried Aura out of the room, blowing out the candle in the lantern. Shoving them both into the nearest alcove, he was very aware that this was the closest they'd been since she'd held a knife to his throat (or since the moment on the stairs, though they were even closer now). Her dress made the space awkward, and he pressed his back up against the wall so hard that he was sure it might swallow him. The voice grew louder, and Lock recognized it not as a voice but as a hum—Lady Hollisworth was humming. Now, if this was a regular occurrence or if she was under the influence of champagne or some other drink, he didn't want to know. Regardless, it was out of tune. He grimaced before he focused his attention back on Aura, who was almost entirely hidden by shadow.

"May I ask what's with your dress?" he whispered, desperate for a distraction.

"Why? Are you going to judge my fashion choices as well?"

"Not unless you want me to."

Lock felt the annoyance roll off of her. "Idiot. Rien was planning a dinner this evening. One I'd rather die than have to attend."

He *tsked*. "My lovely Aura, if you're not one for handsome, young detectives, you should've told me. I'll need a moment to change my character morals."

"You're not a detective."

"Ah, so I'm not a complete lost cause."

"No, what you are is a trespasser." Lady Hollisworth's voice came from the dark. A lantern burned bright, and Lock squinted at the light. "Now, I ask you to get out. I'd call the police, but it's quite obvious you have authority there. In fact, it should be an honour to have Lord Mortsakov gracing me with his presence."

Lock tensed, but they did as they were told, leaving the Lady's house, and he didn't stop feeling her eyes boring into him until they were safely on the cobble outside. He and Aura strolled along the pavement; her hands folded carefully before her waist. The street lamps burned dim, the night silent, save for the sound of their footsteps on the cobble. Rows of townhouses stretched into the night sky, their windows darkened. London was asleep, a time when the ghosts would play if there ever were such a thing.

"You know it's difficult." Aura said, after a while of not speaking.

He frowned. "What is?"

"Fighting the magic, ignoring the itch for the knife that was supposed to save me, not knowing if my employer will send someone after me."

"They won't."

"You don't know that."

"I won't let them." He crossed his arms, looking ahead. "I would never let anyone hurt you."

Despite his anger, it was the truth. It always would be. Lock didn't believe in the paranormal. Lock didn't believe that someone was watching over them at every moment of every day. He couldn't fathom that someone would willingly want to ruin someone else, shattering them until they were nothing but dust in the ground—he didn't believe it until the gunshot rang out.

TWENTY

SÖREN

Sören hadn't realized how much being back inside a morgue affected him until he found himself spiralling into the memories of his past, a bad dream once more. Nearly three years ago, he'd sat on the morgue table in what he'd later learned was Mr. Wrentroth's laboratory. Candles had burned low, creating just enough light for him to see Aura, who he'd learned was an apprentice, and niece, of Mr. Wrentroth. She'd had a gleam in her eyes, scribbling down notes in a chair across from him. *Madness,* he'd thought at first, but Sören had seen that look in his father too many times to know it wasn't that. No, what the apprentice had was a passion, and he'd commended her for it—living without caring for limitations.

His arms had felt incredibly heavy, the last few days running through his mind, though he only remembered snippets.

A bottle.

A threat.

Poison between his lips.

Laudanum, he remembered Aura saying that to his father. His skin no longer felt like it was burning, however the same couldn't be said for his heart.

He'd felt a great deal ashamed.

He should've fought back, should've said his father wouldn't do something like that—yet he hadn't. *My father did not commit those crimes.* He wished to shout, yet when it mattered, Sören had stayed silent.

"You look rather dreadful," Aura had said, shutting her notebook before retreating into a back room and returning with a bottle, promising it wasn't poison.

Sören remembered thanking her, savouring the liquid in his too-dry throat.

"You saved me," he'd said. "Yet it's quite obvious you're no doctor."

"Correct. I'm a poison scientist, sir. You're lucky I dabble in antidotes from time to time."

Sören had been about to respond when the door burst open. His father's face looked shattered, numb. Sören's heart broke all over again, the sound nearly drowning out his father's next words.

Your mother is dead.

And Sören had been powerless to save her.

"Sören?" Iskra's voice cut through his memories, drawing him back to the present. Concern etched her pale features, her brows drawn together. The girl with a taste for short replies and not known to care was looking at him as if she truly did consider them friends.

"What's this? You're not starting to care, are you, dear aristocrat?"

She crossed her arms. "Of course not. You looked . . . distant."

"Scared that I'm dozing off?"

"Scared you're regretting your past again."

He gaped at her.

"I didn't mean to read your mind, but I was right. You should be thankful I pulled you back to the land of the living." Her voice had returned to its usual sternness, yet Sören couldn't help but smile. Across the table in the small cafe, he hoped she knew it was a silent thank you because he couldn't find the words to say it. Very few people were able to see him for him without his past blinding their view. That was, he considered, one of humanity's greatest flaws—defining consistency and greatness by something as inconsistent as one's past. A mistake doesn't reflect who someone was, yet somehow blame is cast as if everything truly is their fault. Iskra seemed to know that, and while he wasn't entirely sure what her past had been like back in France, he supposed it'd taught her that same lesson. He wasn't broken because he'd been poisoned; he was broken because he'd let it happen when he knew there were people that needed him to be better—to fight for more. There were people that he cared for, and he hadn't even been there when they took their last breath. Sören didn't cry, but for once he felt like he should—he'd lived because Aura had saved him, and now Iskra was saving him. He was loved, and who was he to even think he wasn't?

"Now," Iskra said, once again pulling him from his thoughts. "Have you seen this?"

She slid a newspaper across the table. He moved his cup of tea out of the way, looking around the small cafe, and making sure that no one was about. It was a small place made of beige walls and leather armchairs. It looked like a gentleman's club, not that either of them particularly cared. What they needed was the proximity to Lady Hollisworth's estate, and this was it. Looking at the newspaper, his eyes widened at the heading:

ATTACK AT HOLLISWORTH TOWNHOUSE: NO FATALITIES, FEW INJURED.

He stared at it a moment longer before skimming the rest of the article. Apparently, a local beggar shot at the lady, and although police were investigating, the public speculates that Hollisworth knew her attacker. Of course, that hadn't been confirmed or denied. Sören frowned. First, Lady Liang was unconscious, and now someone was trying to shoot Lady Hollisworth. It would seem someone was trying very hard to keep things quiet. Instinct told him to look at the facts, yet his mind could not help but wander to the third suspect. He shook his head; he could care less about idle gossip.

"This is quite the scandal," he said slowly.

Iskra made a face. "More than a scandal. Sören, this seems to me like the killer is trying to keep their secrets."

"That would mean we'd need to evaluate our suspect list."

"Or not. I'm just saying, I think we've been doing this wrong. Instead of looking at this from the point of view of the murderer, we need to look at it from the victim. What, other than the coronet, could they have that the killer wouldn't want them sharing?"

"Aura mentioned that Lady Hollisworth was talking about some sort of deal with Kian the night he was murdered. Perhaps someone else heard them and decided to do something?" he suggested.

"Perhaps."

Sören nodded. "Well, dear aristocrat, I think it's time we continue our investigation."

Iskra knocked sharply on the door before letting her hand fall to her side. Sören stood beside her, his hands tucked behind his back in what he hoped was the image of proper confidence. Lock had sent a letter first thing this morning informing him that he wouldn't be joining them today and that Aura was on business with Rien, so it was up to him and Iskra to do most of the charm. The butler opened the door and let them inside, guiding them to the drawing room. Sören desperately wanted to get a look around, but one thing that Lock had mentioned in his brief letter was that Lady Hollisworth would hardly be in the mood to do such a thing. Sören knew now that it was because of the shooting, and he also knew that Lock had been here last night. Sören wondered if he saw anything of interest. More specifically, if he saw the face of the shooter. Lady Hollisworth strode into the room, all politeness they'd faced last time replaced with a cool demeanour.

"What can I do for you?" she asked.

Sören smiled as best he could. "We'd like to ask you a few questions."

Lady Hollisworth sighed, and he noted a bandage peeking out from her shoulder. "If you must."

Sören looked to Iskra to begin the plan they'd discussed on the way here. Iskra stood, pacing the room. They'd chosen to leave the shooting out of it.

For now.

"Were you going to tell us that Kian didn't choose you?"

Lady Hollisworth stood. "You two should leave. And while you're at it, stop spreading these ridiculous lies."

"You know this only implicates you more?" Sören said, not moving from the chair he sat in, in what he hoped was the image of a perfect, could-care-less, kind of gentleman.

Grudgingly, she said, "Fine, I lied. I was with him in the yard, but that was because he was planning a surprise for Lady Erika, and he wanted my help."

"And we are supposed to believe you?" Iskra asked, pausing to look at her.

Lady Hollisworth stood and exited the room, coming back a few moments later with a letter, handing it to Iskra. Sören stood, looking over her shoulder. The letter was from Kian asking the lady for help, and it was most certainly written by Kian, his signature matching all those Sören had seen before. Still, they'd have to give this to Aura to make sure what Lady Hollisworth was saying was true.

"And did you pass out before or after Lady Erika arrived?" Iskra asked.

"After. That's when I believe the Duke saw me. But just because he chose someone else doesn't mean that I didn't love him."

"That hasn't stopped others before," Sören pointed out.

"You're sick if you think I'm a murderer." She clutched her throat; the blue gem dull at her wrist. "Yes, I was jealous. Yes, I wanted him. That I don't deny. But he didn't choose me, and I have to live with that. Those are facts, but they do not make me a murderer."

Sören couldn't argue with that.

"You were heard arguing with Kian, over some deal—" Iskra started.

"Before you get ideas, it was a simple argument over the proposal, that is all." She gave them a look that suggested she was done answering their question, and neither of them tried to fight.

They thanked the lady for her time before leaving. Iskra departed with the letter, telling him she'd be in touch before the next suspect. Sören hopped into a carriage and rode back to his house, his mind trying to find links between all sorts of information, but none could be found. He felt as though he was wandering in a maze. The thing about mazes, though, was that there would always be a correct answer. One just needed to work for it. The sun was beginning to set as the carriage rolled to a stop outside the red-bricked house he and his father inhabited. Sören's father was away for an investigation for the week, and Sören's heart spluttered to a stop as he saw a curtain move in the window of his house. Carefully, he alighted from the carriage and unlocked his door. Inside, there was no noise, and everything felt normal—perhaps it had been a trick of the light. However, tricks of the light usually involved light, and considering the sun was setting . . . he shook his head, not wanting to think about horrors. He'd had enough anxiety for one day, and he certainly didn't need more. Sören bounded up the stairs to his room, eager to write a letter to the detective inspector about the progress of the investigation, or lack thereof.

"Hello, Sören."

Sören spun to see Xavier sitting in a chair by the window in his bedroom.

He stood there frozen, a million emotions running within him. His father's voice echoed in his head—that Xavier couldn't be trusted. Sören, frankly, found that hard to believe, considering Xavier was the same person who'd spent his party night drawing in the courtyard instead of celebrating Kian. Still, he didn't move from the doorway.

"What are you doing here?" he asked, as it seemed to be the only words he could form. He chided himself for not saying hello, but the words were already out. Besides, being straight to the point would be good.

"My father thinks you're a bad influence on me."

"Does he?" Sören said, finally moving to sit at his desk and pulling a piece of paper from the drawer. "And why is that?"

"Because of what your father was accused of."

Sören stiffened. No one knew about that but he and the police. Sören half-turned. "I haven't any idea of what you're talking about, Xavier. Now, if you please, I need to write a letter."

Xavier stood. "I burned my father's files on your father, if you must know. The secret will stay in the grave as far as I'm concerned."

"You what—"

"I burned them. It isn't any of the Order's business if your father was put under suspicion for influence during the Ripper Murders. Besides, it shouldn't matter. The police realized their mistake, and your father is one of their most prized detectives."

Sören stared at Xavier, not knowing what to say. Why had Xavier been looking at the files himself? A knot began forming in his stomach, and he clenched his fist on the desk.

"I believe a thank you is in order, but I'll let it slide." Xavier crossed the room before muttering a goodbye.

"Xavier?"

The heir paused.

"My father had to work to get his position back—to get to be the inspector he is now. That situation—wrong place, wrong time. If I ever hear the news about this, I'll not hesitate to burn all of your paintings one by one, do you understand?"

Xavier smirked. "You can try, Sören."

"Xavier—" *Please don't be the person my father thinks you are. Please don't fool me. Please–*

"Sören." The heir crossed the room, sticking his pinky out. "I promise. I'm not cruel. A person cannot be defined by their mistakes. Besides, we still have a deal to fulfill."

Sören didn't know what to say, still hanging on the boy's last words, their fingers clasped together. Xavier nodded to him once before letting go and striding from the room without another word. Sören waited until he heard the front door click shut before standing abruptly, almost knocking over his chair.

He needed to get to Scotland Yard immediately.

Detective Inspector Thornsbury fiddled with his blond moustache in thought. Sören had been sitting in the chair for a good fifteen minutes, and he was frustrated. Annoyance wriggled its way up inside him, and he had no idea what to do.

"You're asking me to commit a crime?" he said slowly.

Sören shook his head. "No. I'm asking you to make sure that Xavier isn't connected to Kian's death. Why else would he have stumbled upon my father's files?"

"Perhaps he didn't stumble."

Perhaps he waltzed. Sören had thought it a million times, and the last thing he wanted was for that to be true. For Xavier to have a motive, for Sören to have let another person in only for them to destroy him just as he had started to heal.

"Can't you take him in for questioning?"

The detective shook his head. "It's not enough evidence, Sören. Your father's claims and a break-in aren't enough. I think you're forgetting that you're falling quite deep in with one of the most influential heirs in London."

Falling indeed. He had been since he'd walked into the courtyard the day Kian had been murdered. Sören rested his head in his hands. He should've known not to mess with someone so beautiful; it would ruin him, and perhaps he would let it. Sören had always been like that, letting destruction play with him until he was on his last breath, but this time Sören didn't want to wait. He wanted to live because if he waited, it would only prove that he was back where he started, and Sören didn't want to fall.

Not again.

Detective Inspector Thornsbury sighed and rounded the desk, sitting before Sören. He had stopped playing with his moustache and now rested his hands on his knees. "I cannot promise anything, but if it makes you feel better, I'll try."

Sören lifted his head to see the inspector looking at him with kind eyes. They were eyes that reminded him of his mother, always kind, always trying because he wanted to, not because he had to. Sören smiled because he knew Thornsbury didn't have to do anything, yet he did. *Mr. Niaheartson, I am a fair man.* That was what he'd told Sören the day they'd struck the deal of their apprenticeship, and Sören only hoped that he could repay the detective for all he was risking because if there was one thing he was sure of, he wouldn't let down another person he was beginning to care for.

TWENTY - ONE

ISKRA

Loud shouts from the entrance hall sent Iskra running. Her boots echoed on the floor, furious at the late-night interruption. Though, all feelings seemed to pause as she reached the bottom of the stairwell. Her associate, one meant to keep guard of the house, was glaring daggers at a flush faced Zoialynne. Iskra felt her own cheeks heating, taking in the girl before her, but Iskra seemed to regain herself, the anger turning into a sick feeling as she stared at Zoialynne. The last time they'd met, Zoialynne had made it very clear whose side she was on. Iskra's hand instinctively went to her wrist, where a fresh bandage was hidden beneath her sleeve. *Incroyable*. She had some nerve showing her face here. Iskra waved a hand at her associate, indicating they could go back to their post outside and watched, wordlessly, as they slipped out into the cool night beyond. Iskra desperately wished she, too, could step out with them. Perhaps the cold weather might help her forget the sting as the gem was removed from her wrist without even trying to be gentle. Iskra clasped her hands behind her back, not offering for the traitor to stay.

"What do you want, Miss Adrennha?" she asked, her voice hard. It was all she could muster, considering the alternative would be to beg Zoialynne to stay. Something painful flashed behind Zoialynne's eyes, but even she knew that she'd ruined it all for them——not that there had ever been anything other than a week on a ship and memories that would haunt them forever. A kiss of a memory seemed to dust her lips, but she ignored it. Zoialynne wasn't the same person as she'd been three years ago. But then again, neither was Iskra. They were broken and molded back together by the cruel hands of the world.

Iskra waited as Zoialynne reached into her jacket and pulled out a letter. Unfolding it, she read, "Adrennha, as you are aware, we've lost the Storenné family. They haven't been found anywhere in their empire, yet their political army is strong. After a narrow escape and a discovery of our own, we've discovered one thing—"

Iskra did not need to hear Zoialynne read the rest to know what it said. And, as the world crashed around her, she said, "They're in England."

Zoialynne nodded. "I've sent—"

"Thank you, but it's best if you forget our acquaintanceship," Iskra said, the words spilling out of her mouth before she even had time to stop herself. She looked away, not surprised it had come to this. Her parents were here to destroy her, and it was best no one became collateral damage. Iskra had long since stopped caring—stopped letting people get close to her—and yet her heart cracked all the same. She'd come to England to run from her fear. She had allowed her heart to relax: her first mistake.

Her second had been running.

She should've just stayed to fight her parents in France and died, knowing she hadn't hurt anyone but herself. No, instead, she'd come to England, and now she was going to have to put a wall between herself and her connections

—her friends. Perhaps, it was better that way, easier to pretend the weight in her heart didn't hurt. She shook her head, pulling herself from her thoughts.

Zoialynne's face hardened. "I'll be dead before I let you push me away, Iskra."

Iskra huffed a laugh, striding over and opening the door. "I'm not worth dying over. You, of all people, should know that."

Zoialynne looked like she was about to say something, but Iskra signalled for her associate outside.

"Iskra?" Zoialynne said, making a small sound as Iskra's guard grabbed her arm.

Iskra met her question with silence, not trusting her voice.

"I begged him not to hurt you."

"Why?"

"I—"

"The Duke didn't hurt me, Zoialynne. You did."

Iskra's gaze was unflinching as her heart cracked within her chest. It was cruel of her, but it was the truth. Zoialynne had ruined Iskra, and perhaps it was Iskra's fault for letting her in all those years ago. But when love holds a knife, it is no longer love; it's venom. It is a toxicity so willingly drunk that one doesn't realize what's happened until they lay dazed, wondering what they could've done wrong.

Zoialynne was escorted from the house without a second glance backward. Iskra stood on the steps for a long moment before she let herself wander back up to her room, where a blanket of regretful words and anxious thoughts would suffocate her into a restless sleep.

Or at least she wished it would.

◊

The White Hart was busy this time of night, but Iskra didn't care. Her eyes were on the boy who sat in the corner, picking at his fingernails, making it clear that he was uncomfortable. She'd had an associate locate him and tell him to meet her here at ten. Iskra was late, her fault, but she didn't want to be in this place any longer than necessary.

Sören looked up as she sat down.

He looked tired; his jacket worn half-open revealing a wrinkled shirt. Dark circles plagued his under eye.

Sören let his hands rest on the table. "I'm assuming you haven't called me here to be social."

Iskra regarded him. He was right, she hadn't, but something in his tone made her wish she had. He seemed used to this, which made what she was about to ask of him, worse. Iskra shook her head, preparing to start.

"The night I left France I remember bursting through the doors of my parents' embassy." she started.

"What *are* you? Royalty?"

"No, Sören. My father is a viscount, mother a viscountess by marriage, and they run the majority of the politics amongst the higher circles of aristocracy. They are feared by many, and sometimes, when I was young, I used to think they did such a good job of it, that they even scared themselves."

"I'm sorry—"

Iskra shook her head, cutting him off. "They spread my face on posters and handed it out to their circle and the police. It was clear, I'd been made a criminal in their eyes." It should have hurt, the accusation and her name given to the authorities by the people she was supposed to love, but she'd only felt angry. "They wanted me to become something I wasn't, something I am not—wanted me to take the throne of the kingdom they'd spent years building on nothing but a foundation of lies and deceit.

"That day, I remember being angry. I struck the match before they even had time to stop me and left, without turning back, though I knew the place would go up in smoke. I didn't stop until I reached the docks, before I boarded a boat to America, knowing I'd be chased, but at least I was free, if only for a little while."

Iskra's mind whirled back to that day. The smell of smoke stinging her nose. *This is for you,* she remembered thinking, meant for a girl who'd taught her love so long ago—a girl who'd never see the light of day again. *This is for you;* she'd thought again as she'd gazed out onto the waters; it had been for Iskra alone because ghosts didn't feel sentiment. Besides, Iskra didn't believe in them anyway.

"Iskra," Sören's voice pulled her out of her thoughts.

"I need your help." she said, staring at him, as if she were daring him to pity her.

He only regarded her levelly. "With what?"

He was earnest. Like he'd truly drop down anything he was doing to help her, and it fractured something inside her, knowing what she was going to do. She'd been warned of people like him, but somehow instead of keeping her mouth shut like she'd been taught, the words came spilling out.

"You're very well connected, an asset I need. You have access to Scotland Yard, and when the time comes, if I don't get it, I'll need you to get the coronet for me."

"Xavier—"

Iskra squeezed her hands against the table. "I'm not sure I'll be breathing for much longer if I don't get the coronet, Sören. I need it, and you're going to help me do it."

Sören seemed to have withdrawn into himself, and she sat back. She hadn't meant to snap, but she didn't know anything else. She hadn't been taught how to love, how to make friendship easy, if she could call Sören that. Sören was silent for so long, Iskra wasn't sure he'd agree.

His gaze met hers. "I'm your friend, Iskra. Use me. Don't use me. I'll help you either way."

"You're an associate, not a friend," Iskra said. "You should learn what friendship is."

"Or you should," he said. Without another word, he stood, muttering something about visiting their next suspect tonight. He disappeared into the tavern's crowded room, and Iskra was left staring at the empty space where he'd been.

The carriage rattled to a halt as Iskra alighted from the carriage, her limbs aching from the long train ride and carriage ride it had taken her to get to Brighton. Her mind reeled with the echoes of last night, of her conversation with Sören earlier, but she couldn't focus on that—not while a more important task was at hand. She was to meet the others inside, where they'd investigate Lady Erika Elsder. Lady Hollisworth had provided a dead end while she continued to analyze the letter. She'd given the letter to Aura in hopes of her finding something, but Iskra had yet to receive word of anything. Lady Hollisworth had seemed to admit that she hadn't committed the crime, yet it was a claim made for the guilty.

    Lady Elsder's manor was two stories of elegant arches and pale brick. Light danced in the windows, casting shadows onto the cobble of the front yard. The distant sound of waves crashing together, a calming symphony on an even calmer night, came to her, and Iskra found her shoulders relaxing. After all, the idea of the sea always calmed her and reminded her of the times when she'd been free. The sea was the only place that kept her secrets and rocked her into an endless sleep—well that, and the grave—and for all Iskra knew, she might end up there very soon, considering her parents were in England. The waves crashed into the memories of her nights with Zoialynne upon the ship to England, and she immediately ignored it. She couldn't afford to think of her past, not while the present seemed so intent on ruining her as well. Iskra walked up a grand set of stairs, where she was let in by a butler. She paused upon entry, surveying her surroundings. The entry hall was made of polished marble, with a crystal chandelier hanging above and a twisted staircase spiralling up to the second floor. It reminded her of an empire that lay shattered in France. However, the decor wasn't what had made her pause. Hundreds of colours floated around, music floating out from a room beyond. Laughter and the smell of rich perfumes hit her, and she wrinkled her nose. She'd never been one for strong scents, and she could already feel the headache coming on. Iskra paused because these people were happy, or at least looked like it. They had no idea of the sinister motive Iskra had for being here—that Lady Elsder was a suspect in a murder case. Iskra shuddered. Parties seemed to be a perfect place for murder, and Iskra only hoped it wouldn't happen tonight.

Lady Elsder, a pale woman with red hair, strode around the room speaking with her guests, and if she seemed bothered by her presence and possibly the others, she made no indication. Iskra narrowed her eyes, wondering if this soiree had been an opportunity to hide something. She crossed her arms over her chest. Iskra had been promised a murder investigation, not a dance. Then again, Lady Elsder had also provided a perfect opportunity for sneaking about without being noticed.

"Apologies for the inconvenience. I hadn't known you were coming this evening," Lady Elsder said, moving into Iskra's line of sight.

"Well, it is better to observe in a natural environment. Though, we'll need to ask you some questions."

"That's all well and good. However, I'm busy—"

"Later, then," Iskra told her. This woman was getting on her nerves, but Iskra kept a polite smile plastered on her face. She needed to find Sören, and she needed to get out of this entrance hall.

Lady Elsder waved to a couple and turned to go, but paused before she did. "Feel free to let yourself enjoy the party. I'm sure it's what Kian would want."

Iskra watched her go, taking in the women's grey dress and the party. It didn't look like people were mourning, but she supposed everyone had their different ways of coping. Still, she noted it for later should the woman walking away turn out to be a cold-blooded killer.

Iskra earned a few looks as she strode to what she presumed was the ballroom, two goals echoing in her mind: find the others and get a much-needed glass of champagne—this was a party.

A melody cascaded over the crowd in waves, the tune making Iskra want to dance. Well, except that she had told the only person she would want to dance with to forget about her. *Thank you, but it's best if you forget our acquaintanceship.* The words she had said to Zoialynne were the same words she'd heard so many years ago—words she knew would hurt because once upon a time, they had. Her mother's maid had said those very words as she lay dying as a result of poison. Iskra had promised then never to love someone for fear of how they'd end up. Her parents had destroyed anything she had ever loved, and she was destroying herself by forgetting it. Iskra cursed herself; she couldn't take back yesterday's words no matter how much she wanted to. This time those words were meant to keep Zoialynne safe, just as her mother's maid had done to keep Iskra safe. She clenched her hands into tight fists as if it could switch off the memories. She was too burned—no amount of trying to forget what happened could change that. Instead, she stepped into the crowd, letting the music take her between the crowds of people, guiding her to the champagne. Iskra felt like she was floating—like a ghost watching the mortals dance without a care in her eyes. She weaved between the partygoers, knowing that she was alone because she had to be. She was halfway to the table laden with drinks when someone called her over. She turned to see who'd interrupted her mission, but it was Sören striding towards her.

"Glad you could make it," he said once he caught up to her.

She scoffed. "Are you the hostess, then?"

"No," he replied. "You'd know if this was my party." He looked around the room with what Iskra could only describe as a mild form of disgust on his face before turning back to her. "I believe it's time we start our investigation. I received word from an associate two days ago that Hollisworth is cleared. The Duke confirmed that he saw her."

Iskra nodded absentmindedly, "And what of Lock and Aura?"

"Not here yet."

Iskra grunted in annoyance. Lock and Aura were making a habit of being fashionably late, and she hoped it was because they were forgiving whatever had happened between them.

"About earlier," Iskra trailed off, unsure how to continue.

"It's okay," Sören said. "I'll help you, Iskra. But I cannot promise that I won't also help Xavier."

"What if you can't?"

"I will."

Iskra didn't tell him otherwise, and she supposed it wasn't her place. Iskra ran her hands down the front of her waistcoat, anxiety washing over her.

Sören seemed to pause, feeling the change in the atmosphere as well. The lights dimmed, but no one else noticed as they continued to laugh. Venom clawed its way inside her head and opened its mouth to strike.

A ringing as loud as a bell tower tolled in her ears, and she clutched her head, Sören doing the same. Iskra shut her eyes, feeling the Twisted getting ready for another attack. She pulled at the threads of magic within her and guided it towards the Twisted. The magic seemed to revere it and disappear. Iskra was left somewhat out of breath. It would seem the Twisted were tired of waiting. Somewhere in the ballroom, the drinks table folded and glasses upon glasses spilled onto the floor, and Iskra could just make out a pale pink skirt dashing from the room. Some people stopped to clear it up, while others paid it no glance, even as the music momentarily died before starting up again on Lady Elsder's instruction. Iskra watched the lady hurrying to fetch a butler to clean the mess, the only worry being that she was embarrassed. Her eyes connected with Iskra across the room, and she gave Iskra a pointed look that suggested she wanted Iskra to know that it was all an accident, and she believed Lady Elsder, but murder and broken glasses were two very different situations.

Sören tapped her shoulder, and she followed him out of the room. Iskra cast one last look into the ballroom, and even though she was hardly ever unsettled, in this manor, it felt like the walls were watching them, sensing their next words, and it created a sinking feeling in her stomach. As she and Sören exited the ballroom and weaved their way through guests, Iskra couldn't help but feel as though a shadow loomed above them just waiting to pounce.

TWENTY - TWO

AURA

The bullet had grazed Lady Hollisworth as she'd been exiting her townhouse, just enough to sting, as she watched her attacker retreat. Aura hadn't seen the gunman, and she and Lock spent the better part of three days trying to trace the bullet back to a buyer, but had no such luck, even with the bribery they'd pulled at the Yard. Three days filled with short words and strict talk about the investigation. Aura had spent days casting glances at him, only to find him already watching her, his face unreadable and cold. Aura couldn't grasp what he was thinking, and she couldn't stand it. In fact, as the bullet had shot out, Lock had looked so normal with his worried gaze dropping to her face. However, it'd been ruined when he stepped away, his face twisted in anguish as if he was at war with himself. For all Aura knew, perhaps he was—deciding if their friendship was worth the blood she'd spilled. Aura swallowed, brushing her hands down her dress as if that could scrub off the invisible blood stained on it.

Now, she found herself in Lady Elsder's estate; her back pressed too hard into the wall as though she might disappear into it—in fact, she wished she would. Aura hadn't been expecting a party, though she was dressed fairly in a dress of the deepest crimson, not unlike the colour of blood. Her knife was tucked underneath her sleeve, despite the vow not to use it. She hadn't heard from her employer in weeks, which automatically made her nerves worse.

"If you're going to be sick, might I suggest you do so outside," Lock said, stepping up beside her.

She rolled her eyes. "Scared I'll be ill on your shoes?"

"Now that you mention it—"

But Aura's thoughts tuned out before she heard what he said. What if the bullet hadn't been meant for Lady Hollisworth? What if her employer would be waiting with a knife when she got home tonight? What if Rien was in trouble? What if she couldn't resist the itch anymore and gave in? The thought terrified her. The thought that she could lose control at any moment made her feel like she was walking a slippery slope, knowing she was about to fall. Aura shuddered, crossing her arms.

"My darling scientist, your worries are plaguing me." Lock sighed dramatically.

"You should learn to control your magic, my lord."

Lock nodded thoughtfully and Aura gazed into the crowd, searching for Lady Elsder. She spotted her near a group of older ladies and gentlemen, talking to them with excitement. Lock took a step closer, and for a moment, she felt as though tension hadn't wrapped itself around them and made a mockery of their hearts. Lock rubbed a hand over his face and muttered something in Russian, though she didn't understand.

"I do believe that I still owe you a dance," Lock said. "We may use it to get a vantage point on our suspect."

She looked at him, "It would be quite improper."

He rolled his eyes. "You cut dead people open on an apprenticeship looking for Twisted Magic. Would you really wish to argue about what is improper?"

Aura took his offered hand, cursing his impossible nature. Guilt settled itself beneath her bones, but she ignored it. This was strictly to get a better look for any suspicious activity that Erika might want to keep hidden against the backdrop of a party. With one hand on her waist and the other in her hand, Lock spun them into a dance. The music wrapped itself around them as if it, too, were waltzing. Lock guided her in the space as if they were the only two that existed. His movements seemed planned; each step was calculated perfectly in advance. There was a sort of elegance about the way they danced as if they weren't shattered, held together only by an ever-fraying string. As if there was no blood on their hands, staining their pasts red. Aura ignored the rapid beating of her heart and tried to focus on the investigation, though it was all too difficult. Instead, she let her magic flow through her, the blue glow illuminating her eyes—it was easier than having to look into his.

She stood in a circular room with a glass-domed ceiling showing the night sky above. Inside she watched as Lady Elsder tucked a flash of silver beneath a tile before rushing from the room. The knife hidden beneath the tiles practically called to her, and Aura let her magic fade before looking back at Lock.

"What is it?" he asked, twirling her before bringing her close once more. "Is it my dancing?"

"You know very well your dancing is perfect. If what I saw is no trick, I think we'll be needing to call Scotland Yard down here."

"Oh?" He raised an eyebrow. "Must we postpone this dance a little longer?"

She nodded. "Only if you wish to catch a murderer."

The dome looked out over the vast gardens, where a few plants were placed inside to keep warm over the winter months. Aura looked for the tile she'd seen Lady Elsder hide something underneath while Lock made slow circles in the center of the room before pausing to look out into the yard.

"Perfect place to bury a body, no?" he asked.

"It might be if Kian's body hadn't been found already," she said, but shut her eyes, steeling herself. The sentence had brought the ghosts of her brother back, his body never to be seen again. Alon had been one death that Aura couldn't bring herself to try and investigate because she knew she wouldn't find anything—or at least not anything she wanted to. He was dead along with her parents, and Aura was left missing ghosts. Lock began pacing again, and her nerves frayed. He was so impatient, and she wished she could tell him to calm down but doing that might only worsen what was already cracking, and she wasn't willing to risk it. Aura crouched down, her skirts piling around her, and she lifted the stone.

There was nothing there.

Lock crouched beside her, a look of puzzlement on his face. He stood and began to look out into the yard beyond once more. Aura sat staring at where she could've sworn she watched Lady Elsder place the knife that'd been used to murder Kian. Her heart sank; Twisted Magic. She pushed herself off the ground just as a rock slammed through the window, shards of glass sparking through the air. She moved out of the way, nearly bumping into Lock, whose hand had braced itself around her lower back to keep her from stumbling back, as it skidded to a halt in the centre of the room, a letter tied to it with red string. Aura looked into the yard, though it was too dark to really see anyone. Her heart was in her throat as Lock brushed past her, adjusting his coat.

"I do love surprises."

"You're a horrible liar."

"And some might say you're *too* good." And despite the way they'd held each other in that dance, the way Lock's eyes had shone, there was still a cool mercilessness to his tone. Aura didn't bother responding as she crossed the floor, picking up the letter.

```
           The knife isn't there.
         You are being followed.
Be wary, they have a way of playing puppet master.
```

Aura handed the letter to Lock, who took it with gentle hands. She began to pace the room, frustration clawing its way up inside her. If these people knew so much about the murderer and the investigation, why didn't they just do the work themselves? Aura wanted to scream but settled for clenching her fists. She had no idea if this was her own anger or poison being injected into her mind by the Twisted. Trust was becoming a feeble thing, and Aura hated it.

Laughter and the distant sound of chatter growing closer pulled her from her thoughts.

"Aura. . ." he trailed off, his tone full of suggestion, like a final breath before getting caught. She didn't even think as she found her hand entwined with Lock's as they ran from the room. She didn't remember when she had taken hold of it, but there was certainly no letting go now. Lock's hand squeezed her's as Aura used her other hand to pick up her skirts. She silently cursed the bulkiness of them as Lock gestured for her to go first through a doorway. She pounded up the stairs as fast as she could, Lock behind her. Aura burst into the room beyond, though instead of finding themselves back in the ballroom, they found themselves hidden away in Lady Elsder's drawing room. A secret passageway, by the looks of it. Aura couldn't complain, grateful for the quiet. It hung in the room, blanketing them from the uncertainty beyond the four walls, and Aura let herself breathe for a moment. The room was white-walled, with plush velvet sofas in the centre around a small table littered with books. A lamp in the corner lit most of the room, flickering every so often. Aura wanted nothing more than to plop herself down into a chair and let sleep take her, but her mind was far too busy and far too frustrated to even think about shutting her eyes. She began to pace the length of the room, clasping her hands tightly behind her back. Her thoughts seemed to pull her in every direction, and Aura was sure if she thought anymore, her limbs would give out. She needed to think as if this were all some science experiment: the letters, the murder, the all-knowing, but even then, there were too many variables to even try and make sense of the problem. She could see no way out of her frustration, and she turned again, but paused to find Lock standing before her. She glared up at him.

"You're in my way of pacing."

"You're making me dizzy," he countered.

She crossed her arms but didn't move. They were awfully close, and should anyone come in, it would ruin both of their reputations. His hair fell onto his brow, and Aura thought it made him look beautifully terrifying. Lock's dark eyes searched hers, and an apology came to her lips but died as he opened his mouth.

"You're frustrated," Lock said, and his voice sounded distant despite standing before her.

"Yes." She paused. "I'm not entirely sure why."

It was a lie, and they both knew it.

Lock scanned her face for a moment longer, and Aura felt her pulse quicken. "Yes, I think you do."

Aura sighed, knowing that she couldn't lie to him. Not again. "The letters are another connection my mind has trouble figuring out. If the senders know so much, why not catch the killer themselves? Why not reveal themselves to us and offer to help? We've just been following blindly. How do we know they aren't the murderers or the followers they claim are behind us? They seem to be very good about solving mysteries, so where were they when I was forced to kill at the hand of Twisted Magic? When I was breaking again and again? Where were they when Alon lay dying? I'm worried—well, I suppose I'm worried that we won't figure this out, Lock."

She felt as though she was grasping at the air as she fell, her fingers barely missing the ledge of a large mountain as she continued her descent to death. She was drowning from too many possible answers and what felt like not enough space to calculate. The Duke had gone silent, Rien was seeming more distant, she and Lock were fraying, and they were running out of time to find the coronet. *Lock* was running out of time. Her heartbeat sounded loud in her ears as tears welled in her eyes, and whatever was happening between them, Lock seemed to forget as he reached out, brushing a single tear from her face. She smiled at the small gesture as his finger slowed before pulling away to rest at his side.

"Aura," he said quietly.

She looked at him again.

"Do you know how often I think about that? Listen to me, Aura. If we let the doubt take us, we've already given up. We can't have room for doubt. I know it's complicated when we can't even seem to trust our magic anymore. We still have each other, and that has to mean something. Even when our hope fails, we still stay standing, and we have to keep going. Even though you and I are at odds, I trust you with my life, and I'm sure it's likewise for the others. Even if we are broken, I'll catch you if you fall; all you need to do is let go. Just because you've spent your life dimming your emotions because it gives you a clear head doesn't mean you can be emotionless. You cannot be cold when the world around you is made of fire. Perhaps we're no closer to figuring out the truth, but isn't that an investigation? It's all anticipation and trust in yourself until the last piece clicks."

She had a feeling his words were about more than just the investigation. "But what if it doesn't?"

Lock looked at her with a determination that she hadn't seen in a long time. "It will."

She wanted to ask him how he knew, but she didn't have to. She realized that he wouldn't let this go until it was seen through. That was how he always had been. Aura needed to do this. She needed to pull herself from the waves because she wasn't alone—she was not the only one who was frustrated, and she wouldn't be the last. Yes, perhaps the Twisted were creating a line between reality and illusion, and perhaps their contacts had gone silent, but that didn't mean that solving the mystery was impossible. It meant that they had to know their truth because it was the only one that mattered in the face of delusion. Still, trust was beginning to become blurred, and she sighed, moving to sit on a chair, the velvet hugging her. Lock settled in a chair across from her, crossing his ankles. Aura inhaled.

"I don't trust my feelings anymore."

He looked at her through lowered lashes. "Your emotions seem real whenever I'm near." It was barely more than a whisper.

She looked away, hoping he wouldn't see how red her face got. Her emotions were real because it was easy to trust him. It was easy to follow him blindly because they were connected by a trust that cradled each of their darkest secrets. They were connected by cracked hearts and kept promises, and Aura wouldn't give that up for the world, even though she almost had. Her heart slammed against her chest, and she only hoped he couldn't hear it. He looked at her and Aura shut her eyes before meeting his gaze.

"Why must you get the coronet, Aura?"

He'll kill you if I don't, she wanted to say, though the words never left her lips.

"Aura, please—"

"I—" she stopped, the glimmer of something catching her eye. She stood suddenly, causing Lock to stand and direct his view to where she was looking. She started towards the bookshelf, pulling a book from the shelf, and there sat a tiny blue gem. Lock pulled his gloves from his coat and put them on, reaching for the gem. It glittered in the dim light of the room, and Aura could just make out a spot of blood. She took the gem from his outstretched palm, all memories of their conversation forgotten.

Lock clapped his hands. "Well, shall we continue our investigation, my lovely Aura?"

She nodded, avoiding his gaze and processing his words. He stuffed his hands into his coat pocket, and Aura wanted to reach out and tell him she was worried—that she was tired of ruining herself, but she bit down on her tongue. He hadn't spoken to her, other than small talk, about what she had shown him. He hadn't spoken to her about her crimes, and she almost wished he would, even if he called her a monster. Aura already knew what she'd done was unspeakable, but for once, she needed it to be. Lock watched her for a moment as if trying to figure out what she was thinking and frowned, but she marched ahead of him, her skirts twirling furiously. Aura let out a huff. She shouldn't get her emotions involved in the investigation; it would only end up with another variable that she'd need to fit into the equation. They exited, Lock's words echoing a reminder in her head. *If we let the doubt take us, then we've already given up*. She wouldn't give up, and she had every intention of trusting her friends, even if her magic wasn't to be. And, even if she'd end up losing it, trust was all they had.

TWENTY - THREE

SÖREN

Sören pulled Iskra into an alcove as the voice behind them grew louder. She gave him an annoyed look before pushing him away. He rolled his eyes—it wasn't his fault that he didn't want to get caught sneaking around Lady Elsder's manor, despite the woman knowing of their presence. It felt wrong to conduct an investigation so, well, out in the open. She couldn't fault him for being cautious. Truthfully, he'd much rather be at the sea, stargazing—anything would be better than investigating with Iskra. She was in a state, and Sören wouldn't want to be there when she exploded, like she almost had back in the tavern. He waited until the voices faded down the staircase at the end of the hall before he, too, slipped away from the safety of the alcove. *The sea, the sea, the sea,* he thought, pretending he was there instead. He and Iskra passed several intricate wooden doors but paused when his magic flared, walking itself down the hall and into one of the rooms beyond. Sören shut his eyes, focusing on the magic. Vaguely, he felt Iskra push him into an alcove while she kept watch on the door he nodded at.

"Erika," a man's voice was saying. "We've all seen them. They're way too influential to be attending any party of yours."

Sören held back a snort. He wouldn't consider himself influential by any means. Iskra must've noticed his barely contained amusement because he winced as the heel of her boot connected with his shin in warning. Sören sobered.

"Are they? Perhaps they're nice people."

The man scoffed. "They are here because you were tangled in Kian's sheets, weren't you? Do they know about the library?"

"I beg your pardon?" Lady Elsder's voice was ice cold. "I think it's best if you leave."

Sören's magic was cut, like a knife being brought to a thread. He signalled to Iskra, who strode towards the door. He had half a mind to stop her until he understood what she was doing.

She was going to catch the man on his way out.

He watched from his hiding spot as the door opened, and a man with his hat tipped low, and a long overcoat left, bumping into Iskra.

"Excusez moi," he heard Iskra say, and the man disregarded her completely, but not before Sören noticed her touch his arm. The man hurried down the hallway, his footsteps a fading symphony. Sören hoped that Iskra had gotten the chance to hear something before the man had set off. He pushed off the wall and strode to Iskra.

"He thought something about getting back to his master," Iskra told him, a French accent slipping slightly in her English, an indication that she was tired, and Sören wondered how long it had been since she'd rested. Her eyes were unfocused, and Sören wondered what'd happened for her to be in such a state. If he didn't know better, she may as well have been unconscious for the lack of the fire in her eyes—and motivation. Usually, she might have gone after the man, but today she leaned against the wall of the alcove as if it might let her disappear inside of it. He thought over Iskra's words, his gaze flicking to the direction the man had gone.

He crossed his arms. "Like to a lord. . ."

"Or to the Twisted," Iskra said, saying what Sören had been afraid of. Still, he supposed it didn't matter. They'd be gone by tomorrow, and the Twisted didn't have enough evidence that they really were investigating. The Twisted were certainly a pain, and he needed to figure out how they fit into the investigation, other than the fact that their magic had infected Kian upon death. There had to be some other reason they were keeping an eye on them because even if they found out who killed Kian, the Twisted were too hidden to be arrested. He frowned at the newfound thought.

"Look who it is," said a smooth voice from behind them. Sören spun to see both Lock and Aura walking up to them. Sören practically sagged in relief, glad that they were here. He examined his friends; they still seemed stiff around each other, but at least they were speaking—a sign that he took as a good one. Aura's eyes were puffy as if she had been crying, and Sören wanted to ask her if she was alright, but Iskra spoke first, catching them up on what she'd learned. She let Sören explain what he'd heard, his mind working at a fast rate. He even told them about his new question concerning the Twisted.

"Wouldn't it be obvious?" Aura asked.

He gave her a puzzled look.

Aura shrugged. "They're probably protecting one of their own."

Sören thought over Aura's words, but it seemed improbable. Unless the Duke was working with the Twisted, he wouldn't have let one into his party, especially with his views on the Society. That was unless the Twisted were good at keeping inconspicuous.

Lock and Aura shared another letter, though they believed it'd been pointless. Sören thought the point that they were being followed seemed pretty important, but no one seemed worried about it. Perhaps it was normal for them. A small smirk touched his lips as he imagined Lock sprinting away from a follower, all long legs and tall frame. *Focus.* He chided himself, ignoring the low sound that came from Iskra as she brushed past him. *Curse her.* Sometimes he forgot she could see into his mind, even with the slightest of touches.

Sören strode past them, deciding that if they were being followed, they'd need to be out of this house before something went south.

"Where are you going?" Aura called after him.

"The library."

Lady Erika Elsder's library wasn't a particularly large room, but the grandeur made up for it entirely. A large crystal chandelier hung from the centre of the ceiling, casting rainbows dancing on the glossed mahogany shelves, filled with dust-covered books that took up three of the walls. The fourth wall was blank except for a desk. A picture hung above the desk depicting a flower wilting in a rainy backdrop. It was surprisingly beautiful. Sören wondered what the man had meant by the library, considering this seemed quite normal. He might find such a thing in Xavier's house if he'd bothered to look for it. He shook his head. He shouldn't be thinking about the lord, especially now that Detective Inspector

Thornsbury was doing some digging. Sören shivered, remembering what Thornsbury had told him after he'd found Xavier in his house. *It's not enough evidence, Sören. Your father's claims and a break-in aren't enough. I think you're forgetting that you're falling quite deep in with one of the most influential lords in London.* It was true, and Sören hadn't decided when he should start treading lightly around Xavier, and he wasn't entirely sure he wanted to continue this game either.

Sören wanted very much to get close to him.

"Sören." Iskra's harsh tone sent him snapping out of his thoughts. She gestured to Lock, where a section of the bookshelf had opened, a newer-looking book sitting apart from the rest of the dull covers.

"Well, well," Lock mused. "It'd seem our suspect does have reason to be nervous."

Sören crossed the room to where the others were gathered, his footsteps near-silent on the ornate rug that lay in the center of the office, pausing upon the sight of what was inside the hidden compartment. The compartment, little more than the size of a crate, velvet lined, cradled a silver coronet—the very same one that had been taken from the Order and again at the Liang's. It's silver looked duller than Sören would've thought, though the red gems set into each of the spires practically glowed, velvet lining the inside. Sören only stared at it—this was the object that was going to help save him, if he turned it in to Xavier, the lord would put in a good word. He couldn't help the small smile that came to his face.

"There's minimal dust," Aura noted, her voice puncturing the silence that had befallen them. "Meaning, she was the one that took the box from Lord and Lady Liang."

"Or they gave it to her to save their necks because the Duke certainly didn't give it to them." Sören finished. So, the coronet was missing from the Order, delivered to the Liangs, then to Lady Elsder, but why such a complicated hand down? Sören frowned.

"I know what it looks like." Lady Elsder's voice came from the doorway. Sören spun, unaware the door had been opened. "The Duke ordered the coronet to me as a gift. He said that Kian would've wanted me to have it. Clearly, he was wrong, considering you are all looking at me like I've done something."

"Because you have. The Duke didn't give this to you—it was taken from the Liang's," Iskra said carefully. "This implicates you heavily in Kian's murder."

"You must believe me. I'm being framed." She stalked over to the desk and unlocked a drawer, pulling out a knife.

"What are you doing with that?" Lock asked.

Lady Elsder looked up. "This was found in my greenhouse a few days ago, and I didn't put it there."

"Do you believe us to be fools?" Aura asked. "I have Optical magic. Now, I thought it was Twisted, but now that you tell me, I can see it was the truth."

The woman shook her head. "You have to believe me."

Sören sighed. "Did you see Lady Hollisworth faint?"

A nod of her head.

"Where were you when the emergency bell went off?"

"In Kian's room. He told me to wait there."

"Then how could you have seen Lady Hollisworth faint?" Iskra asked. He watched as reality sunk into Lady Elsder's face, tears welling in her eyes. Sören was almost sorry for her, but judging by the recent evidence, it looked very much like she was the murderer.

Aura handed something to Lock, and he approached carefully. "Lady Elsder, would you like to explain what this gem was doing in your drawing room?"

Lady Elsder looked down to where her own blue gem glittered. "I can't."

Sören quickly went and grabbed the knife from the desk should anything happen. "Lady Erika Elsder, I'm afraid you'll need to be brought down to London for questioning." Aura nodded to Iskra in an indication to send for the Brighton police, and Sören told her to send a telegram to Detective Inspector Thornsbury. Sören looked back at Erika, tears staining her eyes and silent sobs racking her body. She was looking at the coronet as if it held all her answers, and a look came to her eyes but vanished as fast as it had come, her crying becoming louder. Sören wasn't sure it was all an act. If she was being framed, the evidence did a fine job lining up with her movements. Lock picked up the book he'd dropped on the floor and dusted it off, resting it back on the shelf.

"I loved him," Lady Elsder whispered.

"Or perhaps you'd mistook poison for butterflies," Aura told her as she led the way out of the room. Erika watched her go, and Sören gave the knife to

Lock so Aura could check it before the Brighton Police came. He watched Lady Elsder, and although she wasn't tied, she made no move to leave.

Perhaps she knew it was over.

Perhaps she was fighting with despair.

Whatever it was, Sören couldn't ignore the sinking feeling in his stomach.

TWENTY - FOUR

LOCK

The Brighton police got there by the time the party ended, taking Lady Elsder away, promising to take her directly to Scotland Yard. The night was still far from over, yet the party seemed to have died the moment whispers of the police arriving got out, and Lock suspected many of the guests had done their fair share of illegalities. Lock leaned against one of the walls in the entrance hall, arms crossed, watching as Lady Elsder left, looking deflated, chains dangling at her wrists. Lock supposed that was what happened when one's faults caught up with them. A moment after the police left, a middle-aged man with bright blond hair and an extravagant moustache came striding into the manor, brushing his hands down his impeccably clean suit.

The same man Lock had seen at the Nighvengale's with Sören.

Xavier trailed behind him.

The man made a direct line to Sören, and Lock suspected this must not only be his acquaintance but the Detective Inspector he had told Iskra to send a message to. Lock uncrossed his arms and strode to join them. The Detective Inspector looked up when Lock approached, bowing at the waist slightly—it was stiff as if he'd learned to bow at school and had never done it since.

"Lord Locklyn—"

He put up his hand. "Call me Lock. A pleasure to finally meet Sören's inside man."

The Detective Inspector nodded. "I got here as soon as I could. If you wouldn't mind showing me the library."

Lock let Sören take the Inspector and Xavier, who hadn't yet spoken a word, to the library, where Iskra had spent most of her time as if the coronet could get up and walk away. The detective grabbed the coronet and struck up a quiet conversation with Sören and Xavier. Lock handed over the gem found in the library and waited until he made sure they didn't need him before he went back to the greenhouse.

A lantern had been placed in the centre of the room, casting long shadows across the windows. Aura stood there, her back towards him, and even if it weren't for the reflection in the window, he could've guessed she was using her magic, a glow emanating softly from her face. His own magic wrapped itself around the room, sensing the guilt radiating from Aura in waves. He didn't need to ask her what she was remembering; he'd felt this guilt before—she was looking at her first night as the Queen of Spades. His gut twisted, watching as her magic faded. He'd watched that same scene and replayed it in his mind every night since, yet every time he couldn't bring himself to be mad at her. No, instead, he found understanding written between the lines of magic—he needed to tell her that they were both broken doing things for the right reasons. Lock watched Aura as her hands shook at her sides, and his heart shattered.

Aura's eyes met his in the glass reflection, and she started. "What are you doing here?"

"Do I need a reason to check on you?"

Aura didn't respond, looking away from his eyes.

"It's over now," he told her, entering the room fully and going to stand beside her. "Your employer won't hurt you anymore."

Aura was silent, and Lock took that as a sign to continue. He inhaled, preparing himself to say what he needed to.

"I'm sorry, Aura. I know those words mean very little to you, but I must say them. When you told me you were the Queen of Spades, I was angry with you for not telling me, but I was even more furious with myself for letting me take my broken past out on you. The Queen of Spades—I relate to her. She killed because she had to, and I let my guilt control me." He looked away. "I shouldn't have. I hurt you, and I might have even hurt us. Aura, I'm your best friend, and the day I walked in on you, I should've told you about my guilt right then and there. I should've been there—I should have told you that I understood. I won't stand here and pretend that I did not hurt you, just as I will not stand here and tell you that I hate you because God only knows my feelings are anything but."

Aura reached into her coat, handing him her knife. "Please take this. I cannot be trusted, Lock, under any circumstances. The poison crawls inside my mind, and I hold on to reality for dear life. Otherwise, he'll break me, as if all this healing I've done means nothing. I trust you with that because a few moments ago, I'm afraid I may have hurt you."

He took the knife, hiding it in his coat. Lock turned then, facing her, only to find she was already watching him. Her concerned gaze, searching, though, for what, he wasn't entirely sure. Gently, he reached out and touched her cheek. "My lovely Aura, I'm sorry."

Aura scanned his face. "You're forgiven." — a pause — "For you; that day in my room, I was doing it for you."

He frowned. "I'm not sure I understand."

"I tried to ignore the itch, the Twisted Magic, everything my employer did because I knew that we would end up like this—two bruised souls. I knew I was hurting you, and for that, I could not stand myself. I lost that control the night Kian died. I slid a knife into a poor man's heart and then put on a dress as if it was nothing."

"Dearest Aura," he trailed off. "I don't blame you. I forgive you. I will not let you lose control again—that's a promise. But even if you do, I've always been good at saving you, haven't I?"

Aura let out a scoff, but she was smiling, even as she closed the gap between them, resting her head on his chest. Lock tucked her against him, letting the feeling of her in his arms engrave itself within his mind. Gently, he stroked her hair, and silence encircled them, but he was glad for it; he hoped the silence was enough to say all the words he didn't know how to. Together, they stayed like that in each other's embrace until they heard Iskra calling from within the house. Lock smiled as he followed Aura out. Forgiveness between them was easy, but he needed to forgive himself. Aura paused in the hall, causing him to halt.

"You saved me that night—the night after Alon died, that is. I'm sure that makes you a better person than I ever was."

"Perhaps," he said, holding his arm out to her. "But the past has a way of haunting you, doesn't it?"

Three years ago, he and Aura had sat in the corner of Rien's laboratory, his coat wrapped around her shoulders. Her hands had been clasped as if the single action could keep her from falling apart. It had been the only moment he'd ever wished to take her pain and make it his. And, had his mind not still been reeling from burying an old friend in the ground only a month prior, he might've found a way to do just that.

"Poison?" he remembered Aura asking him, as if to confirm she'd heard him correctly.

"Poison." He'd told her, an urgent madness running though his veins.

That night, they'd gotten away with murder, and they'd made a vow, to keep a secret, to keep them free. She'd been there for him at his worst, and the night Alon had died, with Aura huddled in his arms, he vowed he would do whatever it took for her to never feel like that again. It had been well past midnight when she'd burst into the laboratory where Lock was finishing up some notes, though Rein had long since gone home. Her eyes had glittered with tears, and his first instinct had been to hold her, as he'd just done moments ago. Three years ago, Lock had danced with her, an attempt to distract her from the pain, and although Lock hadn't known it then, that dance had been a lifeline for his spiralling mind. The curse on his heart hadn't been as strong then, and he could afford to stay up next to her, without worrying when it would claim him. If he hadn't done what he'd done, bloodied hands and all, he and Aura wouldn't have had a thousand more dances, a thousand more shattered moments, and a million and one moments where they'd save each other from drowning.

The train station was packed, an assortment of people crowding the platform. From ladies in their day dresses and gentlemen in suits preparing for trips into London, to people who looked like they were just making it by. The night was beginning to fade into the day, and Lock suspected that many of these people were waiting to get into the city. He wondered how many of these people did this every day, because Lock was exhausted from his lack of sleep, and he couldn't imagine waking at such ungodly hours. Smoke from the train billowed into the air, and the group pushed their way through the crowd after giving their tickets to the porter. Lock tugged his coat tighter around him as the cool air snapped its jaws. He glanced at Aura, whose own coat was pulled tightly around her. Aura tucked herself closer to him while Iskra pushed ahead with Sören.

"Remind me, when did Iskra start to treat us like people and not business associates?" Aura asked.

Lock shrugged. "I think somewhere along this dangerous path, she realized that she does indeed like the idea of friendship. That, or maybe she's too invested in our dramatics—"

Aura rolled her eyes. "Yes, I'm sure our quarrel is what made her stay the moment things got bad."

Lock smiled, looking ahead at their friends, who were now bickering about which compartment their tickets had said. In the end, Iskra pulled out her chopped ticket and led Sören to the correct compartment, followed by Thornsbury and Xavier. He and Aura followed after them, pushing their way through the crowd, earning a few grunts and curses as they passed. Aura muttered something about watching their surroundings, and Lock threaded his arm through hers. Societal rules be damned, he led her to where the others were already waiting. The train vibrated with energy as an attendant opened the compartment door for them, and they filed their way into their first-class compartment, minus the Inspector and Xavier who'd gone to a second one to discuss the coronet.

The compartment was comfortable, with mahogany panelling and two lamps stationed just above the sliding door that led out into the hallway. White curtains were drawn, blocking him from seeing anyone else, and he much preferred it that way, considering the dishevelled state is was in—his dark hair messy, face hollow from the little sleep he'd gotten since the night the gunshot that almost pierced Lady Hollisworth rang out—where he'd thought the worst about Aura and still couldn't bear to think what should happen if the bullet had hit her. Lock situated himself near the door, Aura taking the window beside him. He was glad that they wouldn't need to spend another journey rattled with tension and strung with the knowledge that hung between them. Lock smiled slightly; that was how it always had been between them, the secrets that bonded them. Sören took a seat across from Aura, looking out the window like a child who never got tired of the world, leaving Iskra to sit across from Lock. She looked more miserable than usual, but he doubted that if he asked, she would tell him.

Contrary to what Aura said about Iskra treating them like friends, Lock also knew that just because she might act like it, no amount of words about her private life would be shared, and Lock only hoped it wasn't eating her up. He looked out the window at the people still boarding the train with frowns on their faces, a sight which reminded him that not a soul knew about their success except for the people he sat with. Lock thought he caught a flicker of movement near the rear of the train, but a blink and it was gone. Beside him, Aura wrapped her hands around her body as if a chill were creeping into her bones. Lock pressed a hand to his inside pocket where her knife was being kept, a silent promise to her that he wouldn't let her employer destroy her again. He watched Aura lay her head on the wall near the window, brown waves falling into her face, rising slightly with the rhythm of her breath—a sight that sent his heart beating faster. He was glad she could rest now and that her demons would hide away for a while. At least, he hoped that was the case.

  Taking one last look around the cabin, Lock noticed that Sören had curled himself into a ball and was still looking out the window, even though the tiredness had set in. Iskra was tapping her fingers against her knee, looking as though she were trying to figure out something, though he knew better than to ask her what was taking up her mind. Outside their compartment, he heard the quiet waves of conversation and the pounding of footsteps of other passengers. Settling his back into the seat, he shut his eyes. His mind was too awake for him to get any real rest, but shutting his eyes was good enough for him, knowing he'd sleep soundly once back in London. Lock remained still until he felt the train shake with the ear-pounding blow of a whistle. Beside him, Aura startled, looking somewhat disoriented before crossing her arms over her chest, annoyed at the disruption. The slow tug of wheels pulled the train forward, and he turned his attention to the window, watching as they moved out of the station. A flicker of a cloak disappeared from the station, though it would seem Aura had already seen it.

"I need your help," she murmured as she brushed past him and into the corridor. Lock cast a quick look at the others, though they hardly seemed to be paying attention before he stood and slipped from the cabin, careful not to draw too much attention to himself.

The vibration of the train beneath him sent his hand clinging to the wall. Ahead of him, Aura had no such qualms, but she was used to walking on rooftops. Quiet conversation reverberated from the first-class compartments, and he and Aura carefully slipped into an empty cabin where Aura reached up towards one of the lamps, pulling a candle towards them. He shot her a questioning look.

Lock sat across from her, eyeing the candle in her hands.

"I didn't think now was a good idea for a candlelit dinner, but if we must," he said, watching her roll her eyes.

"If you must know," Aura said, twisted the bottom of the candle, revealing a small compartment. "There are three bullets in here that I won't hesitate to use on you if you don't stop jesting this instant. Anyway, I'm not sure you noticed, but there were several Twisted on the platform, and I don't know if they made it onto the train, but I'd rather not risk it."

Aura handed the bullets to him while she screwed the candle back together and placed it back in the lantern. He stuffed them into his coat, looking up sharply as a wood panel fell to the floor. Aura clutched the hilt of her knife, where she'd used the blade to pry the wood from the wall. He looked at her, then felt the inside of his coat. "How did you get that?"

"It wasn't hard."

"That is not what I asked."

Aura made a face. "I reached into your coat when I walked past you in the cabin. Don't worry, my lord, I will not kill you."

Aura turned away reaching into the compartment and pulled out a metal revolver, handing it to him. Lock accepted it, taking the bullets from his coat and slowly loading it. He felt Aura watching him, but only met her gaze when he'd safely tucked the firearm into his coat, followed by her knife, which she'd handed to him. They stared at each other for a moment before the door to the compartment opened, a shadow floating before the doorway, and Lock stood, only to blink as glass rained into the cabin, a tiny wince coming from Aura as she fell backwards back onto the bench where she'd been sitting only a moment ago. Lock pressed his lips together, drawing on his magic as he sent their assailant to sleep, the magic buzzing within him. A moment later, he heard a thud as the Twisted collapsed to the floor. He crossed the small space, dragging the Twisted into the next empty compartment over and locking the door. Lock returned and slowly shut the door behind him. In his absence, Aura had seemingly begun fixing the hidden compartment back into place. Worry creased his brow as she went to continue, and he knelt before her, reaching for her hand.

Blood ran down her knuckles, and he pulled a handkerchief from his coat, beginning to wipe the blood away, making sure no glass shards had wound up in her skin.

"Are you okay?" she asked quietly.

"Are you?"

She stayed quite still, and he was glad for it as he wrapped the handkerchief around her cuts. And for a brief moment, he felt anger; towards the Twisted, or for not reacting faster, he didn't know, and he supposed it didn't matter much now. Lock finished with the handkerchief before he shut his eyes and kissed her hand, letting it drop again.

"Thank you," Aura whispered, her face flushed.

Lock smiled. "Just being helpful."

He pushed himself to standing, leaning out of the cabin to make sure it was clear before gesturing for Aura to follow.

"Lock," she said, but he knew what she was about to ask, and he bent down, jamming the lock on the compartment. She nodded after inspecting it, and he rose. It was better to be safe than dead, so he and Aura hurried back to their cabin. She sat, watching the scene through the window once more, her hand stroking her make-shift bandage, and he paused.

"Aura?" he asked.

She hummed, indicating he should continue.

"I truly am sorry for the things I've said; things I've done. I became the worst part of myself, a part that you were never meant to see."

Aura turned to him, forgiveness in her eyes that he didn't deserve. "I don't think you need to apologize to me again, Lock. I think it's yourself. We've both been the victims of a life we thought we wanted, and I cannot get angry with you for showing that." She reached out and squeezed his hand but winced at her injured one. Lock smiled at her, then felt himself mold into the cushions behind him, ready for their long trip back to London.

TWENTY - FIVE

AURA

The train sped towards London; the gentle tug of the engine more calming than Aura wished to admit. She hadn't felt this kind of peace in quite some time. Part of her wasn't sure what to do with it, so she sat in silence, only for her thoughts to take over. *One, two, three.* She counted the rhythm of the train and thought of the Twisted Magician unconscious in the train compartment *Four, five, six.* She imagined Lady Elsder plunging the knife into Kian's heart—a feeling Aura wished she didn't know. *Seven, eight, nine—*

"What if Lady Elsder was telling the truth?" Iskra asked suddenly, stamping her feet onto the floor and leaning her elbows on her knees, blond hair hanging over her shoulder.

"What if she was?" Sören said. "It wouldn't matter. The evidence strongly points toward her. Besides, she had the knife. *And* the coronet."

Aura raised a brow. "Why the sudden second-guessing?"

She had to admit the whole affair had seemed so simple, all the evidence connecting, but, she supposed, they'd solved the puzzle. Lady Hollisworth had been too dismissive, yet everything she had said was true, and Detective Inspector Thornsbury had told them as much as the Brighton Police handled Lady Elsder. As for the Liangs, Lady Liang had woken around two days ago and had given a statement that she knew nothing. While that didn't explain the Twisted, Aura didn't believe that either Izumi or Kano would be searching to start trouble, especially with the police.

"Because when I was a member of the Order, Erika and Kian would spend a lot of time together. You could tell that Kian fancied her. The Liang's might have the motive, you know, for Kian supposedly loosing their money, but Lady Hollisworth might equally have a motive. Think about it. She claimed to have loved Kian and wore black to prove it to us. Erika was in the middle of throwing a party—she didn't care what we thought of her. . ."

"Lady Hollisworth went to great lengths to play the mourning lover." Aura finished, thinking about what Iskra was saying, her feeling of peace slowly disappearing. Lady Hollisworth had played the victim of the Twisted, but what if it had all been an act? "Sören, did Detective Inspector Thornsbury ever tell you about what Lady Hollisworth told the constables the day she visited the Yard?"

Sören shook his head, "I never asked. But I did see her there."

Lock, who'd stayed quiet for the majority of the conversation, furrowed his brow. "She took great pains to make sure that Aura and I left her house, but that isn't unusual if someone broke in unannounced. I'm not convinced she is guilty. Think about it. Lady Erika has the same motive as Lady Clara: Jealousy. You said it yourself, Aura. Perhaps Erika took her love for him too far—if she cannot have him, no one can."

Perhaps, you'd mistook poison for butterflies. Aura remembered saying it, and the evidence made sense. Perhaps Lady Erika took great lengths to make it seem like she didn't care, thinking it'd make her less of a suspect. Perhaps she claimed to be framed because if she didn't, it would give her too much motive. Aura sat back, her mind once more a jumble of thoughts.

Iskra sat back as well. "You make a good point. I just—all the times I spoke with her she was kind to me."

"So would anyone if you looked like you were about to bite their head off," Sören muttered.

"But regardless, it doesn't matter," Lock said. "Lady Elsder had the coronet, and unless she can explain to the Yard how it came to be in her possession, I fear she will be found guilty."

Aura frowned at something Iskra had said earlier. "Iskra, you said *'when I was a part of the Order.'*"

Iskra hesitated before pulling up her sleeve, revealing a scar where her blue gem had once been. "I've been banned. Some rubbish about me working with the enemy."

Aura was about to respond when the door to their compartment opened and Thornsbury entered. He shut the door slowly behind him, leaning against it, attempting to save what little space was left in the cabin.

"Lord Brittenworth has," the detective inspector trailed off. "Discovered something."

"What is it?" Sören asked, sitting up from where he'd been leaning against the window.

Thornsbury avoided each of their gazes, and Aura had the distinct feeling that she wasn't going to like what she heard next.

"The coronet is forged."

She couldn't breathe. Silence descended over the cabin, the walls pressing inwards. That meant that Lady Elsder had been telling the truth. That someone had framed her, and they'd been too quick to assume.

"Of course," Thornsbury added. "I will be questioning her when I get back to Scotland Yard, see if she has any information that she could offer. But I'm afraid we are back to the beginning."

"Thornsbury," Sören said suddenly. "You need to go back to your cabin. Don't come out. Keep Xavier in there."

The Detective Inspector did not ask any questions. Sören's tone didn't necessarily provide any room for such. Aura knew by his tone that he'd heard the Twisted. Iskra opened her mouth to speak, but a letter slid itself under the doorway, and it was like time froze as they stared at it. Lock pushed the curtain aside but quickly closed it when he saw that there was no one.

Aura picked it up, the paper feeling heavy in her hands. She unsealed it, pulling out the letter in the familiar typed ink. The words made Aura's blood chill, her heartbeat stopping before picking up. It read:

```
           My Elegant Elite,
   Lady E was in love with him—the blame is
                undeserved.
    The one with the wrong blood hunts you.
        At the sound of the gun, run.
```

My Elegant Elite. Aura's frustration grew. If they knew they had the wrong person, why didn't they just do the work themselves? Let alone pretend that they worked for these mysterious letter-senders. Aura read the letter to the others, and Lock reached out and took her hand. She squeezed, grateful for his touch. It had a way of pulling her from the depths of her ever-sinking mind. *If we let the doubt take us, then we've already given up.* She inhaled, letting her frustration hide behind a mask of adventure.

"What do they mean by gunshot?" Sören asked as an eruption of voices sounded from the hallways. Sören shut his eyes, and Aura took the letter when Iskra held it out to her. She stuffed it inside her coat and stood. If they were going to run, they'd have to be fast about it. Only, there was no way they could run without getting in the way of crossfire. She was sure Sören had a gun on him, but it would be too risky, especially with all the passengers on board. Sören's eyes snapped open as a loud voice echoed over the chaos:

"Knock, knock." The voice was unfamiliar. Aura squeezed Lock's hand, more out of habit than anything. His gaze was steady, indeed, he looked like he was ready to solve another puzzle, with his jaw set hard, eyes assessing the cabin. Aura looked pointedly at his jacket, where he'd stuffed the firearm from earlier.

"Hello," the voice said again. "I must say you did a lovely job locking away Erika, but what I desire is the coronet. I know you have it. Kian would want my associate to have it."

Lock motioned for everyone to be silent as nausea coiled in Aura's stomach. The conversation was proof enough of who'd killed Kian, and a confirmation that *jealousy* had nothing to do with it. Aura shut her eyes, pulling herself back to the task at hand when the unsheathing of a blade sounded. Lock readied his gun, and Aura noted that Sören had also drawn his, keeping it aimed. In one fast movement, Lock drew the door back, but before he could shoot, a loud *bang* reverberated through the air and the man toppled, face down onto the floor, agony written over his face. Blood streamed from his leg, from where a bullet was lodged in his shin. Aura grimaced, more out of understanding than pity before she and the others ran from the cabin. If there was anyone else in the cabins, they'd been wise not to look. Aura and the others hurried down the centre of the train, not pausing to look although at least two sets of footsteps followed behind them. A gunshot rattled from somewhere behind them, the bullet sticking to the wall in front of them. Aura's mind strayed to the way their own cabin had been designed, her mind working quickly. Turning to Iskra and Sören she told them what to do before they hurried into a cabin, thankfully empty. Aura grabbed Lock's hand and pulled him into another. Aura surveyed the door that led to the outside. It would be even riskier, but it could buy them some time.

"Lock, the door," she said, as she unlatched the door that led to the outside, pausing as the pressure entered the cabin. The door handle rattled but Aura ignored it as she looked out into the night beyond. The train wasn't that high up, perhaps only eight meters, still it did nothing to calm her fraying nerves. Aura stepped forwards, gripping the wall for support, her fingernails making indents. Her skirts whipped as the train continued forward, and she silently cursed herself for wearing them, seeing as balance was already difficult enough. Lock stood beside her, his own hand holding onto the train. Her bandaged hand ached, but she ignored it as best she could. The fear that rattled in her core would make the pain disappear soon enough. The wind was blowing violently as the train sped forward, and Lock stuck his head out of the door, just as a bullet radiated into the night and clattered right before Lock's shoes. Aura swore to herself, her heart in her throat, her pulse almost as wild as the train that whirled along the tracks. Ahead, the tracks curved onto a bridge, the water below not moving very fast. Her brain began its calculations. The bridge appeared only a little taller, perhaps ten meters, which should be safe enough for them to jump if they timed it right. Aura started as a voice filled her ear.

"What exactly are we doing? Enjoying the view? I thought I should remind you that we are in presumable danger."

"We are going to jump."

"My darling scientist," Lock said, half shouting to be heard over the wind. "You mustn't be planning to kill me; I haven't even proposed yet."

Aura smiled. "It won't kill you. Believe it or not, I don't want to die either."

"Lovely."

"Three shots," Aura told Lock. "That's the signal."

The train started to curve, and Lock, aimed the gun into the night air. The train moved onto the bridge, the rhythmic beat of the wheels settling into her core.

It all happened very fast.

The door burst open behind them.

Lock made eye contact with her and winked. Aura wanted to roll her eyes, but water streaked down her face from the chilly winds that stung her face.

Three shots.

They jumped. Aura swallowed her scream as she crashed into the water. It felt as though the water was squeezing in on her, and Aura's breath was beginning to run out. The water was freezing, like a million ice-cold daggers piercing her skin. Her dress was heavy, and she felt as though she was sinking.

She felt a hand around her back, dragging her upwards, and after a moment, she resurfaced, gasping for air. Aura's limbs were heavy and threatened to drag her under once more. The others were already up and swimming towards the grass-lined shore. The hand removed itself from her waist, poking her face, and she looked to see Sören motioning for her to go; it'd seem that he wouldn't let her go, just as she had done for him. She smiled and began her slow swim to the shore, willing herself to move forward.

Aura hauled herself on the bank before collapsing from the sheer exhaustion of it all. Her skirts were soaked through as well as the rest of her. She peeled off her coat, despite the cool air to let it dry. The bridge provided some protection from the foul winds, which was a relief. Iskra walked over to Aura and gave her a tight hug, and Aura paused out of surprise.

"Thank you for not killing us," Iskra said before pulling away.

"No problem," Aura said as she watched Iskra go help Sören make a fire. She wasn't sure a fire would be enough to help the dread that seeped into her veins.

Gentle hands turned her to face him, and Aura looked into Lock's worried gaze. His hair fell onto his brow, his coat slightly ripped, but it didn't seem to matter to him as he scanned her.

"I'm alright," she said after a moment. "I wouldn't have jumped if it hadn't been safe."

He brushed a strand of wet curls from the side of her face. "I know. But if I don't care, how else am I supposed to compete with those handsome detectives?"

Aura rolled her eyes, clutching her arms around herself. "There are no handsome detectives in my life, and you very well know it."

Aura turned around at the dim flare of light to see that Sören had successfully started a fire and was now laying down beside it. Iskra rolled her eyes but moved towards the fire all the same. Aura wanted nothing more than to let sleep take her, but her mind was much too busy for it.

"Mortsakov," she said quietly, thinking of the probably soaked letter in her coat. "Please tell me that we didn't just accuse an innocent woman of murder."

"I wish I could," he whispered back as if the hills around them might wake from slumber. "I wish I could."

He tenderly brought a kiss to the top of her head, and Aura's cheeks warmed with the gesture. Leaning into him, she wished that the warmth would be enough to stop her from shivering. He wrapped his arms around her, and Aura felt as though all was safe——the world wasn't out for revenge, and all was well. She inhaled, taking in the minimal warmth the embrace offered.

"If you two are done," Sören said, still laying down. "Are we going to speak about what the hell just happened?"

Aura stepped away just as Lock rolled his eyes.

"Always ruining the moment, isn't he?"

Aura smiled. "At least he has his priorities straight."

Lock feigned offence. "Is our blossoming love not a priority, dear Aura?"

Now, it was her turn to roll her eyes as she strode to the fire. The heat was welcoming, and she leaned towards it, craving every inch of the flame. The weight of the situation sunk in as if the fire soaked a sense of reality in with the warmth. They'd accused an innocent woman of murder. Better yet, the real murderer was still out there and wishing for the coronet. They all agreed that as soon as they got back to London, they needed to visit Scotland Yard. Aura had no idea how they would go about catching Lady Clara Hollisworth, considering she'd made sure all the evidence pointed toward Erika. She wrapped her arms around herself, imagining all the ways this could have gone right, but that was just it.

It couldn't have.

They were tricked from the beginning—from the moment they'd all attended the party, to the moment they had decided to investigate. Lady Hollisworth had this planned for a long time, should she have known that Kian wouldn't choose her. Somewhere, the Twisted had become experts at playing the hiding game, and Aura hated it—that feeling of intoxicating poison dripping into her mind as they plant another lie inside the mind. Silence stretched between the group, save for the crackle of the fire. It was soon consumed by the soft sound of Sören's snoring, and she wondered how he could be sleeping when there was so much at stake. How could he be sleeping when they were still away from London with no easy way of getting back quickly? Aura turned her back to the fire, looking over the water at the hills beyond. The water was a gentle flow, and Aura wished she was as calm as the waters because then maybe she, too, would be able to let sleep take her. As a child, she'd imagined playing in wide, rolling hills such as these, but now it only made her feel so far away from everything. She felt so far away when she would rather be anywhere but here waiting for hope. Somewhere beyond, Rien would be getting ready to either do the Order's bidding or for a meeting at Scotland Yard, providing notes about his most recent post-mortem. Somewhere beyond, the city of London would awaken with no idea of the mistake she and the others had made. Somewhere beyond, Lady Clara Hollisworth would be smiling, knowing she had just gotten away with murder.

TWENTY - SIX

ISKRA

The train ride back to London was miserable. After a long walk to the nearest station, they were able to catch a train the rest of the way. Thornsbury could have gotten them, but he wouldn't know *where*, and so they'd endured a walk. Iskra sat, her hands folded in her lap. Her pants were mostly dry, but it didn't make her attitude any better. She scowled at the window as if it might be the source of all her problems. How could they have been so blind? Better question, how could *she* have been so blind? Her parents had done the same thing to her as Lady Hollisworth had done to Lady Elsder. She had betrayed a friend and played the short game of manipulation, and the thought of it sent Iskra's anger bubbling. Powerful people had it in their head that they could move other people around like chess pieces—that people were easily discarded until it was time to call checkmate. Iskra was tired of it.

Iskra's veins were made of ice by the time the train had slowed down, her mind a ball of flames. She had departed from the train without so much as a goodbye to the others and walked back to her townhouse. Somewhere along the way, with her chaotic thoughts, she strayed off her course and walked towards the Thames, simply because the water might be the only option to calm her mind. The water was choppy, but she didn't care as she sat on the ledge of a walkway.

She looked out into the waters, her thoughts lost amongst venomous words and pitiful glances.

"Iskra," Sören sat down beside her, digging his hands into his knees. "Stop whatever you're thinking."

"I don't think you have any right to tell me that." Iskra looked away, pretending he wasn't there.

"Maybe," Sören said. "But I know that look."

Iskra turned again, squinting at him. "Everyone needs the coronet."

"It seems that way, yeah."

"But—"

"you need it *more*?" He asked, raising a brow. "I will help you, Iskra, but I will not get in the middle of this."

"I know." Iskra stiffened. "Do you know how sick it is to look at your own bounty with a total of five million more than you thought you were worth? It changes your life, that sort of thing, ruins it. That's what my parents did, ruined everything."

Sören was silent, and Iskra's veins were pulsing with uncertainty. She'd never been good at this. Mostly because she had never learned how to. Iskra continued.

"The coronet is possibly the only thing powerful enough that physically gives me the upper hand, ancient magic and all that. It gives me a reason to stay, to prove to them that I'm not going back. I meant it when I told you if I didn't have it, I might die. Because when they find me, they'll bring me back home, make me take over their criminal empire, and I will be *stuck*."

Desperation leaked from her tone, and she hated it, but for once she did not try to hide it.

"I already said I'd help you," Sören said. "And I'm sorry."

"Sometimes I think you'd help everyone if you could."

"Maybe." Sören looked down. "You know, in another life, I hope I meet you earlier. When I need a friend."

Iskra frowned. "You had no one?"

Sören shook his head, laughing slightly. "No. Imagine it. Getting a second chance at life and being entirely alone."

Iskra did know, except she'd pushed everyone away. Sören didn't need to know that, however. Indeed, she'd told him much more than she planned to. Sören must have sensed her withdrawing because he grinned.

"Did you just admit to being my friend?"

"*Non.*"

"Iskra." His grin faded. "Are you going to hurt the others to get the coronet?"

"Whatever it takes."

"Then I can only help you half-way. I can get you the resources, on your parents perhaps, but that's it."

Iskra didn't let her disappointment show, but she supposed in one way or another she'd suspected it.

"I need a cup of tea," Sören said suddenly and stood, striding off without another glance. Iskra stared at the Thames for only a moment longer before she stood and began to walk to her townhouse, her thoughts somewhat calmer. She wasn't sure how long she and Sören had been sitting by the river, but it had been long enough for wind to finally make its way between her bones; long enough for her heart to freeze, to pretend nothing bothered her. Iskra's footsteps echoed off the cobblestones as she dipped into a side street that'd bring her a block from her street.

When had she ruined it all?

She hadn't meant to push people away, she never did. It just happened. Iskra supposed she did it in the name of saving everyone, but how good it could feel not to be alone. How good it could be to no longer be drowning. When she'd hugged Aura the night prior, she'd also felt a warmth in her chest . . . a warmth she hadn't felt in a very long time. It came again when Lock said something that made so much sense or when Sören sat with her by the Thames. It was what she believed was called love, a pride for the ones she cared about, and she was addicted to the feeling. Iskra was addicted, yet she knew it would never last. But, if her parents were to ever take it away, she would fight. This time, Iskra wouldn't be distracted by a shiny diamond of a future without the cracks and imperfections.

If she would need to bleed for it, then so be it.

Her townhouse came into view, its brick seeming a little brighter despite the clouds above. She crossed the street, ignoring looks from high-class ladies eyeing her outfit. Carriages lined the curb waiting to move into the next large street. A small smile touched her lips at the familiarity of it all. Despite the world coming down around her, there were still moments that were so routine she could've done them with her eyes closed.

Iskra bounded her way up her townhouse steps, knocking before being let in by her attendant, a grim line set to his face. He shut the door behind her, and Iskra whirled on him.

"What is it?" she asked, suddenly not in the mood to speak with anyone.

"You, um, have a visitor, Mademoiselle. They wait in the drawing room."

Dread wrapped itself around Iskra's heart until she was sure it had stopped beating entirely.

One moment.

Another.

Iskra willed herself to move, straightening her spine, mustering a confidence she didn't quite feel. All the same, she took her time getting to the drawing room, her parents' faces flickering before her eyes—the life she'd created taken just as soon as she was starting to feel normal again. Just as she was starting to love again.

Her parents had chased her down with knives, and she had aimed her gun only to find there was no gun at all. She was trapped. Her mind was a maze, and Iskra had been stuck for so long that she forgot how to retrace her steps.

She shut her eyes as she entered the room, wishing to hold onto her freedom for as long as she could. *This is it,* she thought bitterly, *and it is not enough.*

Iskra opened her eyes, staring at the person who sat in her drawing room. She relaxed, if only slightly, though, it was quickly replaced by a familiar ache within her heart. A hesitant smile ghosted over the girl's face, and it twisted Iskra's insides even further. *It's best if you forget our acquaintanceship.* A flicker of emotion passed over Iskra's face, though she quickly schooled it to one of strict professionalism.

"Zoialynne." Iskra nodded but didn't make to move further into the room. She stood, her back rigid against the door. "I thought my instructions were clear. You don't work for me anymore."

"I never really did. Iskra, I'm here because the Duke informed me of a place that might aid in the investigation of Kian."

Iskra crossed her arms, remembering the day another person she'd trusted called her a traitor, and she lost another part of herself. As if in response, her wrist seemed to burn where the gem had been removed, a scar that probably would never leave. "In case you forgot, I don't take orders from Duke Brittenworth anymore. Why would he offer you information that could help?"

"Because I also know things about the Duke that could ruin him."

Iskra stared at her, a stunned silence settling around the room. Zoialynne had threatened her own employer, a risky move on her part. Iskra couldn't help but feel something was being kept from them, but she could see in Zoialynne's eyes that she didn't know either.

Or maybe this was all some cruel trick.

Maybe, Iskra would find a knife in her back.

Or maybe, she was just looking for an excuse to hate a girl who'd never given her a reason to. Either way, Iskra couldn't ignore the fact that Zoialynne had stopped Iskra from hurting the Duke. Zoialynne had watched as Iskra's soul was ripped from her for the second time, and she had done nothing. Perhaps, this was all a ploy to get Iskra into the ground, head caved in, a promise dead within her heart. But Zoialynne was still Zoialynne, and Iskra doubted that she would come to see Iskra if there wasn't a possible chance that the Duke was telling the truth. The girl that sat across from Iskra saw opportunity in truth, and it was this reminder that made Iskra finally cross the room and take a seat opposite her.

"What is this place he speaks of?"

Zoialynne told her about a manor owned by one of the attendants at the party and how the attendant hadn't been seen after he arrived the night of the party. The Duke didn't tell Zoialynne which of the lords it belonged to, but if Iskra and the other's investigation proved anything, it was quite probable that it belonged to Clara Hollisworth. But why wouldn't she have mentioned it when they had talked to her? Iskra dumped her head into her hands, a headache starting to form. Iskra thought it odd, but if the Duke wanted to play his little games, then so would Iskra. She got up to leave with Zoialynne to the address the Duke had provided but paused. An apology formed on the tip of her tongue. *I'm sorry,* she'd whisper. *I'm sorry.* And then she might collapse into Zoialynne because Iskra wasn't sure she could say all she needed to. She should begin her forgiveness now, should she find herself gone.

"Zoialynne?"

"Yes?"

Everything she had planned died on her lips. "Any news on my parents?"

Iskra knew that by the look Zoialynne gave her, her parents were still nowhere to be found. *Nowhere to be found* might very well mean found too late. Iskra knew her parents well enough that they knew how to get around if they wanted to.

If they wanted to find her, they could.

If they'd come to kill her, they would have already done so.

Something was different, and she wasn't entirely sure she wanted to find out what. Once this investigation was over, Iskra would see to it personally that she wouldn't have to worry anymore. She stood silently, calculating the number of days she might have left until her house was burning, she was dead, and the world crumbled. However, even Iskra knew that it wasn't possible to calculate the future. Fate was often cruel, but keeping death a secret, she supposed, may be one of the cruellest things of all. Zoialynne shook her head, and Iskra turned and walked out the door. She didn't need to look to know that Zoialynne followed after her, and as Iskra's carriage pulled up at the curb, she couldn't help but recite an apology in her head so that the world may speak it when she wasn't around.

TWENTY - SEVEN

AURA

The slamming of her bedroom window sent Aura jumping from the warmth of her sheets. She recoiled at the chill in her room and reached for her robe, which she'd tossed haphazardly onto a chair the night prior. Morning light streamed into her room peacefully, though her mind was anything but. Aura's eyes landed on the desk below her window, where a letter lay, inviting a sense of dread into her soul. Her heart jumped into her throat as she moved to the window. She looked out, although all was as it always was.

Normal.

The letter called her to read it, and Aura sighed, opening it as if the paper didn't burn her skin.

```
A familiar face is a liar.
The cuts they make are deep.
Caution, dear one.
```

Aura frowned, reading the letter over and over until the lines began to blur. *Liar.* The word echoed in her head like a taunt. She could have once been described by the very same words, but she couldn't begin to think who might be lying to her. Aura set the letter down and wrapped her arms around herself. Somewhere out there was someone who knew it all, and that was dangerous. People who know without evidence will always end up dying with the secrets on their lips. After all, wasn't that what had happened with Alon? He'd lied about where he was going the night of his death and his act had been so good that even Aura would never find out what had actually happened that night, no matter how hard she looked.

A knock pounded at the door.

Aura jumped from her thoughts and called for them to enter. Rien's secretary, who took care of Scotland Yard correspondence, poked her head in.

"Apologies for the intrusion, Miss Wrentroth, but Rien wishes for you to join him at his laboratory."

The door shut just as quickly as it had opened, and a small smile ghosted her lips. After all, there was nothing like watching Rien cut open the dead in the morning.

The air was crisp as she strode down the pavement on her way to the laboratory. After dressing herself in a maroon skirt with a matching vest overtop of a white blouse, she had hurried from the house, leaves crunching beneath her boots. However, her mind was hardly focused on the scenery, but on the tasks ahead. She wondered what Twisted act Rien needed her for. Perhaps it would be auditory; that was one sense she hadn't found in a while. Her skirts whipped at her feet, thoughts growing into anticipation. Rien didn't usually wake her unless it was important, a notion that had curiosity wrapping itself around her mind. The wind whistled on the streets behind her, though she was shielded from most of it by the townhouses lining the road. Perhaps it was good to be working with Rien this morning, considering Detective Inspector Thornsbury was taking the investigation head-on and had told them to stay away until he got more information on the whereabouts of Clara Hollisworth. She trusted the detective especially as she and the others were practically being hunted. At first, she wasn't sure how she felt about Sören going to the detective, but it was very clear the detective was interested in protecting them, which she much appreciated.

Rien was waiting for her when she arrived, a body laying between them on the metal table. The entire room smelled of cleaning supplies, and Aura breathed it in, the smell reminding her of simpler times, ignoring the sting as the chemicals hit the back of her throat. Aura perched herself in a chair and pulled out a notepad from a nearby drawer. Rien nodded his appreciation, though he looked more tired than she'd seen him in ages. His greying hair seemed to be more faded than usual, dark circles plaguing his under-eyes. She was about to ask him why, but he opened his mouth first.

"Patient aged twenty-two, named Rena Levensmith."

Aura scribbled in her notebook, looking at the body before her. The girl was pale, her blond hair hanging over the examination table in waves. Her complexion was fair, and her hands seemed soft—not a worker. Perhaps, a lady. Her nose had a tilt to it that Aura recognized, although she couldn't place it from where, and there was a circular scar hidden on the inside of her wrist. *Ex-Order member*, she noted. The woman's body seemed to have been killed with a slit to the neck, blood dripping to her collarbone, covering most of her chest. It was stark against her pale skin, the red having dried into something darker. The wound was deep as if the blade had been pressing hard against the skin, as if making sure to severe the jugular vein—as if to ensure there was no way for the victim to live. Rien spoke again, cutting her scrutiny short.

"Found on the side of the Thames by Scotland Yard officers. Come here."

Aura scribbled her notes before standing and grabbed an apron from where it hung on a stand by the door. She tied it around her waist before stepping up to the cadaver of Rena Levensmith.

"First, look at the wounds."

Aura nodded, examining her slit throat and the blood that seemed to be staining the woman's lips. Rien hummed in approval before gently bringing his fingers to the woman's chin, forcing her jaw open.

Aura winced.

Lady Rena Levensmith's tongue was cut off, the job jagged, like it was hurried.

Without taking his attention away from the mutilated body, Rien asked, "Now, what Twisted Magic would make this kind of crime possible—to make them go unheard, even by the shipyard workers?"

She frowned. "Nothing would take the pain away. That is, unless the victim was already dead, but the blood on the lips suggests she was not. So, perhaps Emotive, to inject the victim with a sense of calm. Or Perhaps Auditory to distract the dockworkers?"

"Exactly. Shall we test that?"

Aura nodded before moving away from the table and scribbling in the notepad.

Rien began a 'Y' like incision into Miss Levensmith, and Aura scribbled down the findings, all showing her body had shut down. Rien started his incision into the brain, muttering something Aura couldn't understand. She took that as her cue to join him beside the body, pressing the notebook into his hands, which she noted, were very dry.

"The brain," she reported to Rien, taking out the poison with a syringe. "The brain has been affected by Twisted Emotive magic. Rich purple implies a stronger magician."

"As you predicted."

Aura stoppered the vial, watching out of the corner of her eye as Rien wrote that note down. He was silent for a moment, and a feeling twisted itself into her gut and settled there. Did Miss Levensmith have any connection to Kian's death? It wouldn't seem so. She leaned forward to get a look at the brain, but she knew it wouldn't give her any more information than she knew. Rien seemed to know what she was thinking and spoke as he removed the organ and set it on a tray.

"I doubt this relates to Kian. If it were, why would the victim have been murdered?"

Aura straightened. "Because the murderer knew the victim."

Rien raised his brows, slowly setting the notebook down near Lady Levensmith.

"Perhaps," Aura conceded. She'd need to find proof, but she suspected it had to have been Hollisworth. Miss Rena Levensmith might very well be a mockery of the idea that she and the others had accused an innocent woman. Aura grimaced at the corpse, but the dead didn't speak. Rien opened his mouth but closed it again as a knock sounded at the laboratory door. Rien's secretary popped her head in and whispered something to him. Rien cast a look at her, or perhaps it was at the cadaver; she wasn't sure.

"Aura, get my Scotland Yard report book for me. It's in the back room, and start writing our findings, but make no mention of your suspicions. I'll be back. I have a visitor back at home."

"Yes, sir."

Without another word, Aura watched as Rien ducked out of the carriage house. She frowned after him for a moment before placing sawdust on the floor to soak up some of the body's fallen liquids before striding to the back room.

It was a small space, no larger than a storage room, where a square desk had been set up in the corner, scattered with papers and the red Scotland Yard Report log Rien liked to keep. At the other end of the room was a large cabinet where Rien kept his extra tools and a place where Aura was forbidden to go. She suspected it was because the tools in there were a gift from the Queen, but her imagination went wild when a piece of fabric peeking out from below the door caught her attention. She shook her head. Rien was a good man, and yet Aura couldn't help but keep the Duke's accusations out of her mind—that Rien was giving information to the Twisted.

She laughed.

Perhaps the lack of sleep was getting to her if she believed her long-time teacher and *uncle* to be Kian's murderer when it was clear that Lady Hollisworth was somehow involved. She took a seat at the small desk, flipping to a new page of the logbook and began reciting their findings on Miss Levensmith. A whisper slithered its way into her mind, a doubt that Aura couldn't stop. Ink splattered on the bottom of the page as she sent her pen down with a huff. She pushed herself up and yanked open the cabinet.

Aura froze.

The shock of seeing something she didn't want to was petrifying. Her body locked as she collapsed to her knees, left kneeling with no chance of running to the police. Aura's soul ached at the thought of a liar who offered her a home, a liar who she had loved. Last came the tears because she'd wanted to be wrong. Aura reached into the cabinet and pulled out a black cloak, a cursive T engraved into the neck. It was silken as if it were fit for a king rather than a murderer. She sat back on her heels, and that was when she noticed a bloodied handkerchief and knife tucked into the very back.

It hadn't been Clara Hollisworth who had killed Kian.

It just had to look like it.

Rien was a smart man, and it made sense why he had wanted her here. He'd wanted her to suspect Hollisworth. Or perhaps he had only killed Miss Levensmith, but she knew better than anyone that a killer was still a killer. She folded the cloak over her arm, leaving the knife and handkerchief for the police to find. Rein was not Twisted, she knew that, but the evidence—he had the resources to have the Twisted within his reach if that was what he desired. All those years, investigating them, that wasn't what he was doing at all. Perhaps he had been investigating the Duke or the Yard. Her heart broke. Rien couldn't be allowed to walk free, especially after what he'd done to her. She ran from the room, her sorrow turning quickly into demanding anger. She pushed her way out of the morgue, the smell of it all causing a wave of nausea. Her footsteps pounded against the ground as she ran, picking up her skirts to allow her more movement. *A familiar face is a liar.* The letter's words came to her, and she slowed; it all made too much sense. *The cuts they make are deep*—an ironic saying, considering less than thirty minutes ago, Rien had been cutting open a cadaver. She felt sick, but bounded up the stairs, nonetheless. The door was opened by Rien's secretary.

"Miss, is there anything I might be able to assist you with?"

"I need to speak with Rien," she said, managing to keep the bitterness from her voice.

"I'm afraid he is in a meeting."

She rolled her eyes and marched towards Rien's office anyway. The secretary protested, but Aura was too fast and too determined for answers to let the woman stop her. Aura didn't hesitate as she burst into the office.

She paused in the doorway.

"Ah, my lovely Aura, how nice of you to join us." Lock's words were quickly drowned as she faced Rien.

He was staring at her hands.

Lock's intense inhale indicated that he, too, noticed what she held.

She scowled at Rien.

"Apologies for interrupting your meeting, but I must know when you were going to tell me. Or was I just going to end up in the grave next? Did you kill Kian? Levensmith? Tell me!" The words came out hurriedly and left Aura scrambling for her breath. *And some semblance of sanity,* she thought bitterly.

"That's not mine," Rien said, pushing up from the desk.

"Please, don't lie." Her resolve was breaking. "I saw the handkerchief and the knife. Did you do it?"

"No."

"Lies will bury you, Rien," she said, a cool tone to her voice, one Aura barely recognized. She made eye contact with Lock and saw her own expression mirrored in his. He turned to face Rien, and Aura didn't wait to see what he would say as she left the room. Perhaps she was cruel for not hearing him through, but she didn't have the heart to. Not if the evidence pointed to him. The door clicked shut, though the sound was distant. She might as well have been standing on an island waiting to be swallowed by the sharks that fed her lies. A Twisted, her uncle—Rien. He'd been there for her from the beginning, and she wondered when lies had begun to separate them. Rien, who'd cared for her after her parents died. Rien, who'd let her cut open bodies and begin science even though it was considered a man's job. Rien, who'd saved her without even knowing it.

Rien, who was a liar.

She started a slow ascent to her room, where she stopped to put Rien's cloak in his room. It seemed to burn, but it was only a piece of fabric. Once in her room, she collapsed into the chair at her desk where the letter from earlier lay open. It suddenly felt hollow, more like a house and less like a home; less like love and more like sickening betrayal. How could she not have noticed earlier? He'd been quick to show to the scene. He'd known Aura would be out of town. He worked with Avery. Aura wiped a set of tears from her eyes. She was spiralling into the past, filled with dinner conversations and walks in Hyde Park, even though he had always had work to do. Rien had made time for her, and Aura wondered when that had changed to lying to her. A gentle tap echoed from the other side of her door before opening and shutting just as quietly. Aura didn't need to turn around to know that it was Lock. Her mind was drowning, and he had a way of pulling her away from the waves just as she was beginning to sink. Impropriety be damned that they were alone together in her room; she could care less. Lock leaned against the door, his ankles crossed and his expression much softer than down in the office.

"We aren't going to tell the police," Lock told her. "Not yet. There's not enough evidence. He has no reason for needing the coronet."

She had suspected as much. "I know. I don't like that the Duke is right."

"He may not be."

Aura looked at him. "You did see the Twisted cloak, did you not?"

"Twisted doesn't equal Kian's murderer, my dear scientist." He pushed himself from the door and walked towards her. "That said, I've made it clear to Rien that should any harm come to you, I'll personally see him punished."

"Yes, and my ghost shall make sure to haunt him."

Lock frowned. "My dear Aura, I should think you insane for thinking that if you die, I'm not coming with you."

Aura smiled. It was tentative, but her heart felt light despite the dire situation. Lock braced his hands on the back of her chair, pressing a kiss into her hair before straightening. "Rien is a reasonable man, Aura. I'm sure there's a perfect explanation for all of this."

"How can you be certain?" Aura questioned, ignoring the warmth spreading up her cheeks.

Lock looked at her. "We must all hide our true feelings at one time or another. What if Rien has simply discovered a rather excellent way of avoiding his—killing?"

Aura met his gaze, noting the seriousness of his tone.

"What happened?" he asked. "In the morgue?"

"A new victim, Lady Rena Levensmith. She appears to be an ex-Order member." Aura swallowed. "Throat slit; tongue cut out."

"Like she was killed to keep secrets."

Aura stayed silent, the weight of his words pressing in on them, the room feeling claustrophobic. She took a deep breath. "I don't want to believe he did it."

Lock shrugged. "Then don't. Up until an hour ago, Lady Hollisworth was our prime suspect, and she will remain as such until we can prove that Rien is not being framed."

Aura nodded slowly. They were running out of time to try and prove anything, but she didn't say as much. Lock reached out and squeezed her hand, his skin warm against hers. A small flush crept up her cheeks before looking away.

"If you'll excuse me, I have dinner with my parents at the estate and would hate to make a bad impression, especially after I failed to show up at the coronation. Would you like your knife?"

"No," Aura replied. The answer was quick. "I have other ways of keeping my life."

Lock nodded, and Aura watched him go. She smiled. Her heart longed to follow him out, to make sure that she really was safe, but she stayed sitting.

She hadn't lost everyone she loved, and that thought was enough to keep her alive more than any poison she kept hidden beneath her floorboards.

TWENTY - EIGHT

LOCK

Lock brushed a strand of hair away from his face as he started his walk down the cobbled streets toward his parents' estate, dodging a carriage. The thoughts of Rien rang in his head, though they weren't nearly as loud as the thoughts of the meeting he'd had. Lock had walked into the office to ask Mr. Wrentroth for permission to court Aura and left confused. *I am the wrong person to ask*, Rien had said. Out of all the responses Lock had been expecting, that hadn't been one of them. He supposed he should ask Aura if it was something she wanted, but Rien had always struck him as a traditional kind of man. He supposed he could turn around and march back into Aura's room and confess the fact that he was too scared of losing her and that despite their shattered pasts, he wanted her to be his and he to be hers, but he had a dinner to attend, and frankly, he was scared to tell her such a notion. *I am the wrong person to ask.* Lock didn't know if that was a blessing or not, but he took it to be. He shook his head, ignoring the weight of Aura's knife in his coat as he made his way towards the manor.

"Locklyn Henry Mortsakov," Lada said, waltzing into the entrance hall as he handed his hat and coat to the butler. "If I didn't know better, I'd say you've been to see Aura Wrentroth."

Lock rolled his eyes. "You're right. I have been to see her, but that's quite normal, considering we *are* friends."

He ignored the raised eyebrows she made at him and stalked to the drawing room where his parents sat. His father was in an armchair, spectacles pushed far down his nose to read the book in his hands, while his mother had an embroidery frame in her hands. He paused when Lada didn't follow him in. His sister was pulling on an evening coat.

"Where on earth are you going?" he hissed.

"I'm going out," she said, and at his incredulous look, she added, "Mrs. Darcy will be there."

Mrs. Darcy, Lada's chaperone, was one of the laziest people Lock had ever met. For all he knew, Lada could have a secret dalliance, and Mrs. Darcy would be absolutely clueless. He didn't have time to question why his sister was leaving before his father called him into the drawing room. He had set down his book and motioned for Lock to sit. Lock did as he was told and watched as his mother set down her embroidery and eyed him.

"How was your day?" she asked.

"Fine." What on earth were his parents playing at? "I spoke with Aura."

His mother clapped her hands. "How's she doing? The last time I saw her, she was in tears, due to you, might I add."

He held back his retort. "She's just as lovely as always. Might I clear up that those tears were due to a mutual problem and not all my fault?"

"Of course, of course."

"Lock, your mother and I have been very considerate when it comes to you and Aura—"

"I'm not having this conversation," Lock said, starting to stand. He didn't need to hear a rant about the long list of reasons why it was considered frowned upon for Lock to even consider Aura more than a friend, and in truth, in this society, even the word friend was pushing it. Lock hated it. He had already heard this lecture enough times to recite it as a theatrical performance. Perhaps he'd put on a play for his parents.

His mother rolled her eyes. "Locklyn, sit down. We invited Aura to dine with us tonight."

"Oh." It made sense why Lada was leaving. Lock hadn't been prepared for his parents' confession, and he'd been stunned into silence.

His father smiled. "Well, should you not go get ready?"

Lock straightened his dark red waistcoat as he waited at the base of the staircase. His parents stood behind him, and Lock suspected they looked more like a threat than a welcome committee. A kind knock sounded at the door, and the butler hastily opened it before shutting the door and disappearing from sight. Aura, dressed in a gown of rich purple, stood with her hands clasped behind her back. Lock motioned for his parents to leave, and they did as he said, much to his relief.

He waited until they disappeared before walking up to her.

His head was spinning.

"*Моя дорогая* Aura.*"* He was clearly going insane if the first thing that came out of his mouth was Russian. He shook his head. "My darling Aura, I'm very sorry for my parents. I do believe that they are up to something. Only, I don't know what."

Aura nodded. "I thought as much, considering you are thinking in Russian, which only happens when your mind is clumsy."

He shrugged. "Or perhaps it's because I'm too distracted by you."

Aura rolled her eyes, though they both knew he might as well be telling the truth. He offered her his arm, and together, they walked into the dining room. Lock's heart was a fast rhythm in his chest, and he couldn't tell if that was because of Aura or because of the way his parents watched them with almost murderous eyes.

Lock desperately wished to duck underneath the table and hide. After four courses and several servings of small talk, he was done. He wanted to push away from the table, get Aura, and leave whatever this purgatory was. His father's eyes were glowing, not from any magic, a sure sign of the alcohol he'd downed during this meal, while his mother spoke with Aura about God only knows what. Lock took a long sip of tea, which had been served with dessert, before crossing his arms.

"Aura," his mother said, "Rien has always been there, hasn't he?"

He cast a glance at Aura, but there was no sign that she was uncomfortable.

"Yes," Aura replied hesitantly. "Amelia, where might this be going?"

Silence swallowed the table whole, and Lock shut his eyes, hoping that this was all some bad dream. The grandfather clock in the drawing room struck nine, and Lock jumped before coughing awkwardly into his elbow. He had no idea where his parents were going with this dinner. He'd assumed they'd been giving him an opportunity to ask Aura about a blessing, but this was far from the romantic atmosphere he would have liked.

"What my wife means to ask is that you've never been told about your parents' death?"

Lock stood so fast he nearly bumped his teacup over. "*Father*. That's quite enough. I've put up with your games, and I think it is time you fold. You're truly cruel if you believe that asking someone that I care for how she is fairing, knowing that death has a way of taking what it wants."

"Locklyn, do calm down."

He glanced at Aura, who nodded once. Lock sat down. Chills pricked his skin, and he clenched his jaw. He didn't pull his eyes away from his father. Though instead of seeing his pale-skinned, dark-featured father, he saw a large monster. He hadn't recognized when he started seeing his father as the person for who he was, but that was just it—a mask always slips. For his father, it had cracked as soon as Lock had decided to take up permanent residency in London, and with that crack had come a long list of expectations—expectations that had just been another knife to his torn mind. He tore his gaze away from his father, just as the sound of the front door opening echoed into the room. Lock brushed himself off, muttering a quick apology to his father, as the dining room doors suddenly opened.

Marquess and Marchioness Nighvengale stood in their doorway.

Lock stiffened, but Marquess Nighvengale's gaze floated right over him before landing on Aura or somewhere above.

"I hope we're not late to the party," he said, his voice velvet, and what Lock thought was a note of venom.

"Not at all," Lock's father replied, and as the Nighvengale's moved into the room, Lock found his mind wandering to Shakespeare. He had been right, of course. The devils were here, and they sat right at his dining room table.

TWENTY - NINE

ISKRA

The manor Zoialynne had directed the carriage to wasn't anything grand, though it did look like something out of her own nightmares. Leafless trees creaked before the house that loomed behind them. The dark roof was lined with thick spires, and as they got closer, Iskra could see the paint chipping away at the windowsills. To make things worse, they were in the middle of nowhere, the lights of London glistening in the distance. She watched as Zoialynne slowed her pace as they approached the stairs to the front entrance.

"Scared?" Iskra asked, turning around.

Zoialynne put a finger to her lips, and Iskra understood.

They were not alone.

Together, she and Zoialynne moved into the shadows. It wasn't a good cover, Iskra knew that, but it was something. Iskra forced her breath to slow, despite the fast, rhythmic beating of her heart. Zoialynne shifted, the fabric of her sleeve brushing Iskra.

One breath.

Another.

"I think it was nothing. Just a shadow of the trees," Zoialynne said, pushing past Iskra and bounding up the front steps. Iskra hastily followed after her. *J'ai fait une erreur,* Iskra thought to herself. She'd made a mistake coming here. It seemed obvious that Zoialynne knew something that Iskra didn't, and the thought twisted her insides. She didn't want her invisible apology to mean nothing. No, in fact, she wanted it to mean everything—everything neither one of them was strong enough to say to the other. She caught up with Zoialynne at the door, who pulled a key from her waistcoat pocket.

"The Duke gave me this. He was very clear that there wouldn't be anyone home. Well, that he knew of, anyway."

Iskra nodded, watching as Zoialynne opened the door. She didn't question why the Duke had a key. He knew the locations of all the Order's members, and subsequently knew how to get inside if that is what he so desired. Her hands shook, and Iskra clenched them into fists. If Zoialynne were to betray her, Iskra would be right back where she started. Trust would become feeble, love would become a void of nothing, and Iskra would be nothing but a cold statue again. She would be ready to set the world aflame just to feel again. She would be ready to feel her heart shatter just as it had begun to fix itself. However, she wasn't sure she'd be ready when the inevitable happened.

The inside of the manor was dim, save for a few lanterns that were lit. It was the only sign that the place might actually be lived in. The ceilings arched high above, and a crystal chandelier hung down like tiny teardrops ready to fall onto the polished wooden floors at any moment. A staircase stretched before them, leading up to the second floor, splitting into two curves that continued the rest of the way up. A chill crept its way up inside her veins as Zoialynne shut the door behind them. A phantom brushed her cheek, letting Iskra breathe for a moment. Zoialynne wasn't stupid, she couldn't have brought Iskra here if she was going to betray her. Besides, knowing something and betraying someone were two very different things. It'd been a long time since things had been the way they were on the boat, and she was making a villain out of someone she had once cared for—someone who was the furthest thing from evil. Zoialynne had whispered stories to Iskra about America, and Iskra had fallen asleep to the voice of a girl in awe of life and in love with possibility. Zoialynne was still the same person, but she saw what was real, and that didn't make her a villain. It made her human.

Zoialynne moved towards an opening that must've led to the dining room, a lantern in her hand, but paused when she saw Iskra hadn't moved.

"Did the Duke say where to find this evidence?" Iskra asked slowly. She needed to know, know that she was right, that this was not another trap for her, taking advantage of her vulnerable heart.

"The dining room. Why do you think I was heading there?"

Iskra shrugged. She followed Zoialynne into the room. It was much like the entrance hall, though it was constructed of wooden floors and a beautifully carved ceiling. A large table ran down the length of the room, its places set despite there being no one around. Zoialynne moved towards a cabinet filled with china of all sorts. Iskra stepped towards the table, inspecting the glasses. They were all dry. The gentle noise of Zoialynne inspecting the glassware sounded from behind her, and Iskra turned to watch her, her frame cast in half-shadows from the lantern that Zoialynne had set on the table. Zoialynne still hadn't told her what the Duke said they'd find here. Iskra was about to ask, when Zoialynne pushed a glass aside.

A scream.

Zoialynne was gone.

The floor had swallowed her whole, and without another breath, Iskra was in after her, tumbling into the darkness. At first, Iskra was sure that death could catch her and cradle her, but then she was sliding as if on a decline. She landed with a start on the hard ground. Zoialynne had already stood, brushing off her uniform. Above, the light showed where they'd fallen through, and Iskra could see no way out as she pushed herself up from the ground. They stood in what looked to be a wine cellar, barrels lining the walls of the long hall. Three wooden lights hung from the ceiling, casting flickering shadows off the walls as a cold draft breezed along the stone. Iskra ignored the urge to wrap her arms around herself. It felt haunting down here. Iskra moved further into the room, her fear quickly replaced by curiosity.

"The Duke didn't mention anything about wine, did he?"

Zoialynne didn't answer.

Iskra turned to see a look spreading across her face. It was the look of someone who finally understood they'd been tricked. The pleading eyes told Iskra that whatever it was, Zoialynne had known.

She'd known.

"What is it?" Iskra asked more harshly, wanting nothing more than to reach out and shake the girl before her.

"*La cruauté creusera ta tombe, Iskra,*" a cool voice bounced off the walls. *Cruelty will dig your grave, Iskra.*

Iskra froze.

It was a voice that would chase her through the streets of France a million times. It was the voice that wouldn't rest until a knife was in her back or she was wearing the crown of an empire born to destroy. The echo of shoes on the stone made Iskra want to be sick. She kept her eyes on Zoialynne; she had known. She had known, and she had led Iskra down here to die. It would seem pain was perpetual, and Iskra was the sole target—a victim of the very stars she'd thought cradled love. Zoialynne shook her head, but Iskra was tired of lies. She was tired of betrayal and the visceral, never-ending rip that was tearing her own heart to shreds. She was tired of the trust always being the poison she so willingly drank.

She turned to face her parents. They looked the same, her father's blond hair sporting too much grey and her mother's eyes scanning her in disapproval. She wasn't the same person she was when she'd run, but it felt all too much like she was.

"What do you want?" Iskra asked, too tired to make herself sound like she was trying to fight.

"You know very well," her mother said. "We need you to take our place, Iskra. We need you to be the one to set the world ablaze. Do it, and we'll rescind our accusations."

Iskra scoffed. "You think I care that I am a criminal? As if I haven't felt like one all my life."

Her mother only stared back at her, and despite her trying to keep her composure, tears welled in Iskra's eyes. Once upon a time, her mother would've at least pretended to be hurt. Now, it was clear that her parents were done playing games. It was clear that Iskra was playing a game in which she couldn't win, and perhaps she'd already lost a long time ago.

"You come here fighting. For what? In the time that I've been gone, you could have found a replacement for me. You could've had a funeral for the child you never loved, only ever destroyed. You have what you want, I suppose. I was a child with a heart that only wanted the world to pretend it wasn't cruel. I only wanted love, and you ripped that away along with any hope of me returning to France."

"Your blood is the only heir we will accept, and you know it," her father spat.

"Then I'll have to die. Take my blood in a jar back to France."

Her father made a sound in his throat. "This is ridiculous. You'll come back to France or," he brandished a gun, pointing it at Zoialynne, "I'll shoot her."

Iskra kept her back still. *Show no weakness, and they cannot hurt you.* Her mother moved to one of the barrels while her father stalked closer.

"You'll do what I tell you," he said. "Or you will be responsible for your friend's death."

Iskra shook her head. She was tired of this manipulation. "I will not. And you will not harm her."

Her father watched her, and Iskra kept her gaze locked with his. He cocked the gun, and Iskra swore under her breath.

"One more time," Her father said slowly. "You know how good my aim is, *Ma chere fille.*"

Her father backed up and began adjusting his aim. Iskra watched as he placed a finger on the trigger and—

"I'll do it," Iskra said. Her father grinned, but not the type of grin that someone would give a daughter he hadn't haven't seen in years. It was the kind a wolf made before they pounced. Her father pocketed his gun before he clapped his hands together.

"Good. We'll be on our way in three days. Don't even think about asking for help."

"Yes, sir," she said.

"And Iskra," her father finished, "you should know by now I don't keep any loose ends."

Iskra whirled just as her mother brought a knife through Zoialynne's back. Zoialynne screamed, and Iskra felt hot tears pierce her skin. She looked for her father, but he was already gone, another ghost in the catacombs. And when she looked back, so was her mother. It was only her and Zoialynne, both bleeding in different ways. Iskra rushed to her side as a small sob racked her body. Iskra was cruel, and she was sick. She shouldn't have ever let her emotions stop Zoialynne from letting her in. Zoialynne's eyes were shut, the pain obvious on her sweat-stained face.

"Zoialynne, please," Iskra whispered. "I'm sorry."

A small smile touched Zoialynne's face, like a ghost. "No. I'm sorry. I didn't know. The Duke—"

It was obvious she was in pain, but Zoialynne didn't have to say more for

Iskra to understand. Her parents were in the Duke's pocket, wrapped around his finger. How could Iskra have believed the worst in someone who only ever gave Iskra the world? Iskra brought a hand to Zoialynne's face.

Zoialynne breathed in. "You ought to try breathing, Iskra."

Iskra laughed, a tear falling down her pale face. The words she'd told Iskra on the boat now seemed like a distant memory. Iskra watched as Zoialynne smiled, and the look in her eyes was one that Iskra had only ever seen in one place—when they looked out into the vast sea and swore to each other that they'd see each other again soon. It was a look that Iskra knew meant goodbye, and Iskra didn't know how to ask her to stay.

Zoialynne's body stilled beneath her.

She looked so peaceful. Iskra's quiet sobs echoed in the cavernous chamber of a wine cellar, and she wanted the floor to cave in and swallow her whole. She wanted to rip apart the universe. She wanted to break her parents one by one until they knew what this felt like. She wanted to lie next to Zoialynne and tell her all the things she never got to say.

She couldn't do any of that.

Iskra had never known love like the kind she had felt with Zoialynne. *I love you until the stars die,* she thought, because it was what Zoialynne had said her parents told her before she fled to the Americas. Iskra had never been taught to love, never been good at it. But maybe, in another life, she might've loved Zoialynne.

Perhaps, she did now, but she would make a mess of it, if she even tried.

Her tears fell onto the body of someone she'd never see again. Death was a cruel servant of time, taking life whenever it pleased. For it was when a heart began to slow, and the tears began to fall that time stopped caring. The world didn't care that Iskra had been destroyed again, for what did it matter if there was one more broken girl in the world?

"I love you till the stars die," Iskra whispered again because stars are infinite, and perhaps somewhere in the universe, Zoialynne might hear it. *Zoialynne.* The name sounded so sad on her tongue. They'd spent the better part of their life in cages, guarding their hearts against one another; fear, keeping a hand over their hearts. They were assets to each other, Iskra supposed, but somewhere along the line, she couldn't keep her heart in line. Perhaps that made her weak, or perhaps it made her a better person than her parents ever were. Iskra tasted bitterness before, but it was nothing like this. This was an agony she couldn't shake. Iskra bent before someone who'd taught her what it was like to be loved despite how much the world had taught her to hate. Iskra smiled; life was feeble, and she'd live it until she, too, took her last breath, because love was worth living for, even if love and her had never quite gotten along.

Iskra stilled.

Zoialynne couldn't be dead. She would need to report back to the Duke. Her parents would know that, surely. She kept her face schooled should her parents notice her discovery.

Then, she felt the cool tip of metal at her neck.

THIRTY

SÖREN

Sören bounded up the stairs of the manor, kicking his way inside. Iskra and Zoialynne hadn't come out in fifteen minutes, and Sören was beginning to think they might never come out. He prayed to God that he'd made the right choice following Iskra. He shouldn't have. He knew that. But he also knew a thing or two about sinking, and Iskra was barely holding her head above water. Just as he knew he didn't have to be here, he was—he was because he cared all too much about people for his own good. Besides, he'd felt bad for leaving so quickly.

When Iskra passed by the tea shop he'd been sitting in, he'd assumed she'd be going home, but then Iskra had come back out with Zoialynne. And thus, following had ensued. Zoialynne had almost caught him outside the manor, but he'd ducked around a bush just in time for him to pass off as a shadow. Now, as he barged into the entrance hall, his heart was practically in his throat. He'd heard enough to know a trap, and he only hoped he wasn't too late. The sound of an invisible clock chimed off in his head, and he forced himself to ignore it. *Tick, tick, tick.* Sören's head turned sharply, looking into the dining room where a lantern was left on the table. It looked as if it had been burning for quite a while, judging by the wax that pooled at the bottom of its holder, but Sören moved into the room regardless.

Then he saw the gaping hole in the floor.

"Hell," he muttered, scrubbing a hand over his jaw. Iskra would have to repay him for this, perhaps a game of cards which he won, or perhaps simply a large feast in his honour. He cursed before sliding into its shadowy depths. Sliding down was what Sören imagined his time spent under poison would've looked like in his head—starting in the light and watching as the shadows swallowed him whole. He shook his head as if trying to shake his past from him. He landed on a rocky floor with a wince before standing, brushing dirt off his trousers. The room he stood in was cavernous, but his eyes only went to Iskra, who was bent before an unmoving Zoialynne, and the man that stood behind her, who was holding a knife to her neck. The man, he assumed, was Iskra's father, though her mother was nowhere to be seen. Iskra looked nothing like her father, save for the blond hair and posture. Without a second thought, he pulled out his gun and pointed it at the man. Sören hadn't known Iskra long, but he knew her enough to know that this man had hurt her.

"Step away," Sören said, a threat in his tone that masked his fear. He was pointing a gun at what was probably the most influential man in France, let alone the criminal network.

Iskra turned to him, her face tear-stained, and Sören offered what he hoped was a reassuring smile, meeting the panic in hers. His gaze flicked to Iskra's father, who hadn't removed the knife from Iskra's neck.

"I said, step away," Sören repeated, mustering a sense of authority he barely felt. "If you don't speak English, well, I don't know what I'll do, but it'll be bad."

"Stupid boy," Iskra's father muttered. "First, you should address me as *my lord*. Second, you truly must be foolish to get yourself tangled in this. You understand that death will come for you, much as it did for the poor girl." He indicated Zoialynne. Sören noted the blood but forced his eyes back to Lord Storenné, swallowing in a sorry attempt to muster courage as the reality of the situation sunk in. Y*ou have a wild heart, Sören. Don't lose it*—his mother's voice. Long ago, he'd lied, but tonight, he would do no such thing.

Sören placed his finger on the trigger. "Will it? Death and I are close friends, my lord. Threaten me again, and I'll see my good friend comes for your wife next."

The only indication that Sören's words bothered the man was a slight slip of his wolf-like smile. But his mask was back in place before Sören could relish the feeling. Marquess Storenné went to push the blade into Iskra, and Sören's mind cleared, focusing on the tip of the silver—a snake zeroing in on his prey.

Sören pulled the trigger.

The bullet hit the knife, knocking it out of the marquess' hand. Iskra rolled out of the way and stood, her moves effortlessly practiced, despite the way her hands shook. Sören pointed the gun at her father next, gripping it so hard it hurt.

"As you can see, it's difficult for me to miss. Leave my friend alone."

"Stop getting in business between my daughter and I."

Iskra took a step forward, looking at Sören with what he could only describe as agony. "Sören, please—"

But he couldn't hear her over the rush of blood in his head.

"Daughter? Is that what she is to you? That's interesting because the last time I checked, you don't hold blades to your family's neck." Footsteps echoed on the floor above, and the Marquess looked up in horror. Sören only smiled, an imitation of perfect innocence. "Did I forget to mention that I brought along some friends from Scotland Yard? Don't fret. I'm sure they still brew tea in prison."

Marquess Storenné scowled at Sören, a threat that Sören wouldn't forget, but he'd done what was right. Marquess Storenné pushed around Iskra and all but ran for the back of the room where Iskra's mother had appeared behind a stone, holding Zoialynne. It would seem neither of them particularly cared that Zoialynne's blood was dripping onto their finery. Before Sören realized what was happening, the wall turned and then it was as if they were never there.

Sören put his gun back inside his coat and rushed towards Iskra. Her demanding demeanour was replaced by the face of someone who'd watched the world shatter before them, as she crumbled, once more, to the floor. Sören knelt beside her, keeping his distance should she try to bite his head off. She opened her mouth, her shoulders sagging. She looked at him. Her eyes were red-rimmed and swollen, and he pulled a cloth from his coat, handing it to her.

"She's not dead," Iskra said, taking the cloth from him and wiping her nose. "She can't be."

Sören frowned, his heart sinking for her. "Iskra. . ."

He knew what it was like to lose someone. He may have even believed her, but the blood—there'd been too much of it; he didn't need to be a medic to see that.

"*Good Lord.*" Detective Inspector Thornsbury's voice came from the entrance to the cellar. Sören turned to see him taking in the blood where Zoialynne had laid only moments prior. The Inspector's gaze flicked to Iskra and then to Sören, his face morphing into a grim line. Sören nodded, and Thornsbury slowly walked to where they sat and knelt on one knee.

"Loss is cruel to you, isn't it?" he asked, and Sören sat back on his heels. Watching the Inspector speak with such sorrow was something Sören hadn't expected. Iskra turned to the Detective.

"It is to everyone. However, I need you to help me get her back."

Thornsbury frowned. "Miss Storenné—"

"Iskra."

"Right, Iskra. You're in denial. Please allow Sören and I to escort you back to Scotland Yard. My associates can clean up he—"

"Take me. But she cannot be dead. My parents wouldn't disobey Duke Brittenworth."

Detective Inspector Thornsbury turned to Sören. "Parents?"

After a quick trip to Scotland Yard, Iskra gave a description of her parents, though Sören doubted they'd be back for her after today's ordeal. They didn't strike Sören as the kind of people that were to be labelled as fools. The Detective Inspector offered to take them back to Iskra's townhouse. Sören had never been there, but he needed to make sure that Iskra was alright. She'd watched someone she cared for die and was presuming she was alive because of what she thought the Duke's motives are. Sören knew it was foolish to try and argue. He just hoped it wouldn't end up destroying her when she found out she was waiting for a ghost.

Sören plopped himself onto a plush cushion across from the detective, who'd been invited in for tea by Iskra, and accepted the cup Iskra handed to him. He was more of a coffee person, but the tea might help calm his racing mind. It was steaming, but Sören was only half aware of how the mug burnt his skin. He took a deep sip, letting the flavour sit on his tongue before swallowing it. Across the way, the Detective Inspector fiddled with his moustache.

"You know you shouldn't have gone without informing the police," Thornsbury said, taking on a tone that reminded Sören of his father. "What would've happened if Sören hadn't been there?"

"My parents would've played their game, and I would be either rotting or on my way to France. Besides, I'm not sure you get to demolish me for my actions when I've been helping with your investigation."

Detective Inspector Thornsbury sighed. "Stubborn girl. So, get on with it. Explain to me why you and Miss Adrennha were in the manor in the first place."

"Zoialynne told me the Duke had told her that the manor belonged to one of our suspects—"

"But if our suspects are all cleared except for one," The detective trailed off. "You knew it was too good to be true, but you went anyway to make the Duke believe you trusted him. That is why you believed Ms. Adrennha isn't dead, because she needs to report back?"

Iskra nodded. "I must admit, they had me fooled until my mother didn't freak out immediately when she saw the blood. My mother's always had problems with blood. She can't stand to look at it. My father, on the other hand, is a different story, but he didn't put the knife through her, did he?"

Sören nodded, following. "Where would your parents take Zoialynne?"

"The Duke most likely. But I wouldn't try finding her."

Sören gaped at her. "You're just going to leave her in, as far as I know, what are considered enemy hands. What happens when the Duke doesn't need her anymore?"

"Sören is right. It's too risky," Detective Inspector Thornsbury said, taking a sip of his tea.

Iskra leaned her elbows on her knees, steepling her fingers. "Zoialynne is my informant. We know how to get out of sticky situations. I don't know when I'll see her again, but I know that she won't leave this world as easily as a stab to the back."

"Just make sure you aren't waiting around because regret wishes to speak to the dead, alright?" Thornsbury told Iskra, and Sören found himself wishing the same. Iskra nodded, and it was clear their meeting was done. Thornsbury got up to leave, but Sören lingered, watching his friend carefully.

"What is this really about?" he asked.

Iskra looked up at him from where she sat. "Nothing."

Fine. He turned to go.

"Sören?" Iskra called once he was at the door.

He faced her. "Yeah?"

"We need to get that coronet back."

He only nodded. He knew they did. Time was pressing thin, and the longer they waited, the easier it would be for Lady Clara Hollisworth to escape.

Once outside, Detective Inspector Thornsbury told Sören to meet him back at Scotland Yard later to receive the information on Xavier he'd asked him to look into.

"Is everything alright?" Sören asked before the Detective called for a carriage.

"Don't get into a knife fight, Sören."

Sören stared at the Inspector as he tipped his hat before pulling himself into a carriage. The carriage rolled off, and Sören was left to take a long walk back home.

A match was struck and placed inside a lantern, illuminating Xavier's face. Sören stood in the doorway, watching the young lord who'd, once again, found his way inside Sören's home. His father would be home from Scotland Yard soon, and he hated to think what he would do if his father walked into the drawing room where Xavier currently was. He stayed in the doorway for fear of moving any closer to the damnably handsome boy that sat in a chair at the far end of the room.

"It's my understanding," Xavier said, pushing himself from the chair, "that you've had some interesting conversations with the police."

Sören's heart stopped, but quickly resumed a fast pace within his chest. It'd seem he was forgetting how to breathe. "Have I? You do know I'm working to solve your brother's murder?"

"I do, which is all well and good. What I have an issue with is you looking into me."

Sören swore, wishing Detective Inspector Thornsbury had informed him what exactly Xavier was guilty of. Certainly, he didn't look like a criminal, but Sören also knew that many people wore masks to protect those shattered souls beneath.

"I have issues with," Xavier stuck a hand into his coat pocket, "you not trusting me. I've done nothing to make you believe otherwise. We have a deal, remember?"

Sören crossed his arms, his elbow hitting the doorframe. "Xavier, you must know that you know too much for me not to take precautions."

"Precautions? I have a past, Sören. That doesn't make me any worse than you." Xavier crossed the room and stopped only a few feet away. "That said, why should you think me untrustworthy?"

"Because you've been holding onto a knife for this entire conversation, and I know for a fact that my father's crime accusations were entirely in a secret conference room to protect the Yard from the news. So, you nor your father could've known unless you did something."

Xavier pulled the knife from his coat, setting it on the side table next to the chair he'd been in. "You'll never learn to love, will you?"

Xavier swept from the room, and only when he heard the door close did Sören sink onto the floor. His mind was reeling because Xavier had done something, and it couldn't be good if the innocent-seeming boy clutched a knife in secret. *Even the devil can wear a smile.* He rose from the floor and picked up the knife Xavier had left behind. Sören shuddered, not because of the action itself, but because it meant one thing. He couldn't trust Xavier. And, unfortunately, Sören had already made the mistake of falling.

THIRTY - ONE

AURA

Aura fiddled with the fabric of her skirts, watching as the Nighvengales spoke with the Mortsakovs. Something about the pair made Aura uneasy as she lifted a glass to her lips and drank swiftly. She made eye contact with Lock across the table, whose face was unreadable. It'd seem that their presence had shocked him as much as it did her. For all the years she'd known Lock, she hadn't seen the Nighvengale's once.

So why now?

Marquess Nighvengale barked a laugh at something Lock's father had said, and Aura jumped, a shiver running down her spine. *What was wrong with her?* Marquess Nighvengale was a slender man with spectacles resting on his pale face and brown curls hanging over his forehead. His wife, the marchioness, was similar in complexion, save for the lighter brown of her hair. Aura had never seen the couple in person, only heard about them, like most people. They were the whispers that waltzed around London's streets—the shadows that danced with the ghosts. Lock's gaze on Marquess Nighvengale was hard, and Aura couldn't help but think there was something he knew that she didn't.

"Miss Wrentroth, is it?"

The voice startled her as she met Marchioness Nighvengale's gaze, her hand resting on her husband's arm. "Yes. Please, call me Aura."

"Aura, it is. Please, call me," she paused like she was at war with her mind. "Lady Nighvengale."

It was a strange notion to think that Aura should call her anything other than that. Perhaps she wasn't used to speaking with people such as Aura, as that was the only explanation she could come up with.

"Miss Wrentroth," Marquess Nighvengale asked, ignoring her comment to call her Aura. "Might I ask how Rien is? The last time I saw him, he was carving out a cadaver in the study hall of a university."

"I didn't realize you knew each other. He's well." *And a liar*, she added in her mind, but did not say out loud. Marquess Nighvengale nodded before taking a bite of the food before him. She cast a glance at Lady Nighvengale, only to see her already watching Aura, fiddling with a red ring on her middle finger.

"Apologies," Lady Nighvengale said. "I was simply admiring your dress. It truly is very elegant. I wonder how many knives you could hide within it."

She nearly knocked her glass over. Across the table, Lock stood from his chair to catch the glass, but it only teetered. Aura felt as though she, too, was spinning—the Nighvengale's couldn't know about her past as the Queen of Spades, about the blood on her hands.

"You must forgive my wife. She does have a sense of morbid fascination."

The couple shared a look as Aura nodded, her heartbeat quickening. She smiled, "I don't think you'd want to wear a knife in this dress, my lady. You wouldn't want to risk cutting yourself."

The Marchioness returned the smile. "I'm sure you're right. That'd be the sensible thing to do."

Aura felt her breath return to its usual pace. She dared a glance at Lock, who gave her an encouraging nod and patted his coat where Aura's knife was being kept safe from the tortures of Twisted magic.

And safe from her.

"Might I ask you a favour?" Marquess Nighvengale asked. It sounded like a bargain from Hell, but Aura gestured for him to continue regardless. "First, you're investigating the Duke's case, yes?"

A nod.

"Lovely. I'd like you both to stop investigating. Trust me, you don't know what you're getting into. The Order of Crowns is filled with *danger*, and I don't want any of you to get caught in their crossfire."

Aura wanted nothing more than to tell the marquess she'd drop it, but Aura had seen it this far, and there was no amount of threat that would get her to stop. She needed the coronet. *Lock* needed it. She and Lock exchanged a glance but didn't remark on the Marquess's comment. It didn't look like he wanted one either, seeing as he'd quickly turned back to his conversation with Lock's father about business. How nice it must be to think they'd speak, and people would obey. Aura fought the urge to roll her eyes as she picked up her glass and took a long sip, hoping that it might wash down the unladylike remark she was considering giving the arrogant devil of a man.

The rest of dinner passed in painful stabs to the brain. Aura desperately wished to run from the room, although the Nighvengale's didn't attempt to address her again. Instead, she endured a polite, if not awkward, conversation with Lock's mother about how her most recent scientific studies were fairing. She was glad that, despite the presence of the marchioness and marquess, Lock's family was still as comforting as they'd ever been with her, which wasn't much, but it was something.

After the last course had been served, they'd retreated to the drawing room, where she and Lock quickly excused themselves, leaving for a much-needed walk. Lock had helped her into her coat before tugging on a pair of gloves and leaving the cursed atmosphere behind them. The night air was crisp, a cool wind blowing down the streets, playing with her skirts. She stuffed her hands into her coat and tucked her chin into the collar. Streetlamps lit the pavement, a luminescence that Aura was grateful for with the dark skies above. Despite the street being nearly empty, Aura could hear the effervescent sounds coming from a few blocks over—people, out for the night, gaudy with drinks or their friends. They walked in silence, and Aura let her thoughts slip away as if they might be taken away by the wind. The Nighvengale's had known they were investigating Kian's murder, so either they had the Duke's ear, or they were more present in society than everyone thought they were. Surely, the Duke wouldn't associate with the marchioness and marquess, considering at dinner, they'd made their views clear on what they thought of the Order. *The Order of Crowns is filled with danger.* Aura should think with their views that they might stand a chance of fitting into the Society. That was improbable, considering if the Nighvengale's had the Twisted on their side, London would've started burning a long time ago.

"Aura," Lock started, dragging her from her thoughts. "I'm very sorry for tonight. I didn't know that the Nighvengale's would show up, and I certainly didn't know that you'd be invited to such an odd dinner."

Aura smiled out at the street. "It's not your fault. I'm rather unnerved, but I suppose the Nighvengale's have that effect on people."

He chuckled. "That they do. Did I tell you about the time I got into a fight with the marquess in his carriage house?"

"What?"

"Apparently, trespassing is not something someone enjoys. Long story short, I put him to sleep."

"Lock, you cannot just put the most influential man in London to sleep,"

"And you cannot simply stand there looking that lovely, yet here you are."

They passed into shadows—a break between the street lamps—and Aura was grateful Lock couldn't see the way a blush crept up into her cheeks. She didn't notice Lock had stopped walking, looking back the way they came until she was quite a few paces ahead him. She was about to call to him when an arm reached out from the shadows of the alleyway beside her, locking its grip around her neck. She kicked backward, but they dodged her attempt. The shadowy figure was quite a deal taller than her, an advantage she didn't enjoy. It felt like the air was running out. *Fight*, her head screamed, but her mind was hazy. Twisted magic, she knew, yet she didn't have the energy to try and ward it off. The smell of rich cologne clogged her senses, and she stifled the urge to cough. The shadowy figure used their free hand to shove a letter at her feet.

"Power is created by words that cut and actions that push the dagger further; you should do good not to envy it," they whispered before letting her go and running in the opposite direction. Aura all but collapsed, gasping for air, picking up the letter with shaking hands. No one should know that saying. Her father had taken it to the grave with him—it was the only thing she remembered about him. Not how he looked, not his love. That saying—death had allowed her to keep. Her heart slammed against her chest in a fast rhythm. She stuffed the letter into her coat pocket just as Lock's footsteps echoed around her, and before she knew what was happening, he was kneeling before her, searching her face.

"Are you hurt?" he asked, his voice panicked.

"No." It was all she could manage to say.

Lock swore violently before muttering something about "giving the fool a piece of his mind," and Aura thought about telling him it would be no use, but Lock was already sprinting in the direction her attacker had departed. She walked slowly to stand beneath a streetlamp, and with still-shaking hands, she pulled out the letter, unfolding it.

Aura's heart stopped.

In fact, she was quite sure the world around her was starting to go black. It was a correspondence between Lord Nighvengale and Rien.

Dear Rien,

The use of first names caught Aura off guard, despite the marquess mentioning they'd known each other—another fact Rien had failed to inform her of.

Our world is becoming much too dangerous for our daughter. Our demons are catching up, and I cannot think what I shall do should any harm come to her. I've seen how you care, your heart is wide, and you have a safety that Liza and I cannot provide. Our daughter has a curious mind, as you know, and I think she should do good at all that science you preach of. Do keep her from the blood, my friend. Regarding your previous correspondence, Liza and I will disappear, leaving you the rightful inheritors, and I will contact you when the devils have left us. Rien, you're a good man, and I leave you one piece of advice for our daughter. Please, don't let her believe she is anything less than loved. See you Sunday,

Charles Nighvengale.
February 10, 1871

Aura stared at the letter, the date only seven days after her birthday. *Our daughter.* She shook her head and was about to read the letter again when a slip of paper fell out of the envelope.

Aura Elizabeth Nighvengale
Born February 3, 1871
Rightful parents: Marquess Charles Nighvengale, Marchioness Liza Nighvengale
Parent of tragedy: Rien Wrentroth

No, no, no, no. Aura was used to tricks, but this was cruel. This was a sick hoax, but the evidence was hard to ignore. Her heart was once again beating against her rib cage. She feared it might fall out. She put both letters into the envelope and shoved them into her pocket, hoping to burn them when she had the chance. There was absolutely no way she could be related to the people who she'd sat in a dining room with not less than half an hour prior. She supposed she should feel relief that her parents weren't dead and that they were truly here. But she felt none of that. The buildings around her seemed to close in, the bricks ready to smash her to pieces.

Liar, liar, liar.

The words pounded in her head, anger twisting itself within her. Her parents were liars. Her parents had run, left her, and Rien had been left with Aura to manage the world all alone. Rien had been a good parent, and she'd lived without the lord and lady for so long. Why on earth would they come to her now? Lock jogged around the corner, his breath heavy and jaw set in a hard line. He suggested they return home, and Aura agreed, but in truth, she would rather go to Hell itself than have to sit in the room with the closest thing to the devil on earth. Lock offered his arm to her, and she took it, holding onto it more tightly, but if he noticed, he didn't say anything. Aura was grateful for the warmth shared between them and the invisible string that bound them together because she wasn't sure what she would do if she had to face her parents alone. *Parents.* The word tasted bitter.

"My lovely Aura," Lock said, pausing and turning her to face him, and for a moment, she forgot all about her anger. "Your vexation is slicing me in the heart. Might you share what plagues you?"

"When we return to London."

He nodded, and they quickened their pace back to the manor where they made work of saying goodbye before hopping into a carriage and travelling back to Lock's townhouse. Aura had avoided the Nighvengale's gaze; she could hardly even look at them, even if she wanted to.

The Mortsakov's library in Lock's townhouse was extravagant and just the place she needed to find peace. Located on the second floor, it had four walls of books filled with stories. A soft seating area was arranged in the centre, a chandelier illuminating the space. Aura stood near the large window that overlooked the brick wall next door, it wasn't much of a view, but she didn't feel like sitting down, not while her mind raced. The door clattered open behind her, and she spun to see Lock carrying in a tea set and placing it on the table. Aura smiled softly before turning her attention back to the window.

"'Power is created by words that cut and actions that push the dagger further. You should do good not to envy it'," she quoted, and Lock moved up beside her. "That's what my father said in his will. That's what the stranger tonight told me before running off."

Lock frowned. "How should they know if it was in your father's will?"

"That's a question I don't have an answer for. However, I have a sick feeling that they will." She pulled the letters from her pocket and handed them to him. She crossed her arms, watching as he read it. His face was etched into a frown, his dark hair falling onto his brow. If this moment wasn't so filled with the venom she felt towards the truth, she might've taken more time to admire him. He met her eyes a moment later, his eyes sorry.

"Aura, where did you get this?"

"The stranger gave it to me, but I've thought about all the ways that could be forged. None of it makes any sense. That is my real name, real birthdate; I can't bring myself to forgive them."

"Do they even know that you know?"

She didn't and told Lock as much. He paced the room for a few excruciating moments. "If they don't know that you know, we won't say anything. They lied to you. They let you believe they were dead, and as far as I'm concerned, I don't think they can expect you to forgive them. I just don't want them to pull you into their waters because of your blood." He took long strides towards her. "I won't let them."

"I know." She shook her head. "It'd seem lying runs in the family."

"Don't say that. You know very well your situations were different. They didn't need to fake their death, that's quite extreme." He brought his hands to her face, and Aura relished the feeling. His dark eyes were steady as he looked down at her.

"My lovely Aura, no matter what happens, I will be here. You have overtaken my heart, and if I must destroy myself to see your suffering end, then so be it." Aura smiled, her heart pounding inside her chest. He smiled. "Plus, how is someone going to teach you how to dance if I'm not here?"

Aura rolled her eyes. "You know very well that I'm a good dancer."

He removed his hands from her face and walked to the tea set, pouring two cups. She moved to sit on the couch and accepted the tea he handed to her. She took a sip, and he looked as though he was about to say something, but a knock sounded at the door. Lock sighed and made his way to the door, his long stride sending him across the room in seconds.

Lock came back a moment later, looking grim.

"Detective Inspector Thornsbury is here," he told her. "Rien has been arrested."

THIRTY - TWO

LOCK

Detective Inspector Thornsbury showed Lock and Aura to his office on the upper floor of Scotland Yard. It was relatively large, with wooden panelling and a desk that stood at one end of the room. Iskra and Sören sat in two of the four chairs that had been placed on the other side of his desk, each with matching expressions of confusion. Aura hadn't had the chance to tell them about Rien, but by the looks of it, they wouldn't have had time to hear it. Iskra's lip sported dried blood, and Sören's outfit looked slightly ruffled, and Lock could only begin to guess what had happened since he'd last seen them. Detective Inspector Thornsbury shut the door behind them and drew the blinds on the windows to his office, letting the silence stretch thin. Lock, who'd been holding Aura's hand since the Inspector had called on them, let go as Aura moved to sit in a chair. He took the one beside her as the Detective Inspector took a seat with a sigh across from him. He looked weary; the last time Lock had seen him, his hair had been neatly kept, and his suit had been pristine. Now, his hair stuck up on odd ends as he twirled his moustache with a finger, his suit jacket wrinkled, and his eyes sported dark circles. Lock didn't know the inspector well, but he knew him well enough to know that he'd been working harder than usual. Sören seemed to notice it too, as he instinctively started to clean off the desk for the detective, separating the papers into neat piles.

Lock hadn't known Sören to clean up other people's messes, but he supposed the detective was a friend. Detective Inspector Thornsbury smiled slightly at Sören's attempt to make him look put together, and Lock suspected that he hadn't had many people treat him the way Sören did. Beside him, Aura shifted uncomfortably, playing with the fabric of her skirts, mouth pressed into a thin line.

"You said Rien—" Aura started, pausing to collect herself. Lock went to reach for her hand but paused to see she already held Iskra. Lock settled back into his chair, the ghost of a smile touching his lips. Iskra had never been one to show affection, but something had changed, and if Lock didn't know better, it would seem she was treating them like the world was about to end. At that thought, he frowned but didn't ponder it further because the Detective Inspector dropped his hand onto the desk and nodded.

"He killed Lady Hollisworth."

Lock sucked in a breath, an invisible bullet striking the room into shock.

"What?"

"He was arrested late this afternoon, shortly after I came to get you and Lock. He turned himself in, in fact. He brought the cloak, the handkerchief, and he confessed to killing Hollisworth and framing Elsder, all because he wanted the Order for himself—he explained how he couldn't live with himself after you found out about a woman named, and he was specific about this, Levensmith. He was on about something to do with not wanting to watch Kian destroy the world and his new wife would not get the power of the Order. He explained that he hired the Twisted to cover his tracks to protect you. He confessed to passing along the coronet to make you believe it was the prized motive. And finally, he said he was sorry—that he couldn't be the person your parents expected him to be."

"Everything he told you is a lie. You must know that?" Aura asked, tears welling in her eyes, and this time Lock did reach out and take her other hand. "You must know that he's a part of some cruel scheme. I thought he was guilty, I did, but hearing him say it, confess to it, he wouldn't. He helps solve the puzzle of death, not cause it."

Detective inspector Thornsbury looked at her with sorrowful eyes. "We had no choice."

Lock thought Aura would argue, but she did not. She didn't move, only stared blankly at the desk, her expression unreadable. His magic flared for just a moment to feel enough pain to drown the entire office. He squeezed her hand, and she squeezed back; a sign she was holding on above the waves. She stood suddenly and began pacing the room.

"What if they put the Twisted up to this?"

Lock frowned, as did the rest of them, watching as her skirts billowed with her hurried strides from one end of the room to the other.

"Who did?" the detective asked.

"My parents." Aura turned to Lock. "What if this was their way of making sure we stay off the case because they figure I'll accept that Rien did it."

He supposed it was plausible, and he considered it when Sören chimed in.

"Aura, your parent—"

"Are dead?" Aura shook her head, nodding at Lock. He slipped the piece of paper from his coat pocked and passed the letter to Sören, who read it along with Thornsbury and Iskra. Iskra swore in French, and Lock felt the same way when he'd found out. Aura continued pacing the room.

Thornsbury sat back in his chair. "That was unexpected."

"Imagine them showing up to dinner," Lock muttered.

Thornsbury looked at the letter. "I suppose it's possible. However, like I told Sören, the Nighvengale's, and I suppose by extension, you, are some of the most powerful people in London. We couldn't accuse them of anything even if we wanted to."

"What about Hollisworth?" Iskra asked, her accent thick. "She was a strong suspect. In fact, we are pretty sure she'd done it after all of that."

Detective Inspector Thornsbury grimaced. "About that—"

He then explained where he'd been all afternoon. The Detective, along with a couple of constables, had been assigned to bring Clara in for questioning. Only when they got there, Clara Hollisworth's door was open, and they entered cautiously. It was then that they found her in her drawing room, a knife through her leg where the detective thought it'd hit the femoral artery causing her to bleed to death.

Lock sat back; his chest heavy. Out of all the news he'd expected to hear, that hadn't been one of them, and her death made it look like Rien really was the culprit—that he was a murderer. The more Lock thought about it, it was clear that Rien was being framed. He would never do anything for power, not ever, and certainly not to rid the world of its flames, because that'd already been done long before. Besides, murderers didn't tell a suitor to ask their niece instead. They didn't laugh and hug their niece when finding out the truth about her secret classes. They didn't let their apprentice learn all the skills they would need to deduce their crimes. Only a fool would do that. Detective Inspector Thornsbury explained how their inspection team spent hours looking for a clue, and that was when Rien Wrentroth showed up on the steps of Scotland Yard preaching his sins. Aura all but fell back into her chair, shaking her head.

"This cannot be. There's an answer, and I just can't figure it out." She rested her head in her hands.

"Then I suppose it's very good you don't have to do it alone," Sören said, rising.

"Where are you going?" Iskra asked.

"To get some tea. In the meantime, Thornsbury? Might you pull out the files on the case?"

Detective Inspector Thornsbury nodded before pushing back from his chair and walking over to one of the many file cabinets in the corner of the room. Lock turned to Aura, whose hand had found his, and stroked it with his thumb. He knew that she blamed herself, but for what? He had no idea. Iskra turned to face both of them.

"I have a lot to catch you up on, but I do have a quick question."

"Go on," Lock said.

Iskra turned so that she addressed Aura. "Would you wish to be called Lady Nighven—"

"No." Aura's response was precise, but Lock understood. He didn't particularly like being called a lord—it was all too formal. Though, he suspected Aura's reasons for not wanting the title had more to do with her dislike for her parents and less with the formality. Lock tapped his free hand against his knee. For the first time, it was sinking in that she wasn't Aura Wrentroth, she was Aura Nighvengale, and even though it didn't matter to him, it felt odd. Aura would always be the girl he knew, regardless of the last name, and he smiled, but it only lasted for a split second as a horrible thought struck his mind. He was going to have to ask the devil himself for his daughter's hand, and that was horrifying enough, especially after the way he left things the last time, magic and all. He swallowed, putting that out of his mind. He needed to focus, to solve this mystery before they found themselves lost in a maze of emotions. Detective Inspector Thornsbury dropped the files onto the desk, six in total: One for each Lord and lady, one for the Order, and one for information that seemed to connect, but they didn't know where to. As the Detective Inspector explained each folder, Lock saw a glimmer of the usual detective, the kind that'd light up at the chance for some good organization. Iskra reached across the desk and picked up Clara Hollisworth's folder. In bold letters, she scribbled two words onto the paper: *Décédé, deceased.* Lock frowned. Even if Hollisworth had been the murderer, he supposed it hardly mattered because someone had killed her.

Detective Inspector Thornsbury stared at Iskra's writing. "You just ruined a perfectly good folder."

"With the French language? *Non.* If anything, I made it better."

Thornsbury crossed his arms, but a smirk played at the corners of his lips.

It was, he decided, the closest that Lock had ever seen to a smile. Sören burst through the door carrying a tea tray, and Aura laughed at the sight of him. Lock looked to see him, his chin stuck in the top teacup for balance, as he walked, a step at a time, towards the desk. He smiled at Aura's momentary happiness, and it swelled within him. He recalled his words to her earlier this afternoon. *You have overtaken my heart, and if I must destroy myself to see your suffering end, then so be it.* He meant those words and would always mean them. Her happiness was most important to him, and although hope felt lost amongst the piles of paper before them, he'd make sure this investigation was done right. If not for Kian, if not for him, then for Aura, because she deserved to look at the world with ambition again. She deserved it. Her happiness would always mean more than any title he had or any trouble they faced. She deserved to be happy, just as much as Iskra deserved to be free from expectation, and Sören to shed his past.

If not for Kian, then for them.

If not now, then never.

And Lock wasn't one with the term *never* in his vocabulary. Beside him, Aura stood, helping Sören pour the tea, the smell of peppermint reaching his nose. The delicate sounds of papers flipping reached his ears, and at that moment, Lock wouldn't want to be anywhere else. Aura handed him a teacup, and he accepted with a nod as he reached for one of the files. It was going to be a late night tonight, but it would be worth it if the people he cared for found hope again —if he found it again. Detective Inspector Thornsbury took a sip of his tea and sighed before he flipped open a file. Silence fell over the group, and Lock silently prayed that this would lead to something, lead to anything that might set their passion alive and their doubt to flames. *If we let the doubt take us, then we've already given up*, he thought, and this time he truly did believe it.

Iskra slammed a file back down on the desk, startling Lock. He'd been quite invested in the Duke's recount of the party when Kian had died; it was slightly romanticized, but other than that, it was accurate. The clock had long since struck midnight, his teacup emptied, and the pounding in his head had started to worsen — he wouldn't have much longer before everything went black. Aura, who'd been practically falling asleep in her chair, snapped at the sudden ruckus, and Sören let out a snore. Iskra lightly slapped his cheek, and Sören glared at her through half-open eyes. Detective Inspector Thornsbury looked at them as if they were all children but sat up straighter.

"Inspector, is Lady Elsder still in the holding cells?"

Thornsbury shook his head. "Afraid not. We let her go after Rien confessed. We had no choice. Why?"

"You didn't release her after you found out the coronet was false?"

"No. I wanted to ask her a few more questions. Then, Rien turned himself in. Again, why do you ask?"

Iskra rose from her chair, spreading the pieces of Lady Erika Elsder's file onto the desk. "This whole time, I've been pondering the question of motive. It's obvious that the coronet is what everyone is after. I think that the murderer's goal was never to *marry* Kian but to kill him for it. Presumably for its power, symbolically or magically, it's hard to say. My suspicion was further confirmed when you explained what Rien said."

Beside Lock, Aura shut her eyes, her face stilling in concentration. "'He confessed to passing along the coronet to make you believe it was the prized motive.'"

Lock recognized them as Detective Inspector Thornsbury's words. Aura opened her eyes.

"There was never a question on if the coronet was the motive. We knew it was. I believe that Rien phrased that carefully, to give us a hint."

"A hint to what?" Sören asked, crossing his arms.

"If Erika believed the coronet she had was the real thing, it would be a disappointment if the police took it away. She must've then taken out Hollisworth, who was in danger of getting in the way. Because Rien was in contact with the Yard and the mortician on the case, he would've been in the perfect position to claim *he* murdered Hollisworth in order to help us."

Lock understood. Rien had delivered the answer to them on a silver platter: power, the lengths that one was willing to go to get it. That was why Erika had wanted Kian and why she wanted the coronet. Lock nodded slowly. "And the only way to catch her is to give her what she wants."

Lock made eye contact with Detective Inspector Thornsbury, who rubbed a hand over his face.

"Dear Inspector," he started.

"You want the coronet to set a trap, don't you?" Thornsbury asked, once again fiddling with his moustache.

"Smart man."

"It's evidence. I cannot. My superiors will be furious, and I will lose my job."

"And I'm apparently the daughter of the most influential people that can stop that from happening," Aura said, rubbing at the tiny scars on her knuckles from the incident on the train.

Detective Inspector Thornsbury stared at her as if trying to decide if she was serious. In the end, he seemed to trust her as he pushed up from his desk with a sigh.

"The things I do for you—"

"Because you love us," Sören interrupted.

Amusement sparkled in Thornsbury's eyes as he left, shutting the door behind him. Lock wished that their plan worked because if it didn't, he didn't know what they would do. Then again, it had to work. He wouldn't accept any other option. Iskra reached around Aura and squeezed his shoulder, giving him a nod. He rolled his eyes at her.

"I thought we spoke about reading my thoughts," he said.

Iskra shrugged. "I didn't mean to. Besides, at least you were thinking something good."

Sören snorted just as Thornsbury strode back into the room, a piece of paper in his hands.

"You better hope this plan works because Rien is gone from the holding cells, and I'm afraid I don't have time to ask for permission."

Lock shook his head, a smile growing on his face. Yes, it had to work. Any other option for saving the ones he cared for was unacceptable. And even if it didn't, they'd find another way because that was what they did. They would keep trying until the calculation was perfect, and there was no room for error.

And they'd fight, broken pasts, unshed tears, stained hands, and all because they had no other choice. Too much hope was dangerous to have, but tonight he should wield it like a weapon.

The carriage rattled past the darkened streets of London as they began their journey to a storehouse the Yard used for ambushes like these. They'd made a real show of Thornsbury handing them the coronet and loading it into the carriage. The Inspector himself would be riding with constables and had gone ahead to await their arrival at the storehouse—a place where it was estimated that Erika would be waiting for them.

The coronet, stored safely in a box, sat beside Lock and Iskra with Aura and Sören on the other side. Silence had placed its blanket over the group, and Lock checked out the carriage window every so often to make sure they weren't being followed. Soon, they left the main London streets, and empty fields took the place of the buildings. Lock's heart beat fast as he dared yet another glance out the window. The night would soon give way to morning, and the city would awake with no idea of their reckless plan. A shadow danced in the distance but drew closer. A carriage, much like the one they rode in, came up the rear. He frowned.

A gunshot rang out into the silent night.

Lock glanced at Sören, who already hugged his own firearm tightly, ready to fire. The carriage drew closer until it was parallel to theirs. Lock could just make out a large black cloak as they aimed their gun for the window. Lock saw Iskra pull the coronet into her lap. One shot, directed at their driver, who screamed in agony as the horses began to slow.

The carriage tipped.

Lock didn't even think as their perpetrator aimed the gun a second time. He dove for Aura just as the carriage severed.

The gun fired as he wrapped his arms around her.

Then, the world disappeared.

PART THREE
HERE LIES: LOVE

Emmaline Leigh

THIRTY - THREE

SÖREN

Smoke filled the carriage, and an ear-splitting noise filled the cabin. Sören groaned as he clambered out of the carriage, blood trailing down the side of his face where he'd hit it when the conveyance had tipped. Iskra stumbled out after him, her arm clutched to her chest, followed by Lock and Aura, who looked as though they'd seen death—Sören was sure they all had. He laid on the ground, unable to move; it felt as though he'd bruised a rib. He stared at the greying sky, trying to figure out where it had gone wrong. The coronet was in the hands of the enemy, their horse circling to finish them. Except that it wasn't the real coronet—and that if Erika was behind this, her desperation was making her mad. Detective Inspector Thornsbury would be waiting for ghosts, and his future would be ruined. Sören would've failed at proving to his past that he was more than his pain.

Beside him, Iskra tried to sit up, but collapsed again. A slight wince and a French curse escaped from her mouth. He heard Lock mutter something in Russian, though he didn't even know Lock knew the language. Sören shut his eyes, remembering the face of a blond boy as handsome as he had ever seen. *You'll never learn to love, will you?* He'd asked, and Sören stayed silent because he had. He had found the beauty in life, fallen for forgiveness and played games with fate. If death called on him again, he would leave with no regrets. Because regret, he found, were the words that reminded him to act differently next time, and if not now, then in the heavens.

A hand dug into his shoulder, and his eyes opened to see Iskra looking at him, a single tear streaking down her face. He didn't need to speak to know she'd heard his thoughts, and she didn't need to speak for him to understand she knew —knew the cruelty of the world and that all it took was one person to distract from it. His hand found hers, and he was surprised when her fingers didn't move to let go. Sören offered her a weak smile before turning his face to the sky once more. Around him, a thousand butterflies swarmed, showing him the kind heart of the world before the pain took his body. Their red wings flapped, and Sören could no longer see the darkness of their attacker nor the sound of the horse he had ridden upon.

Was he dying?

He squinted as a butterfly floated before him.

He blinked.

There were no butterflies, but an army of coated magicians beyond fighting their attacker.

A figure in a crimson high collared coat stood above him. It was double breasted, silver buttons in the shape of what appeared to be the suits of cards, starting at the waist and trailing up to the collar. Their face was concealed by a sheer red veil, eyes covered by a strip of crimson lace, but Sören could've sworn he felt a look of impatience pass over their features.

"I'm not sure how long we can hold them off, sir. It should do you and your friends good to get out of here."

Sören smiled. "Right, because it's easy to walk with your head spinning. Who are you?"

"That doesn't matter." Their voice was sweet and reminded him of a voice he'd almost forgotten. A voice who'd sung him to sleep—a voice that had sung one last time while he was too far to hear it.

The figure muttered something about "doing this here," and then Sören was dragged into a magical showing—a stage set to show the truth, as the blue haze of Optical magic filled his vision. He'd never been shown an Optical event before, only heard about them. He stood in a dining room, a long table stretched, taking up the length of the room. A man with a pale face and straight blond hair sat at a table across from a Scotland Yard officer. The man seemed to be muttering to himself as if he were praying. The officer flipped open a book.

"Go on, tell me what happened."

"She's gone, sir. My wife—" The man shook his head. "When I woke up, she was gone, her stuff still here—all but a dagger. I don't know where she would be, but yesterday she mentioned something about meeting with a man named A.N. Catcherheart."

The officer scribbled in his notes. "And who is this, A.N. Catcherheart?"

"I don't know."

The officer nodded again before standing to leave. "We'll set out a search."

Sören knew that might as well be the same as saying they wouldn't even begin to look into it. Not with the evidence comprised of a gentleman's word, they had nothing tangible.

"Sir, one more thing?"

"Yes?"

"I think she's gone insane. Playing with the damned, she is."

The blue haze lifted, and Sören was back in reality, staring up at the sky. The cut on his head had been bandaged and he slowly, if somewhat painfully, pushed himself into a sitting position. Lock and Aura were already sitting, the blue light fading, bloody hands clasped in each other's. Iskra rocked herself to sitting and winced, muttering to herself. Sören squeezed her hand before letting go, but paused when he saw the letter before him, and it was only then that he realized that the red coats were gone, with their attacker collapsed on the floor. With careful fingers, Sören picked it up, now used to the sinking feeling in his stomach.

```
A clue.
Now run.
```

Sören read it to the others, his voice hoarse. Iskra plucked the letter from his hands to read it for herself while Sören pushed himself to standing, ignoring the pain that shot through him. Certainly, when this was done, he'd need to find himself an infirmary. The others stood on shaky legs, and Sören felt as though he, too, might be on the verge of collapsing again. His head spun as he looked at their destroyed carriage, the dead driver hunched over in the front seat, and the horses having calmed a few strides away. While their attackers' carriage remained in tatters, their horses were fine, if not shaken. *Think*, he scolded himself. Now wasn't the time to be of no use. There were four horses in total—an idea popped into his head. Sören told his plan to the others and slowly walked to get the other two horses so they could continue to their destination. Sören's bones were weary, but a setback didn't mean they were done. One thing was clear: whoever had sent that Twisted had fallen for their trap, just not in the way they had expected. And now, if they wanted the coronet, the enemies were going to have to pry it from their fingers. Even if it wasn't real, they still had something Erika needed. Sören reached the horses, stroking them gently with his fingers, letting them know that it was over. It was as much a reassurance for the animals as it was for him.

Footsteps approached behind him, and he turned to see Lock. His face was cut, blood dripping from the corner of his brow, trailing down the side of his face. Some was dried against the corner of his mouth, and he smiled, his hair in wild disarray. Sören thought he looked half-insane. Clearly, the red coats hadn't deemed his wounds severe enough. His jacket was torn slightly, and Sören noted that he'd probably got the brunt of the damage when he'd blocked Aura. He continued stroking the horse as Lock stopped beside him, smile fading.

"You know that we wouldn't have let you die, right?"

The question made Sören pause. Out of all the things he'd been expecting, that hadn't been one of them. "Of course. Why?"

Lock crossed his arms. "Because you were ready to let go back there. I'm not sure if you notice, Sören, but we're as much your family as your own father is, if not more. I just wanted to make it clear that regardless of who you've been and who you're going to become, we have no plans to pretend our friendship with you didn't happen after our investigation is over. We're not cruel."

Sören smiled. "I know that, don't worry. And back there, I could've let go, but it wasn't my time. Death has made that clear. Besides, I care too much to leave."

Lock let out a laugh. "Maybe on our way to Thornsbury you might explain to us why I felt regret bouncing off you for a split second."

"I don't have to. All you need to know is that I fall for danger, and it'll be my downfall."

Lock frowned. It was clear he didn't understand what Sören meant, but Sören wasn't going to offer up any more details. The lord looked as though he was going to say more, but Sören was already grabbing the horses and leading them back towards Iskra and Aura, who were checking the reins on the other horses. Sören handed the reins to Aura, who offered to check them, while Iskra picked the box off the floor, checking to see if the false coronet was still inside. She nodded in reassurance, and a silence descended over the group: the kind of silence that came with loss, although they hadn't truly lost anything. Their plan had been thrown away by something different than what they'd expected, but that was no reason to mourn. They still had the chance to get to Thornsbury with the coronet. Hope had wound itself around them like a promise, only to let go when they needed it most.

"Are we going to speak about who those people were and what they showed us?" Iskra asked.

"When it's safer," Lock told her, and Sören agreed. They needed to focus on getting the box to safety before they could focus on their saviours and the people who were sending them those mysterious letters. Sören turned, his hands gripping the saddle, ready to mount. In truth, he hadn't ridden since he was a child, but this would have to do. Memories of a life he had forgotten flashed before his eyes: his mother teaching him, their rides in the English countryside, all things that had seemed insignificant but had left a gaping hole in his heart after she had passed.

A pain in his neck.

The world around him spun, and as he went to reach for his neck, he found darkness surrounding him once more, like an old friend. He should be afraid, but it wrapped itself around him like a hug, pulling him gently to the floor. It was an odd source of comfort; the kind one gets when they've read something that they've read before or done something so routine they forgot how they used to live without it. Blindness threatened to take him, and the last thing he saw was their attacker pocketing a package of throwing darts, blood running down the front of his stiff-collared shirt, and Sören could have sworn he was looking at Death himself.

THIRTY - FOUR

ISKRA

Iskra was remembering a life that seemed so distant from her own. She felt her hands tied behind her, though it was the only thing she registered as she was dragged under. She was remembering a life where the waves had been her home, her worries were left in France, and a girl with a kind smile stood beside her on a ship's promenade. Her head felt hazy, and she found herself wishing she was back there now.

"What happens when we dock? I know you've found work, and it's selfish of me to ask, but would you allow me the honour of asking you to help burn down my parents' empire?" Iskra remembered asking, desperately wishing that she didn't have to get off the boat.

"Iskra, I've spent my past playing with fire, and I don't want to do it again. While I must refuse your invitation, I can offer you a piece of advice." Zoialynne had turned to face her then, bringing her mouth close to Iskra's ear. Iskra's heart stopped, only to pick up its erratic rhythm. "Be careful not to get burned."

A chill involuntary wound its way down Iskra's spine, and she refrained from hugging her arms around herself.

Maybe it was the idea of their hearts becoming forgotten amongst new memories.

Maybe it was because only the waves could hear them, but Iskra had whispered, "I've never felt a love like this—I've never had a friend as you have been to me."

Zoialynne's eyes were glassy then, and Iskra wondered if she had made a mistake like her parents had warned her about. Friends were a liability, but here, at this moment, Iskra could not believe that. Zoialynne laid a hand on Iskra's.

"I love you until the stars die, Iskra. Don't forget that. If we forget each other where humans walk, then let us find each other in the stars—forever vast, forever infinite."

Iskra's mind whirled, her vision still as dark as the night sky had been on the night Zoialynne had promised her they'd see each other again. Zoialynne might've loved her that night on the boat, but Iskra hadn't known how to care in a way that wouldn't hurt them both. She started to come to it—sounds coming to her in pieces, but it was nothing more than a conversation that made no sense to her muddled mind. Her head ached, and Iskra wasn't sure if that was because of the damage the carriage had done or of an injury she'd sustained in whatever hell she was in now. She blinked, the shadows before her eyes slowly inching away, and Iskra looked upon their purgatory.

She sat with her hands tied to a support beam behind her in what looked to be the basement of a manor. Bricks lined the walls, their uneven pattern leaving lots of places for mice to hide away from the world. A small lantern had been set on a wooden table, casting the room in a dim glow. It reeked of dust and dirt, and she wrinkled her nose before continuing her examination. Iskra blinked as two shadows in the doorway caught her attention, each with what looked like a dagger attached at their hip. Iskra almost scoffed at the sight of them, for all she knew, they could be playing the part of illusionists—that they held power when they had none. A distant buzzing sound seemed to reverberate throughout the basement, and Iskra wondered where they were and what might be going on above them. Somewhere behind her, Sören let out a wince as he banged his head against the pole. She pinched his finger, or tried to, as the rope that had them all tied was unforgiving. He slapped her hand. Lock, who must've sat closer to Iskra's left shoulder, huffed.

"Could you two get it together? In case you haven't noticed, we're tied up."

"That we are," Iskra replied. "Thank you so much, Mr. Mortsakov, for enlightening us, once again, on our dire circumstances."

"Did I hit my head, or is that a hint of sarcasm I sense?" Lock retorted. "And it should be *Lord Mortsakov*. You're lucky I don't care."

Iskra scoffed, and to Iskra's right, Aura said, "perhaps we might all stop for a moment and realize that the coronet is missing."

All seriousness was snapped back into place as if it were the last gear in need of turning before the clock struck its timely toll. A quick glance around the room proved that the coronet wasn't there. It was false, there would have been no consequence, but there was no sign of Erika either. Iskra's heart raced, guilt clawing its way up inside her. If only she had—

"Don't do that," Lock whispered. "None of us expected this."

She nodded, but not before she cursed his Emotive Magic. Ignoring the lingering emotion and focusing on the real question, Iskra let her mind clear. Where was Erika? Wouldn't she want to confront them? Perhaps she'd gone back to Brighton between the time she'd been let go by the Yard, but that seemed a waste *especially* if she needed what she thought was the real coronet. Iskra didn't know her well, but she did know the lady was a practical woman. She wouldn't want to make two trips.

"We agree that this couldn't have been Erika, *oui*?" Iskra asked. The others hummed their agreement, and if Iskra's hands were not tied, she might've held her head in them. Her thoughts were a maze of unconnected lines—a feeling she'd thought she'd never have to feel since fleeing France. Clara was dead, and as far as they knew, the Liang's hadn't left their house in weeks, scared of the Twisted. There was no one else.

The clue the Twisted gave them popped into her head.

"Who was that man at the kitchen table?" Iskra asked.

"I've had a while to ponder that," Lock said. "You've all heard about the missing woman in the city, correct?"

Iskra nodded, despite Lock not being able to see her. Horrid business, it all was. Thousands of upper-class ladies had gone missing in the past decade, yet there was nothing being done about it. Surely, Lock didn't think they were connected to Kian's murder, and she told him as much.

"No," he conceded. "I think we need to re-evaluate every situation that might implicate Erika or Clara as a runaway. I think the Liangs are out of the question, considering they've been married for a while. Think about it. If I ran, the first thing I would seek is security. The coronet and the Order could provide that."

Iskra understood and began to think through every detail that she'd witnessed their two suspects do. And yet, she couldn't think. Her mind kept straying to something Lock had said. *If I ran, the first thing I would seek is security.* Iskra shuddered because she had done just that, and now there was another scar she would never be able to remove. The pull on the rope around her wrists shoved her from her thoughts. She recognized the feeling of Sören's hands as he worked to undo her bounds while Aura worked on Lock's. Iskra took her cue and started helping Sören. The rope slid from her wrists, but she stayed seated as the shadows from the edges of the room moved around them. Two more hooded figures filed in, and Iskra realized they were Twisted. Black cloaks covered the majority of their bodies, hoods low over each of their faces.

Venom wedged itself between her heart and her head, thoughts screaming at her to act. Her veins pulsed with the echo of a past version of her, and not one she wished to have back.

Iskra fought because she had to.

Her mind separated from her body. Pushing herself up from the beam, Iskra swung her fist at the nearest Twisted with what little strength she had left. Once upon a time, the Twisted would have been glowing, red as the blood they craved, but that was before they'd been forced to go into hiding. Iskra's fist collided with air as the Twisted sidestepped her attack, shoving her roughly in the back. She stumbled forward, teeth gritted, but she didn't fall. The magic inside her pulsed, angry and ready to burn the world, but now was not the time. Iskra whirled, ready to destroy the cloaked figure before her with all the pain they injected her with. Sweat dripped down Iskra's brow, and the effort of keeping her mind sane was causing her to grow weary. She paused, but only for a moment. The people she'd come to know as friends had also begun their attacks, their eyes hungry. Lock's jaw was clenched so hard, she thought it might snap, but it was clear he was hearing things—the whisper of a ghost of the past perhaps. Tears ran down Aura's face, her eyes flickering blue, normal, blue, normal, and back again, the agony from her own sense being used against her. And Sören, the first person who had seen Iskra as a friend, looked scared, and Iskra knew all too well his thoughts were at war, pushing and pulling at a constant state of indecision and false desires. Iskra ducked out of the way just as the Twisted's boot struck the air where she had been moments before. Iskra steeled herself for a breath before rushing at her attacker. Placing a hand on their heart, Iskra let their tormented heart feed into her head.

"Why?" Iskra whispered. It was simple enough. The Twisted tried to shake her off, but the thoughts found their way to her anyway.

"*I had no choice.*" It was a whisper, and soon the venomous magic pulled itself from Iskra, letting it rest, once more, inside its sorrowful heart. "*I was born into poison, and poison I've become.*"

Iskra took her hand from the Twisted's heart. "You don't want my blood on your hands. I'm no expert on poison, but it can lose its toxicity if you let it."

"My family—" It was a harsh whisper from beneath the cape.

"Will thank you," Iskra said.

"No, tell them I'm sorry."

The Twisted removed their cape, and beneath was a girl who looked only a few years older than Iskra. Tears streamed down her pale face, and a soft smile touched her lips.

"Thank you," she said, "if only for a moment, for showing me what it was like to be human."

The girl's face shattered as she drove a blade into her side. The silver was so quick that she hadn't had time to stop it. Iskra watched as the girl's eyes began to shut, and Iskra shook her head. She wouldn't let her die. She couldn't. Time was cruel, and for a girl only a few years older, she still had time to live. Iskra had wished for freedom at a time when her wrists were shackled by a cruel empire reigned by even crueler people. When she had finally gotten it, it felt like she was breathing for the first time. Iskra knew that the girls magic was never to be accepted by the world, but perhaps she could leave for a while, feeling the water flow beneath her and the wind at her hair, even if just to feel for a moment like life was fair and the men that inhabited it weren't born holding knives.

Iskra pulled the blade out as the girl fell. Kneeling before her, Iskra ripped a piece of the cape she wore and tied it around the wound. By the looks of it, she hadn't hit anything major, but Iskra was no doctor. She sat back on her heels, discarding the bloody knife beside her. She stared at the girl, and whether she'd make it or not, Iskra didn't know. But she did know one thing. These people were all broken and shattered by society. They were on the run, turning themselves into weapons just for respect—power in a world destined to hate them. They'd been set aflame so many times by other people's hatred. It was no wonder they hardly felt the pain anymore. *Why,* Iskra had asked, and she wondered how many times someone had begged to hear that. They weren't villains because they wanted to be; it was because they wanted to survive—a feeling that Iskra knew all too well. A feeling that'd dug itself a home inside her soul as soon as her own parents had looked her in the eye and deemed her a criminal. A criminal, she was wrongly accused of being because she hadn't wanted to play a part in their venomous empire of lies and deceit. Still, there were people who crossed the line and got blood on their hands for the wrong reasons. There were people who played mind games with innocent players, just so they could get a laugh. They were the reason why tortured innocents with magic had been cast from society, the words of the devil going with them. They were the people who were cruel just to be so. To hurt someone with such intentions was something no one in their right mind would do—to cause pain because it made them feel better and more powerful. For it was not good and bad magic that made people evil; it was powerful people and how they wielded it. For all the evil in the world, Iskra would never understand them as easily, and perhaps she never would. The line between good and evil was blurred, and Iskra only hoped it wouldn't be the thing that would end up destroying them.

THIRTY - FIVE

AURA

Fighting off magic so similar to her own was something much more effortless than magic that was not. The pain was less, though she faded in and out of reality. Reality: a threshold she'd learned meant little when people were always trying to escape from its many horrors. Aura used to feel that way—used to want to run from the pain—but she found that running was the worst option one could ever consider.

  She swung her fist at the Twisted's head, colliding with velvet. It was odd how something could feel so good, yet the wearer beneath was consumed by hate, wearing cruelty like a crown. Aura hadn't asked Lock for her knife, despite knowing he still held onto it. Even though he cast her careful glances in between his own attacks, she didn't want it. The blade was something Aura wasn't sure she'd ever be able to risk having again, as it was becoming increasingly apparent that her employer had found she was fighting them off with the minimal strength she could muster when it came to her past. Aura's mind tumbled into theories about their suspects, how they might be runaway's, how they might be liars. A fist collided with her gut, and she was sent stumbling backwards, the wind knocked out of her. Tears threatened to spill from her eyes, the pain making its way through her entire body.

From the corner of her eye, she could just make out a purple glow coming from Lock. It seemed to calm her, if only for a moment. Aura stood, her ache slowly receding as she marvelled at him. He was brilliance trapped by shackles made of blood. He was a prince upon a throne of glass waiting for one wrong move to let it shatter—and shatter he'd let it because he didn't see his true worth. Calculations filled his mind, wrapped by the poetry of his heart, and it was beautiful. Aura watched the purple incandescence flow up his veins, his glowing eyes steady and purpose-filled, and for a moment, it was like all the cruelness in the world was gone.

The remaining Twisted collapsed into sleep, and Aura had no idea how long they had, but Lock had bought them time, and that was enough. Aura took in the aftermath, her breath caught in her throat. Iskra leaned over a girl, her hands streaked with blood. Sören looked as though he had won a war, but only by becoming the last person on the front, tortured by regret. And Lock, he was watching her take in the damage. Fresh blood had started dripping from the cut at his mouth again, and he brought his thumb to his chin, wiping it away as best as he could. She offered him a small smile, but it was one she wasn't sure was real. They stood in a battle zone of prying eyes and false hope, blood streaked on the floor, a sickening silence hovering over them. It was the kind of place where whispers were welcome to place their rumours, and their hosts accepted them gladly. She shook her head. Now was not the time to mourn the way the world played its game. Aura placed her hands on her hips, pretending she was back in the laboratory with Rien, inspecting Twisted poison. She needed to detach herself from emotions, especially now that time was running out. Her fingers itched, but it was not the kind that made her fear, it was the kind that longed to search the Twisted's blood for their magic. That was, of course, if she had the right tools. Instead, she'd have to settle for finding the murderer without the help of their henchmen.

"Lock," Aura said slowly, "you said that you thought Clara or Erika could be a runaway. You included Clara because you don't think she's dead, do you?"

He nodded his head. "I did. Our attacker's carriage was bothering me. I felt like I'd seen it before."

Sören snorted. "What idiot pays attention to carriages?"

"The same idiot who might be onto something," Iskra said.

Aura couldn't help but keep the smile from her face. Lock nodded at the exchange before continuing.

"Anyways, while I waited for the rest of you to wake up, I thought about it. Then, it hit me. I saw it driving behind us to Scotland Yard, just as I'd seen it in a carriage house not a fortnight ago."

Aura stared at him, all connections clicking in her head. The bowing of her head, her quiet manor. How had she not seen it?

"My dear Aura, must you stare at me like that? I'm afraid I might pass away," he said, a teasing hint in his eye.

Aura rolled her eyes. "You think that Clara faked her death, don't you?"

Lock nodded. While the Twisted were out, there was only one way they could see if Clara had truly faked her death. Aura hadn't been able to view the day she'd died, and she suspected now that was because of the Twisted they had hired. What Aura didn't understand was why. She didn't like using her magic to show others' scenes, but it was the only way they could know if they were right. Aura motioned for them all to come together, linking her hands between Lock and Iskra, Sören across from her. She inhaled, preparing herself for the strength this would drag out of her. Lock's hand gave a reassuring squeeze, and she shut her eyes.

Magic spread throughout her, moving between her and Iskra's connected hands. She waited until it'd made its way back to her before calling for the past—the night Clara had planned her own murder. They stood in Clara's drawing room, the dim light of a candle flickering from the centre of a table. Surrounding it was a team of four Twisted and Clara. Across the room stood a shadow, but Aura couldn't make out their face. Lady Hollisworth lay face down on the floor, and the Twisted walked to their respective spots. Sticking their hands out, they let their magic flow, although she couldn't see it. The shadow moved from the wall, a top hat on his head, pulled low over his brow so only his lips were visible. He bent, placing two fingers at Clara's neck.

"Dead," he said, not that Aura or the others could hear him well, but Aura could read that word off someone's lips no matter the silence that embraced them. The Twisted molded themselves into the shadows, their blackened capes blending in perfectly. The mysterious shadow nodded at each of them before walking out of the house. A breath later, a maid walked into the room, her face screaming in horror. She was so focused on her mistress that she didn't see the Twisted that held their place in the darkness where one directed their magic at her. With trembling fingers, the maid turned Clara over, and her face paled. Although to Aura and the others, Clara looked perfectly normal. She suspected the maid must've seen death written upon her mistress's face. Aura shuddered just as her magic drew back into reality. Her head spun violently, and she felt as though she might collapse at any moment. Her vision swam, much worse than the last time she had projected her magic onto anyone. Then again, it had been a long time since she had shared it with a large group. The last time had been the night Alon died, sharing a vision with Rien, desperately trying to figure out what happened. Lock's arm wrapped around her waist, and as much as she hated to admit, she needed it. She tucked herself into his side, shutting her eyes in an attempt to control herself.

"My darling scientist," Lock murmured so that only she could hear. "I must say I'm honoured to have you swoon over me."

If Aura hadn't been leaning into him, feeling as though her legs were about to give way, she might have rolled her eyes. "Locklyn Mortsakov, I am *not* swooning."

"I think he was being sarcastic," Sören said.

Iskra made a rude noise. "You don't say."

Aura opened her eyes a moment later to see Sören casting nervous glances at a door that must have led out of this basement.

"What are you looking at?" Iskra snapped.

"I hear footsteps," he said.

Iskra clamped her mouth shut, and Aura pushed away from Lock so that she stood straight but still, but he was supporting her, his hand resting gently around her waist. Aura's heart raced, her mind struggling to find a reason why Clara would lie. Why she wanted the coronet, and if she really was a runaway. The last time they'd seen Erika, she had pleaded innocent, and they hadn't believed her. Now, Aura wondered why she'd covered for Clara. Surely Erika would have known she was being framed by her friend at the time. Aura wondered what Clara's movements had been on the day of the murder.

"Just so we agree," Sören said. "Clara is the murderer, right?"

Slow applause.

Lock stiffened beside her. She cast him a quick glance, but his face was unreadable—the only sign that he was feeling true emotion. Aura fixed her gaze back on the doorway.

Clara Hollisworth held a knife in her pale hands.

Her blond hair was bound into a knot at the base of her neck, pale pink dress pristine, as if she were going to a ball rather than a basement turned bloodbath.

"Go on," she told them, an amused tilt to her mouth. "Where did I go wrong?"

"I don't know," Sören cut out. "Maybe by murdering Kian. By the way, care to inform us why you did it?"

Clara looked as if she were on the brink of laughing, and it grated with Aura's nerves. She moved from the doorway, starting in a slow circle around the room. She flashed Aura a grin, and Aura noticed that on Clara's wrist, where there should've been a gem, the skin was smooth as ever. Aura frowned but kept her mouth shut. Silence weaved its way through the room so that the only noise that could be heard was the relentless sound of Clara's shoes on the floor. This was taking an excruciatingly long time, and if she wished for them all to go insane, Aura was sure her plan was working. Her patience was running low.

Aura swore. "Why did you do it?"

Lady Hollisworth *tsked*. "Lady Nighvengale, you might wish to watch your foul mouth."

She bristled. Lady Nighvengale was someone she was not, despite her recent knowledge of who her parents were. Discomfort settled itself in her stomach. How did Clara know who her parents were?

Lock rolled his eyes. "Just bloody answer her."

"Very well. I killed *Kian* because he knew my secret, and God he was easy to kill. He knew who I was, so he had to go, much as you will be soon. We made a deal that he'd choose me. He didn't follow the plan and he paid for it. You should have seen him, so full of desire it practically suffocated him—"

Aura was going to be sick. The woman before them wasn't Lady Hollisworth. She wore a facade, most likely from Twisted Magic. This woman had not been the same woman that had bumped into Aura on the night of the party—this one was the one that had taken her place. "Where did you put her?"

Lock looked at her, but Aura kept her face at the imposter. "And who are you?"

The amusement returned to her pale face. "Smart girl. As you might have guessed, I'm a missing woman. A runaway from my husband, too many expectations, you see."

Aura glanced at Iskra, but there was no sign she understood what the imposter spoke of.

"With Kian already knowing Clara, I had to act quickly, but he noticed the absence of my gem. Let me say his kiss died pretty fast after that. Anyway, my next plan was the coronet. If I could get that, then I could take the Order to put as much distance from me and my husband as possible, the unloyal bastard. The coronet would've made me powerful, I would've had the authority to have him locked away if I wanted to. Besides, I needed the magic—I was infected by Twisted Magic for too long trying to secure Kian. As for my name, why must I tell you?"

"Because if you don't—" It was the first time Iskra had spoken since the imposter had entered the room. "If you don't, there's a policeman upstairs that can take you right to your husband."

Aura knew very well that there was no policeman, but the imposter didn't need to know that. For the first time, all humour vanished from the woman's face.

"My name is Lady Beth Levensmith."

Aura stilled, "As in sister to Rena?"

Lady Levensmith nodded. "A shame she's dead. She and I never had a relationship, but I didn't kill her."

"Ah yes, because we believe the words of liars," Lock mused, and he unwrapped his hand from her waist. Aura felt the absence but watched as he paced the room. "You can't stand the sight of yourself. You killed Kian because he was the last person that could link you to your family and husband. You chose vengeance, but was it worth it? I mean, here you are, still looking for an escape."

A glint of madness showed behind Lock's eyes, the kind she knew was an act, but a very convincing one.

"Liar," Lady Levensmith hissed.

Lock pretended not to hear. "You can't outrun what you refuse to face, milady."

Aura watched as Iskra took a step up beside Lock.

"What if we told you that you could heal?"

Tears dripped down Lady Levensmith's face, and at that moment, she was fragile, bombarded with too much pain. Lock turned and nodded at Aura, and she took that as a cue to ask her questions.

"Beth," Aura said, taking a gentle approach, "tell us where the real Lady Hollisworth is."

"She's upstairs, in the garden shed." As she said it, her shoulders sank.

"Where is the coronet?" Lock asked.

Lady Levensmith's gaze turned hard. "Don't know. That *bastard* took it from me."

"Wh—" Her mind falling into a reverie, before she had time to ask who Levensmith was talking about. A kind of calm that caused her to panic. Sören collapsed, and Aura glanced back at Lady Levensmith. She was staring at the floor.

"I killed Kian Brittenworth," she whispered through her spilled tears.

Aura's eyelids became heavy, her knees gave way, and fear wrapped a hand around her heart. Had they not gotten through to her? Had this all been a ruse while the Twisted worked to deteriorate their minds? She glanced at Beth, who was looking at the door, but a glance backward proved there was nothing. Lady Levensmith seemed to remember herself, taking small steps towards the door. Her face had morphed, unguarded by Twisted Magic. The woman's hair now a deep shade of brown, her skin pale as if she were to be ill. The woman with a hard demeanour had been shed and left a hollow shell in its wake. She was just a broken woman who'd been forced to grow up too fast. She reached the door but paused in the doorway and looked down at her feet as if willing them to just let her collapse too. Aura's eyes began to close, but she willed herself not to fall into her dream state yet.

"I thought you wanted to be saved? I thought you wanted to be forgiven?" Aura rasped.

Lady Levensmith smiled sadly. "Some of us can't be saved. I don't deserve to be forgiven, not after all I've done."

"You have to try."

Beth just shook her head and moved to take a step out of the doorway, but something made her pause. "I want you to know that I didn't order this upon you." She waved her hand at them. "I never actually meant to hurt anyone, not at first. Then *he* claimed he shouldn't have hired me, and I was tired of you lot getting in the way. *I* still need the coronet, and I'm not going to let you stop me. I'm too far into the grasp of greed to deserve any pity. For that, I'm sorry."

She was gone, leaving the door swinging behind her.

And Aura was left sinking in the powers of her own poison-filled mind.

THIRTY - SIX

SÖREN

Sören's head throbbed. Around him, his friends gave in to the power of their minds, collapsing to their knees. Weariness spoke its soft words, a lullaby for the tired, taking its victims without a struggle. His own vision was fading between the realm of the living and that of his head.

How dangerous that could be.

It was here that his mind was filled with ghosts, waiting to jump from the shadows of his past and haunt him once more with a vigour that becomes worse with magic. It was here where being out of control scared him. He could jump from carriages and face a threat without losing the spring in his step, but it was here, when his mind risked deterioration from pain, that he was truly and wholly afraid.

This wasn't supposed to happen.

They were supposed to be saviours.

He was supposed to be.

And yet, Sören was losing a grasp on his mind as the magic wrapped its unforgiving hands around it, searching for his greatest fears. The Twisted painted his mind with nightmares in an attempt to break him so he'd run—run from them and their mind of horror. And, well, they certainly did their job.

There was something to be said about the ones who run. They were cowards, too afraid to face the fact that they were worthy of redemption. Sören had realized that quite some time ago, yet he couldn't help but feel for Lady Levensmith. Yes, he was spiralling down into Twisted Magic because of her, but she was a scared individual, and Sören could relate to that all too well. Still, it was what she'd done with the fear that had made her a horrid person. She'd kidnapped the real Clara, forcing her away while she lived out her selfish dreams.

Lady Levensmith had killed for the same selfishness, and that was something that sympathy couldn't fix. It was twisted and wrong, and Soren only hoped she wouldn't be gone when he awoke from the nightmare in which he had fallen. Although Lady Levensmith had long fled the basement, her last words haunted him. *I am too far into the grasp of greed to deserve any pity.* The words left a hollow feeling within him, engraving themselves on his heart. Not because Sören connected with them, but because he knew they were wrong. Her actions were cruel—there was no denying that. But no one was ever too far gone so long as they kept their head from their own self-pity. Greed might follow Lady Levensmith to the grave or the cells of Scotland Yard, but sooner or later, he hoped she realized that it was her that held onto greed's hand. Sören's head felt heavy, his eyes no longer fighting to stay open. He lowered himself onto his back, feeling as though the floor was swallowing him whole, the magic taking its winning blow.

He was falling.

Sören's eyes shot open, and a ticking filled his head. Tick, tick, tick, tick. It was a relentless pounding against his skull as he stared at the muraled ceiling above. Trees made of the richest viridian took up the majority of the scene depicted, but in the centre rose a large ghost made of shadow, its piercing red eyes staring at Sören from above. He shot to standing, or rather, he was pulled. This nightmare —a result of the Twisted—had control over him, not the other way around. At least, not when he was too far inside. He stood in an antechamber, the tiled floors alternating between crimson and black, an odd choice and a rather unpleasing sight, but Sören supposed he would be lucky if the poor decoration choice was the only nightmare he faced. The rest of the chamber was relatively plain, with white walls and a lone crystal chandelier. A small table stood in the centre of the room, and atop it stood a single rose. An invisible force pushed him towards the table, and he nearly stumbled over the thing entirely but caught himself before he could. It was as if Sören were a marionette. His hand picked up the flower, small thorns pricking his fingers.

"You ought to be careful with what you touch."

Sören froze. His back stiffened, and despite not meaning to, he squeezed the rose. A voice that had haunted his heart until he had let go, a voice that he hadn't heard in a very, very long time. He stole himself before turning slowly to face his mother.

This isn't real, *he reminded himself, but it was too easy to wish it almost was. His mother looked the same as always, her dark brown skin as soft and as glowing as he remembered, her dress void of any wrinkles, and her ring still sparkling on her finger. He should say something, but he could not; his mouth had been sewed shut by magic. He wanted to run to her, hug her, apologize for all the horrors he'd done—for not being there when her face finally lost its smile and her heart had enough of its beating. Still, he stood frozen.*

This is not real.

"You should be careful of who you hurt," she whispered even lower. Her eyes flashed before a wave of anger filled the room. "Perhaps if you were, I would not be dead."

Sören struggled against the magic. Crying out was not an option, and he supposed the illusion before him did not care how sorry Sören was.

"You should know that there is no forgiveness for what you have done. You have forsaken me, child, and for that, those thorns will find themselves buried within you forevermore."

The rose wilted in Sören's hand, and he involuntarily jumped back, tripping over the table, and he was once more sent for the floor. He squeezed his eyes shut, wishing very dearly to be back in reality.

Sören had been expecting horror, a nightmare, but he hadn't expected to see the very thing that haunted him most. There were, he supposed, many kinds of ghosts, but pain was the worst of them.

Sören groaned at the blue haze of the illusion that still had not left him.

He rolled onto his back before pushing himself into a sitting position, almost teetering off the balcony rail he found himself sitting upon. The view was rather spectacular, buildings covered in snow beyond. The sun sparkled, dancing along the roofs and the ground. Shadows moved along, people doing ordinary activities in Sören's own creation of hell. A chill ran down his spine, and he turned to see Xavier sitting in a chair, his legs crossed. A heavy coat wrapped around him, fur drawing up near his throat, his blond curls free. Sören was pulled off the balcony ledge, walking to the centre of the balcony, only pausing when he was unable to move.

"You never will be able to love, will you?" Xavier asked, and Sören inwardly cringed.

Not real.

Not real.

The slow chime of a clock rang from somewhere in the distance. Xavier pushed up from the chair, walking slowly towards Sören. He was so close, Sören would be able to touch his face. The boy smiled, and Sören wanted to smile back, his heart melting slightly. "It's a pity,"

Xavier stabbed him.

As the young lord yanked the knife out, Sören pressed a hand to his stomach, his hand coming away bloody.

"What did you do?" he croaked, surprising himself when his lips formed the words. Sorrow ripped him apart.

It's not real.

The chiming of the clock became louder.

Across the way, Xavier wiped the blade before giving Sören a slow smile.

Then he was gone. Sören looked back at his wound, but where he should *have been bleeding out, bloomed a purple hyacinth. He wasn't particularly known for understanding flowers, but this specific flower had been a favourite as a young child. He swore. The bells were so loud they were practically in his head. The blue haze of the magic began fading to black, and before Sören knew it, he, too, was gone.*

"Sören Niaheartson, wake up, or I'll stab you," Iskra whispered harshly as Sören was pulled from a daze. She knelt a few feet away from him, her trousers dusted with dirt, and her hand rested on his shoulder. He sat up slowly as if he truly had been stabbed. But there was no blood, no wounds on his hand from the thorns. A few feet away, Aura still lay as still as a corpse, but Lock was sitting up, his back against the wall, a contemplative look on his face. He would do anything to capture the look of his friend and laugh about it when they all made it out alive. He'd even make sure to capture Iskra's annoyed look she was currently regarding him with.

"What's this about stabbing?" Sören asked, much more cheerily than he felt. "Dear aristocrat, I think I've had enough of that for one day."

Iskra looked like she wanted to question him about it, but he pushed himself to his feet.

"Very well, you and I are going to find Lady Levensmith before she does something disastrous," she told him. Sören turned to look at her before tossing a quick glance at Lock and the still rather dead-looking Aura.

"And them?" he asked.

"We're going to look for the real Lady Hollisworth. That is, once Aura wakes up." Lock replied, dragging a hand over his face. Sören suspected it had as much to do with their weariness as it had to do with their poison-filled minds. His own mind was thinking over what he'd seen, trying to make sense of it all. But that was just it—there was no sense in madness. The Twisted had shown him his worst nightmare, and that was that. It was cruel and dark and crooked, but so was Sören's head. He shouldn't be so scared of losing love again, but it terrified him more than death itself. Sören shook his head.

"Well, *mon ami*, let us go," Iskra said, already heading towards the door. Sören followed soon after, realizing that Iskra had called him a friend, one of the few—and arguably, one of the only things—he knew about French. He wondered what Iskra had seen in her terrorized nightmares because whatever it'd been, it'd been enough to make her consider him a friend, or at least admit it. The cool air outside was fresh on his face, and as he trailed after her, a small smile touched his lips.

THIRTY - SEVEN

ISKRA

Wind slapped at Iskra's face, the crisp air biting her skin. The cold seemed to seep into her veins and stayed there, along with her ever-cold heart. She'd hoped the fresh air would ease what she'd seen in her mind, but it'd only caused the pain to stab more icicles into her chest, dripping with Twisted Poison. There weren't any words that needed to be said, yet it was as if the magic had heard the ones Iskra wanted to say anyway.

It meant nothing.

The blood that had blossomed onto the floor as the love she feared so great of losing lay, truly dead, before a raging fire. Iskra knew that her grief was slowly killing her, but she wouldn't believe her parents would kill Zoialynne, not if they knew she had information on Iskra. The next nightmare had been far worse. Iskra had sat upon a throne, a crown of serpents placed upon her head, and a golden card sat in her lap. She looked upon a crowd of shadows, the ones who were crooked and wrong and had no moral line or awareness of sorrow.

And she'd been their leader.

A leader she'd fought her life never to become. She'd rather die than have to find herself playing the Devil to a crowd of those hungry for agony. Iskra knew that there was good in this world, but eclipse it by evil, and one finds themselves alone with a knife to their back.

A knife that'd crack one's soul in half if that's what it took to forget the world is beautiful and vast and a place where freedom shouldn't have to be fought for, but given. Iskra was tired of fighting, but she would if it meant that the ones she'd started to call home were safe. It was always like this: the slow cycle of realizing there wasn't much left she could do. Zoialynne's words floated into her head from a time when the worst had seemed so far away. *Be careful not to get burned.* Iskra had made a silent promise, not knowing that it'd be the only one she couldn't keep. Iskra couldn't stay away—she was burned by a cruel memory of a father who had loved her, a mother who had wished her well. Burned by the Duke who'd promised her a home and burned by the sight of Zoialynne dying as a result—and she would get burned a thousand more times if it meant love would wrap its arms around her again. And she would do whatever it took to get it back.

Iskra wrapped her arms around herself as she walked up the stone steps that led from the basement to the grassy front lot of the manor. The manor they'd been trapped in was relatively simple, red brick towering high above them, and its windows arched almost as if it were Renaissance; however, it did nothing to keep the icy chill from her veins. She scolded herself for not wearing anything warmer than her coat, which was meant for early autumn.

Behind her, Sören's soft footfalls trailed after her, his mutterings hardly reaching her ears. Their footsteps soon gave way to silence as they reached the grassy lawn. Trees boarded the entire perimeter, a pathway leading away from the house, disappearing into the darkness beyond. Iskra spun, making sure Sören was still behind her, but her gaze froze on the manor again. It loomed above them, all elegance for the cruelties that lay inside, and far in the distance, smoke piled into the sky, the distant smell of a bonfire reaching her nose. Iskra would rather be there now, letting the warmth seep itself into her bones. Movement caught Iskra's eye in an upstairs window, but it was gone as quickly as it had come. Sören sauntered up beside her, making a slow circle around himself. His own hands were stuffed into the pockets of his coat, dancing slightly on the spot. If her nightmares hadn't reminded her how fragile life was, she might've been tempted to ask why he looked like a total idiot. Instead, she turned to him, his gaze now on the manor.

"Are you okay?" she asked as she rolled the unfamiliar question over in her mind. Sören seemed to be doing the same, but when he glanced at her, there was only that usual glint of amusement.

"Magic has a way of getting to you—ways you don't think you're scared of until your mind is stripped and vulnerable."

Iskra nodded, knowing better than to read his mind, but she didn't have to, because Sören was not a liar, and he had told her what he was feeling. "It makes a devil of us all."

Sören hummed his agreement before turning. "Well, dear aristocrat, I'm thinking we should get a move on before Lady Levensmith gets the coronet."

Sören moved in the direction of the woods, and Iskra followed, a slow smile reaching her lips. It was a shame that she'd be willing to give it all up if her parents did anything to hurt the ones she loved again.

Iskra hated the woods. She wacked another branch off her face, nearly hitting Sören in the process. Sören swore, cutting her a glare. She only smiled back at him, though she suspected it looked more like a grimace. Fallen leaves crunched beneath their boots, the eerie atmosphere even worse in the darkness of the woods. Each branch looked like the shadow of a person Iskra didn't want to remember. Her sleeve was ripped from stumbling through a bush on her way into the forest, strands of her hair hanging before her face.

The trees loomed above as they found themselves in a clearing. Here, the trees seemed to stand at attention, the silence commanding as if waiting for an order. All branches were behind them, already hidden in the darkness. Iskra couldn't see the manor anymore, and the only safety line she held onto was the moon high above and Sören, whose gentle breathing sounded from beside her. The wind wound its way around the surrounding trees, like serpents curling around one's neck. Iskra stiffened, her heart hammering within her chest.

"You know it's strange," Sören said, his voice quiet, taking in the clearing, "how the beating of one's heart calms me. Even when it's as terrifying as yours."

"It's even more strange when someone else's thoughts are the paradox to their words."

Sören looked at her then. "I'm sorry for what happened to Zoialynne."

"Yeah, I am too."

Sorrow wrapped its cruel hand around her heart, but Iskra refused to let it take her again. Zoialynne wasn't dead; she couldn't be. There was too much evidence that said otherwise, but as the days went by, even hope was starting to walk away. Iskra shook her head, placing her walls back where they belonged around her heart. Movement across the clearing had Iskra tensing and Sören reaching for his gun. Lady Levensmith stumbled out of the clearing, her dress in even more disarray than before, a small cut on her cheek dripping blood. Even in the moonlight, Iskra could tell that Lady Levensmith had been crying. She looked so fragile, like the girl she was—forced around at every moment. Even now, she was controlled by her own greed, pushed by a drive for revenge. Iskra noted that even as Levensmith took a step closer, Sören didn't remove his hand from his gun, and then she realized it.

He was truly afraid.

Sören, who'd always been so carefree, and had a will for danger, was afraid of the one who held revenge in their heart. She supposed it made sense. Revenge, after all, had been the person Sören hadn't wanted to become. Iskra hadn't wanted to become it either. She was pulled from her thoughts by Lady Levensmith sinking to the grassy floor of the forest, her skirts pooling around her.

"You truly are fools wandering out here alone," Lady Levensmith whispered. "I *need* the coronet. Where is it?"

The woman seemed to have gone mad, though neither she nor Sören made comment on it.

"Not fools," Sören corrected. "We're the mad ones who believe you are capable of saving."

"I don't know you. I don't—"

"Don't want to be saved," Iskra said. "We know. Yet, save you we will because even those too far gone can be."

"*Liar.*"

Iskra shook her head. "Not a liar, just another person who needed saving."

It was the truth, and maybe it was because no one could hear her. Maybe it was because she knew that Sören was scared too, but vulnerability had seized her heart, forcing words out into the open air. "There was a time when flames blinded my senses, and in truth, they still do, but there was someone who saved me, someone who I hadn't asked for help. I'm not a monster because of her. I'm alive because of—" Iskra looked away. *Her.*

"Perhaps." Lady Levensmith inhaled sharply. "When you see him next, tell him I'm sorry."

Iskra frowned, but then Sören was rushing forward, as Levensmith pulled a blade from somewhere Iskra didn't notice, driving it into her stomach. She let out a cry, as small knife slipped from Lady Levensmiths hands, blood blossoming quickly onto the woman's bodice. Iskra was no doctor, no scientist, but she was losing a lot of blood. Lady Levensmith was fading in and out of reality, and Sören was wrapping a torn piece of her dress around the wound. Iskra stayed where she was.

"We tried, Sören. Just—"

"No." The words were strong and had Iskra staring at him. "I won't let her die. I can't, Iskra. I spent a lifetime wishing someone would save me, and I was ready to lose myself again until they finally came—until Aura saved me. She isn't dead yet."

Iskra cursed herself. "Fine."

She helped Sören pick up Lady Levensmith, Sören at her shoulders and Iskra at her feet. They manoeuvred her through the forest of hell, dodging branches sharp as knife blades. Iskra kept her eyes on the fading woman, so carefully believing she wasn't good enough for this world. And perhaps she was not, but at least she would have another chance. Iskra knew that Lady Levensmith would need to be arrested for Kian's murder and the manipulation of her scheme, but she would get justice for her crimes and Kian would get the rest he deserved knowing his murderer had been caught. They pushed out of the forest and laid Lady Levensmith onto the grass. She was dying, her breath shallow. Iskra tightened the makeshift bandage before straightening.

"Sören, I think you should go fetch Thornsbury."

Her friend cast a weary glance at the woman between them.

"I'll handle her," Iskra reassured him. "I won't let your wish be in vain again."

A soft smile touched Sören's lips, and Iskra tentatively returned it. He cast one last glance at the dying woman before running towards the manor. Thornsbury wasn't in there, but he could find a telegram or a letter that he could send to the inspector. Iskra watched him retreat before looking at the blood blossoming on Lady Levensmith's makeshift bandages. *Please,* Iskra thought, *forgive me.* She inhaled the cool night air, looking into the darkness. Iskra only hoped she could keep her word to Sören. For Iskra was no God, and she could not tell time when to take its toll.

THIRTY - EIGHT

LOCK

Locklyn Mortsakov was lost in his head, wandering a maze of remembrance. Nightmares cracked in his mind like a strike of lighting, there one moment and gone the next. No matter, he would not dwell on his fears now or ever. Lock tapped his fingers against his knees, an erratic rhythm as Aura stirred. She looked at the ceiling, and even as he watched her, he couldn't help but wonder what she'd seen. Aura pushed herself up and looked at him, and he swore he was frozen under her stare. Anything he'd wanted to say, any sarcastic comment, disappeared on his lips as she reached for his hand. He ran a finger over her knuckles, the scars from the indecent on the train already beginning to fade.

"Aura—"

"I just want you to know that I'm sorry. For my past. For what I did—the pain I might have caused."

He squeezed her hand. "I know, lovely Aura, I know."

And he meant it. She shouldn't be apologizing, but he let her. In some ways, he'd been worse than her; it should be he who atoned for his actions. Gently, he reached across and brushed a loose piece of hair from her brow, her eyes flicked to him, and he pulled his hand away, fearing he'd made a mistake. But he had needed to make sure she was real after what he'd seen. *Her dagger inches away from his chest, her forever gone.* He shook his head. It hadn't been real; that was what the Twisted did, played with one's heart, watching in amusement.

"Well, should we find the real Lady Hollisworth, then?" he asked, changing the topic. "I'd wager good money that the coronet is also being kept there."

Aura frowned. "If Levensmith doesn't already have it."

He nodded, standing. His head was spinning slightly, the Twisted Magic beginning to take hold of his system. He didn't have much longer before it would take him for the night, and he shut his eyes for a brief moment, trying to focus on what Lady Levensmith had said, but, in truth, he was having a hard time remembering anything since he'd faced his personal purgatory. Lock opened his eyes, stumbling as he looked around the room, all the blood around him. Aura, too, seemed to take it in as a small gasp escaped her before looking down at her own hands. His magic burned, running towards her and yet he only felt one thing: fear.

"I have your knife," he told her, patting the inside of his coat where he'd kept her knife ever since she'd given it to him, and where it would remain until she asked for it. Aura nodded at him, and he moved around the bodies, heading towards the door that he assumed led out of this basement and into the manor directly. Everything was still—a sight that haunted him more than anything. Stillness, he found, was the worst kind of reaction. One was still when they found out horrible news, still when they were scared, and still when one dies, consumed forever by silence. Some of the Twisted's hoods had been removed during the fight, and here, now, they looked so peaceful, and not like the people they'd been forced to become, fighting just for another chance at air.

He tried the lock on the door Lady Levensmith had first emerged, and it was no surprise to find it locked. He swore silently, wishing Sören was still here. Aura moved up beside him, removing a pin from her hair, causing it to come tumbling down in waves around her. Ты такая красивая, *you are so beautiful.* He almost said it out loud but kept himself in check. This was an investigation, a place not meant for feelings, but for focus and probable bloodshed. He watched as Aura tried the lock, and on the second time, the door swung open.

"Shall we?" she asked, lifting a curious brow at him.

He pressed a hand to his heart. "Dear Aura, are you mocking me?"

Aura rolled her eyes, but he didn't fail to notice the small smile that touched her lips.

The hallways of the manor above were as dark as the nightmares Lock had faced in his mind. The floors of polished mahogany creaked with the smallest breath and echoed with the step of a shoe. The walls were painted a dark grey, and chandeliers hung from the ceiling like stalactites. He instinctively moved closer to Aura as if to shield her from any monsters that might be lurking in the shadows. Logically, he knew there was no such thing as monsters, but at present, he didn't care; he would do anything to make sure they made it out of here with their heads. Despite the darkness of the decor, he couldn't help but admit there was a certain pull about it—a calling to the broken boy within him. This place was a palace for the damned, a shell to carry out the Twisted's deeds, and for that, Lock scolded himself for feeling any sort of resemblance to these horror-filled corridors. It was easy to imagine death in a place like this, so macabre and twisted.

Lock shook his head, just wanting to find the real Lady Hollisworth. They turned down a hallway, trying to locate the back of the manor that would lead them to the garden shed. Lock had no idea who would do such an absurd thing, hiding someone in a shed, but then again, he supposed it had worked. He dared a glance at Aura, but when he looked back ahead of him, it was as if the walls were closing in on them. He stopped walking at the same time a knife whizzed past their heads, connecting with a vase at the end of the corridor. Aura flinched, and Lock reached for her hand as they turned to face their assailant.

There was no one.

Lock tensed, preparing for a fight, but not even the shadows moved. His head felt hazy, but he would not fall again.

"Love; such a feeble thing in the face of danger," a familiar voice said from the shadows. "You two will die tonight, and it will be by my hands."

Sir Avery Waltzeen stepped out from seemingly nowhere and gave them a slow, wolf-like smile, his red hair falling wildly onto his brow. Lock took a step in front of Aura, knowing her past with the devil before them. Her hand clutched his, and he longed to face her and tell her that it would be fine.

"What are you doing here?" Lock ground out, the menace in his eyes not artificial as when they had been with Lady Levensmith. Rage sparked within him like a match to a flame, and there was no extinguishing it. He was tired of people who hurt the ones he cared for, tired of watching as their hearts got stabbed over and over again.

He would not stand for it.

Avery took a step towards them, and he and Aura moved back.

"My job. I *did* warn you." Waltzeen didn't elaborate, only flicked his gaze to Aura, which only ground out Lock's nerves more.

"Oh, go to Hell, would you?" Aura said with ice in her voice that Lock wasn't used to hearing. It was the voice he'd only heard once; *your heart is cursed.* She'd now stepped up beside him, glaring daggers at Avery.

Amusement flashed in Avery's eyes. "I'm afraid it will be you going first."

Avery reached into his jacket, and Lock didn't hesitate to turn and pull Aura with him as they fled in the direction of what Lock could only hope was the outside. He cursed under his breath as a bullet hit the wall closest to his head. His coat whipped behind him, legs aching. He turned sharply, entering a door on his left. He and Aura found themselves in a room void of anything. He swore violently, realizing too quickly they'd been set up. He tried to move from the room but was met with a barrel at his brow.

"Lord Mortsakov, Lady Nighvengale, it's with my regrets that I must inform you that you will not see the light of day, not after this. In a world of locked rooms, there must be a way out. Shouldn't there? Not here, not in this house of secrets." Avery shot the gun just above Lock's head, hitting the opposite wall. The rapid sound of what sounded like the flipping of a million switches echoed from every direction.

Avery smiled. "Be sure not to scream."

They were falling, then. And Lock could've sworn that Avery's eyes had flashed at Aura, almost as if in warning. He didn't have time to ponder that. The pit they descended into swallowed them whole, and a few seconds later, he hit the ground. He just had time to hear the echo of the floor closing before he let the darkness claim him.

"Lock," Aura's voice called to him from the depths of the darkness. He forced his eyes open, searching for her. The pit they'd fallen into was too dark and too damp.

"Aura?" He hated how raw his voice sounded.

The only light source came from two lanterns hanging on either side of a door. Lock's eyes caught on the shadow moving towards him, a slight stiffness to her gait. He pushed himself up, his muscles aching. Not a breath had passed before Aura all but collapsed into his arms, and he did not let go. His hands circled her waist as she rested her head on his chest. His magic wrapped its arms around them, and he only felt one thing: hopelessness. He felt a void within his heart, but there was a door, a door and a way out. He rested his chin on Aura's head, and for a moment, they weren't broken, they weren't cracked—they were just two people who cared too deeply about too much to mess it up.

Then she stepped away.

A smile touched his lips as determination flickered behind her brilliant eyes, that not even the darkness of the room could dwindle.

A series of clicks sounded from somewhere, like thousands of gears turning, before the room started to fill with fog. Lock jerked his head in the direction of the door, neither of them speaking for fear that the fog might be more than harmless. The door had no handle, and Lock had half a mind to kick the door in, but he was far too exhausted to even try. He patted his pockets for Aura's knife and pulled it out. Beside him, Aura watched him, her gaze careful.

"You're not going to be able to open the door with that," Aura pointed out.

"I can. I just need to stick it into the lock."

Aura nodded. "Right, my lord. I should've thought you smarter than this."

Lock made a face. "Don't you, *my lord*, me, dearest, it could—" he coughed, the fog beginning to sting his lungs.

"It's a puzzle," Aura breathed hurriedly. "We need to find the key, preferably before the timer on the wall runs out."

Lock spun around. He had not noticed the timer before, but now, he could just make out its dim, hourglass shape, its ticking almost melodic in his ears.

"Don't just stand there, Mortsakov. I don't know about you, but I'd rather not die down here."

Lock pocketed Aura's knife, bending down to inspect the door while Aura moved from his side. *There has to be some way out of this,* he thought. He could not let them die down here. A few more heartbeats passed, and he thumped his fists against the metal in frustration.

"Lock," Aura rasped. The fog was so thick in the room he could barely see her.

Carefully, he grabbed a lantern and moved towards the vague shape in the gloom.

"Here," Aura said.

She was kneeling in the centre of the room, bent over the floor. Lock knelt beside her, setting the lantern down with a small metallic thud. There, in the centre of the floor, was a tiny silver box engraved into the ground, a gear lock sitting in the centre, a loud ticking filling his ears.

"You have three chances to pick one number," Aura said hurriedly. They were running out of air, and he feared that if they didn't crack this puzzle in the next thirty seconds, regardless of the minute they still had on the timer, they'd be dead either way.

Lock forced an inhale. "So, we need a clue?"

A nod. "Or—"

He knew the look she shot him—it was the look of someone who knew something. So, he prompted. "Or?"

"Mechanics like this," — a pause — "are built with fail-safes, as Lord Liang pointed out. We have to jam it, that is unless you can think of a code."

"Risky, no?"

"Extremely."

"So, how do we do it?"

Aura reached over, her fingers reaching inside his coat, pulling out her knife. Her eyes met his, and he knew it: it was now, or they were both dead. He nodded, though whether it was in reassurance or a signal to go ahead, he wasn't entirely sure. Aura tightened her grip before she raised her hand above her head.

She stabbed the knife right into the centre of the gear.

Lock held his breath, his vision starting to blur. Lock wasn't particularly religious, but at that moment, he considered praying. *Please*.

Everything was silent.

Lock blinked, gasping in air as dim light spilled into the chamber. Before he could ponder the miracle, Aura was already tugging him up by the sleeve, her breathing heavy. Together, they pushed out of the door, clutching each other as if they feared that if they let go, they'd lose their grip on their sanity. The door to the chamber slammed shut as they clutched each other, breathing in gasps of air. They stayed like that, huddled in silence for a few moments. Lantern's mounted onto the wall cast the slim stairway they stood in a dim glow, the only sounds coming from the steady intake of their rapid breaths. Quickly pulling apart, they bounded up the stone steps, bursting into the frigid air beyond.

Ahead stood what Lady Levensmith had described as the garden shed. It looked much more like a pavilion, its brick walls rising high, met with a coned glass ceiling. A large glow shone through the glass, and as much as Lock hated to admit it, it looked rather welcoming. He inhaled the air, taking in the oxygen as if it might be his last before he and Aura made their way towards the pavilion.

Inside, plants grew, covering the entire circular space, some common, but most of the flowers Lock had never seen before, but none of that mattered as his eyes met the vault door at the opposite end of the room. Aura's hand found its way into his, and he paused to look at her.

"My dear Aura, it's just another adventure."

"What if it's a trap?" Worry creased her brow, and Lock wished to wipe it away. He wished he could tell her that he didn't have the same doubts, but he had to believe that they hadn't come this far for it to be a trap. But in truth, after what they'd experienced in the manor, he had no idea what to expect. *If we let the doubt take us*—he cursed.

"And if it is? We'll work it out, like always. Though I must admit, you're the more calculative of us, so I'll just stand there looking pretty, offering my expertise when needed."

Aura rolled her eyes, letting go of his hand and starting towards the vault door. "How about you stop *looking pretty* and help open this door."

He sighed, feigning indignation. "If you wish."

Lock turned the wheel, clenching his jaw with effort. Even with him and Aura working together, it took them the better part of three tries to get the door open, it finally swinging open on its hinges.

They paused on the threshold.

The room was larger than he'd first anticipated, with stone walls climbing high to the ceiling, no sign of the domed glass of the pavilion behind them. A wooden chandelier hung, and candles cast the room in an eerie glow. In the centre of the room sat a pedestal, where a golden cage stared back at them, and a girl sat blindfolded behind its gilded bars. They rushed forward for the girl, but in a flash the pedestal lowered into the floor, the girl's screams becoming more and more distant.

Silence.

Like the kind before an explosion.

Lock's heart was thumping wildly in his chest as the horrid sound of gears clicking together filled the air once more.

The walls were closing in.

The room seemed to be fill with warmth as the walls trapped them in. Even if they tried running, the vault door had clicked shut behind them.

They were trapped.

Lock wanted to tear his jacket off in the heat that suffocated them. He turned and met Aura's panicked eyes.

There was no way out of this, and it'd seem they both knew it.

He gently took Aura's face with his hands, wiping away the single tear that dropped. The sound of the gears seemed so distant, and Lock shut his eyes because if they failed, all hope would truly be gone, the line of justice left uncrossed. Aura's hands wrapped around his neck as he moved his arms around her, tears welling in his own eyes.

"Aura–" he paused. Lock needed to tell her—what? He couldn't. Instead, he wished he could find the right words to say that she was lovely in everything she did. She was beautifully broken, but not so broken that she couldn't have shown him love, especially when he hadn't deserved it. Yet most of all, Lock wished he could tell her all the words he couldn't say—the ones he was too much of a coward to say. He wished he could thank her for saving him from dying, saving him when no one else could see it. Lock met her gaze, the gears once again drowning out his thoughts. He looked at her, so shattered by the world, yet still standing, still fighting because she refused to lose again. So damaged, and yet he loved her impossibly. She was his best friend; he had been a fool to have lost sight of that. He removed a hand from her waist, brushing it down the side of her face, taking in all the details before it was too late. It was like time had paused so they could look at each other—it was like time knew that when he looked at her, all opposing sides in his head stopped and forged peace. The walls were too close, and—

Aura's lips pressed into his.

He brought his other hand to her face, kissing her as if the world were to end today. Aura's hands moved from his hair to his waist, pulling him as close as her skirts would allow. They'd always been able to find a calculation, a way out of a problem, so why not this? *If we let the doubt take us, then we've already given up.* At this moment, nothing else mattered but the invisible string that held them together. She tasted of love and shattered pasts, and she was so enchanting that he never wanted to wake up. He pulled away slowly as if to savour the feeling of her hands in his hair, on his waist, their hearts fused together as one. Lock looked at her, his mind racing, hands still cupping her gentle face.

He needed to speak before the weight of the end crashed over them. He needed to speak because the words were so loud, consuming him until he was afraid his heart might explode. Doubt crept into Aura's features.

"Aura," he tried again, because if they were to die, these words could not be left unsaid. He lowered his head so that his forehead was against hers. "My lovely Aura, you can carve out my heart, rip my soul from my body, murder me if you must, but there is nothing that could convince me that I'm not taken, wholly and devastatingly, by you."

She stared back at him, and Lock longed to kiss her once more. Aura leaned her head against his chest, but not before he saw something unreadable pass over her face. Lock tucked her closer to him, one hand against her back, the other against her head. They were truly trapped, the walls forming a box. If everything were to end, at least Aura was here, in his arms, her frantic heartbeat against his slowing one. He shut his eyes, preparing for it to be over.

Silence.

He opened his eyes to find the walls slowly retreating. The golden cage started to rise from the floor, and Lock turned his gaze to see Sören standing near the vault, a lever beside him, sweat slicking his brow. Lock almost melted from relief. He gave a nod to his friend, and Sören strode forwards, Aura taking a step backward, her face still slightly flushed.

"Iskra?" Aura asked once Sören had joined them.

"With Lady Levensmith."

Aura nodded, and Lock only hoped that she'd be alright should Avery decide to show up. Sören strode towards the cage, unlocking it with a key and removing the blindfold from the real Lady Hollisworth. Relief flashed over the woman's features. She looked exactly like the girl Lady Levensmith had pretended to be when her facade had been applied, her blond hair falling over her shoulders. She stood on shaky legs, a grateful smile playing on her lips. She didn't speak as Sören held out his arm to her, helping her down from the raised pedestal. Lock slowly trailed after them, Aura beside him.

"I'm quite pleased that we're not dead," he said, hoping to lift the sombre mood that seemed to have dispelled them.

"Quite," Aura replied, taking his offered hand as she stepped from the room before letting her hand drop to her side. "You're a good man, Locklyn Mortsakov."

He raised a brow, but she did not continue, and before he could prompt her, Lady Hollisworth paused, her skirts spiralling with the movement.

"You—" she said, shaking her head. "Before I forget, I must give you this." She pulled a letter from a hidden pocket in her dress and handed it to Sören. He read it before handing it to Lock. Lock froze at the familiar ink-pressed font.

```
It's all just a game.
```

It's all just a game. Lock had no idea what that meant and exchanged a look with Aura, then with Sören. He suspected no one wanted to find out, but if all was just a game, he would sure as hell play if it meant keeping the ones he cared for safe. And, as they left the garden pavilion behind, he had the feeling that he was going to have to do just that.

THIRTY - NINE

AURA

There is nothing that could convince me that I'm not taken, wholly and devastatingly, by you. Aura's head spun, recalling Lock's words as they walked through the manor, everything echoing in the hollowed space. Sören spoke in hushed tones with Lady Hollisworth, her face still deathly pale, red skirts trailing after her, blood-like in the dim lighting. Aura glanced at Lock, an air of confidence radiating off him. The feeling of her lips pressed against his came rushing back all too suddenly, and she looked away, her cheeks heating, but not before she caught Lock smirk at her. The fiend. As if they hadn't been horrendously close to dying only moments prior, and there were simply too many apologies that couldn't have been said. At that moment, it hadn't mattered about her sins. It had just been her and him bound together by shattered pasts and a love she hadn't thought she could have. He'd held her, and Aura believed that she was worth the kindness in his eyes. They were both bound by bloody deeds, but that didn't mean they were incapable of love, incapable of forgiveness. Aura focused her attention forward, quickening her pace. She wanted to leave this manor and all its horrors.

Footsteps.

She swivelled, barely missing the gun that swung at her head. Distantly she heard Lock order Sören to get Lady Hollisworth out, but she didn't hear his reply as she stared into Avery's cold eyes. She had no idea *what* he was doing, perhaps he'd figured out she intended to disobey anyway. That was, if she had any control left. A gunshot rattled her ears, and Avery stumbled back in shock as his gun teetered to the floor. He glared past her, presumably at Sören, and Aura half turned to see him nod at her before shutting the door—a barrier between danger and freedom. Lock moved to grab the gun, stuffing it into his coat. Amusement sparkled in Avery's eyes, the kind that was sick and full of madness. And, as if on cue, four Twisted stepped out from the shadows, and Aura could only guess these were the only ones Avery had left at his disposal.

Avery circled them slowly, and bells started ringing in her head. Rage flowed into her bloodstream, eyes flashing red with violence. Lock seemed to cast a worried glance at her, and she wished to ask him for her knife.

They deserve it—the violence you could cause them, a voice whispered in her head. She had been afraid of this moment. Her hand closed into a fist, willing herself to relax. Movement near the window caught her eye, but there was nothing but darkness beyond. Her employer was quite good at making sure never to get caught. She clenched her hands harder, sure that half-moon shapes were beginning to form on her palms.

She was better than violence.

She was better than her past.

But how easy it would be to let her mask slip.

Focus.

A blow to her gut had her launching back to reality. Avery was nowhere to be found. Aura brought her boot to the first Twisted's stomach, using the momentum to stumble a punch to the other. She cast a quick glance at Lock, who fought gracefully as though he were fencing instead of at a disadvantage. She cursed her skirts silently, dodging a blade and bringing her elbow sharply into the Twisted's side.

Successful—then she was losing.

A push had her stumbling forward, flashes of horror in her eyes. Her arms ached as she tried to fight, but it would seem they were destined to make her bleed. A blade pressed itself to her neck hard enough to draw blood.

"Go!" She heard someone bark as she bit down hard on her lip, all but collapsing to the floor. She brought a hand to where she knew blood would be blossoming on the collar of her blouse. A grunt from beside her told her that Lock had also fallen. Avery was before them in an instant, a slow smile spreading across her face. He looked as if he wanted to speak, but Aura wouldn't give him that satisfaction.

"Why?" she asked, shocking herself at the strength her voice held. "Why are you doing this?"

He clapped his hands. "Because it's fun. Revenge."

"Revenge?"

"You know how it feels, Aura; That need for violence, that drive to turn your pain into madness. Do you want to know why I did this? For power, for glory, for *justice*—for the ones I lost to you, Aura. Forgive me, *The Queen of Spades*."

Aura stared at him, suddenly wanting to sink into the floor. Hatred crawled up inside her heart, burying itself because she knew exactly what he was talking about. She bristled. She was better than that.

"You didn't lose anything to me," Aura said evenly.

"Didn't I? But you wouldn't remember wielding the knife, would you?"

This isn't possible, she thought. But she knew it was Avery's magic, hiding out in polite society, using his Perceptive Magic for evil. He had heard her thoughts. How much he knew, she didn't know, and that terrified her. All that time he'd spent giving her order's, he was gleaning his own information. Her blood ran cold. Avery only smiled wider.

"All those thoughts, Lady Nighvengale. Surely, you'd be put in the Yard for some of them."

Aura's blood boiled, and in one step, she pushed off her feet and swung her fist at his head, hoping to do damage. He caught her fist, pushing her backward. She tripped on her skirts and would've fallen all the way if Lock hadn't stabled her, his hand going to her back. Avery began his slow circle again.

"Power; isn't it lustrous? The envy it plants in your soul, so much so you will do anything to get it? That is what I did. You, Aura, killed someone I cared for very much, and now I will rip you apart. What was it you did before you arrived at the Order? *Killed my brother?* Perhaps. You see, my partner, your employer, he and I helped Lady Levensmith, and she owed us. With Kian out of the way, we could have gotten the power we wanted, if you hadn't lied about getting the coronet for me." He laughed a harsh sound. "Even the Duke was in on it. The Order is a place for the cruel, and it wasn't hard to orchestrate Kian's death to create room in the hierarchy. Long story short, you have gotten in the way too many times. You destroyed me, and now I will show you what it feels like to be destroyed."

As if she didn't know how that felt.

"What about what *he* wants?" Aura said. "He wouldn't want me dead, I'm too *valuable.*"

Avery's amused look turned bitter. "*He* doesn't have to know, Aura. He and I—we don't want the same things."

Aura raised a brow. "What is it you want?"

"I've already told you. I want you to *feel* shattered." Avery continued. "you see as we've been speaking, word of the Queen of Spades has slowly been making its way through London. Such a mess, Lady Nighvengale. London wants your blood. Well, the Queen of Spades. I'm not so cruel to share your real name. After all, this is still a game, and you're still a key player."

"You're insane," Lock said. It was the first time he'd spoken, and Aura started at his voice. She cast a quick glance at him, proving that madness had once again set into his eyes, his jaw locked hard. He had pushed himself off his knees, his back as straight as someone who had true authority.

"You, Mr. Mortsakov—"

"It's *Lord Mortsakov*, to you, if I recall."

Avery grunted. "You, *Lord Mortsakov*, are that. I can see how you two are made for each other. What with the hunger that crawls inside you? In fact, I can see how you crave so much to hurt me, but you won't." Avery continued his circling, and Aura felt as though the walls were slowly closing in. Avery was right, she craved violence, but she was better than that. How easy it would be to let the madness take her, but if she did that, then she might never return. She shook her head. She wouldn't let Avery get to her. She needed to focus. This was a problem, and all she needed was the solution.

"Insane?" Lock said, his cool mask in place. "Most definitely. Or perhaps my dearest Aura and I are tired of you." Aura wanted to roll her eyes, but she knew he had said what he did to pull her back to the task at hand. Aura took a shaky breath. "And the coronet? Where is it now?"

"Are you so naive to believe I'd tell you?"

No, she didn't. Her veins were buzzing, and she must've stiffened because Lock was beside her in a moment, pressing her knife into her hands. The metal felt familiar in her hands, her hand tightening around the hilt. She didn't even glance at him as strode towards Avery, and it only took a moment before the tip of her knife was pressed against his chest, a tiny drop of blood spreading on his shirt.

"Where is it, Avery?"

"You're not yourself," Avery said, looking bored.

She pressed the knife harder, hard enough for his face to twitch. She smiled. "Where *is* it, Waltzeen?"

He sighed, though she didn't miss the pointed look he shot at her. *This is an act.* "You truly are no fun, just like he said. It's under the oak tree at the far end of the lot. Not that you will have the chance to find it anyway."

Aura paused as Avery side stepped her knife. She stared at where he'd been, her knife dropping to her side. Who was this *he* that Avery spoke of? Surely not anyone she knew of. Her employer hadn't met her so he wouldn't know. Aura's insides twisted; her heart caught in her throat as the world crashed around her. She distantly noted Avery speaking, but she hardly heard it. Instead, her mind screamed at her, Avery's words rushing at her. *Word of the Queen of Spades has slowly been making its way through London.*

She felt sick.

She'd just begun to find herself, starting to forget about the damage she had caused, but now it faced her, bared teeth and all. The Queen of Spades had destroyed her, and now it would soon be her greatest downfall. It had been her escape, a house for the violent girl hidden within her soul, but it had never been home. Home had been Rien; home had been Lock. Home had been her friends. Home had been her, and she had refused to see it until she was laying on her own bedroom floor, watching as Twisted magic ripped her soul apart. The Queen of Spades had been the girl who hadn't wept for Alon because she hoped he would still be alive and the girl who had when the police had pronounced him dead. Aura didn't know what she would do if London found out about the Queen of Spades—she couldn't go back to that. They would order her dead, and there would be no way around that, whether the public knew her name or not. Aura was doomed for destruction the moment she had listened to that poison that had found its way into her heart, and even more doomed when she had started to justify her actions. She was a monster. Or she had been one until Lock held her close. He made her forget that she was angry and horrid and wholly undeserving of anything he gave her. He made her forget that life was cruel to people like her; he made her feel like she was not tortured. She loved him because he was love, with his cursed heart that beat for her, his eyes that shone with unshed tears whenever he was proud, or the way his smile could light up the room as if he called the entire galaxy to him. Together, they were infinite. A calculation that cannot be solved nor proven; simply existed in time to prove that broken doesn't mean irreparable. And yet, she would not drag him into the mess she made because he didn't deserve that. *You are a good man, Locklyn Mortsakov,* she'd told him, *and you do not deserve me.* She was pulled from her thoughts as Avery lunged at her.

    Thunder reverberated throughout the room. A luminous purple glow came from Lock, his eyes as bright as she had ever seen them, and she wondered what he and Avery had spoken of while she had let her thoughts carry her away. Avery dropped to his knees, the amusement leaving his eyes as he searched frantically for the Twisted, but they were nowhere to be found. His eyes began to droop as if feeling heavy, and all Aura could do was watch Lock. Magic travelled through him, peeking out from above his collar before making its way up to his hairline. She wondered what kind of dreams Avery would have. Not that it mattered, but part of her hoped for something that would have him wondering where he had gone wrong. Aura thought back to his words. *But you wouldn't remember wielding the knife, would you?* She didn't, and perhaps she didn't want to, but it had not been her fault. She had been propelled to drive that knife through her victim, but she hoped she could find out why before Avery did something that would destroy all of them in the end. Lock's magic finally faded, and Sir Avery Waltzeen collapsed to the floor with a thud. She stared at him for what felt like an eternity. He wasn't dead, but he wasn't alive either—no one alive could be that driven by hate. But even as she thought it, Aura knew it was a lie. Hatred was greedy and fierce, and it could control anyone if they let it. Lock was before her in a moment, gently taking the knife from her hand before hiding it away in his coat, though she only half-registered it. She wiped her hands on her skirts, surprised to find them shaking, but then they were grasped by warm, familiar ones. She didn't look at him at first, for fear that if she did, she wouldn't be able to save herself from the depths of his heart. He squeezed her hand, as he had always done when the world felt as if it were on the verge of toppling over.

"My lovely Aura," he said with a sad tilt to his mouth. "Shall we get onto finding the coronet?"

She nodded and didn't remove her hand from his as they walked. It was a comfort, their friendship kindling a love so vast that silence was comfortable. She shut her eyes because she knew that Avery had trapped her, put her in an impossible situation, and she was not going to get out of it unscathed. A fire burned around them, and Aura would do anything to make sure that no one she loved got burned, even if it meant burning herself in the process. She looked at Lock, only to find his gaze already accessing her, a frown deepening on his face. He didn't speak, only turned back towards the direction they walked in. They pushed out into the frigid air, and Aura shivered. Silence blanketed them—a silence she wasn't used to. The weight of the night surrounded them, and Aura felt as though she was back in the entrance hall of the Order of Crowns. *The Queen of Spades strikes again!* That was what they would've said about the facade she hid herself behind. Except for this time, it would be true. The public would make sure she paid for her injustice as if she hadn't already paid tenfold.

At the far end of the lot, just like Avery said there would be, sat a tree, its limbs creaking in the breeze, whispering words only those of ancient worlds could even dare to comprehend. Its roots grew deep into the ground so that the tree might tell of the centuries past—the love that came and didn't last. What Avery hadn't spoken of, was the lone headstone that sat beneath the tree, like a ghost leaning against its trunk for an afternoon to rest from the heat. But it was nearly winter, and ghosts weren't real. The coronet box sat at its feet, hardly damaged by the rain London had received in the past weeks, a silken cloth of black laid over the mahogany. Aura imagined it looked like a coffin just before a funeral where death would finally get what it wanted. But this wasn't a funeral, and the coronet wasn't a human. Lock's hand brushed hers, a reminder that he was still standing beside her and a silent wish to continue on their way.

One look inside the box proved that Avery had told the truth. For a moment, the red gems set into the silver coronet seemed to glow, a thrum echoing at her fingertips, but a blink and it was gone—she shook her head, she must have imagined it. She couldn't, however, deny that she felt magic pulsing, even through the now-closed box.

A silhouette trotted up over the hill, her gait immediately recognizable. Iskra was before them in minutes.

"The police are on their way."

"How kind of you to inform us. It would also seem you brought visitors," Lock said, his voice void of all emotions. Aura glanced at him, but this time, Locklyn Henry Mortsakov didn't want her to see him. Aura cast all worry from her mind as she gazed at the shadows slowly making their way toward them. Aura nearly groaned. Had the Twisted not fought enough? She assumed this was their attempt to stall while they waited for Avery to arise from Lock's magic, but it would not work. She should suggest Lock use his magic on the few Twisted that dared come closer, but Aura was no fool. They wouldn't make the same mistake of letting their gracious magic flow through the air, not after Lock had let Avery fall into a dream state. Iskra swore in French, and a small smile ghosted Aura's lips. Iskra gave her a look as if to say *quit your smirk before I do it for you.* Aura bit down on her lips, just as thoughts that were not her own crowded into her mind. *Love is your weakness. You will die tonight. He will leave you, just as they all will and have done.*

A fist swung at her head, and she caught it just inches before impact

The Twisted were fools to believe that Aura wasn't used to thoughts as they once fed her. No, Aura was used to them—the voices that told lies. She used her free fist to punch the Twisted before her, and the sounds of fighting slowly broke out around them. She'd dropped the box upon impact and a Twisted dove for it, but not before Sören came leaping out of the shadows, picking up the box and running. Had she not been mid-battle, Aura might've stopped and stared at him. For all his recklessness, he had a way of saving the day, and Aura had to admit she admired him for it. The Twisted pulled out a knife, and then time was moving slowly. The knife went for her heart, and Aura braced herself for the impact, ready to face death.

Nothing happened.

The knife had dropped to the floor, the Twisted retreating into the shadows. Aura stared at them, hand pressed to her heart where a knife would have been lodged. Iskra crossed her arms, a slip of blood falling down her cheek before starting up the hill muttering to herself about getting back to London. Aura, too, started her way up, and Lock fell into step beside her. No words passed between them, and she longed to ask him what was on his mind, but she didn't. The feeling of his lips against hers came rushing back, and she fought against the blush that crept up her cheeks.

Word of the Queen of Spades has slowly been making its way through London. She and Lock were infinite, and while infinity could not break, there was one thing that could prove that it wasn't as endless as everyone thought it was. The solution was simple: death. *You are a good man, Locklyn Mortsakov.*

A small tear slipped down Aura's cheek as she and Lock caught sight of Iskra and Sören in the distance. *And you do not deserve me.* Infinity wasn't perfect, and Aura would shatter it again and again if she had to—to save them from Hell. And, as the sun crested over the tree line and the toll of bells wailed in the distance, Aura knew what she had to do.

FORTY

ISKRA

The manor's drawing room was elegant for a place that had held such horrid events this evening. Iskra tightened her grip on the red velvet chair she sat in, tilting her head to the ceiling. It was gold, as was everything else, save for the blood-red settee the group sat in. They'd been ordered inside as soon as Scotland Yard's constables had arrived. She thought back to the letter Lady Hollisworth—the real one—had given Lock and Aura. *It's all just a game.* They'd shown it to her after they had gone inside, Sören included, and Iskra was still puzzling over it as voices echoed from the entrance hall. None of them had spoken much since Lock had pulled the letter from his waistcoat and showed them those four words. They pounded in her head. *Allons, c'est juste un jeu. Come on, it's just a game.* She scolded herself in French and again in English, hoping it'd make her see sense.

It didn't.

As if the universe sensed Iskra needed a distraction from the statement of the hour, Detective Inspector Thornsbury pushed open the double doors of the drawing room like he was the most important person there. His moustache curved into an elegant swoosh above his top lip. He clapped his hands, giving each of them an earning smile.

"Well done," he said, then his smile fell. "What happened?"

Iskra sank into her chair as Sören explained the details of everything.

The kidnapping.

The Twisted Magic.

The Letters.

Lock and Aura took turns filling in the detective about what had happened in the pavilion, and he collapsed into a chair with a weighted breath, his shirt wrinkling with the motion.

"I'm quite glad you're alright. Now, to business. My constables are taking care of Lady Hollisworth, and Lady. . ."

"Levensmith," Iskra said, recalling the girl dying on the ground before her. Iskra wasn't sure what the constables would do, but she hoped that the imposter served her time. Across from her, Aura shifted in her chair.

"There is something else you should know. Avery Waltzeen is the leader—or whatever you may call it—of these people. He and his partner orchestrated the crimes. This means that the Order is worth a true investigation. From what I can gather, Avery and his partner hired Levensmith before Avery got greedy. I'll also need protection for a while," Aura explained.

Iskra watched Thornsbury frown. She knew where Aura was going, and the Detective, bless him, fell right into the trap.

"With what?" he asked.

"I was the Queen of Spades, and Avery—"

"Has told people." Iskra cast a glance at Aura as Thornsbury finished her sentence. Aura's face filled with acceptance, knowing that Avery hadn't lied.

"And you want protection that I cannot give. Aura, I'm sorry, I truly am, but when it comes to this, my hands are tied. Unless you want the entirety of Scotland yard knowing the Queen of Spades' real identity."

Iskra pushed to her feet. She, just like everyone else in the room, said that there'd be no easy way out for Aura, no matter how much the poor girl wanted to find one. She strode towards the door, the room feeling sickening. Iskra had known the night of the opera who Aura was—she hadn't meant to, but mind-reading comes with a price, she supposed. It made no difference to her back then, whether Aura had lived or died for her choices. But now? Now, there needed to be a way to fix this. She didn't hear the others stand, but she knew they followed her and suspected it was each for their own reasons. Iskra pushed out again into the blooming dawn, a peaceful scene that felt as though it should be anything but. Lady Hollisworth was in tears again, explaining her captivity to a set of constables, while a doctor worked on Lady Levensmith as another constable tried to coax answers out of her. Detective Thornsbury gingerly stepped in and filled the constable in with what they had told him about the imposter before joining their group again.

Silence seemed wrap itself around them once more. Iskra watched the sun continue its ascent into the sky, and it was at times like this when Iskra could forget about the world. In fact, being here, Iskra had had little time to think about the situation she was in. Her parents had taken Zoialynne and wouldn't finish until Iskra gave them what they wanted. She wouldn't give them it, no she would get what she needed. *The coronet.* She walked over to where she had placed the box inside one of the constables' carriages. Flipping the lid open, she marvelled at the sight before her. A crown of silver sat in a deep velvet cushioning, red gems set into the spikes. She picked it up delicately, watching as the early sun sparkled off it, making it shimmer.

Iskra smiled.

She was no criminal.

Yet, part of her could do it—take it and go back to France to burn her parents from the inside. Part of her wanted to be greedy, to allow her heart to lead her. But she had made that mistake once and knew better than to make it again. Still, how easy it would be to take the devil's hand if it meant her heart could feel alive again.

But even as she thought it, she knew that was cruel.

"I understand," Sören said from behind her, "if you wanted to betray us all. I'd bloody hate you, but I would understand."

I would never do that, Iskra wanted to say, but instead, she said, "How can the heart long for something so ridiculous as another person?"

"Not the person as much as the memories you don't want to forget. The memories you imagine making." Iskra turned to him, but for once, his face was grim. "Love is greedy and hungry, but you should be wary, as it has a habit of turning into something more like insanity."

Iskra should say something, but there wasn't anything that could console two fools with love wrapped around their necks, choking them until they felt nothing but its bliss—bliss that could turn into a burn. Instead, she placed the coronet back inside the box, making a silent promise to get it when there were fewer constables around. "I'm not going to betray you."

When she turned towards him, his easy smile was back in place. "I know you could never stay too far from me, the kind friend and, dare I say, handsome genius."

She rolled her eyes. "Save your remarks for Xavier."

Sören opened his mouth to retort, but movement on the tree line had Iskra's attention over to where constables hurried around, orders slicing the air in loud voices. From the distance at which she stood; she could only hear snippets.

"–Avery."

"Escaped—"

"Get—"

"—him!"

She had understood enough to know that Avery had been spotted. She also knew enough that Scotland Yard couldn't touch him as long as the Order of Crowns was on his side. She should chase after him and help those incompetent fools before Avery could get away, but she was sinking. She sat on the step of the carriage, exhaling sharply. She had barely had a chance to breathe since Kian had died, and sitting here, letting it all sink in, was horrible. Memories of the manor came flying at her, Zoialynne's fading breath. Iskra had wanted to believe that she was still alive, but hope was just a game, like everything else. *She has to be alive,* Iskra told herself again and again; even now, she believed it, but she couldn't help that sliver of doubt that crept into her mind. She looked past Sören to where Aura was speaking hurriedly with Detective Inspector Thornsbury, Lock lingering not so far away with Lady Hollisworth. They were tying up loose ends, she knew, but Iskra had learned long ago that if they tried to tie them all, they'd end up with a knot, or worse, one string left. Soon, echoes of the constables faded and Iskra was consumed in darkness.

Three years ago, when Iskra had docked in England, she'd found herself, along with Zoialynne, sitting at the long table in one of the Order of Crowns various meeting rooms. Fire had bubbled inside her then, screaming at her to let it out. An hour later, Duke Brittenworth had embedded a blue jewel into Iskra's wrist, promising her safety and the needs for her destruction so long as she helped them first.

"Promise?" she remembered asking.

"With my heart."

Iskra should've realized that people like him don't have hearts. She should've realized that the only person who could cause a fire great enough to destroy was her. Iskra should've known that power was sick, and she should've known sooner or later, it would end up taking her soul as well. *I am going to betray you.* Iskra should've told Sören that, but she couldn't, and now she was going to cause trouble.

It was only now that Iskra realized what had driven her all those years ago: desperation.

Desperation to understand.

Desperation to destroy.

She was no longer that person. Now she was doing it because she deserved to live a life of freedom, a life where she didn't need to look over her shoulder. She was doing it for her friends because contrary to what she had thought, she didn't want to do this alone. This mystery was just beginning, and she wouldn't let her selfishness get in the way. Her parents wanted her? They'd have to pry her from her grave. Zoialynne might be gone, but Iskra would spend every waking minute making it up to her. All she needed was the coronet.

"Iskra?" Aura's voice pulled her from her thoughts as the carriage rumbled towards London. She had been so caught up in her thoughts she hadn't remembered climbing in, let alone sitting with Aura, Thornsbury and Hollisworth. She blinked slowly.

"Apologies. Where are Lock and Sören?"

"Following," Detective Inspector Thornsbury replied.

Iskra turned her attention towards Lady Hollisworth. Her blond hair had been swept back, her face cleaned, though her dress skirts were still torn in some places. And, as if Iskra had remembered why she was sitting in this carriage, she asked, "How did it happen?"

Aura shifted beside her, fiddling with the fabric of her skirts where a patch of dirt hung.

Lady Hollisworth clasped her hands in her lap. "I went to the Order the night of the party." She turned her wrist to show the blue gem that was still pressed into her skin. "After pleasantries, I received a note from Kian to meet on the terrace. This wasn't unusual, considering he always had something to catch me up on while I'd been away."

"Only it wasn't Kian when you got there, was it?" Aura asked from beside Iskra.

Lady Hollisworth shook her head. "No. It was Lady Levensmith. I had never seen her before, but I had heard of her husband. She asked how Kian and

I's relationship was, and then I was struck. Before I passed out, I saw myself staring back, presumably the Twisted Magic already set in place. Then, I woke up in that cage, and the rest was blurry until you came."

Iskra nodded.

"Apparently, a Lady Cordzig and Miss Rena Levensmith snuck into the Order that night—tried to stop Lady Levensmith. But their pleas landed on deaf ears," Thornsbury said. "And they both ended up dead as a result."

Iskra set her mouth in a grim line. They mostly fell into silence for the duration of the ride, Thornsbury asking Lady Hollisworth the occasional question, and Iskra could only help but wonder about the clue their rescuers had asked. The carriage slowed as they entered the late afternoon London traffic.

"Do you know anyone by the name of A.N. Catcherheart?" Iskra asked. She felt Aura's gaze slip to hers, but Iskra ignored her.

Lady Hollisworth frowned. "No. Should I?"

"No, just something I heard once," Iskra told her, then continued her look out into the streets. A.N. Catcherheart could be someone who didn't matter, or they could be the person set to ruin them, and the thought made Iskra uneasy. She shook her head, trying to relax into the cushions for the remainder of the journey.

Iskra handed her coat to her butler before heading up the stairs to her room. She was desperate for sleep. Scotland Yard had insisted on hearing her and the others' accounts of the events.

As the clock had rung twelve bells, with the promise to speak with them soon, Iskra had slipped into a waiting carriage and watched the passing darkness until she had made it home. Now, as she washed her face and twisted her hair into a braid, she couldn't help the calm that washed over her. *It's all just a game.* The words echoed in her head, but surely a game could pause for rest. Dark circles bruised her eyes from days of not sleeping; every time she tried, images of death and people in coats that might as well have been ghosts haunted her thoughts. Iskra covered herself in a silk robe of rich maroon, one of the things she'd brought with her from France and one of the only things that didn't fill her with hatred. It reminded her of a love long passed, but not the kind that was rooted in tragedy. Iskra pulled it tight over her before heading back downstairs.

Her butler was nowhere to be seen, so she brewed the tea herself. Not that she minded, as scents of smooth peppermint filled her senses. Sleep could wait for just a few more moments, just to let her sip delicately to drink away the day, letting the calm make its way back into her veins. From somewhere beyond, a cool draft sent shivers down Iskra's spine, and she jumped as the tea whistled. Pouring herself a cup, she let the scorching sensation bleed through the cup and into her palms. With her tea in one hand and a lamp in the other, Iskra started her ascent back upstairs. She didn't believe in ghosts, but her door hanging open when she was sure she had closed it might have given her a reason to start.

Iskra carefully made her way to the top of the stairs, listening for any noise, but nothing greeted her, and that was almost worse. A silence so deafening that even the streets beyond seemed to be holding their breath.

Iskra shook her head. She was going insane. Walking the rest of the way to her room, she ignored how fast her heart pounded.

Her teacup smashed to the floor, lantern crashing roughly to her desk. In a wingback armchair facing her sat a coated figure dressed in deep red, the familiar lace covering their eyes, veil fixed over their face, a letter held between their gloved hands. Iskra stood in the doorway, wanting to run, but her feet stayed frozen in place. The figure simply sat there, motioning for her to join in the chair across. Iskra's feet moved regardless of whether she wanted them to. *These people saved you from the Twisted,* she reminded herself, but that didn't stop trepidation from eating away at her mind. Iskra sat slowly, as she'd done a million times. The figure reached forward, handing the letter to her. She took it, her hands surprisingly steady. The letter was like they always were, folded, and Iskra could just make out the ink on the inside. Iskra looked up as if to ask the figure how they'd gotten in, what the letter said, or to ask who they were, but they were gone. She looked at the door, but it didn't move. Iskra breathed a sigh, letting the tension in her shoulders relax. Unfolding the piece of paper, her heart continued a violent rhythm within her chest.

```
She is gone.
```

Iskra didn't have to ask what the letter meant. She knew. She knew even as she sunk to her knees that hope had once again blinded her. A tear shed down her face and onto the words. Memories, of blood soaking through her shirt and Iskra holding her until the heartbeat had long faded, ran through her mind. *She's gone.* This time truly, alone in her room, Iskra let herself scream at the air around her. *She's gone.* Iskra read the letter over and over as if it could bring Zoialynne back. But it would not, and she knew it.

"Miss Storenné?" Her butler's voice came from the doorway. "There's someone here to see you."

Iskra had half a mind to ask him to send whoever it was away, but instead, she rose.

At the door, Xavier stood, a sorry look on his face. "I tried," he whispered.

Iskra looked at him, her grief momentarily replaced by confusion.

"I tried to stop them." He rubbed a hand over his face. "Zoialynne's on her way to France."

Alive. She nearly collapsed, and Xavier reached out a hand to steady her, his hands ink stained.

"Why?" Iskra managed, but she knew why. For leverage. Xavier only nodded at her, confirming what she knew. After a moment or two, he left, and Iskra watched him leave just as she had when they'd met three years ago—Iskra seeking a home and Xavier wishing he didn't have one at all.

She's gone. Iskra thought again, because love was insanity, and she was alone again, fighting to stay sane.

FORTY - ONE

SÖREN

Sören Niaheartson was not known to worry, but as he lingered by the entrance of Scotland Yard, that was exactly what he found himself doing. Detective Inspector Thornsbury would be out any moment, and Sören needed to ask him something that had plagued him all the way back from the manor. He scratched his temples, where the beginnings of a headache was starting to form. Beyond, the rest of London was laying their heads down for rest or getting ready to hit a pub, neither of which sounded particularly interesting to him at the moment.

The doors suddenly swung open, and Thornsbury stepped out, placing a hat on his head. He began walking in the opposite direction of where Sören stood, and without another thought, Sören ran to catch up. They walked in silence, Sören counting his breath. One mystery left to solve. It should be easy, but all it left was a weight inside his chest.

"Evening, Detective," Sören spoke slowly as if trying to cause the anticipation within him to rest.

Thornsbury nodded. "Hello. I assume that since most of your friends went home nearly two hours ago, you want something from me? Sören, it's past midnight, and I'm hungry. Please don't ask about anything illegal until I've slept at least eight hours."

"Ah, the detective needs his beauty rest, does he?" Sören quipped. "Don't worry, old man. I won't keep you up. I just have a simple question."

"Why do I doubt that?"

Sören frowned. "What do you mean?"

Detective Inspector Thornsbury sighed. "Nothing is ever simple with you. But, by all means, enlighten me."

Sören crossed his arms as he walked. "I need you to tell me what Xavier did."

His father would kill him if he found out Soren was inquiring about the new lord. His father thought that Xavier was dangerous, and from what Sören could gather, he was. But Sören had long since stopped caring about danger. Besides, he needed to know if he'd once again trusted blindly. Sören needed to know if he was better, and he needed to know that he wouldn't go insane with the feelings that stirred in his chest whenever he thought of the pretty boy with the curly hair and the smile of the sun—he needed to know that the sun was not going to burn him. *Love is greedy and hungry, but you should be wary, as it has a habit of turning into something more like insanity.* That was what he'd told Iskra, words his mother had once again told him when Sören had been crying over a girl who'd moved back to her home. He'd sobbed, but the love he'd held for her had not nearly been what he felt pounding inside his chest.

Sören felt like his heart was burning him, but the kind of pain one never wanted to end. He bit his lip, and Thornsbury watched him closely. Sören looked back at him and watched as conflict flashed across his face. Thornsbury treated Sören like his own son, and he suspected the detective was at war—the battle that all parents must face—to protect or to let life teach its many lessons. In the end, it would seem the latter won, and Thornsbury's shoulders relaxed.

"Are you sure you want to know?"

Sören nodded, even though he wasn't sure he would like what he heard.

For the second time that evening, Sören found himself in a situation he normally wouldn't. He sat in an armchair by a large window that looked over a darkened street, the street of the Order of Crowns. Breaking and entering, Sören had done before, but sitting here in the dark waiting for a boy that might not be in for another hour or so, was new.

Sören shifted uncomfortably.

This might've been a mistake, but Xavier was no danger. Well, not an immediate one, anyway. While he waited, he ran the conversation with Thornsbury over in his head.

"Xavier," Thornsbury had spoken quietly as if Sören might bite his head off. *"Is not a pure-blooded Brittenworth. Xavier's mother is off the grid from what I can tell, but let me say that the young lord has done many illegal things to try and find her."*

"Including a knife fight?" Sören had asked, remembering when Xavier had held a knife during their last conversation.

Thornsbury nodded. *"A knife fight on a noble party of Duke Brittenworth's most trusted advisors."*

Now, as Sören sat in the dark, he couldn't help but ponder Xavier's very existence. How long had he known about his mother? The sound of familiar footsteps sent every single one of Sören's thoughts away as he reached for a match inside his pocket. The door opened, and he struck it, lighting the lantern on the small table beside the armchair. Had this been any other situation, Sören might have applauded himself on the dramatics of it all, but this—well, it wasn't a jesting matter.

Xavier Brittenworth paused in the doorway; his face unreadable.

"Xavier," Sören said. "I'm only here to talk, so I wouldn't pull a knife on me if I were you."

Xavier moved into the room, lighting the rest of his room so that they could see each other fully. The lord's movements were methodical, practiced, and, Sören noted, held a hint of what he could only describe as fear. Sören didn't move as Xavier finally plopped down on the edge of his bed, his eyes significantly more tired-looking in the light.

"What is it you want?" Xavier asked, a weariness in his voice.

Sören ignored the flutter in his heart. "I know about your mother."

The boy's face before him hardened, but he said nothing.

"Tell me about the knife fight," Sören prompted.

Sören wasn't sure Xavier was going to say anything, but after a moment, he spoke. "I had understood that my father's advisors had information on . . . my illegitimacy. I pulled a knife on them, the first time I'd ever dared harm another. I hadn't meant to draw blood, but I needed to get out of here—"

I needed to get out of here. The words echoed in Sören's head, but he ignored them as Xavier spoke again.

"As you can imagine, attacking your father's advisors with a small audience wasn't something that made him happy." He paused, looking at Sören then. "He hired Twisted to make them forget it happened. Do you know what it's like to feel trapped in your own house? My father hated me afterwards, keeping me only because I hold this place's assets at the tips of my fingers. Others, well, they weren't so lucky."

Sören looked around the room as if he could glean some of the information Xavier knew. But the walls weren't visionaries, and they certainly didn't whisper, so Sören nodded for the lord to elaborate.

"From the time I'd found out about my mother, I was ditching my tutor and scouring for anything that would help me get back to her while my father was off on Order business. I went back to France to see if I could find her, but all I discovered were burnt ashes. I should have stopped then, but I—" he paused as if remembering a time he'd long since left behind. "I couldn't."

"Why feel ashamed? Why let me believe you were a criminal? Why let your father speak of you as such?"

"I'm not ashamed." Xavier paused again, and Sören suspected he was gaining his composure. "I'd rather have people think of me as a criminal than have me tossed out of here before I can find her."

"What if she doesn't want to be found? What if—"

"She's not. *Non-exieris.*"

"Never surrender?" Sören asked, silently thanking his father for forcing him to take a Latin class.

"Just something I received in a letter." Xavier stood and strode to his desk, rummaging before finding what he was looking for. Sören stood, accepting the letter from Xavier, laying it flat on the desk. It was a letter he'd seen a million times before. Behind him, Xavier began rearranging pillows on his bed, and Sören's head swam. He folded the letter, committing it to memory. He wondered how long Xavier had been receiving these, and as if Xavier could hear his thoughts, Xavier added, "I started receiving them after the knife fight, nearly a year ago to this day. Always said the same thing. It was odd. The first time I received one, it reminded me of something I had told Iskra when she first arrived."

Sören stared at him. "I hadn't realized you knew each other."

"Not many do. I only wish my father would have been more forgiving to her."

Sören nodded slowly, his mind returning back to the letter. Xavier had been receiving them for quite a long time then. *Always said the same thing.*

"Is your mother the reason you needed the coronet? The power that everyone tells me it holds?"

"Yes and no." The heir spoke slowly. "Not for the power, literally. Symbolically, it would have given me power to *demand* my father for information. I couldn't be seen getting it, the police would think it had something to do with Kian's death."

"So why the night of the party?"

"Because I knew Iskra would ask Zoialynne to step away. She'd try to take it, but if you could get it—"

"The coronet is with Thornsbury. I'm not going to steal it from him, Xavier. Everyone needs that coronet, you know."

"I know. I suppose I don't need at anymore, though I will fulfill my end of our deal. I've been in contact with someone who may be able to help." Xavier didn't elaborate, and he didn't ask. Sören frowned as he placed the letter back on the desk, as another question came to his mind.

"Would you do it?" he asked, keeping his back to Xavier. "Would you leave?"

"Eventually. There's business I need to take care of here before I do—if I ever do. One of which is to continue to break my father piece by piece."

Sören whirled. "What?"

"You don't honestly believe I'd let my father hurt anyone else? Not long after he had started viewing me as something less than a son, I realized that he was the villain." Xavier drew up his sleeve, a scar where a blue gem had once been. "And as far as I'm concerned, I'm just my father's stupid illegitimate son who spends his afternoon drawing ghosts."

Sören slowly turned back to the desk, taking in a pile of drawings all of the same man. He looked to be about twenty, grey shading his face in angular proportions, his eyes always covered by a hat. He looked *exactly* like the man that had been present when Levensmith had faked her death as Hollisworth.

He sensed Xavier wanted to speak, but when Sören turned to face him again, Xavier was staring at the floor. He looked at his pale face, not fragile as one might expect, but edged with quiet determination.

Xavier Brittenworth was not dangerous.

He was fighting for freedom, a feeling that Sören knew all too well. Perhaps they were both insane, driven by love, by liberation, but maybe that was what also made them human—chasing a dream that was only so far from their fingertips.

Xavier's eyes snapped to Sören's, an intensity hiding behind his eyes. "Let's play a game."

Sören was done with games, but he didn't speak. He didn't dare move.

"I'll keep your secret." Xavier paused. "And you keep mine."

"If you mean the secret about my father—"

Xavier took a few strides towards him, making Sören pause. "I mean your secret about the poison. You tell no one about my mother. I mean, Sören, *we* did not have this conversation."

"And I'll keep your secret," Sören repeated Xavier's original phrase, not wanting to focus on what the lord had just said. His heartbeat rammed against his ribcage, but Xavier took a step back and nodded an invisible hat to Sören. Sören waited a moment until he understood he was being dismissed. He walked towards the door but paused in the doorway.

"I want to help you," he said quietly. Not because he was ashamed but because the last time he had heard those words, his father had spoken them as Sören lay breaking apart at the seams.

"And you will," Xavier said. "Just not now."

Sören wasn't sure whether feeling in debt to Xavier was a good thing, but he was willing to take a chance. Love, liberation, and him. Sören would do it because he wanted what Xavier did. He looked back at the spy of his own father, a lopsided grin on his mouth. Sören smiled.

"You're rather determined. Has anyone told you that?"

"I seem to remember you calling me cocky. But no, only you've called me determined."

On the way back towards his house, Sören couldn't help but smile. A smile that only lasted for a few precious seconds as he was hit from behind. Sören stumbled, his knees striking the cobbled streets.

He tumbled into darkness and found himself searching for someone to help him, but no one was there. He was alone. A heartbeat reached his ears, and he wasn't sure if he wanted to know whose it was or where it would lead him.

FORTY - TWO

ISKRA

Iskra refused to let grief take her. This was the consequence of letting love wrap its arms around her, and for once, she wouldn't regret it.

She couldn't.

Not when she'd found value in her friends, just as she wouldn't go through this alone, just as she would make sure she would live. If she had to hold hands with memories then she would, no matter how much she ached to feel them again. She would not let Zoialynne leave this life without her mission being fulfilled; Iskra owed her that much. She might not have told Zoialynne everything she had wanted to, but the universe was vast, and Iskra only hoped Zoialynne could see how Iskra felt.

It had been three days since she had received the letter. *She is gone.* Perhaps the letter spoke of Zoialynne, but perhaps, it also spoke of Iskra. Iskra was gone, the one that spoke of love and weakness. She was better than her old self, better than the girl that had run from France. If anything, she was ready to face Hell. She was going to get Zoialynne back, even if that meant facing the devil himself.

The last time Iskra had been inside the Order, she'd been stripped of her position, leaving a scar where a blue gem used to be. She should've been nervous, stepping into a place that has broken every promise it had made, but even as she took a seat in one of the several offices in the manor, she felt nothing but anger. Her fists curled into balls on the chair arms, and she pursed her lips, trying and failing miserably not to scowl.

The office she found herself in was one of the few she hadn't been permitted to enter as a member, though it looked mostly the same as all the others. Four walls of bookshelves surrounded her, and a mahogany desk near the far end where she sat. Behind her was a large fireplace, though it looked as though it hadn't been lit in some time despite the cold weather dawning London's streets. The servant that had shown her through hovered in the doorway, and Iskra wondered if they thought Iskra was going to do something rash. Well, she supposed they had good reason to think that, but Iskra was here to discuss one thing: her parents. The Order had made it clear that they would protect her from them, and although that promise had gone out the window, she knew that the Order kept tabs on them.

And she needed to know everything.

At that moment, Iskra felt like she was younger, sitting in on her first Order meeting, a meeting that should have taken down the Society. The Society, that was just a whisper, yet the Duke was set on destroying them. She'd been living in the Order at the time, innocent to the cruelties that hid behind the Duke's careful face. She'd been too naive to question the Duke, what they spoke of, and instead spent her days with Xavier. He'd been her first friend, and Iskra hadn't even realized. She remembered one day in particular; Xavier had just painted her a painting, and she and Xavier had spent the afternoon making cookies. Her heart has swelled, feeling almost happy.

It only ever lasted so long.

Duke Brittenworth had discovered them, and thrust her painting into the fires of the wood oven. Iskra had remembered wanting to scream, but she knew better than to do so. It was the first day she'd realized the cruel side of the Duke, but even as he'd scolded them, neither of them moved. Neither of them dared to. He was just a broken boy shunned by his father and she was just a runaway French girl who knew nothing better.

She wasn't that girl now.

"Miss Storenné," Duke Brittenworth said, pulling Iskra from her thoughts as he strode into the room, nodding at his servant to leave them. *Pathetic,* Iskra thought. He couldn't even call her by her own name, as if he hadn't treated her as a daughter, even at least for a little while. "I must admit I was surprised to hear you came here."

"Don't flatter yourself. I'm only here because you have the information I want."

The man chuckled. "Dear Iskra, when will you learn that all information comes at a price."

"Who says I'm not willing to pay?"

Duke Brittenworth regarded her levelly as he sat backwards in his chair.

And, for a moment, Iskra was sitting across from her father, demanding to know what he and her mother had done. She swallowed as if to shove down the bitter memories. Iskra supposed her parents and the Duke were one and the same—both promising things they knew they couldn't keep. In her parents' case, they had promised love and given her anything but, and in the Duke's case, he'd promised safety, and now Iskra was running. *Again.* She pushed that last thought out of her mind.

"I know that my parents were here with Zoialynne. I know that they are bringing her to France. I know that you work for them, and I need information. What are they going to do with her?"

A low laugh echoed throughout the office. "They broke my staff down one by one. I don't work for them, not anymore. It was clear that our intentions were never the same and never will be, not while they are looking for you. As to what they will do, they gave me this."

Iskra tried not to dwell on the fact that her parents had suspected she would see the Duke. She also tried to ignore the sincerity in the Duke's voice. Pity, almost. Though, she wasn't sure if it was pity for her or pity that her parents and his principles didn't quite align. She accepted the letter from the Duke, ripping open the black seal on the top—her parents' seal, etched with a crown, a crack through the centre. In swirly font, the message felt taunting, as if they were inviting her to a tea party rather than issuing a threat.

This is far from over, ma petite Etoile.

Iskra tucked the letter into her pocket and said nothing as she stood and left the room. The Duke did not call after her, nor did she wish him to. She had almost reached the door when Xavier stepped from the shadows, his pale face looking better than it had nearly two weeks ago. She suspected that Scotland Yard had informed him that his brother's murder was solved. In his arm, he held a painting. She stared at him.

"I know that you and I may as well have been strangers, but I spoke with Sören the other day, and that got me thinking about the painting. And, well, you were the first friend I ever had besides Kian. I just wanted to thank you for helping put him to rest."

"You're welcome," she said, and she meant it. Xavier deserved to be at peace, just as much as Kian did in his grave. She could say that he was her first-ever friend, but the last thing she needed was a reason to be linked to his house again.

"I'm sorry," he said, but she didn't understand what for. He reached out and squeezed her hand before letting go, Iskra's magic wrapping itself around him at the small contact. *I'm sorry for letting you think you were alone.*

Iskra didn't know what to say. Instead, a small smile touched her lips.

Xavier returned it and left, switching his canvas to another arm as he walked, but not before Iskra saw the beginnings of what looked like the image of a boy surrounded by flames and another holding them away. Iskra smiled before she opened the door of the Order and walked out. This time, there was no malice in the memories she'd made, only a longing for the people she could have saved if only she had realized she needed to save herself first. *This is far from over.* He might very well be right, but Iskra was no longer afraid of losing, because she knew that she would win. It was a very risky gamble, but one she was willing to take in the game that she had been forced to play.

Somewhere between dusk and dawn, between home and nowhere, between North and South and the stars and the grass, Iskra found herself falling into darkness. The sounds of the London streets disappeared, and Iskra let a little red bird guide her into a place where reality was non-existent. Her head ached but only for a moment, and then, Iskra saw the sea once more.

Iskra was jolted awake by the sound of a loud thump from behind her, head aching, vaguely remembering passing out next to a pub. Perhaps she'd had too much to drink, but Iskra wasn't known to drink at all. Blinking away the blurriness, her heartbeat returned to normal, she took in her surroundings. She was in a tunnel made of stone, lanterns hanging every few feet, lighting the way. Iskra sat frozen as she gazed upon a person in a flowing red coat. They didn't move, nor did they speak, but Iskra had the distinct impression they wanted her to stand. After a few breaths, she did, her muscles protesting ever so slightly. The tunnel looked like something out of a medieval textbook, a renaissance painting without the allure. The wordless figure turned and began walking down the hallway. Iskra followed, trying to gauge how far they were underground or where they were. She followed behind the figure, their red coat flowing behind them like blood, Iskra's head spinning.

She shook her head as if trying to shake off a dream. After what felt like nearly an hour, they came to a large wooden door that the figure promptly pushed open. Iskra followed, but paused upon entry. It was darker in this room, a chandelier hanging from the high gold-gilded ceiling. Around were red theatre seats, faded over time, all facing a stage where seven red figures now stood. Iskra's gaze locked on her friends, each sitting in a red chair facing the stage. Iskra almost wanted to laugh. It looked as though they were sitting down for a performance without a clue on what it was about. Aura had a troubled look on her face as Iskra sat down, but before Iskra could ask her about it, one of the red figures stepped forward.

"Ah, my Elegant Elite." A pause, "How nice of you to join us."

"Join you?" Lock scoffed from where he sat on the other side of Aura. "I don't believe any of us actually came here of our own will."

The first figure — the one who'd spoken — only shrugged off his comment. Their lips, just visible beneath their sheer veil, seemed to twitch before resting.

"Why are we here?" Sören asked.

"To ask your questions," another figure said.

"Who are you? Under the disguise?" Lock asked. He stared at them with such intensity that Iskra knew was the look of a man who was trying to figure something out.

"We cannot say. But we are the people who helped you."

"The letters," Aura murmured.

The only confirmation was a slight nod of the head by seemingly the leader of this group.

"Why us? And if us, then why haven't you helped us prior to this investigation?" Aura asked.

"Because you take action when something strange happens. You see a knife where it isn't supposed to be, and you investigate. You also—how did you put it to the Duke? You are the most powerful. As for not helping you earlier, we had no proof. Especially of you, Aura, that you were helping our cause."

"And what is your cause?" Sören asked.

"To keep the mystery alive. To get justice for those who have died and been put aside, ruled as insane—to make sure that our streets are safe. We have reason to believe that Kian is only the start."

Iskra wanted to tell them that the streets would hardly be crime free. That the upper class was willing to go to great lengths to sweep murder away from the eyes of the public, but she suspected that they already knew that; they just didn't want to believe it.

"Who do you work for?" Lock asked.

"You'll know that in time."

"You just sit waiting until someone gets murdered?" Iskra asked. That hardly seemed fair.

They didn't say anything.

"*It's all just a game,*" Lock said. "That was what in the letter you gave Lady Hollisworth. What does that mean?"

"It means that everything you come across is a gamble of luck, everything you thought you heard or saw could be a trick, everything is a hoax, a practice of manipulation, and most importantly, everything has a rulebook," They replied. *Everything you come across is a gamble of luck.* The phrase repeated in Iskra's ears, but she silenced it only by listening to the sound of her heartbeat.

"If you knew who the murderer was, why didn't you go after them yourselves?" Sören tapped his fingers on his knees.

"Because we're under the law. We are a group of people who cannot be caught and who will be killed if our faces are shown amongst the public. We are the Twisted that want to do justice rather than pain. Our leaders are different, but we shall let them explain it to you when you meet them. It is because our presence must remain secret except to those who can help us and those who work with us."

Iskra took in their words carefully. Her whole life she'd been told that Twisted were bad, murderous beings. "You're the Society, aren't you? The ones the Order wants gone."

A brittle laugh sounded from behind a veil. It was answer enough. *Yes,* the silence almost seemed to say. "The Order was never out to get us, so you say. No, the only goal of the Order was power, and we could give it to them. Poor souls never stood a chance."

Iskra watched them. They'd proven she could trust them. They'd proven that they were not out for blood, but to help save it. She shifted in her chair, frowning.

"Why are we here?" she asked them.

"Isn't it obvious?" The leader of the group asked. "You've proven yourselves. We want you to work for us."

No. Iskra would not be let down again. She couldn't.

"Are you mad?" Lock asked, his voice accusatory. "You've built yourself on flimsy ideals and expect us to follow? My apologies, but I am respectfully going to decline."

An expectant silence filled the air, but when no one said anything, the figure clasped their hands together. "Very well."

"Wait," Sören said. "Why tell us about yourselves? Even though you couldn't ensure we'd believe you."

"Only time will tell."

There was a pause before another one of them spoke. "Now, if you think you can find your way back, you may leave. Don't come looking for us. We know how not to be found. Remember, this meeting never happened. Understood?"

Each of them nodded in turn and stood, but Aura paused and turned back to them. Iskra watched as they looked at her expectantly. Well, at least, that is how she thought they were looking at her.

"What do we call you?" Aura asked them. "Surely, you have a name other than the Society?"

"We do. The name shall never leave this room, just like the rest of the information. We are but a rumour whispered in the wind."

"Understood."

Iskra could feel her palms starting to sweat, and she clasped them behind her back. Surely, this was the part where they were going to get trapped and would never see the light of day. Surely, this was the moment they revealed that this was all an evil scheme. The part where the promises were broken. Instead, they all stepped off the stage as if they had planned it and looked at them head-on, even through the strip of crimson lace covering their eyes.

"We are the Kingdom of Cards Society."

FORTY - THREE

LOCK

We are the Kingdom of Cards Society. They were the people who Lock had been warned to stay away from. They were the people who he'd been convinced were the villains, the ones who hadn't a care for the lives they took. And yet, they were the people that had helped them solve Kian's murder. The Kingdom of Cards Society went against everything Lock had ever been told, every lie the Order had told him. The Society sure had their way of going about their business, considering Lock had to black out before entering their lair, but they were not necessarily the villains he'd believed them to be—as far as he could tell anyway. The theatre wasn't one Lock had been in before, and in truth, he wasn't all that focused on the decor, but on the red-coated beings themselves. They'd floated before Lock and the others like blood-red ghosts professing they were protectors, and Lock shouldn't have believed them.

But he did. They hadn't given him a reason to think otherwise.

They had given them a choice to stay or leave, and as far as the Order was concerned, the Duke had never given Lock that choice. Not that Lock was really even an Order member to begin with. Regardless, he wouldn't work for them. He shook his head; the Kingdom of Cards Society was a lot to take in. Why would they reveal themselves to them now? Why put so much faith in them—a group so broken they were still trying to piece themselves together? *To keep the mystery.* That was what one of them had said, and Lock had furrowed his brow. The mystery of what? For the first time, he didn't pretend to understand—he wasn't sure he wanted to. Trusting came at a price, and if half of that was staying oblivious to what they hoped to accomplish so long as it wasn't malicious, then so be it. He'd play their game; he'd play because his cards were dealt a long time ago, and if everything Lock had done had led him to this moment, he had to follow it through. He wasn't broken anymore. He was beginning to piece himself back together, and he would do whatever it took to be a better man for himself and his friends. *Everything you come across is a gamble of luck.* And, Lock supposed, luck would just need to bend in his favour.

    Now luck, as it happens, was just what he was hoping for as his carriage pulled up a block away from the Nighvengale's estate. While the mystery of the letters was solved, one thing was not: whatever was behind the wall that the fool of a marquess didn't want Lock to know about.

    He alighted from his carriage and into the cool night air. For once, the streets were quiet, the late hour working to his advantage. *Perfect*, he thought. No one around to witness his crime. Lock had never claimed to be a saint, but breaking into the Nighvengale's felt like a sin, especially since Aura found out they were her parents. He still remembered her face when she had learned that her grief had been wasted on people who had lied, wiped any memory of themselves, and ran with their regret. That is, if the Nighvengale's were capable of feeling such emotions.

    Lock shook all thoughts from his head as he neared the manor. He needed to focus. The manor, unlike the last time he'd been here, was deathly still. It didn't breathe with life as it had on the night of the party, but instead stood still and unmoving. He checked the windows of the surrounding houses, confirming they all seemed to be dark, before slipping around to the cobbled area at the back. In the darkness, Lock could just make out the shape of the carriage house. He took his time walking over, partially because he didn't want to be spotted and partially because he didn't want to stumble. Movement flickered from the corner of his eye, and he quickly ducked behind a tree, willing his breath to stay silent. He reached into his coat pocket, where he still held Aura's knife. He pulled it out with ease, letting his hand wrap around the handle as he listened for anyone on the streets beyond. The knife felt weighted in his hand—a weapon not made for his skin, yet he kept his grip firm on the silver-hilted blade. After a few moments, he dared a glance around the tree. When he found nothing, Lock continued his trek towards the carriage house, though he did not put the knife back into his coat. He knelt at the door of the carriage house, ready to use Aura's knife to aid him inside, but found that the door was already unlocked. He slipped the knife back into his pocket and entered cautiously.

Stillness.

That was what he was met with. But unlike the house and the streets beyond, this felt like hell—like the shadows were waiting for the right moment to pounce. Lock mentally kicked himself. He'd survived many Twisted attacks, but he was scared of the dark? He almost laughed. Moving into the room, he let his eyes adjust carefully, avoiding the centre worktable. The door to the office was closed, and Lock gripped the handle, only to see a soft glow emanating from the crack beneath the door and what was perhaps the faint smell of smoke. A wave of anger took over Lock's senses as he burst through the office door. At the far end of the room, the wall opened up into what appeared to be a small cabinet. And, in the middle of it all, stood Marquess Charles Nighvengale, a flame in hand, burning the remnants of whatever secrets he seemed set on taking to the grave.

"Hello, Lord Mortsakov," the marquess said in a serpent-like tone, his back still turned towards Lock. "I'm surprised you didn't show up with the authorities."

"You know just as well as I that they cannot stop you," Lock replied, his own tone a mask of calmness slipping into place.

The marquess grunted a laugh. "I suppose you're right. Yet, you still decide to show up."

"And you still decide to be a coward," Lock said, lowering his tone. "But rest assured, I'll find out what you keep so dear to you. After all, I'm not sure if you noticed, but liars and I are old friends."

He could've sworn he caught an uncertain glimmer in the marquess's eyes, but it was gone before Lock could truly get a look at it. Lock took a step forward. "Go on, dearest marquess, confess. I promise I won't fault you."

"I don't make promises."

"Come now, acting like a stubborn child? I would've thought you better." Lock hummed. "Is it because you've only ever been let down? After all, didn't your child promise to be around forever? Didn't your children promise to love you? Or perhaps it is because you promised them, and you lied."

Marquess Nighvengale pocketed his match, stomping the remaining flames out with his boot before turning, a simmering anger in his gaze. "That's enough."

"I don't think it is."

"Yes," Marquess Nighvengale seethed. "It is."

The marquess picked something up off the floor, a memory of a remaining piece of evidence. He pocketed it and headed for the door. Lock caught his arm, and despite being taller, the marquess seemed to shrink. "Your daughter knows what you did. I hope you're happy knowing what you've done."

"What I did was something you'll never understand." Hurt danced in his eyes at the mention of Aura, and Lock almost felt sorry for the man. He let go of the marquess only for him to pause.

"I don't want to hurt you, Lock. I don't want to fight; I've never been that sort of man. Yes, I'm ashamed of what I did, and she may never forgive me. I know that you care for her, just as I know there are some things you will never understand."

Marquess Nighvengale swept from the room, and Lock was left to find his way back home. He had come searching for answers and had somehow left with more questions than he had arrived with. The Nighvengale's were hiding something. That was clear, but Lock wasn't sure they were the criminals he'd originally believed them to be. *Perhaps*, he thought, thinking of the crimes that he'd committed, the blood that stained his hands. He thought of the way he'd been so cruel to so many people he'd believed were sinners. Lock shook his head. *Perhaps I am wrong.*

Upon arriving at his London townhouse, he found Aura still huddled in a chair. The chair she'd barely left all night. Her eyes stared into the fire as if at war with herself. Lock eased himself into a chair across from her, but said nothing. Instead, he took in how the fire cast her in a glow so angelic he might've believed he was dying. He watched Aura carefully, but she only fiddled with the necklace at her throat, a gift from Rien after they had gotten back. He supposed it had been an apology of some sort, a necklace shaped like an anatomical heart. Lock smiled to himself, but it was short-lived. Rien was Aura's uncle, and Lord Nighvengale was her father. Lock didn't want to tiptoe around Aura; he wanted to dance, but Marquess Nighvengale was clear about his hatred for Lock, and Lock supposed he deserved it. Aura looked at him, and he hadn't realized he'd been staring until her dark eyes latched onto his.

He blinked, his gaze softening.

"My lovely Aura," he said. "Might I ask what worries you on this fine evening."

"A letter I received from an old friend," she said. Lock stared at her for a moment, but before he could ask anything, she spoke again. "Is love a sacrifice?"

"No," he said it with such determination that he almost believed it. "Love is many things. It is wondrous and infinite and tragic, but it is also fair. If you must sacrifice for love, one is left thinking why they did it, and the other is left wondering if it was truly worth it. That hardly seems fair to me."

Aura nodded slowly as if taking in his words bit by bit. Lock shook his head because he needed to speak before time took advantage of them.

"And if saving someone is a sacrifice?" she asked him.

"Does saving someone need to be equated to sacrifice?" he asked, not answering her question. He didn't have an answer. Aura watched him for a few heartbeats more, and Lock almost forgot how to breathe. "Dearest Aura, sacrifice is greedy, used to rip love apart, but if saving someone is worth sacrifice, remember that you must also be saving yourself."

Aura fiddled with the fabric of her skirts. "Thank you. I've just—the world feels very much like it's crashing, and I cannot help but think if I had done things differently—"

"Regret nothing," Lock said. "Everything that has happened, it's a guideline. A reminder for you to improve, to change if you want to."

Aura smiled then, and he sat backwards. "Has anyone ever told you, Lock, that I'm wholly and devastatingly taken by you?"

"As a matter of fact, no."

Lock smiled back at her, his head beginning to grow dizzy. And if this moment was the last one before the Twisted Magic claimed him, if he were to die in this moment, it would be enough.

An hour later, Lock dropped Aura off at Rien's townhouse, a promise to see her soon. They had walked, the cool air wrapping around them, letting a chill creep into their bones. All was solved, yet Lock couldn't help but feel as though the world was threatening to end. He shoved his feelings aside as Aura stood before him, her face red from the cold. Gently, he watched as she reached around his neck. She watched him for a moment, and Lock could have sworn he saw what looked like sadness, but it was gone as soon as he had seen it. Slowly, she pressed her lips to his. Immediately, the world seemed to stop, his heart beating rapidly in his chest. He brought his hands to her waist, and after a moment, he pulled away, leaning his forehead against hers just like he'd done in the pavilion.

"My lovely Aura," he whispered so that not even the ghosts could hear. "My heart is cursed, but it is yours."

"And our hands are blood-stained, but I would let them waltz us into a dance if you offered."

They stayed like that, huddled together for a few precious heartbeats before he wished her goodnight. He turned and began to walk but paused upon hearing Aura call back to him. He turned. She stood in her doorway, her face glistening in the gentle moonlight.

"I'm sorry," she said, but before he could ask her what she meant, the door was shut behind her. He stood there, only for a moment, before turning and walking back home. Lock could have sworn he had seen a tear trail down her lovely face, but it was dark, and she was cast in a shadow. *I'm sorry,* Aura had said, and as he crossed the silent streets, he found a response coming to his lips.

"It's alright," he responded aloud to no one but the ghosts and the beggar on the corner. He pulled his coat tighter around him as the wind picked up. The air felt heavy with untold secrets and hearts dug out with daggers. It felt like the night beneath a tree where a shovel hit the dirt, burdened by the weight of a lie as a girl cast in shadows watched. It felt like forbidden love, risky and yet so full of affection. The night was crisp and spoke of the dead who'd never speak back. Maybe it was the way the light formed shadows against the near-silent streets. Maybe, it was the wind that whispered of a better future. Or maybe, it was the memory of a girl who tasted of love and shattered pasts. For the first time, Lock felt as though all was a game, and he was ready to play. Had his mind not still been reminiscing over the feeling of a too-short kiss, he might've realized the weight of his coat was lighter, the glint of a dagger no longer visible.

FORTY - FOUR

AURA

Kill Locklyn Henry Mortsakov. Aura didn't remember slipping the knife from his pocket, but she stared at it, the glimmer of candlelight reflecting off its sharp blade. The letter she had received last night sat open on her night table, each word like a stab to her heart. *Or Aura Nighvengale being the Queen of Spades won't just be another rumour.* Her fist clenched hard around the hilt of her blade, and she hated the way it felt comfortable in her hands, the way it felt familiar. She hated that last night she'd lost herself amongst poison, waking only to find a knife in her hands and her heart a moment away from shattering. Whether her employer or Avery sent the letter, it didn't matter.

Kill Locklyn Henry Mortsakov.

Those were the orders.

Orders she wouldn't follow.

She would find a way out because she had to. Aura knew that once the magic took hold, she wouldn't be able to stop it. Not again, anyway, which meant that she needed to stop the magic from happening in the first place. Still, she didn't move as she watched lantern light flicker over the blade. *Is love a sacrifice?* She had asked Lock; *No*—that was what he had told her.

She almost believed him.

Almost.

She saw no way out of this. It was either he was dead, or she'd be labelled a killer. Setting the knife under the floorboards, Aura stood and pulled a coat from her dresser. She needed to find the Kingdom of Cards Society. They were tricksters, masters of hiding, and what Aura needed to do was to pull the biggest deception of them all.

A knock sounded silently at her door, and although Rien had gone to bed hours ago, Aura still expected to see him there. They'd apologized, Rien giving her more opportunity in the morgue, and Aura half expected to see him with a crooked smile on his face, asking if she wanted to sit for some tea like they used to. Aura did not expect to see Iskra standing there.

"*Je suis désolée,*" Iskra said, not moving from the doorway. "I can leave —"

Aura shook her head, opening the door wider. "It's alright."

Iskra looked almost relieved as she walked straight into the room and all but collapsed onto Aura's bed. Aura smiled before taking a seat at her desk and pulling out a piece of paper. She dipped her pen in ink, holding it there, thinking of all the words she didn't know how to say. A rustling came from Iskra, and Aura turned to see her face skimming the letter. She looked up at her, and Aura watched as heartbreak passed her face.

"You're not . . ." She trailed off. "Going to do it."

"I'm not," Aura replied. "About the Queen of Spades—"

"I knew," Iskra said. "The night of the Opera. I didn't mean to hear you, but I did. I know you tried to stop. I do not blame you, but" — she held up the letter — "what the hell is this?"

"A threat. I have a way of avoiding it, I hope, but I'll need your help."

"With?"

Aura turned away from her and began writing a letter to Lock. A blurriness welling behind her eyes, a tear falling onto the ink as she signed her name. "I need you to give this to Lock. And I'll need you to take a trip to the Society, assuming you can find them."

And if Iskra had any objections, she didn't show it. She only nodded and took the once-dry letter from Aura, stuffing it into the pocket of her coat. Iskra faced her with a determined look, and Aura knew that somehow the world could be crashing down around them, and Iskra would help her, regardless if they were friends or mere acquaintances. A small tear slipped down her cheek, for even as she buttoned her coat, it hit her that sacrifice could do a million things, but in the end, the only thing it really left was an emptiness in the heart.

The attendant at the bottom of the stairs let her in without a fuss, simply stepping aside as he hauled open the door that would lead her to Avery's office. Gravel kicked up against her shoes as she stumbled inside. Her heart was pounding against her ribcage. Like the last time, many of the hooded figures paid her little mind. Shadows lined the walls, only warded off by the occasional lantern that hung on the wall. Aura stalked through the tunnels, not caring for any Twisted Magicians. On her walk down here, all she'd felt was anger.

At Avery.

At her employer.

Aura marched towards the office Avery had shown her only a few weeks prior. It was the same, though she cared very little for any of it, as her eyes zoned in on Avery Waltzeen. He was reading, his boots kicked up on the desk. He looked casual, and the sight made her feel worse. Aura pulled the letter from a pocket inside her coat, practically slamming it onto his desk.

Avery looked up, slowly, before sitting back, removing his feet from his desk. "I was wondering when you'd show up."

"I *hate* you," Aura said, shaking.

"Maybe so. However, I did warn you."

"And you're little performance back at the manor?" Aura said. "What was that about?"

Avery shrugged. "You were never going to do the job, and for the record, I meant everything I said."

"Does *he* know?"

Avery sat forward. "Doesn't matter."

Aura stared at him for a moment, then tapped the letter on his desk. "What is this? If you knew I was never going to do it?"

"Insurance. I said *you* were never going to do it. The Queen of Spades will."

"Avery—"

It was too late. A familiar buzzing entered her veins. *No. No. No.*

It's too late.

Her footfalls were light against the cobblestone streets, although her head was pounding. Her veins were shaking, and she vaguely remembered leaving the Twisted headquarters, a conversation with Avery ringing in her head.

The coronet.

She needed to get the coronet from Scotland Yard, even though she and the other's had just gotten it back, even though Lock had a chance. She remembered nodding, even though something inside her screamed that she couldn't—*wouldn't*—do it, and then everything had gone black, opportunity slipping from her fingertips.

And yet, here she was, on her way to Scotland Yard to get the coronet. As she strolled for the back entrance of the constabulary, Aura couldn't help but think about her traitorous heart. It had been one thing to make a deal with the Society. Whether they knew it or not, it was another to steal the very thing that had caused this mess in the first place. The coronet would be safer in the hands of the police. Aura knew that, yet she was selfish; she *needed* it. Aura shook her head as if trying to clear her thoughts—she needed to focus. Slipping out a pouch of lock picks, she unlocked the back door and slipped inside. It was dim, save for a few lanterns that had been left on for the night crew or police working late, and the silence stretched the air so thin Aura was afraid to move at first, but it was late —late enough that Scotland Yard would be nearly empty. The coronet itself was contained in Detective Inspector Thornsbury's office until the commissioner could hand deliver it back to Duke Brittenworth, earning him a no-doubt, gleaming reputation and compensation for his efforts in finding the coronet. She bit back a scoff. They'd get no recognition for this case, but she supposed she hadn't truly wanted it. She had wanted Kian to get the justice he deserved, and he had—and here she was, stripping half of it away.

Biting down on her guilt, Aura moved quickly through the abandoned halls of the Yard, navigating her way to Thornsbury's office, and it didn't take long until the door clicked shut behind her, and she stood alone in his office.

I'm sorry.

A quick look around the room suggested that the coronet was hidden in the cabinet at the far end of the room, judging by the excess dirt that pooled at the base of the compartment. It would seem that the detective inspector was an abecedarian when it came to hiding prized possessions. That, or he simply didn't expect anyone to break into his office, which was still a mistake on his part. Swiftly, Aura collected the keys from Thornsbury's desk drawer and crossed the room, unlocking the cabinet.

One second.

Another.

The lock gave way with a satisfying click. The coronet sat in a wooden box, a crown etched into the delicate wood, a red gem in the centre, shining up at her, *taunting* her. She pressed her lips together as she carefully lifted the box from its hiding spot and shut the cabinet behind her. A peek inside proved that the coronet was there, sitting upon plush velvet. *Is love sacrifice?* Her words echoed in her head, each word like a stab to her heart. Shaking off her thoughts, Aura shut the lid before hurrying from the room, taking care to keep her steps light, her traitorous heart thumping loudly in her chest.

♠

Aura turned into the alleyway opposite Scotland Yard, finally slowing her steps. If everything went to plan, news of the Queen of Spade's death would make its way around London, and Aura would be safe. *Lock would be safe.* She continued down the alleyway until she turned into a thinner, darker passageway. Ahead, a gambling den sign swung slightly as Avery Waltzeen stepped out from the shadows. Aura approached him slowly, cautiously. He looked smug, though Aura wasn't sure why.

Thank you. The thought slithered into her head before leaving, and if Aura hadn't known better, she might have thought she imagined it. She shifted the box in her hands, reaching it toward Avery.

"He better keep his promise," she said.

Avery looked amused. "Lady Nighvengale, there was never an intention of giving *him* the coronet. *I* need it, and you've just delivered."

No.

Aura willed herself to pull the box back towards her, but the magic was too strong. *No.* Somewhere beyond, a clock chimed three bells, the air shifting.

"You *work* for him?"

She froze.

Lock.

"Aura . . ."

Her hands were still outstretched.

"What are you doing?"

Something snapped inside her, her pulse returning to normal, and Avery took the box from her, and she turned and met his gaze. "What I have to."

Lock took a step forward, looking confused. "I'm sorry, *what?* Aura, that is the coronet."

"I know." It was all she could say.

"Is this—are you being forced to do this? I swear I will—"

Aura looked pleadingly at him, the magic fading from her system. "Please, Lock, I need you to trust me."

His gaze softened, and for a moment, laughter echoed like a symphony; a kiss pressed against her lips, and countless tears fell into the safety of each other's arms. For a moment, she was back underneath a tree, watching as she felt her heartbeat for something she had not wanted to be love. For a moment, maybe she could pretend that what they had wasn't tragic and twisted; maybe Aura could pretend that she wasn't a traitor, that betrayal wouldn't rip them apart.

"I can't let you do that, Aura."

He took long strides towards the coronet, towards *her*, and she had only a split second to think. *It's life or death; him or her*—her knife was at his throat in seconds as she stepped between him and the coronet. She tightened her grip on the hilt, looking into his darkening eyes.

"You're going to have to."

For a moment, the invisible string held them together, and the next, it snapped as the look of betrayal and hurt flashed into his eyes. His back stiffened beneath her touch, his jaw clenching as he looked down at her. His gaze flicked upwards suddenly, warning flaring in his features.

"Aur—"

She gasped as pain shot through her body, her knife dropping to the floor. The cool tip of metal pressed into her back, blood leaking from the back of her bodice and onto the cobble. The Society member who'd stabbed her taking a step backwards, though she barely registered them as she looked at Lock. His face was going pale, his eyes hard.

She collapsed to her knees, Lock bracing her to the ground, looking torn between helping her and going after the Avery. He should do neither—she was not worth his care, and the Society would take care of Avery. She turned her head just in time to see the red coat who'd stabbed her hurrying down the alleyway, the sound of their pounding footsteps fading as they chased after Avery.

Aura waited for the darkness to take her.

The Queen of Spades would soon be dead—for good this time. She was safe and alive, and so was Lock. *This is for you,* she wanted to scream but didn't.

She couldn't.

Her mouth was suddenly too heavy, and she rolled onto her side as Lock finally let her go. And, as if on command, Thornsbury stormed out from the shadows, helping a struggling Lock to his feet. Aura didn't dare look at him. She only hoped Thornsbury would do what he needed to, whatever Iskra had asked of him. *It's all just a game.* If it was, then why did Aura feel like she was losing? This was betrayal; it was sick and cruel, but at least she and Lock would have a thousand more dances, their bloodied hands clasped in unison. Aura smiled, a tear rolling down her cheek. Not from the pain, but from the idea that she was finally free of the broken girl that wielded a knife for power. She was free. Her heartbeat pounded in her ears, and Aura wondered if this really was false, a trick aided by The Society. She wondered if this was what dying felt like, painful and sweet, a thousand memories haunting her heart. *I'm sorry.* Aura had whispered, and this was what she had meant. She was sorry she betrayed him; that sacrifice would wedge its greedy hands between her and love. She was sorry that she hadn't fought harder to keep her sanity. Her head lolled to the side. Vaguely, she thought she heard someone call her name, the cobble shaking beneath her, but whether it was someone coming to her aid, or the earth falling apart, Aura wasn't sure. Her eyes were too heavy, her senses slowly dulling. *Nothing can convince me that I am not wholly and devastatingly taken by you.* The words echoed in her head one last time, like a remembrance of love before sacrifice and betrayal carved out her heart. Aura thought she felt Lock reach for her, but before she could respond, the darkness found her, and then she was falling.

Aura Wrentroth–Nighvengale sat on a bench in the courtyard of Lock's country manor, the day long since gone. The knife had gone just deep enough to pierce her flesh, the point giving way to fabric as it hit her skin, the artificial blood blossoming on her, courtesy of Thornsbury. He hadn't liked the idea, but it was what needed to be done. *Perhaps*, Aura thought as she fiddled with her skirts for the tenth time. *Perhaps, he is a reasonable man, after all.* The pain, Twisted Magic, and equally as numbing.

It was almost midnight, and the sound of footsteps on the cobble announced his arrival.

Lock Mortsakov stepped out of the shadows, his hair dishevelled, his tie crooked beneath his waistcoat. In his hand, he held a crumpled letter. He stared at her from across the courtyard, his face unreadable and as distant as Aura had ever seen it. Aura stood, walking to him slowly. Her heart was in her throat, her mind racing. Lock didn't move, only stood there, frozen, as if seeing a ghost.

"I'm sorry," she said. But even as she spoke, she knew that no words would be good enough to forgive this.

She couldn't tell him why she had done it; the words died on her tongue as he took a step towards her, his hands cupping her face. He brought his lips to hers, and a thousand memories crashed between them, their hearts beating together, but it was gone just as quickly as it had come. This tasted like poison, revenge for what she had done—betrayal hung between them, sweet and venomous. She pulled away, staring into his dark eyes, and for a moment, they were soft and filled with something that Aura could only describe as love.

"I suppose even the loveliest things can hurt like a knife," he whispered. "My lovely Aura, why did you do it?"

He didn't clarify. She'd done many things—none of them had been because she *wanted* to.

"I had no other choice, Lock. You know that."

"Do I?" he asked, a sharpness to his tone, and Aura flinched. His gaze softened, then, "I'm sorry."

She stayed silent, forcing her hands into fists to keep from shaking. *I'm sorry.* The two words that were tossed around almost as much as I love you, but they meant little. Aura knew that words were cruel, and what she had done was worse. She wanted to let him know why she had done it, why she *had* to do it, but the words caught in her throat as if she were bound to secrecy. Aura took a step backwards. They were broken and shattered, and love wouldn't happen so long as it was forged between a lie and bloodshed. It would not be forged between hate and the memory of a kiss, but how easy it would be to let it. Aura stared at him, and for a moment, she let herself pretend that the world hadn't crashed around them—that she was not the one that had let it. And yet, this was what betrayal was; it was visceral, leaving an emptiness and an ache inside a heart, slowly growing until the weight of it was too much to bear. She was completely trapped by the weight of her heart and her head—the war that seemed infinite and never-ending. She could only hope that forgiveness would come in time, but then again, trust was glass: once it was shattered, it could never be the same. If this was a game, she'd have lost the moment she had picked up that dagger. She and Lock's hearts were bound by infinity, or so she had thought. But infinity was not meant to be torn apart. They had always had a solution to a problem, but this was not simple, and problems couldn't be solved with a blade, yet Aura had done it anyway.

"Aura." It was a whisper, and for once, she did not want to hear the rest.

"Locklyn," she said, her heart cracking. "I'll be on the next boat to

France within the hour."

She turned her back on him, her gait more purposeful than she wanted it to be. She wanted to break down in his arms, to have him hold her for one last time. She was the girl with a vengeance too deep to love, and he was a boy broken by blood too weak to ask her to stay. Aura could've sworn she heard the tiny sound of metal clinking against the ground, but she didn't look back. She didn't let herself look back.

"My heart is cursed," Lock said, a whisper in the distance. Aura turned, only to find he was gone, and words hung in the air, silent and aching.

But it is yours, she thought, though no one was there to hear it, the weight shattering her already bleeding soul in half.

The water seemed too calm for the storm that raged inside her. The docks were lit up by lanterns, casting the boat before her in a dim silhouette. The morning would come soon, and London would go about its business as if nothing was wrong. Iskra plopped her bag down beside her and sighed. Aura knew that going back to France would be hard for her, but Iskra hadn't said no. In fact, her eyes had lit up like a newly raged fire. They would only be there for a while, as long as it took for the news about the Queen of Spades to die down, and then they'd be back, and Aura would need to face what she had done. Thornsbury would be making an announcement in the morning that the killer known as The Queen of Spades was found dead, and she would be free—she just didn't feel it. She felt numb, and even more so as Iskra helped her onto the boat, taking up a place by the railing to watch as their home disappeared.

"Do you have a plan?" Aura asked.

Iskra shook her head. "I can fight my parents, Aura. I'll figure it out."

"I'm sorry about the coronet."

"I wasn't the one dying." Iskra said, letting the silence drag on.

Aura let herself sag against the railing—the thrill of a new adventure was distant, drowned by the sorrow that held her heart in its hands. Passengers slowly climbed on board, muttering in languages that Aura could only make out half of. The crew worked their way past, directing people to their cabins or the dining hall, but Aura and Iskra stayed where they were. Aura breathed, sea air reaching her lungs, and Iskra smiled, the feeling of someone experiencing true happiness. Aura clenched the railing, feeling as though the knife really had struck her. Lies were backstabbing, and sorrow had made her hollow. Aura reached for forgiveness, but it seemed so far away. Below, the boat pulled forward, and Aura caught sight of a shadow turning away from the docks, his long coat flowing behind him. She shut her eyes, and when she opened them again, she could no longer see the shore. She wished that she could forget this.

But this was beyond forgetting.

It was not a blade, it was betrayal, yet it had stabbed just as quickly. Because no matter how sharp the knife, betrayal always found a way to cut deeper.

FORTY - FIVE

LOCK

Lock's head was pounding as he stumbled towards his townhouse. He'd been worried he wouldn't make it in time, and he'd been right. He was too late. The boat had already been pulling away from the docks. His veins were thrumming, and his head pounded. His vision swam, the walls of the alleyway seeming to close in on him, though none of it mattered. All he could think about was *her*.

Stay.

He'd needed her to stay.

Lock stumbled then, his knees connecting with the cobble, palms scraping against the ground. Lock let out a hiss, pressing his forehead to the ground. He'd lost his coat somewhere, and a chill racked his body. He was dying. He'd known as much when he'd seen Aura hand the coronet to Avery.

You're killing me, Aura, he wished he'd said. Instead, he'd watched as she collapsed, red blossoming on her chest—a sight he'd never be able to rid from his memory. Lock shut his eyes tight. So tight until they hurt, and when he opened them again, his vision was still swimming.

Stay.

He needed to get up, needed to get to France, needed to see her. His forehead rested against the ground, letting his thoughts float back to her, past the sting of betrayal still echoing in his bones. For if he were dying, he wanted it to be with her. He'd long since decided that he'd love her forever—love her even in death. Lock let his eyes close, the metallic taste of blood welling in his throat.

No. He couldn't be dying. He needed her to come back home.

Lock picked his head up off the ground, dark blood splattering the cobblestone in front of him, a cough racking his body. His head ached, forcing him to press his forehead to the floor once more in an attempt to make the pain subside. It would do no good. No one was coming for him, he knew that. But even as he thought it, a set of heavy hands lifted him off the ground, his vision darkening. It was only then, that he noticed his arms.

His veins were pitch black.

Another jolt of pain shot through him, the poison pulsing through his body. *I'm dying*—the thought was laced with bitterness—*and it is because of her.*

His head was wrenched upwards, by the same hands that had lifted him from the ground only a moment ago, and he bit down on his tongue at the force.

The coronet was placed on his head.

It was glowing, a vibrant white.

Or perhaps he was still dying.

Beams of light shot out, so bright Lock had to squeeze his eyes shut. His heart was hammering in his chest. Lock breathed in a gasp of air; the pain sharp in his head.

Nothing.

Lock's entire body shook, and he might have fallen over had someone not still be holding him up. The light began to fade, his heartbeat still loud in his ears, and he clenched his jaw against the effort.

His knees buckled and he collapsed again just as the coronet fell off his head.

It had been silver before, pristine, now it was cracking, the red gems having fallen out onto the ground. For the first time in a long time, everything felt silent. His skin was unmarked, and his entire body seemed to thrum with energy. He felt *alive*. Slowly, Lock stood, ignoring his dishevelled state and turned to face a red coated being—a member of the Kingdom of Cards Society. They didn't say anything as they moved to crush the red gems. Without them, the coronet was a regular crown, despite all its cracks. The shards of gem lay broken on the alleyway, and the Society member picked up the coronet from the ground and made to leave down the alleyway.

"Thank you," Lock called. It sounded foolish coming out of his mouth, but he felt as though he should say something.

"Thank Aura," they replied. "You owe us."

Lock stared back down the alleyway, where if he walked far enough, he'd reach the waters. *What had she done?*

The Society member held up the coronet, drawing Lock's attention. "This is the start."

"Of what?"

"Of the game."

EPILOGUE

SIR AVERY WALTZEEN

Paris 1889

Aura Nighvengale wasn't dead, and he knew it. Her little act had split her life in half, a ravine placed between the heart and the head, and it would give him just enough time to re-evaluate the situation. That detective had put out a statement on the death of The Queen of Spades as he'd left London, but Avery knew better than to believe Aura would make a martyr of herself. The coronet was in the enemy's hands, unusable—a problem—but not unsolvable. They had other ways of getting what they needed—*patience, Avery,* the master had said. *They don't know. As far as I'm concerned, we have all the time in the world.* Avery tugged at the lapels of his carefully tailored suit, striding into the entrance hall of their operations unit in France. Three chandeliers above cast rainbows along the plain walls and black and white diamond marble floors. The continuous silence was only broken by his boots striking tile in an even pattern. He took the black stairs two at a time, sprinting up to a room lit only by a few candles. A circular table sat in the centre of the space, a draft blowing in from the open doors that led onto a balcony beyond. Avery pulled the hilt of Aura's blade and threw it onto the table with a loud clatter. It would need a new blade, something *sharper,* but certainly, they could manage it—so long as the hilt was attached—*so long as they still had what they needed.* He'd pulled it from that foolish detective she had working for her; Avery *tsked*. The man really should've been more careful about leaving things lying about. He drew in a deep breath, the scent of freshly baked bread and the lingering blood hitting his nose. Avery curled his hands into a fist, frustration begging to be set free.

Their plan had failed.

His plan had failed.

He could think of several people who wouldn't be pleased with such information, but that was a problem for a later date. In one fluid movement, he drew a card from his jacket pocket and flung it at the wall. The four corners had been made into blades allowing the card to wedge itself directly in the wall—a new invention on his part and a bloody useful one. Lady Levensmith had proven a disaster, just as he had expected, but everyone else had thought she'd be great. The master had thought she would be perfect, anything to keep his hands clean. But no—he threw another card—she had ruined their chance at gaining the one thing they truly wanted: power. What *he* needed, and it was becoming increasingly clear that the *master* wasn't just settling for that. He wanted *revenge.* Levensmith had just been another reminder of why he could never trust those with magic born of the saints, of the kind world. No matter, they would just need to choose their next approach carefully, and this time they were going to get their hands dirty. Wind whistled past his ears as he threw card after card, each more forceful than the next. His biggest problem was Aura and her friends, and he had intended to remove her from the equation altogether, but of course, the master had needed to use them first.

"Don't kill them, Avery," he'd said, *"I mean it."*

Avery had scoffed. *"Don't tell me you care?"*

"Of course not. But I do need them alive, just as I will need all cards on the table. Do you understand?"

Avery had nodded, but he hadn't missed the flash of past memories behind his partner's, his master's, eyes before they were replaced by their usual darkness, edged with insanity.

Well, if they'd just killed them when they had the chance, perhaps they would already have what they wanted. The coronet was gone, and they had no hope of getting it back, and Avery wasn't sure when the next opportunity would present itself. Then again, his partner didn't strike him as the kind of person to wait around for opportunities; he would make them, and Avery only wondered when that would be. In truth, he was itching for a fight because he enjoyed *playing*. People were games, easily moved across the board or dealt into a game, and Avery enjoyed it—watching them figure out that there was no way out.

There was no escape.

This was a show, a performance of puppets, and he was the puppeteer. He was God-like in a world of people waiting for a sign, and he deserved the power that would soon find its way into his clutches. He would get it, and if he had to leave the master to do that, then so be it. With that pleasant thought, he plucked the cards from the wall and strode out into the cool night air. On the horizon danced the city lights of Paris, twinkling and star-like. Avery slumped against the railing, shutting his eyes, only then letting his exhaustion take him. He needed a drink. He needed to burn any remnants of bitterness from his soul, just for a moment, because even he could be human sometimes. Turning his back away from the view, he leaned his back against the railing, rolling his neck. A crack rang through his bones, and he relaxed a bit.

A knock at the door sent his eyes flying back to the shadowy depths of his room. In the doorway stood a figure cloaked in black, though their face was pale, a lackey used to send messages. Avery pushed away from the railing, mouth twisting into a sour line.

"What do you want?" Avery snapped, the idea of a drink sounding better and better by the minute. He shoved his hands behind his back, watching as the man flinched at the harshness of his tone. *Weak.*

"*He* wants to know how it went."

"That is between him and me, and not anything I should be passing on through the inconsistency of the spoken word." Avery's tone was dry, almost nonchalant. He needed a drink and certainly didn't need to divulge all the information to the boy.

"But—"

Avery strode towards the door but paused to call over his shoulder. "Tell Catcherheart we are going to have to make a new plan."

Kingdom of Cards

Emmaline Leigh

ACKNOWLEDGEMENTS

I'd like to take this first sentence to formally apologize to my readers for the ending. It had to be done. Moving on. . .

Thank you so much to anyone and everyone involved with the creation of this book.

Thank you to my editor, Erin Young, for all of the kind words, for helping to guide KoC in the direction that it is in now, and for always being sure to have my voice heard. Thank you to my cover artist, Kelly Ritchie. I could not have imagined a more beautiful cover for a book that means so much to me.

Thank you to my parents for being so supportive of my endeavours and being nothing but helpful. Thank you to my sister, Heather, for being there from the beginning. Your support was unwavering.

Thank you to Liv and Sarah—you two are the best friends a girl could ask for.

Thank you to Nicole for helping me with the scene dividers and the helping to make sure Lock's Russian was accurate. Thank you to all the people who followed me on Instagram, who were so understanding when this book didn't come out when it was supposed to, to those who helped me make sure the languages were accurate, and for the constant love and support. To my 15-year-old me, who started writing Kingdom of Cards with a very different image in mind, I think you would be proud of this version—we did it.

And thank you, dear reader. Watch your cards . . . the game isn't over yet.

Photo by Heather McGeown

ABOUT THE AUTHOR

Emmaline Leigh is a Canadian author from Toronto, currently pursuing a degree in English. When she's not writing, she can be found dancing or reading her favourite novels. She started taking writing seriously at 14, though she'd always known she wanted to be an author from a young age. Follow her on Instagram for updates on her upcoming work.

Instagram: @emmaline.l.writes

Kingdom of Cards

Printed in France by Amazon
Brétigny-sur-Orge, FR

20432358R00268